The place you're at is the place I'll go.

Where you're at is where I'll fall.

CONTENT

Falling

CHAPTER 18

TANG Chong had only gotten halfway through when Ye Qin picked up his pace and ran to the street. He flagged down a taxi and pulled the door open, asking, "Where? Give me the address."

At 8 p.m., Ye Qin reached one of downtown S-City's high-end clubs.

The club was very renowned locally and not too private. A film crew had even rented it out for shooting once. Because of this, Ye Qin let down his guard and easily believed Tang Chong's words, thinking that Cheng Feichi was really in here discussing business.

The private room was located on the top floor. Ye Qin knocked and entered, finding the inside quite dim and shrouded in smoke, making him cough continuously. Only when he saw the empty bottles on the table and all over the ground did he realize he might have been tricked. Ye Qin turned, about to leave, but Tang Chong grabbed his arm.

Drunk, Tang Chong used a lot of strength, dragging Ye Qin back with just a tug. "You just came and you're leaving already?"

Ye Qin glared at him. "You lied to me."

Tang Chong burst into laughter before dragging Ye Qin towards the table. "How can I lie to you? We do have a President Cheng here." As he spoke, Tang Chong pointed at a fat, middle-aged man on the sofa. "This President Cheng is also a famous entrepreneur in S-City, no lesser than your old schoolmate. Come, I'll introduce you."

Just as he finished speaking, Ye Qin broke free from his restraint and turned to walk out the door. This time, rather than stop him, Tang Chong waved a wine glass and said unhurriedly, "I hear you're shooting on Cangquan Mountain? Tsk, poor little fallen young master. Our President Cheng happens to be that film's investor. Perhaps he could call the crew and ask them to take good care of you?"

Ye Qin's heart sank, and he froze in his steps. Tang Chong's threat lay bare in his words. Ye Qin knew from the very beginning that Tang Chong wouldn't put what had happened behind him so easily. He just hadn't expected Tang Chong to be so vile as to use Cheng Feichi to bait him into a trick.

He took a deep breath and turned back. "What do you want?"

"What are you saying?! As if I could possibly want anything on your body."

That sentence made the whole room erupt into waves of laughter. Tang Chong tilted his chin at the wine glass on the table beside him. "Since you're here already, shouldn't you have a few drinks before leaving?"

Clenching his back teeth, Ye Qin took big steps to the table. He picked up the glass that had just been filled up, tilted his head back, and downed it all in one go.

Immediately, there was applause. Ye Qin put the glass down, feeling a sting traveling down his throat into his stomach. It burned so strong that his temples pounded and his vision blanked, almost making him fall.

Another glass of wine was now placed on the table. Tang Chong looked on nearby with a wry smile. "As a newbie, you have to drink at least three glasses as a token of appreciation, don't cha?"

Beggars couldn't be choosers. Ye Qin contained the anger churning in his chest and downed the remaining two glasses in one go as well.

The last glass nearly choked him. He only ever had a few sips of red wine with friends. This was the first time he drank such strong stuff recklessly. Clenching his teeth, Ye Qin forced himself to swallow the wine in his throat, eyes turning red from discomfort. A few clear drops that he couldn't manage to swallow spilled from the corner of his mouth, and he wiped them off casually.

Ye Qin stood up straight as he put the third empty glass down on the table, thinking that he could finally leave now. But then Tang Chong filled another glass, tsking. "Why, I almost forgot. I suppose you haven't met most of the people here? Isn't your group known for being modest and polite? At any rate, shouldn't you also give a toast to every boss you're meeting for the first time?"

Realizing that he had fallen into Tang Chong's trap, Ye Qin got so angry that he wanted to rip the guy's head off his neck and kick it like a soccer ball.

"Everyone, take your time and enjoy. I have to go now," he said, containing himself again and again.

It hadn't been easy for Tang Chong to get Ye Qin there. How could he let him go so easily? He picked up the glass and chased after him. "You should at least drink this…"

Ye Qin slapped away the hand Tang Chong put on his shoulder, and the glass dropped to the ground, shattering and spilling red wine all over Tang Chong.

Meanwhile, in another private room in the same club,

Cheng Feichi had just finished with business dealings. After turning down offered wine with the excuse that he still had things to take care of at home, he took his jacket, got up, and bid his goodbyes.

Yan Hong had come at some point and was waiting for him at the door. When she saw him leave, she raised the thermos bottle she had been holding in front of her chest as if presenting him a treasure. "Have you had a few drinks, Feichi-ge? Here, I made some hangover soup."

Upon hearing her call him "ge", Cheng Feichi gave an imperceptible frown. "I didn't drink, but thank you," he said, glancing at the thermos in her hand.

Sensing his indifference, Yan Hong panicked slightly and scuttled to his side. "I only came because Auntie said that you're here... It's still early right now. I know a restaurant next door. Why don't we have dinner there?"

She mentioned Cheng Xin on purpose. Cheng Feichi was indifferent by nature. He already had a tendency to ignore people overseas, but at that time, Yan Hong could at least constantly approach and develop a relationship with him on the pretext that their families had a long friendship. Ever since he returned, Cheng Feichi was constantly busy with work, so it became even harder to find occasions to interact with him, not to mention that his schedule was filled with dinner parties where all kinds of women circled him. Yan Hong felt very insecure.

After all, Cheng Feichi never responded to her pursuit, let alone acknowledged her as his girlfriend. Right now, Cheng Xin's approval was the only thing she could grasp onto.

However, Cheng Feichi offered her no reaction and continued to walk down the hallway to the elevator at a steady pace. "I'm not hungry. You can go by yourself if you want."

"That restaurant's quite special," Yan Hong kept trying to

persuade him. "All the décor is made from Lego, even the flower-pots. Didn't you join a Lego competition back in America? I'm sure you'll love it."

It wasn't until she mentioned this that Cheng Feichi showed a slight change of expression. His eyes focused as if recalling a past memory.

But it only lasted for a moment. Then, everything returned to normal.

"I joined that competition to help a friend," he said and paused for a moment before adding, "I don't like Legos."

As a scrupulous girl, Yan Hong naturally didn't overlook the slight abnormality in his behavior. But he was firm in his refusal, so she could only try another way. "If you don't want to eat, we can go have something to drink? Let's get something here. It's so hot outside right now, and their cold brew is..."

She was interrupted by the sudden opening of a door on the left side of the hallway. Yan Hong covered her mouth and cried out in surprise when she saw two men coming out, shoving at each other. One of them pulled the other by the hair and attempted to slam him into the wall.

"Think you can get cocky just because I gave you a bit of face? You got the guts to put up a front in my face? If I don't teach you a lesson today, you'll never learn who I am!"

People lost control easily after having one too many drinks, and this kind of shouting and brawling was a constant presence in bars and clubs. Yan Hong quickly hid behind Cheng Feichi and grabbed his arm. "Ignore them. Let's go," she said in fear.

But Cheng Feichi seemed fixed to the ground.

The one getting punched also wasn't a pushover. Making use of the few martial arts techniques he had learned for film, he turned and pinned Tang Chong's arm while the latter was still cursing with vigor. In a nimble flip, he pinned Tang Chong to the wall.

His other hand raised up high in a stance that was ready to give Tang Chong a taste of his own medicine. The other men in the private room poked their heads out to have a look. But in the end, Ye Qin's tightly clenched fists didn't land on Tang Chong. He still had to hurry back to the set to shoot more scenes, and he didn't want to see himself in tomorrow's headlines.

Slamming Tang Chong against the wall, Ye Qin rubbed his scalp, which was stinging painfully from the earlier hair yanking, and walked off. Unexpectedly, Tang Chong held steadfast to his sinister designs and stuck out a foot to step on his untied shoelaces. Ye Qin tripped before he got a chance to steady himself. Thanks to his fast reflexes, his hands landed first, saving his face from making close contact with the floor.

Using his arm as support, Ye Qin got back on his feet. The first things he saw were a pair of well-made leather shoes and well-fitted suit pants.

Behind him, Tang Chong sneered and clapped his hands in petty smugness. Tang Chong planned to come up and taunt him some more, but then he saw the man standing nearby, and his face immediately drained of color. "P-President Cheng! You're here too? What a coincidence! Your old schoolmate is here as well. We're just playing around... Ha ha ha."

As soon as Ye Qin heard Tang Chong say "President Cheng," his heart clenched tightly.

He didn't know how he got up from the ground. His brain worked slowly, like it was rusty. He couldn't even decide whether he should turn and flee immediately or say hello and then flee.

While Ye Qin was still in a panic, a jacket fell on his shoulders, covering the red wine stains all over his chest and back.

"Let's go. I'll take you back."

"Just let the driver take him," Yan Hong was still muttering

as they reached the doors of the club. "Let's go find something to eat…"

Rather than changing his plans to placate her, Cheng Feichi had the driver take Yan Hong home and drove Ye Qin back to the set in person.

Ye Qin knew deep down that Cheng Feichi was helping him. With Tang Chong's habit of bullying the weak and cowering from the strong, he would stop stirring up trouble for at least a month. When Ye Qin thought of this, he immediately relaxed quite a bit from the tense state he had been in ever since entering the club.

But being alone with Cheng Feichi made him unable to relax completely. After thanking him, Ye Qin didn't know what else to say. As his eyes skimmed over Cheng Feichi's long, elegant hands on the steering wheel, he suddenly realized that this was the first time he'd sat in Cheng Feichi's car.

Back in high school, it was always him driving Cheng Feichi. Ye Qin even drove him to the competition. When Cheng Feichi left the exam room, the two of them, having just started going out, went on their first date. They grabbed KFC and Japanese and even watched a movie.

Back in those days, Ye Qin still dared to say and do anything. He called all the shots without asking and tacitly decided that Cheng Feichi ought to follow his lead for everything.

Now, Ye Qin lost that courage. "You probably haven't had dinner yet, have you?" he asked in a small voice after debating again and again whether to break the silence. "I've got some biscuits." He searched his pockets and instead of finding any biscuits, he drew out a BB cushion.

Cheng Feichi gave him a silent glance.

Ye Qin got even more nervous, stuffing the BB cushion back into his pocket in embarrassment before straightening out his clothes. "I forgot to put them back yesterday after doing laundry... Why don't we stop and find somewhere to eat? There are a lot of restaurants in the area."

"It's fine. I'm not hungry."

As he spoke, Cheng Feichi turned up the AC.

Yi Qin couldn't stand low temperatures. In the summer, whenever he turned the AC on to cool down, he would catch a cold or get a stomachache. While they had been living together in the apartment in Jiayuan Compound, Cheng Feichi got up every night to turn off the AC and pull blankets over him.

Ye Qin knew that he shouldn't keep dwelling on the past, but Cheng Feichi's every action made him see shadows of who he used to be.

Ye Qin turned to look out of the window. He lifted his hand and touched the circular object hanging at his chest through the wine-soaked fabric. His eyes went red again.

This should have been the perfect opportunity to apologize, but Ye Qin could tell from secretly eyeing him that Cheng Fei-chi wasn't in a good mood.

Cheng Feichi's lips were pressed tight, and the corners of his mouth sank a tiny bit in a line with almost no curvature. The hand on the steering wheel was also clenched tight. Facing front, his eyes were dark and heavy as if he were restraining himself.

Ye Qin didn't blame him. He had run into trouble in a place like that, and even had to take the trouble back to set. Anyone would be in a bad mood.

Especially after getting Cheng Xin's phone call.

"A young lady like Yan Hong went all the way over there to pick you up. Shouldn't you at least take her home?" she lectured as soon as it went through.

"I had the driver take her home," Cheng Feichi replied, switching to speaker.

"She went to find you, and you brushed her off with a driver?

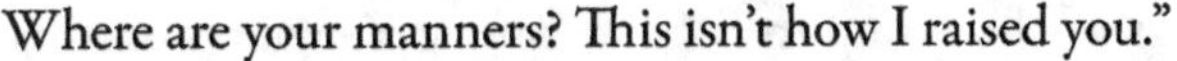

Where are your manners? This isn't how I raised you."

Cheng Xin nagged a few more sentences before changing the subject, possibly out of concern that she would draw her son's resentment. "Where are you now? When will you be home?"

Ye Qin thought Cheng Feichi would tell her the truth, but against his expectations, the latter fell silent for a while. "Home?" he finally asked back. "Which home?"

In the following days, apart from the aftereffects of the strong wine that made Ye Qin's stomach churn every time he thought about it, the other thing that lingered in his mind was that look on Cheng Feichi's face.

He had never seen Cheng Feichi like that, with that icy voice and mocking smile. It was as if he thought poorly of everything, but also as if he had become hopeless and indifferent after enduring the vicissitudes of life.

That day, Cheng Feichi left after dropping him off on the mountain. He didn't even take back his suit jacket.

Thus, Ye Qin kept it for himself. He hung it up inside the closet of his hotel room and admired it for two days before asking his assistant to take it to a nearby dry cleaner to get it cleaned.

The assistant just brought the cleaned suit back today. Ye Qin laid it out on his bed, deliberating whether to use it as an excuse to set up another meeting with Cheng Feichi when suddenly, Zheng Yueyue called.

"Are you done filming today? Make yourself presentable and come out immediately. I called you a taxi. Bring Xiao-Yun with you."

Xiao-Yun was Ye Qin's assistant who oversaw his everyday needs while he stayed with the crew.

It wasn't until after he arrived in a hurry that Ye Qin finally got a rough idea of what was going on. Since there were currently two members of the group in S-City, Zheng Yueyue took this opportunity to accept a mall performance gig and livestream.

He Hansong had just rushed over from another shooting location for an ad and was currently getting his make-up done with a dour face. Song Xu, who had been dragged along for an extra head, was still in a daze. As soon as he saw Ye Qin, he flung himself at him and hung off his shoulders, only to be lifted by the back of his shirt and moved aside.

"Ge... I want to go back to bed..." Song Xu whined at the top of his lungs.

Although the group members' personalities were nothing alike and they often did not see eye to eye, they all maintained a common understanding: it would take a fool to turn down a money-making opportunity.

Fortunately, this wasn't their first rodeo. The three of them quickly adjusted themselves. Before getting on stage, they checked over their lyrics. The acoustics in this mall were quite average, so nobody would catch on if their voices cracked once or twice while singing. When they began to interact with the audience, a few fans actually showed up on the upper level, waving and screaming their names.

Therefore, the boy band that appeared out of the blue successfully warmed up the audience. As their performance was being livestreamed, a lot of passersby joined the audience as well, asking for the group's name.

Ever since the surge of domestic boy bands in the past year, they hadn't appeared on stage together as a group, especially after AOW, a seven-member boy band managed by Starlight Entertainment, emerged as a force to be reckoned with. AOW cleaned up as "Best New Group" at every awards ceremony at the end of the year, making it even harder for their little group with one foot already at death's door to survive. All they were

left with was the occasional mall concert. The remainder of the time, every member left to find work using his own ability.

It had been such a long time since they last enjoyed being surrounded by such a lively group of fans. Even He Hansong, who normally fumed with rage whenever he saw Ye Qin, put a curb on his temper. Still humming after the gig, he invited Ye Qin and Song Xu to stay for a night at a nearby five-star hotel.

Having disliked him for so long, Ye Qin couldn't help but feel that He Hansong was up to something. He searched the lounge inside and out for Xiao-Yun so they could rejoin the crew.

"Yun-jiejie was just called away by Yueyue-jie," Song Xu told him. "Let's go together. I'm here."

He Hansong had just removed his makeup. "Look at you hicks. Are you scared that I'll sell you?" he snickered while spraying his face with toner. Then, he looked at Ye Qin from the corner of his eyes. "Every bit of flesh and bone on your body wouldn't be worth what it costs to stay one night at that hotel."

His family's decline was a thing of the past. As much as Ye Qin was in dire straits, he still had some pride in his bones. To prove himself worldly, he let Song Xu drag him to the hotel.

The two of them shared a suite. As soon as he entered, Song Xu cried out and made a beeline for the pool, diving right in. Ye Qin was nowhere as energetic. He'd run and jumped all morning for his shoot, and then stood on stage for several hours in the afternoon. Now, his waist was so sore it didn't even feel like a part of him.

Out of the blue, Ye Qin remembered what that elderly doctor had told him when he last visited the hospital to have his tail bone checked: "You should take care of your body while you're still young, or you'll suffer when you get old." Ye Qin slowly lay down on his bed and pulled a blanket over his waist.

As he massaged it, he dozed off sleepily.

When he woke again, it was dark all over. Only the scattered lights outside the window lit up the faint outlines of the room décor.

Ye Qin called Song Xu's name several times and got no response. That guy was probably living it up somewhere and hadn't come back yet.

He got out of bed, put on his slippers, and went to get a drink from the fridge in the living room. The cold bottled water slid down his throat, waking him from drowsiness. It also helped clear his vision, which had been blurry from staying in the dark for too long.

He saw someone lying on the sofa.

Thinking that it was Song Xu, who had returned without making a sound and had mistaken the sofa for a bed, Ye Qin walked over and tugged the arm dangling off the sofa. "Don't sleep here. There's a bed in the bedroom."

It wasn't until he touched a tightly cuffed wrist and a steel watch heated by the warmth of a human body that Ye Qin realized something wasn't right. He jumped and went to turn on the lights.

The person sleeping on the sofa wasn't roused by Ye Qin's movements.

Ye Qin tiptoed back. Before holding in his breath, he caught a delayed whiff of booze in the air.

He looked down slightly at the man lying defenseless on the sofa. Bending over, Ye Qin lifted the man's hand gently and put it at his side. Then, he fetched a blanket and covered him, before slowly squatting down next to the man.

He didn't know why Cheng Feichi would be here. He just didn't want to break this hard-won peace.

Perhaps because he had been drinking, Cheng Feichi slept very deeply. His lips were slightly pursed, and his brows were drawn into a deep furrow. Ye Qin couldn't help but reach out

and touch the skin between them, gently smoothing out the crease. But as soon as his fingers left, those eyebrows wrinkled again; as if Cheng Feichi was full of inescapable melancholy and unease even in his dreams.

He hasn't been happy recently, Ye Qin thought. *He doesn't laugh, not because the jokes aren't funny, but because he's unhappy. He doesn't want to laugh.*

But why? With a burden like Ye Qin lifted off his shoulders, shouldn't he spread his wings and soar? Shouldn't he be circling the skies freely, with no one to tie him down anymore?

After leaving his scumbag self, Cheng Feichi should have walked a straight, smooth road. Everyone he met should have been kind-hearted. He was such a nice person. How could anyone have the heart to hurt him?

When Ye Qin thought that there might have been someone out there who hurt Cheng Feichi the way he once did, his heart hurt so much.

As he held Cheng Feichi's hand, Ye Qin accidentally felt an unnatural bulge in his right palm. He carefully turned over the hand and saw a scar in a distinctly different shade than the rest of Cheng Feichi's skin.

The winding scar crossed Cheng Feichi's entire palm. The regrown flesh was a gut-wrenching red. Though it'd already been healed for quite some time, he could still imagine the ghastly sight of when the skin and flesh had initially been cut open.

Ye Qin suddenly remembered the day they broke up. Cheng Feichi's right hand had been wrapped in thick gauze. When Ye Qin wanted to grab his hand and take a look, Cheng Feichi had moved it away. At that time, Ye Qin had been too angry to take note of it.

So had he gotten this wound before that day? Why? Back then, his mother had been staying at the hospital, his father had wanted him to rejoin the Yi family. They'd wanted to send him abroad, and he had refused. *To go to C University with me...*

Many vignettes from Ye Qin's past that he had never really thought about in detail flew into his mind. His heart pounded, and his breathing also became rapid. Just as the truth was in his reach, the hand he held onto shifted.

Cheng Feichi woke up to an unfamiliar ceiling. He didn't know where he was, but having built up vigilance over the years, he reflexively clamped down on the hand holding his, trapping the person immediately next to him.

"Ah!" Ye Qin cried in pain, making Cheng Feichi's eyes shift to his face.

Though he recognized the person, his hand showed absolutely no signs of letting go.

Ye Qin could feel Cheng Feichi's hand shaking, and his palm was covered in a layer of cold sweat.

"Did you have a bad dream?" he asked hurriedly, thinking that Cheng Feichi had gotten a scare. "It's okay now. There, there, don't be afraid."

Grasping at straws, he tried to soothe Cheng Feichi using the same method Cheng Feichi once used to comfort him.

And it actually worked! Not a minute had passed before Cheng Feichi calmed down, his breathing evening out. Yet he still looked at Ye Qin with gloomy eyes that made the latter feel pressured.

Ye Qin tried to wriggle his wrist free several times, to no avail.

He presumed Cheng Feichi was acting this way out of anxiety, having just woken up from a bad dream. Ye Qin was about to offer him water when he heard a low, hoarse voice.

"Are you done?"

Dumbfounded, a puzzled look appeared in Ye Qin's eyes.

Cheng Feichi didn't elaborate further. "How many times

has it been now?" he continued asking instead.

Ye Qin's lips trembled. He thought he somewhat understood what Cheng Feichi was saying, but he wasn't entirely sure. "Wh-what do you mean?"

One man reclining on the sofa and one man squatting on the floor confronted each other in strange postures.

Cheng Feichi stared at him for a while. Suddenly, he hooked up the corner of his mouth, and yet his eyes contained no laughter. "This love game you're playing, is it fun?"

It was as if someone struck Ye Qin with a stick with no prior warning. His whole head buzzed. His heart, too, got knocked into an endless abyss by this violent shock, plunging at ten million times the speed of free fall.

Yes, that was right. After meeting again, they kept running into each other repeatedly. It was such a coincidence that even Ye Qin would have thought it had been arranged on purpose. Wasn't this exactly the same as all those things that he had done before?

Putting on the pouty, docile act at inappropriate times; shamelessly highlighting his weakness and currying favor. There had been a time when he burned down mountains of thorns with a carelessly lit fire. There had been a time when he broke through heavy defenses and entered Cheng Feichi's heart that had once been as calm as peaceful waters. Then, after stirring up waves and storms, Ye Qin told him heartlessly that it had all been a game, a malicious trick that rose from an absurd hate.

Cheng Feichi was kind, but that didn't mean that his tolerance had no bounds. Neither did he forget easily. After getting hurt so deeply, he couldn't even if he wanted to. Every midnight when he dreamed, the past seeped into every crevice of his mind and took form in front of his eyes.

How could he forget? How could he possibly forget?

Unprecedented despair swallowed Ye Qin like a giant wave

at high tide, sweeping away his disordered breathing and putting a halt to his loud heartbeat.

Ye Qin spent every waking moment thinking of how to ask for forgiveness, how to get back to Cheng Feichi, the best person in the world. Yet he neglected the most important thing: Back then, he had been Cheng Feichi's entire hope, a ray of sunlight; one that he would defy his parents without question for, and throw away his future just to hold onto.

Whereas now, he was nothing.

The room was filled with a freezing silence. It was so quiet that one could hear the sound of a needle falling to the ground.

Cheng Feichi let go of Ye Qin's hand. He took a deep breath and slowly let it out of his lungs, so that he could clear his muddled head.

He'd lost control in an unfamiliar room in front of Ye Qin.

His hand started throbbing with a dull swelling pain due to overexertion. He wiggled his fingers and opened his palm. Because the tendon had been severed years ago, it was still stiff to this day. When he heard a low "sorry" from the man beside him, Cheng Feichi only paused momentarily before sitting up and taking in his surroundings.

He was too careless.

Before going to the dinner party, he'd heard that Cheng Xin had single-handedly stormed off to the Yi family again. Cheng Feichi hurried back to stop her from making a scene and endured her hysterics the entire way as he escorted her back. The crying and cursing still rang in his ears after he arrived at the dinner party. With everyone urging him to drink, he couldn't help letting loose and had a few more than he should.

After, his head spun so much that he only wanted to find a place to rest. With his guard down, Cheng Feichi took a room

card that was handed to him, assuming that it was indeed empty as the person had said. As soon as he entered the room, he passed out on the sofa.

Sitting up made the blood rush back to his head. With full clarity, Cheng Feichi strung together the cause and effect of all events that took place. After thoroughly reviewing everything, he pinpointed the fishiness of the affair. Someone clearly planned this. That person must have heard something about him and Ye Qin. As to whether this trap was set up as a pitfall or a way to curry favor, Cheng Feichi could find out with some minor investigations.

It was just that he hadn't expected Ye Qin to be caught up in this.

Cheng Feichi confirmed from personal observations that this was a regular suite in the hotel. He closed his eyes and pinched the space between his eyebrows. There were too many coincidences. He didn't know what role Ye Qin had played in all of this, if he was approaching Cheng Feichi intentionally or if he was simply being used. There was no way to tell just based on the naked eye.

After all, Ye Qin was superb at acting. Six years ago, he had already played Cheng Feichi for a complete fool. Now, as an actor, his skills must have reached new heights.

Cheng Feichi stood up, grabbed the coat that had been slung on the back of the sofa, and left straight for the door.

Flustered, Ye Qin hurriedly followed after him. But his legs, tingling from squatting too long, barely took two steps before giving way, bumping into the marble tea table. He almost fell.

Cheng Feichi heard the noise behind him and turned back. He saw Ye Qin propping up his knee with his wrist. It had finger imprints from when Cheng Feichi's had squeezed down earlier. Ye Qin raised his head, showing red lips and white teeth on a petite face set with a pair of reddened eyes moist with tears, looking both pitiful and stubborn.

Cheng Feichi was reminded of the same look that Ye Qin had given him at their first reunion at that dinner party. His eyes had been moving everywhere in evasion and he bit into his lips so hard they almost bled. And even then, he thought he hadn't been discovered.

"Sorry," Ye Qin repeated in a hoarse voice. "I don't know why things turned out like this. As soon as I woke up, I saw you…"

"I know," Cheng Feichi interjected.

He had no time to figure out if Ye Qin was telling the truth. This was something he would look into later by himself. He didn't want to hear Ye Qin's explanation because he didn't want to let his guard down in this situation. Or perhaps it was because of a subconscious lack of self-confidence.

Once, he had enough confidence to maintain rationality and caution in all circumstances, and he had indeed accomplished that for the past five years. Yet perhaps it was because he was drunk or overtly nervous from falling into someone's trap. On top of that, he had to take caution against himself. Cheng Feichi didn't want to listen anymore, afraid that his excellent judgement would be influenced.

Ye Qin was stunned at his harsh, cold interjection. Seeing Cheng Feichi's right hand slightly shaking as it hung at his side, Ye Qin couldn't help taking a few steps and speaking out of concern, "Your hand…"

This time, Cheng Feichi didn't let him finish, opening the door and leaving without hesitation.

Through the door, Ye Qin heard his steady footsteps fade into complete silence.

He stood in place, shook his head, and muttered to himself absentmindedly, "I wasn't…I wasn't playing a love game."

Ye Qin's eyes stung. He covered his face with his hands, and let his trembling eyelashes prickle his palms. "Sorry..." he repeated to empty air.

Early next morning, as he was having breakfast on the second floor of the hotel, He Hansong gracefully picked up a piece of a waffle and set it down on his plate. Just as he was just about to go back to his seat and enjoy breakfast, he felt a breeze against his back. Completely unprepared for the guy who grabbed him by the back of his collar and threw him against the wall, he didn't have a chance to scream before that person squeezed his throat.

Ye Qin took the plate in his hand, dropped it on the table. "Did you pull that crap last night?" he leaned in and asked in his ear.

So choked he could barely breathe, He Hansong dry coughed and "said, "What...what do you mean last night?"

Ye Qin dragged him off the wall and shoved him heavily. "Don't play dumb with me. Who else could have done it?"

The pain of having his shoulder blades strike the hard wall made He Hansong wince. Furthermore, they were inside a blind angle of the dining room, so no one else saw. To keep up the bluff, He Hansong tilted his chin high and looked down at Ye Qin with raised eyebrows. "You got such a big advantage, so shouldn't you thank me instead of biting the hand that feeds you?"

Anger burnt even more furiously in Ye Qin's eyes. "So it was you!"

He Hansong set his own hands on the wrists of Ye Qin's hands, which were still clenched on his neck. He pushed forward with all his might and gasped heavily, smirking, "Who's playing dumb, exactly? You're clearly on cloud nine from bagging yourself a rich patron. You want to erect a monument of chastity while whoring yourself?"

He had disdained Ye Qin's loftiness for a long time. A young master from a fallen family? More like a packaged trick. Even within their group, he was in the lowest tier, the least popular one, garbage who was only fit for polishing his shoes. Somewhere along the line, he even found the guts to seduce Tang Chong—He Hansong had wanted to teach him a lesson for a long time now.

Ye Qin was momentarily stunned by his thinly veiled insults. A moment later, he realized, "It was Tang Chong! He's the one who made you do this, isn't he? Where is he?"

He Hansong naturally wouldn't tell him. Ye Qin's lost look brought him a rush of joy in his heart, and he sneered as he straightened his crumpled collar.

During the day, Ye Qin used his breaks in between takes to call Tang Chong quite a few times. He circled through all three of Tang Chong's numbers, but none of his calls got through.

That further confirmed his suspicions—Tang Chong was most likely responsible for last night's shenanigans. He'd sensed something peculiar about Ye Qin and Cheng Feichi's relationship and deliberately set a trap for Cheng Feichi.

It was also possible that Tang Chong had tried to earn himself a debt of gratitude from Cheng Feichi. After thinking of this, Ye Qin was no longer angry at being used as a gift to curry favor. Instead, he began to worry about Cheng Feichi's situation. Cheng Feichi had just returned to China. He didn't know of the degenerate mess behind the scenes of the business world here. Tang Chong was just the first to use these twisted tricks against him. There would always be a second and a third.

All throughout the grapevine, it was said that Cheng Feichi had yet to secure his position in the Yi family. Ye Qin could also tell from the manner Cheng Xin spoke on the past phone call. For this kind of scandal to take place at such a critical time, Cheng Feichi could only stand to lose from it.

Ye Qin anxiously opened up Cheng Feichi's chat, contemplating whether to send him a message reminding him to beware the scum around him. For several minutes, he dwelled on the text input, unsure of what pretext to use to start the conversation.

Perhaps Cheng Feichi would just neglect his message. Perhaps he would believe that Ye Qin was playing one of his clever tricks again.

An overwhelming feeling of powerlessness descended on him. Ye Qin was afraid of being misunderstood by Cheng Feichi, but what he feared more was Cheng Feichi ignoring him from then on.

Yet this was the evil fruit borne by what he himself had planted. He could only rely on himself now. He would pull the baleful plant out, even if the process was punishing and painful, even if the plant, having rooted deep in the soil, could only wither and eventually turn into dust along with the luxuriant foliage of memories, never to see the sun again.

By the time Ye Qin finished work for the day, the words that he wanted to say already filled up a page. He folded the slip of paper and stuffed it into the pocket of the suit that he had yet to return.

As soon as he finished packing, a call came from Zhou Feng. "What have you been up to? I couldn't reach you for the entire day."

Ye Qin's voice lacked spirit. "I was up in the mountains. Signal wasn't good."

"You're still in the mountains? Aren't you participating in—what's it called— 'Avancez!'?"

Ye Qin turned on speaker mode and put his phone on the table. Picking up a tube of ointment, he sat cross-legged on the bed. "How did you know?"

"Apart from chasing Yuanyuan, I spend all my free time finding out what you're up to. You know what? I'm the first to sign in and search your Super Topic on Weibo every day. Isn't that so touching?"

Although his scratched skin hadn't healed yet, the coming reality show included segments that involved getting in the water. Thus, Ye Qin had to apply the ointment to his wound three times a day. Grimacing with pain, he answered, "Thank you so much, officer. Your time is *so* valuable. Please mind your own business. Your attention is not required here, thank you very much."

"Not at all. There is a ninety-ten ratio between Yuanyuan and you. I'm not actually paying that much attention to you."

Even Zhou Feng's bad jokes couldn't cheer Ye Qin up. He went silent for a long moment, eyelids cast down. "I ran into him yesterday."

"Where?"

"In a hotel suite."

Zhou Feng fell silent for a while. "Our A-Qin is indeed a true man. You managed to get him alone in a locked room in such a short time! If I had half your courage, I would have already taken Yuanyuan as my wife."

When he had learned of Liao Yifang's thoughts from Ye Qin, Zhou Feng had looked quite stricken. But just when Ye Qin thought he was going to let go of Liao Yifang, Zhou Feng went back to his old self. With his spirits rejuvenated, he came up with a long list of new plans in an entirely invigorated manner.

Admiring Zhou Feng's ability to regain his spirit after continuous defeats, Ye Qin asked him how he managed to do it.

Zhou Feng replied, "Whenever I think about Yuanyuan being someone else's husband or wife one day, I can't eat or sleep. Actually, I don't want to do anything until I get him back."

Ye Qin had similar thoughts, but he didn't dare to voice them.

The more he thought about it, the more he felt ashamed of himself—of his infatuation and wild dreams. He waited for Cheng Feichi to shatter his dreams and tell him, "I don't want to see you anymore." But at the same time, he hoped that these words would never come from his lips because then, he could still find reasons to show up at his side, even if that meant always keeping a low profile and never holding his head high anymore.

"I didn't *get* him behind doors," Ye Qin said unhappily. "I was caught in a trap with him."

After hearing him recount the events, Zhou Feng sighed as if he had just watched a three-hour drama inside his head. "The celebrity ring is degenerate indeed... You know what, maybe you should mention my family when you're out by yourself. S-City is a bit far from the capital, but my old man still counts as renowned. That way, you might be able to intimidate some people."

"Aren't you afraid of being thrashed by your dad?" Ye Qin objected before pausing for a moment. "Speaking of which, there's something else I'd like you to help with."

Five days later, before the actual shoot took place, Ye Qin browsed the school forum with his attention completely focused on the phone screen. Every post that mentioned a certain Cheng, once regarded as the hottest guy in school, got censored. The nasty comments were either reported and deleted or hidden by the admin. The discussion surrounding Cheng Feichi's family and parentage died off.

"Is this what you call...fan comment suppression?" Zhou Feng asked in WeChat as if he had seen through Ye Qin. "Are you going to take credit and seek rewards from our straight-A student? Since you went through so much trouble."

Ye Qin regarded this as him and Zhou Feng lending each other a helping hand. Satisfied with the result, he left the forum page and said, "Would you be able to hold in your anger if they said those things about your Yuanyuan?"

Ye Qin couldn't stand anyone finding fault with Cheng Feichi. Even five years ago, he had had this problem. Despite clearly defining Cheng Feichi as his enemy, he couldn't stand anyone else saying a bad word about him. Back then, he thought that it was because he hated it when someone questioned his taste. Later, he realized his own behavior meant he had taken Cheng Feichi under his wing.

His gege was such a nice person. No one could say bad things about him.

The show they were going to shoot today had also been assigned by Zheng Yueyue. It was a temporary job that fit into their busy schedules. He Hansong and Ye Qin were going to show up on set to shoot as guests. The filming location was in a high-end hotel in S-City where the well-funded crew had rented one of the hotel's indoor swimming pools.

Ye Qin stayed silent from when he entered the dressing room throughout changing and doing his makeup. Several times He Hansong tried to provoke him with jeers but he ignored them all.

"You didn't get this job from his connections. Yueyue-jie also says you don't always need to be so tolerant," Xiao-Yun, his assistant, whispered in his ear.

Ye Qin shook his head. He just wanted to remain unnoticeable. Tang Chong would not have been able to put him and Cheng Feichi in that situation without help from He Hansong. If he pissed off that petty guy again and brought disaster upon Cheng Feichi, Ye Qin would never have the courage to face him again.

Nor did he want to appear in front of Cheng Feichi again, unprepared as he asked, "How many times?"

But despite Ye Qin's refusal to stir up trouble, some people just didn't want to leave him alone.

Today, S-City was rainy and colder than previous days. The swimming pool was well air-conditioned. This indoor temperature, acceptable to other people, became unbearable to Ye Qin who had been afraid of cold since birth. After half an hour in the water, his limbs began to stiffen and his blood seemed to freeze.

As Ye Qin was not a big shot, he did not have a say in this. Naturally, he wasn't naïve enough to approach the staff and request them to turn the temperature up. After two hours of shooting, he was frozen with cold. His face drained chalk-white while his lips turned purple. Wrapped up in three bath towels by Xiao-Yun, Ye Qin sat in the lounge with a cup of hot water in his hand. It took him quite a while to recover.

"The suit has been delivered to President Cheng's personal assistant," Xiao-Yun reported next to him. "I waited for him near the building."

"Did he...say anything?" Ye Qin finally responded.

Ever since he had learned that this hotel belonged to the Yi family, thanks to Zhou Feng's extensive connections, Ye Qin had been planning this. The group's headquarters was in an office building nearby. Afraid that a hasty attempt of reestablishing contact would repel Cheng Feichi, Ye Qin wanted to take advantage of today's shoot. He had taken the suit with him so that Xiao-Yun could deliver it to the front desk of that office building, but he hadn't foreseen that she would bump into Cheng Feichi as he was making an inspection tour.

"President Cheng himself didn't say anything, but his PA said...said..."

Xiao-Yun was reluctant to finish the sentence. Ye Qin, however, was unable to hold himself back. "What?" he demanded.

"He said...he said that there's no need to return it. President Cheng is not short of a single piece of clothing."

Ye Qin sat dumb with incomprehension as if he was still

digesting the meaning of this sentence. It took two or three minutes for him to slowly stand up. "Let's go. There's still some shooting ahead."

Xiao-Yun handed over his clothes. He put them on, habitually going for his pants pockets first.

He lifted the fabric and reached inside. Nothing was there.

He checked all the other pockets. Still nothing.

Ye Qin went into panic all at once. He took the ring that Cheng Feichi had given him everywhere he went. When he first entered the circle, he wore it on his left ring finger and was often asked by fans and reporters if he had a girlfriend. That, combined with opposition and pressure from his agency, made Ye Qin string it up and wear it around his neck ever since. Hidden inside his clothes, it was kept away from the public's eyes.

Not many people knew about this, apart from those who were close. For example, people who once lived in the same room with him.

Burning with rage, Ye Qin stormed into the lounge next door only to find it empty. He took out his cellphone and dialed He Hansong's number. As soon as the call had been put through, Ye Qin demanded hastily, "Where did you hide my ring?"

Knowing that Ye Qin could not physically reach him for the time being, He Hansong took his time and answered with relish, "What are you talking about? That piece of trash you wear on your neck like something precious?"

"Yes, that one. Where is it?" Ye Qin forcefully suppressed his temper.

"Ah, let me think. I saw it on the floor when I entered the lounge today. I thought some other guest lost it... It looked like a Cartier, but you couldn't tell if it's real or fake. There was only one diamond after all, so tiny that anyone with dull vision would miss it..."

He Hansong was deliberately delaying the crucial information. He spoke of everything but the whereabouts of the ring. It wasn't until Ye Qin had almost lost it that he seemed to arrive at the eureka moment. "Oh yes, speaking of which, I couldn't find anywhere to keep it, so I just threw it into the pool before the shoot."

As soon as he heard this, Ye Qin couldn't care less about giving him a thrashing. He put down the cellphone and ran for the pool.

The pool area had just closed. A water pump hummed in preparation for filtration and a water change. Despite his assistant and the staff's attempts to stop him, Ye Qin jumped straight in, afraid that his ring would be lost in the process.

An hour later, Ye Qin bowed apologetically to the pool staff one by one. Afterwards, he returned to the lounge and took off the wet clothes. He squeezed them before putting them back on, still wet and sticky. It felt really awkward.

Xiao-Yun was knocking on the door, sounding flustered, "There are fans at the main entrance. I'll go down and distract them. You take the staff elevator."

Ye Qin sighed. *It never rains unless it pours,* he thought. Normally he couldn't find fans anywhere, only for them to show up when he was least graceful.

...They probably came just to see He Hansong.

Wrapped in a dry towel, Ye Qin quickly crossed the pool with his hair still dripping. Following the staff's instructions, he headed towards the staff elevator.

Ye Qin walked with his back bent over like a thief, not even daring to lift his head. The pool thermostat had already been turned off. He had stayed in cold water for over an hour looking for the ring, and his limbs were still shivering now. Even as he pressed the elevator button, his hand shook uncontrollably.

Thank God he had found it. Ye Qin uncurled his palm. He gazed at the ring, now safely kept in his hand, and pulled the corners of his mouth up into a reassuring smile.

When the elevator doors opened, he was still looking at that ring.

There was already someone inside, so he walked straight into the corner with his head hung modestly. Once the elevator doors were shut, he picked up the ring, blew on it, and put it back on his left ring finger before holding it up before his eyes. Now away from the eyes of fans, he took advantage of the privacy of this little enclosed space to scrutinize it from different angles.

It was only when the other person in the elevator asked, "Which floor," that Ye Qin jolted. In a trance, his eyes focused on the face he had been dreaming about.

Ye Qin was barely able to command himself to press the button for the ground floor. His entire brain nearly blanked out. Sparks danced here and there as if parts of it had gone missing and it wouldn't be long before it fell apart.

Who could imagine that he would meet Cheng Feichi under these circumstances?

During the five years when Ye Qin had missed Cheng Feichi like crazy and wanted to get back together, he let his imagination run wild. He had thought of myriad ways to meet but never dared to picture such a scene.

It was truly bizarre.

Just as he was desperately trying to think of a way to explain his presence with what scattered wits he had left, something even more bizarre happened.

After moving three floors down normally, the elevator took a plunge. At an uncanny speed, it dropped more than ten floors.

Scared out of his mind, Ye Qin simply couldn't control himself. When the elevator finally stopped and the lights overhead

burned out, he had already buried his entire body in the arms of the other person on board.

Compared to him, Cheng Feichi was so calm that he didn't even look as if he was just in an elevator accident.

In only a few seconds, he had pressed the buttons for all remaining floors. Even now, in pitch dark, he not only refused to panic but even had the time to grab Ye Qin's arm, straighten up his limp body, and enable him to lean against the corner. After that, he freed his hand, pulled out his cellphone, and began making calls.

Ye Qin opened his mouth and took a few sharp gasps. His eyes were tightly closed, however, and it was hard to tell whether it was out of shame or fear. The hand that wore the ring was still on Cheng Feichi's body, clenching the shirt fabric around his waist.

Although Cheng Feichi had no intention of pushing him away for the moment at least, Ye Qin loosened his hand after a few deep breaths. He barely just managed to calm himself down.

One by one, he uncurled his fingers and let go of the fabric. No matter how much he had wanted to prolong the entanglement, he didn't take a trace of warmth with him.

By then, Cheng Feichi had already finished calling the rescue team. His phone screen had just dimmed when he heard broken voices coming from Ye Qin, who had shrunken into a ball at the corner. "I...I didn't mean to do that." He swallowed, nearly choking himself as his voice grew even weaker. "This elevator... this accident...I didn't make this happen. I didn't know...I didn't know that you...that you would also be here."

This explanation, seemingly from nowhere, made Cheng Feichi's throat tighten.

He could hear from Ye Qin's voice that he was crying.

CHAPTER 19

IN such a confined space, even a tiny bit of sound could be amplified infinitely by resonance between walls. A little sobbing sound couldn't escape his ears.

Ye Qin hadn't meant to cry. He'd held back his tears when he had stood at his mother's funeral, when he had had no choice but to enter the entertainment industry, when he had been ostracized and bullied, when he had talked about old times with his best buddy. At times, when it became too much to bear, he let the tears circle in his eyes before holding them in resolutely, as if he could deceive both himself and the others that nothing had happened.

He was no longer a child anymore, and he knew that crying would not solve any problems. Crying just made people think he was weak, made himself easy prey; able to be tossed into the mud with a flick of the wrist. He wanted to survive. He wanted to be stronger. He wanted Cheng Feichi to see that he could be steady and reliable too.

The darkness alone was not enough to bring him to tears. He was afraid that Cheng Feichi would hate him. He was afraid of never being able to be near Cheng Feichi again. They were so far away from each other. There were less than two meters of distance between their bodies, but they seemed to be separated by a ten-thousand-foot gulf. Even life and death became irrelevant when it came to such a distance.

The tears gushed down despite Ye Qin's attempt to control himself. He was so afraid. He dug his nails into his palms in a fiercely clenched fist in order to prevent his teeth from clacking. "The first...the first time we met, it was my manager who took me there to say hello to a few big-shots who I'd never seen before. I didn't...know you would come."

Cheng Feichi didn't make a sound to stop him from talking, so he went on.

"The second time, in the hospital, I was there because I had really hurt my tailbone. I wouldn't have taken time off to see the doctor if the plasters worked the way they should. I still have my X-ray. I can show it to you if you want.

"The third time, in the mountains, I planned to visit my mother's tomb the next morning. I didn't expect to get lost. When I called you, I didn't expect it to go through. I booked my own B&B in advance. If you don't believe me, you can look at my order confirmation.

"The fourth time, Tang Chong lied to me that you were with him, drunk. I only realized after arriving that he tricked me. The fifth time, Tang Chong was behind that as well... We have some unsettled grudges between us."

As he narrated their encounters one by one, Ye Qin slowly regained composure.

He was afraid of being in the dark, but the darkness had given him courage. When he could no longer see Cheng Feichi's face, he could let go of his self-regard and dignity as if they did not exist.

After all, it wasn't his first time appearing in front of Cheng Feichi in such an undignified state. He might as well write this one off as hopeless and recklessly pour out what he had always meant to say. That would be better than stammering and dragging his feet.

"This time, I'm here to shoot a show. I heard that you might be around, so I asked my assistant to send those clothes over." Finally arriving at the current situation, Ye Qin felt both helplessness and a surge of relief. "I took the elevator because there are fans downstairs. I am not...I am not playing..."

He struggled for a long time but still could not manage to say "love games" out loud. Cheng Feichi's even breathing reached his ears, and Ye Qin dropped his shoulders, discouraged. "I promise, this will surely...surely be the last time."

For some reason, the words "last time" seemed to trigger a sensitive nerve in Cheng Feichi's brain and his fingers hanging at his side twitched a little. That seemed to be his only reaction to this revelation.

The maintenance crew soon arrived.

The elevator was stuck between Floor 7 and 8, but closer to the upper. The rescuers threw down ropes from the eighth floor.

Cheng Feichi wanted to send Ye Qin up first, but Ye Qin shook his head and shrunk back, dropping his eyes to the ground. "You...you go first."

Standing under the light, he began to stammer again.

Cheng Feichi had no choice but to go up first. Then, he turned around and squatted down, offering his hand to pull Ye Qin up. Ye Qin tugged the rope but didn't dare move. Finally, because he was really scared, he lifted his hand and grabbed Cheng Feichi's for support. Immediately after he climbed up, Ye Qin let go, not daring to linger a second longer.

The tip of his nose was red from the extreme cold. His hands were also cold and his face was streaked with trails of

tears. The bath towel wrapped around his body had already fallen on the ground when the elevator stalled. Now, Ye Qin only wore a wet T-shirt and a casual pair of pants that clung to his body. The outfit revealed his extremely slender waist and protruding shoulder blades. Despite his height, he was too thin for a grown man of twenty-three.

Several staff members explained to Cheng Feichi the cause of this technical failure. Ye Qin more or less grasped that Cheng Feichi had come to inspect their work. The elevator had chosen to break down with the boss inside—no wonder they were scared into such a state.

At this moment, Cheng Feichi looked quite grim. Ye Qin guessed that in addition to this accident, his nonsensical confession inside the elevator just now also played a part. Seizing a gap in the conversation, he quietly interjected, "Excuse me, I... I think I should probably go now."

Unable to think of a gesture to accompany this sentence, Ye Qin bowed habitually. Then he turned and ran.

It took Ye Qin a long time to unlock his cellphone, which had become very wet in his warm pocket. He called Xiao-Yun while walking, turned a corner, and left through the side door. He was promptly welcomed with a heavy shower of girls holding up boards with "He."

The girl in the front row squealed in delight and ran towards him, bringing over everyone behind her. Ye Qin cursed He Hansong a million times over in his head and desperately looked around in search of a hiding place. He saw a sign for the nearest safety exit and was about to go that way when someone grabbed his arm from behind.

Ye Qin thought he had been ambushed and almost began struggling when he turned and met Cheng Feichi's face. His tense muscles instantly relaxed.

Cheng Feichi had the same idea as Ye Qin. He led him to the stairwell usually reserved for the cleaning staff. They went down to the basement, out into the parking lot, and through the winding walkway toward an elevator. No one was there.

At this point, Ye Qin still had a lingering fear of elevators. He shrunk back his neck and took a step backward. "I can just wait at the stairs. They didn't come for me, so they'll be gone in a moment."

Even though Cheng Feichi heard his words, the hand that he slid around Ye Qin's wrist did not loosen. "This is the reserved elevator. You'll be fine," he said.

There was no direct connection between "the reserved elevator" and "you'll be fine," but Ye Qin accepted this logic easily enough. Frozen to the spot, he "oh"ed before following Cheng Feichi into the elevator that took them straight to the top floor.

The top floor of the hotel was a private venue closed off to the public. The hallway was so quiet that one could barely hear the sound of footsteps treading on the carpet. There was only one suite there, and it was not numbered. The door was equipped with a fingerprint lock. Cheng Feichi took the lead and went in, but Ye Qin stood at the door, hesitating with his hands behind his back.

When he was certain no one would see, he secretly used his right hand to rub the part of the skin with warmer temperature. "My feet are dirty...can I take off my shoes?"

Cheng Feichi turned and looked at him. A trace of surprise flashed across his eyes. "Just come in," he said after a moment's pause. "There's no need to take off your shoes."

This penthouse was obviously Cheng Feichi's personal space, for his use only. Its interior decor took after a style entirely different from other bedrooms in the hotel. Things were gray

and white, simple and clean.

In the living room, the wall usually adorned with a TV was instead transformed into a whole wall of bookshelves. There was one mug on the dining room table, and only one towel, one pair of slippers, and one toothbrush in the bathroom. There were traces of life everywhere. Ye Qin assumed that Cheng Feichi came here often.

Ye Qin called his assistant to inform her of his whereabouts. He had just hung up when Cheng Feichi knocked on the bathroom door. He didn't enter himself and simply handed Ye Qin the toiletries through a crack in the door. "Turn the tap left for hot water," he said from the other side. "For cold, turn right."

Ye Qin unpacked a new pair of slippers in front of the mirror. He happened to look up and saw himself with wrinkled clothes and messy hair. His pounding heart slowed down gradually and returned to a normal rhythm.

He looked so miserable that it would probably elicit pity from any good person. Lending him a hand would not be so different from saving a drowning dog.

After a hot bath, Ye Qin felt his body vibrate with warmth and come back to life. Afraid that Cheng Feichi would grow impatient if he took too long in the bathroom, he went out without wiping his hair dry. It wasn't until he saw a glass of water with two capsules of cold medicine on the table and heard sounds coming from the kitchen that his heart fell back into his chest.

The cup was disposable, though, and there would be no lollipops as a reward for dutifully finishing his medicine.

Thanks to the heater, the room was a bit too warm. That, and the fact that he felt nervous and ill at ease gave Ye Qin a thin layer of sweat after sitting still for a short while. Using "adjusting the temperature" as an excuse, Ye Qin walked across the dining room and peeked into the kitchen. Cheng Feichi stood in front of the stove with his back to him. His shirt cuffs were unbuttoned and folded back, revealing the smooth muscle contours of his arms.

The view of Cheng Feichi's back put Ye Qin in a trance and transported him back to the time when they lived together at Jiayuan Compound. Back then, Cheng Feichi also stood like this in the kitchen, cooking. When he heard footsteps, he would even turn around and smile at Ye Qin.

Ye Qin tried his best to hold back and restrain himself so he wouldn't spring forward and take this long-lost figure in his arms.

He was afraid of scaring him away. In that case, he might never get him back again.

What he was even more afraid of was becoming too greedy for the warmth to part with it ever again.

Cheng Feichi never liked to eat out before, and he still didn't.

Two bowls of egg noodles were placed on the table. When he saw Ye Qin eating rather slowly, he asked, "Not to your taste? I'll order room service for you."

It was lunchtime, and the kitchen of a starred hotel offered all kinds of food. Any dish would be more elaborate than this plain bowl of noodles.

"It's very tasty," Ye Qin replied hurriedly. "It's just a bit too hot."

He wasn't very good at lying. When he lied, his eyes drifted, unable to find a focus. Stiffly, he picked up two noodles and pursed his lips, feeding them inch by inch into his mouth as if he was indeed afraid of the heat.

Ye Qin finished less than a third of it before Cheng Feichi finished eating. When he saw Cheng Feichi standing, Ye Qin also put down the chopsticks and stood up.

"If you can't finish, just leave it on the table." Cheng Feichi left to wash his hands and was now putting on his jacket. "Take the reserved elevator to the underground floor and walk along

the aisle," he instructed. "Turn left, then right, and then right again. Go straight up the stairs and you will see the back door where you can get a taxi."

Ye Qin knew he was leaving. The meal was too short. He hadn't had time to say anything.

He wanted to ask if Cheng Feichi had seen the note stuffed into the pocket of that suit. He wanted to ask how he had spent the last five years. *Is your hand okay? Do you still hate me? Beat me, yell at me if you want, and I won't leave. Would it help your anger, even if just a little?*

Ye Qin trailed along with a face full of panic and apprehension. His distress reminded Cheng Feichi of something. Cheng Feichi fetched his wallet from the inside pocket of his jacket and produced a few hundred yuan. "That should be enough to get you to Cangquan Mountain."

Ye Qin raised his hand and lowered it again, torn between taking and not taking it. If he took it, that would reveal his incompetency. If he refused, he didn't know what he could use as an excuse to meet with Cheng Feichi in the future.

When he saw Ye Qin unable to make up his mind, Cheng Feichi put the money on the cabinet in the foyer, and turned, about to leave.

A hand tugged the corner of his coat from behind.

This time, it was probably the bowl of noodles that gave him courage. "What I said was all true. Those things I said in the elevator...I wasn't lying to you," Ye Qin said somewhat anxiously.

And I will never lie to you again. Never, never, ever, lie to you again.

He knew he still had a long way to go to reach the forgiveness he longed for. He just didn't want to add another layer of misunderstanding to their already entangled, badly damaged relationship.

The wall clock ticked in the living room as if hope was also slipping away by the second. Ye Qin silently counted to twenty in his head. Then, when he realized his case was hopeless, he curled up his fingers and slowly withdrew.

It was expected, but he still felt sad.

When he counted thirty, Cheng Feichi, still facing the door, finally moved. He tilted his head a little, eyes falling on Ye Qin's hand with the ring.

"Hmm." Ye Qin heard him answer quietly.

Despite drinking the hot water and taking his medicine, Ye Qin got a cold nonetheless.

When they were shooting that afternoon, he began to sneeze. Then, his limbs began to wobble and all strength left his body. When the assistant finally found a thermometer, his temperature was already 38.5 degrees.

The entire shooting timetable could not be pushed back just for a supporting male role. Ye Qin took his Tylenol and splashed ice water on his forehead to force himself to stay awake and focus on work.

His assistant Xiao-Yun couldn't bear to see him suffering. "All this for a mere ring! The staff there already offered to help, but you just had to jump into the pool."

"So worth it," Ye Qin sighed, smiling sheepishly.

He had found his ring all by himself. Moreover, he had bumped into Cheng Feichi and had eaten a bowl of noodles Cheng Feichi cooked. The experience was so worthwhile that Ye Qin could soak in the cold water for a few more days.

After work, Ye Qin was in great spirits, as if he was never sick. He returned to the hotel after filming but refused to rest. Halfway through browsing a shopping website, he picked up a call from Song Xu.

"Qin-ge, did you fall into the water?"

"How did you know about that?"

"Someone posted it in the Super Topic on Weibo! A photo of you being chased by fans at the Garden Hotel."

Ye Qin was not surprised. Sure enough, He Hansong's fans were as meddlesome as the man himself, posting photos of him in the most awkward moment. *As if he hasn't got a handful of faults already.*

"I didn't fall in the water." Right now, he had no time for He Hansong. Ye Qin swiped across the screen, finding this bottle pretty and that one delightful. In the end, he added them all to his shopping cart. "I jumped into the water myself. How can that be 'falling'?"

"Again because of He Hansong?"

Speaking of this, Ye Qin could not help but feel resentful. "Who else could it be?"

"I'm sorry. I'm so sorry," Song Xu said pitifully. "Before, at the hotel, I had so much fun that I came back super tired. He just happened to come over and asked me to go for a few drinks, so I ended up sleeping in his room. I didn't know he could be so treacherous, stirring things up again and again…"

After Cheng Feichi had left that night, Ye Qin couldn't get through to Song Xu. He had been unable to get in touch with him until he returned to the capital from S-City. He then told Song Xu an edited version of the incident and Song Xu was so alarmed that he jumped up and was about to call the police. Ye Qin, on the other hand, just told him to be more vigilant next time and not believe what he was told so easily. Then, he dismissed the matter.

Song Xu was obviously still full of shame and remorse. If Ye Qin hadn't assured him that no one had actually taken advantage of him, he even said he was willing to offer his body to make up for Ye Qin's spiritual loss.

"It's okay. It's all in the past now." Having finished his search for the bottles, Ye Qin was now browsing folding paper. Now it was him comforting Song Xu. "We three have been teammates for so many years, so it's understandable that you weren't on guard with him. Just be careful in the future. He'll harm me this time; next time he won't hesitate to take you down with him."

At the other end, Song Xu made doddering, affirmative sounds. He acted like a grown-up and told Ye Qin to take good care of himself before hanging up.

There was a courier collection point at the bottom of Cangquan Mountain. As soon as he got better, Ye Qin borrowed a bicycle. He rode it when the road was flat and pushed it when it turned steep on his way down to fetch his parcel. He even bought a few cups of milk tea for the girls.

The female star was the popular actress Liu Yuqing. Having been trapped on this mountain for half a month with only boxed meals and bottled water, she longed for something refreshing. After taking a few sips of iced milk tea, she was almost moved to tears and said she wanted to adopt Ye Qin as a brother—apparently, he was a life-saving Bodhisattva to her now.

"So am I a bodhisattva or a brother?" Preoccupied with unwrapping the package, Ye Qin asked without raising his head.

Liu Yuqing saw him produce a heart-shaped glass bottle and a dozen paper strips for folding stars. "A sister, rather," she said, speechless. "A hopeless romantic of a little sister."

Ye Qin didn't mind at all. People already laughed at him and called him a sissy when he had been folding paper stars at school. They had done the same when he wore pink. But history proved that that trick actually works: didn't Cheng Feichi agree to be his boyfriend because of that jar of stars?

Nonetheless, that'd been a different time, and that blood-stained star had become the deepest thorn in their hearts. Yet

wasn't that the exact reason he was beginning to fold them again? He would make a new jar of them with all his patience and sincerity as Cheng Feichi's compensation.

Originally, he planned to make one every day, but then he found out he would need more than a year to fill the jar. That would take too long. Ye Qin pondered over the matter and changed the plan. He would make three stars every day for each part of a day from sunrise to sunset: the morning, afternoon, and evening.

He thought he would have a lot to say to Cheng Feichi, but when he picked up the pen, he had no clue where to start. The three stars he had made on the first day all hid the same sentence: *I miss you, gege.*

That night, lying in bed, Ye Qin felt the itch to send a text message to Cheng Feichi. Just one wouldn't be overstepping, right? After all, he still owed Cheng Feichi five hundred yuan. It was only natural for the debtor to contact the creditor.

After struggling for a long time, he finally sent three words, "In bed already?" But after hitting send, he felt a trace of regret, like a clown who wanted to replicate the old road to success. Cheng Feichi was not the same teenager who knew nothing about love. He was so smart. He might even suspect that Ye Qin had ulterior motives.

The text message could not be withdrawn. Ye Qin ruffled his own hair and held the phone, waiting anxiously for a reply.

He hadn't actually expected to get one. It came when he was almost asleep: *What is it?*

The simple reply made Ye Qin's heart beat like a drum. He sat up and poured a glass of water down his throat to calm down. Then, fearing that Cheng Feichi's patience would wear thin, he typed hurriedly: *Thanks for your help last time... How should I pay you back for the taxi fare?*

He tried to be as businesslike as possible, not daring to show too much emotion, afraid to scare the other man away.

The reply he got was again brief: *No need.*

Ye Qin looked at those two words for a while with drooping shoulders, feeling listless. Soon, he regained his spirits and chose his words with care while holding the phone.

He decided to be a bit more daring. What if he was greeted with a lovely surprise like last time?

When the phone vibrated again, Cheng Feichi had just started the car and driven onto the road.

Today, he had dinner at the Yi family's residence. Yi Zheng had called him there under the pretense of discussing business. They convened in the study, but Yi Zheng had only dwelt on business for two minutes before he started talking about other things, instructing him to pay a visit to Yan Hong's family tomorrow and spend the night at their family residence.

Naturally, Cheng Feichi didn't give his word. He was still thinking of an excuse to get out of it when the current lady of the house began to toss out thinly veiled insults at him. The gist of her declaration was simple: *Go back to where you came from. A sparrow must not covet what belongs to a phoenix.*

Yi Zheng's face darkened. "Xiao-Chi is now a member of the Yi family, once his place is officially acknowledged. If you can't see him as your own, at least be civil."

But the woman was still sharp-tongued. "Am I wrong? If you don't have a guilty conscience, why don't you bring that woman back to be the lady of the house and let your good son be its rightful young master? You've planned it all out, huh? Preparing a room for him at home, finding him a wife. Do you think that this way, his heart will belong to the Yi family?"

Yi Zheng slammed his chopsticks on the table, shaking

with anger. Ignoring the presence of his two sons, he yelled, "Then what do you think I should do? Leave the entire family fortune to Yi Hui and let him squander it all?"

Cued by his father, Yi Hui, who used to be the only young master of the family, let out an "ah." He began to tap the bowl with chopsticks, while curving his eyes in a smile. "Dad, why are you calling Huihui? Ah, Mom…Mom, don't cry."

The woman's yells and sobs and the smashing of dishes on the floor all combined. It didn't sound like a family home, but rather a magnificently decorated mental hospital.

Cheng Feichi couldn't listen anymore. He got up and was about to leave when Yi Zheng ordered behind him, "Go change your surname tomorrow. Your name should be added to the Yi family tree."

Sneering, Cheng Feichi marveled at the long list of things he should do tomorrow. Unfortunately, none of them were within the scope of his duties, and he had no intention of doing any of them whatsoever.

At the door, he found his half-witted half-brother, who had gone after him to send him off. Yi Hui was holding up an apple. "Gege, gege, you haven't had your fruit for dessert yet."

Though he had grown to six feet tall, Yi Hui still spoke and behaved like an eight-year-old child. Cheng Feichi knew that, apart from the delay in his intellectual development, his unsophisticated looks and straightforward mannerisms came from his family's sheltering.

Once, another person had given him the same impression, and that person had also called him "gege."

After a second of consideration, Cheng Feichi said "thank you" and took the apple Yi Hui handed to him.

Approaching a red light, Cheng Feichi applied the brakes.

He then got his cellphone and saw the text messages.

The SIM card he used a few years ago had been inserted into the phone he was using now. The text messages were unsigned, but he knew that number by heart.

This time, it was four sentences long: *Thanks for your help. Otherwise, I might have embarrassed myself in front of everyone... How about I treat you to a meal? You choose the place.*

The light changed before Cheng Feichi thought of a way to reply. After arriving at his penthouse suite, he first took off his jacket. Then, he went into the kitchen to put the kettle on.

Cheng Feichi hadn't returned for several days, since last time when he left the suite ahead of Ye Qin. He refused the cleaning services from the hotel, out of dislike of letting unfamiliar people into his private space. Normally, he cleaned the place himself and organized his own belongings.

When he passed by the dining space, he was still thinking that the noodle bowls left out unwashed were probably moldy now, considering the hot weather. The table, however, turned out to be impeccably clean. There were no bowls with leftovers, no soup stains from the meal, and no used dishes in the kitchen sink. Even the mug that he often left on the table was put upside down on the cup holder to prevent dust from falling in.

Cheng Feichi then went into the bathroom. It was as clean as if no one had ever used it. The glass door of the shower room was clear and transparent. There were no traces of water left behind by the inevitable splash of the showerhead, and several pieces of extra disposable toiletries, including the bathrobe, were neatly folded and placed at the corner of the washing stand.

He knew that after showering, Ye Qin had stood at the kitchen door for several minutes wearing this white bathrobe.

When he was hanging up the suit jacket that had been left by the door for several days in the closet, Cheng Feichi fished

out a note from one of the pockets. In addition to expressing his gratitude, Ye Qin also told him to be careful of Tang Chong.

Cheng Feichi stared at this unnecessary note for a long time. His eyes skimmed over the signature "Ye Ruan" in the lower right corner, and he picked up his phone to reply to the text message.

For the next few days, every paper star Ye Qin made contained the same message: *Gege, please reply.*

That night, he waited and waited, and when he finally received a message, Ye Qin almost jumped up from bed. His fingers trembled as he tapped the message. But then, seeing a string of nineteen-digit card numbers turned him into a punctured balloon, and he collapsed on the bed with frustration.

He had been too optimistic after all. Cheng Feichi simply did not want to meet with him; did not want to give out his info on personal financial apps like WeChat or Alipay, to which Ye Qin could not only transfer money but also send messages. He would rather enter a long string of bank details.

The courage Ye Qin had mustered, not without difficulty, was now diminished by half, especially after paying back the money. He fell into a complete daze, as if he had lost all direction to move forward.

"Just take my advice. Write a letter and pour in all your remorse and devotion. Better if you can bring yourself to shed a few tears. Let your tears run over the ink and sink in, or you can simply cut your fingers and write with blood..."

"Stop! Stop! Stop!" The description made Ye Qin's hair stand on end. "Is this a love letter or a guilty plea? If I really wrote him a letter like that, he'd probably never want to see me again."

"Considering our current situation, is it really different from pleading guilty? If I wasn't afraid of scaring Yuanyuan, I'd fall on my knees onto a bunch of thorns at his doorstep right now just to offer my humblest apologies."

Recently, the two old friends had again found themselves a shared interest after many years apart. They shared mutual comfort and encouragement, exchanged advice and suggestions. Although plans that actually worked seldom came from their discussions, at least they were able to gain a little confidence from each other.

For example, when Ye Qin accidentally entered Cheng Feichi's suite and shared a meal with him, Zhou Feng was still bunking on the street outside the building where Liao Yifang was living.

"You know how gentle Yuanyuan looks, but he can be so heartless about this kind of thing. He left no room for negotiation. He hasn't left the house since summer! If I hadn't joined law enforcement, I would've really wanted to kidnap his parents just to see if that'd make him speak to me."

That sounded weird, but Ye Qin somewhat shared his feelings.

Cheng Feichi was not avoiding him, nor was he giving any kind of response. It was even more impossible for Ye Qin to take the initiative and advance. That attitude was worse than superficial resistance.

When they were still teenagers, Ye Qin had blindly and confidently thought himself to be the one in control of their relationship, only to later learn that *he* had been the one led by the nose. His happiness and sadness all came from Cheng Feichi, yet he had foolishly thought that all those accelerated heartbeats and shed tears were common reactions to stress.

Now Cheng Feichi had closed that door and ignored all signals from him begging to reconnect. Ye Qin must still be dwelling on the past. Otherwise, how else could he believe that Cheng Feichi's reply would mean giving him a second chance?

Cheng Feichi was so good, so fine, and so calm. Even in their

youthful, hormonal love, he had been gentle and restrained. He'd had his own principles about what they could do and what they shouldn't. The reason Ye Qin had been able to break those principles was that he had broken into Cheng Feichi's heart by sheer luck. And now, Ye Qin was sent outside, barred by the gate, and exiled to a faraway place. He couldn't even find a way back.

Cheng Feichi had always had initiative. It wasn't until he gave the order that a lonely heart, drifting outside like a wandering ghost, could find a place to return to and belong.

That day, they finished shooting early. Liu Yuqing, the female star, invited all actors and staff from Group A to dinner.

One could not escape human contact during this kind of meal, yet past experience cast a shadow over Ye Qin's heart. He wanted to make up an excuse of wanting to go back and rest at the hotel on the pretext that he wasn't feeling well, but Liu Yuqing, who was always calling herself his "jiejie" recently, dragged him into the car.

"Everyone's going. You won't hurt your jiejie's feelings, will you?"

S-city was neither big nor small, and although Ye Qin had promised that to be "the last time," he was still secretly harboring the idea of another chance encounter.

However, the heavens would not allow him to get lucky again and again. This time he encountered the TV series' investor, President Chen, whom he had met in the private box, as well as his old friend Liu Yangfan, whom he had not seen for a long time.

It was not like he hadn't met any of his old acquaintances at the wine table in the past five years.

Ye Qin had been too young to set foot in the business world when his family had gone bankrupt, but Ye Jinxiang was an out-

and-out businessman. Before the relationship between father and son had become so strained, Ye Jinxiang had also taken his son around socializing in the rosy-sounding guise of "introducing him to the world."

Thanks to this familiar face, Ye Qin had been recognized by the big-shots in the capital. Even if they hadn't managed to remember his face, they could still bring themselves to register the name with that face upon hearing it. After a round of introductions and greetings, it was time for the middle-aged bosses to lament anything between "think about the good old days" and their own great achievements, then use the Ye family's decline to showcase the difficulties of starting a business. Finally, they would hand him a business card and end the encounter with, "If you have any troubles, just call your uncle."

At first, Ye Qin only felt embarrassed when faced with this kind of situation. But after a few times, he gradually lost that sense of shame. He had learned to let these words go in one ear and out the other. *You do your grand speech, and I'll have my dinner.*

Could the situation be even worse? Perhaps, but this was no longer in the scope of his consideration. His goal now was to live his current life to the fullest.

Therefore, upon facing an old friend who he had once drunk, played cards, and been mischievous with, Ye Qin was not quite uncomfortable. Between two rounds of toasts, they accidentally met each other's eyes, and he even gave him a wink and a smile.

It was Liu Yangfan, however, who was not quite used to this scene. He was not only avoiding eye contact, but also all contact with Ye Qin.

After several rounds, Ye Qin went to the bathroom to give himself a few minutes to relax, having had his fill of food and drink. Leaving, he bumped into his old friend in the doorway, and his first reaction was to look around.

"You go first. Don't let people see."

"A-Qin," Liu Yangfan, however, called out his name. "Long time no see."

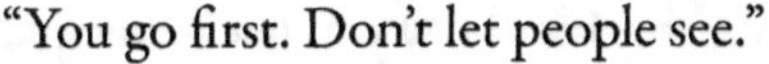

The dinner party was not over yet, so the two of them had a little chat in front of the bathroom.

Having learned that Liu Yangfan had come to S-City to inspect the entertainment company recently invested in by the Liu family, Ye Qin laughed. "The real estate business maintains a strong momentum domestically, but it's good to expand. The entertainment industry also has good prospects for development."

Dressed formally, Liu Yangfan now reined back his former playboy temperament and looked more stable than when he had been in school. He still remembered the past. As the conversation went on, he changed its direction. "Back then, it's not that I didn't want to help. My father, he..."

Ye Qin knew what he was going to say and interrupted with ease. "Well, well, those things in the past have long been laid to rest. Why would you still mention them? You shouldn't take on the blame by yourself. Family problems should be solved within the family. We don't ask others to take responsibility."

Seeing Ye Qin's openness and optimism, Liu Yangfan was slightly relieved, finally becoming more relaxed. "You're filming here now?"

"Yes, it's Director Li's new series. I'm playing Liu Yuqing's brother. She's today's host."

He said it lightly, but Liu Yangfan couldn't accept it easily. No one knew better what Ye Qin used to be like. He might not have been arrogant and domineering, but he was proud and puffed-up. Even when Ye Qin had come to him to borrow money, he hadn't let himself be seen in a shabby, wretched state. He had stood with his back straight and his neck upright and had said, "In less than three months, I will pay you back every cent."

The Ye Qin before his eyes now was smooth and tactful. He kept a low profile and a joyful smile that did not reach his heart. Liu Yangfan didn't know whether his proud bones were broken or hidden. On the one hand, seeing this saddened him. On the other, some weird, unprecedented thoughts popped up.

"Are you single now?" Liu Yangfan asked.

"Huh? Yes, I am. When you ask a question like that, you really sound like a reporter from some entertainment channel, ha ha."

"When will you come back to the capital?"

Ye Qin thought about it. "The end of the month, probably. I'll be back right away after shooting. What, you want to invite me to dinner? We should call Zhou Feng and eat together."

Liu Yangfan did not take the initiative, but said nonetheless, "I have a place in the eastern part of the city that's vacant at the moment, but it's furnished with electrical appliances and everything. The decoration is somewhat luxurious, actually."

That seemed to be only half of what he wanted to say. For a moment, Ye Qin was at a loss. Then he said, "I have a dormitory."

"There was a time when I couldn't make decisions for myself, but now my father can't control me anymore," Liu Yangfan narrowed his eyes and said somewhat arrogantly. "Instead of biding your time in entertainment, why don't you follow me?"

Still in much confusion, Ye Qin quickly waved his hand several times in disapproval. "I can't, I can't. I'm not good with business. You see, I haven't got a very good temper. I'll fight with people at the tiniest provocation. If you're looking for a sidekick, you shouldn't choose someone like me."

From his actions, Liu Yangfan found something reminiscent of the old Ye Qin, and he couldn't help but laugh. "No, I'm not asking you to join my business. You could live there, just as you once did at our club. You can just eat, drink and sleep. You won't

need to have a care in the world. I'll support you financially."

After the dinner party, Ye Qin fled the scene in haste.

Working in the entertainment industry, he had seen many a dodgy, dirty dealing. Just at his side, there was He Hansong, a typical example of someone making his way up by relying on a protector. Since Ye Qin's debut, there were also one or two such patrons interested in buying him off. Even his manager, Zheng Yueyue, suggested that he might as well take such a shortcut.

"In such a relationship, people take what they need from each other. Don't think of it so terribly."

But even though Ye Qin had understood and was used to this, he never thought the "I see you as a brother but you want to sleep with me" scenario would happen to him. Sitting in the car, he took out his phone and opened the front camera as a mirror, taking a look at himself. Two eyes, a nose, and a mouth. Nothing special whatsoever. He indeed looked not much different from his younger self.

Liu Yangfan must have had an attack of conscience and wanted to show him some sympathy after seeing the miserable turn Ye Qin's life had taken. Plus, he had too much wine. He was not sober when he made the offer.

That must be it.

After a good night's sleep, Ye Qin pushed this to the back of his mind. Yesterday's small talk had not even been a proper catch up. He was very clear about the gap between his current status and Liu Yangfan's. Forget about hanging out together. Any more chatting was going to result in cold, awkward silence.

Like attracts like. Back then, common interests shared by their gang had simply been eating, drinking, and fooling around, making mischief. They hadn't done anything good when they were together. They had just been born into a similar sort of family, birds of a feather.

Remembering how he had repeatedly belittled Cheng Fe-ichi and trampled on his dignity in front of that disreputable company, Ye Qin wished he could go back in time and wake his younger self up with a slap.

Granted, his friends' talk had added fuel to the fire and had goaded him to say those disastrous words. But ultimately, he had hurt Cheng Feichi because he had been arrogant, conceited, and ignorant of what cherishing meant. Now, he was suffering the repercussions, so there was no one else to blame.

He had been buffeted by wind and rain for five years now. The present Ye Qin was not only very good at not taking things to heart, but also had the ability to quickly regain his spirits and make a few more paper stars. Having spent the whole day on the set, he had missed yesterday's due. Inside those stars, he wrote: *Yesterday, I was too busy. Another day of thinking of gege.*

Today was not less busy. Ye Qin's role arrived at a critical juncture. There was a scene when the female star decided to fol-low the footsteps of the male star and come out of the mountains, while the third important role, her brother, chased her down the road shedding tears the whole way, unable to let go of his sister.

Ye Qin had never received any official training in acting be-fore or after joining the industry. He was especially bad at crying scenes. After running up and down the road several times, he still couldn't squeeze out a single teardrop. He thought he was going to be yelled at, but the executive director instead handed him a bottle of eye drops that seemed to have appeared out of the blue.

"Come, use a few drops and hold them inside your eyes. Take a few steps and then blink to squeeze them out. Just wait for my signal for the right moment."

Ye Qin felt flattered. Previously, the second female star

had gone through the same difficulties. Her tears just wouldn't come. Yet she had not received such gentle treatment and had only been scolded to tears by the director.

Ye Qin simply thought the director was in a good mood today. But as time went by, he realized something was wrong. It was only upon receiving a bottle of ice water and a small electric fan from the crew's assistant, who was normally stand-offish towards obscure actors such as himself, that Ye Qin finally came to the conclusion that all the staff present today were treating him better than they used to.

In the morning, when he'd arrived on set and greeted everyone, almost everyone had looked up and smiled at him in salutation. Midway through the shoot, when he had been sweating, someone had been keen to hand over a towel, and the electric fan had been fixed to blow cool breezes in his direction. Even when their lunch boxes were distributed, he didn't need to grab one for himself. Someone had placed one on his table for him to enjoy as soon as he finished shooting. It had been accompanied by a bowl of seaweed and egg soup which he hadn't had the chance to enjoy ever since joining the crew.

But why? It couldn't be a sudden attack of collective conscience, right?

Having finished chewing the last few pieces of seaweed left at the bottom of the soup, Ye Qin still wasn't able to solve the mystery. He wanted to ask Xiao-Yun, but after asking around, was still unable to find her. He was just about to call Zhou Feng and boast about his suddenly improved treatment, when Liu Yuqing beckoned him from the window of the lounge reserved for the stars.

"Come in, didi. Enjoy the air conditioning here."

So Ye Qin joined her, bringing along a bottle of orange juice the assistant had given him in the morning.

"Geez, just come and join me. There's no need to bring anything." Liu Yuqing smiled and showed him to the seat, pushing a bowl of cherries in his direction. "Try some. They've just been sent up from the bottom of the mountain."

Cangquan Mountain was essentially inaccessible, so the preciousness of fresh fruit could be imagined. Ye Qin was used to keeping a low profile among the crew. How could he dare to eat anything offered by the leading actress? Thus, he declined with the excuse of being allergic to cherries. Liu Yuqing roared with laughter and said that she had never heard of such a rare rich man's disease.

The break room wasn't big. It was divided into several smaller compartments with cloth curtains. At the moment, the male star was resting next door. Liu Yuqing nudged her chair toward Ye Qin. "What are you afraid of?" She kept her voice low. "Jiejie wouldn't bite you. You should hold your head up and be tougher while shooting. Otherwise, they'll all take you for a softie."

But I am a softie, Ye Qin thought. *Who would they bully if not me?*

Seeing the confused look on his face, Liu Yuqing couldn't help but laugh again. As the two played close siblings in the TV series, she naturally adopted some sisterly care for Ye Qin. Picking up a large, red cherry, she stuffed it in his mouth. "Come, you just eat. Jiejie won't tell your patron."

That whole afternoon, Ye Qin couldn't concentrate on shooting. Even while they were taking breaks, he asked everyone he could think of without a moment's rest.

Who could stay calm when a patron seemed to have appeared out of nowhere?

Someone had overheard his conversation with Liu Yangfan yesterday and the rumor spread very quickly. He would probably

have appeared in the headlines if not for the common practice within the industry that one didn't sell this sort of news to the media, even if everyone in the circle knew.

Or he might not appear there after all, since he was practically an obscure figure. Even if someone was willing to tip off this breaking news to the media for free, no one would likely want to waste their time writing such a piece.

But still, he needed to clear his name as soon as possible. This kind of misunderstanding could be very troublesome. He would never be able to clean up the mess once it was spread far and wide.

When she heard his story, Zheng Yueyue was in disagreement. "Since the rumor is out, just let it be. Anyways, what they want to know isn't the truth. They want some stimulation, some fun. That's all. After all, you were old friends, and he did have his heart set on you. So this isn't a miscommunication. Even if someone takes it seriously, you can stand on your own feet. Why not take advantage of the current situation and get yourself some benefits?"

Ye Qin understood the reasoning very well, but he couldn't get over this hurdle in his heart. To add to that, he was technically still in S-City. What if Cheng Feichi heard about this? Ye Qin didn't even dare follow through with the thought. Even "rubbing salt into the wound" would not be enough to describe how this would worsen their relationship.

Seeing him insist, Zheng Yueyue sighed with a trace of anger at his failure to make an effort for the better. "The harder you try to explain the situation, the more you'll smear your name," she then said. "Right now, the only way to stop the rumors from spreading is to ask President Liu to step up and clear whatever it is between the two of you. Even though others may not believe all of it, it's better than you standing alone."

Ye Qin immediately contacted Zhou Feng to ask for Liu

Yangfan's contact information.

Although Liu Yangfan was still in S-City, he said that he was busy and asked Ye Qin to meet up tomorrow. The meeting place was set to a club in the city center, the one that Ye Qin had once visited.

After all, Ye Qin was meeting an old friend and let down his guard. He gritted his teeth. He had even bought two bottles of expensive red wine to show good faith. As Ye Qin stepped into the club, he was stopped by the security guards at the door for a thorough check. No one came downstairs to meet him, so he had to wait at the door until the waiter inside confirmed with the guests upstairs and let him in.

Ye Qin also didn't take the rude treatment to heart. The only thing he wanted was to hurry up and resolve the matter.

Arriving at the arranged place, Ye Qin knocked on the door. When it opened, he entered. But after taking two steps inside, he looked around the room and froze on the spot.

He hadn't expected Liu Yangfan to be alone, but he also hadn't expected *him* to be there.

"He's here, he's here. Finally." Tang Chong was always the first to stand up in this kind of scene. Taking up the pretense, he came to the door in a welcoming gesture. Seeing what Ye Qin was holding, Tang Chong said in astonishment, "Oh? Looks like the big star spent a lot of money. It's certainly not easy to please the new boss. Those probably cost half the money you made on the drama shoot, am I right?"

People in the background roared with laughter. The situation was not different from the last time here, in another private room. Ye Qin could have faced it openly, but now he felt his face burn hot and wanted to escape.

Because Cheng Feichi was also here. During his first glance after entering the room, Ye Qin saw him in the crowd.

Of course, if you belonged to the elite circles, you couldn't really choose who to socialize with. There were only so many younger heirs of those rich and powerful families. Where on earth did he get the confidence that Cheng Feichi would side with him and alienate the snobs and "villains" like Tang Chong?

His old friend, Liu Yangfan, presently held a glass of wine and sat in silent acquiescence, which was enough to explain everything. He had spoken casually about being Ye Qin's patron. Well, a leopard couldn't be expected to change its spots. Liu Yangfan had probably done this kind of thing many times before.

Liu Yangfan was not the only one. Ye Qin recalled that he himself had once been a member of that gang, relying on his family's wealth and running amok. Now the tables had turned, and it was his turn to bear the maliciousness that he'd once imposed on others. Only now did he personally taste the bitterness.

Retribution finally came in front of his beloved, in its original form.

"I heard earlier that President Tang also took a fancy to this one, and even threw aside his old sweetheart to catch him," someone mocked him. "Now, now, what's going on? The canary is still the same canary, but the gilded cage is now in the hand of our own President Liu?"

Failing to become Ye Qin's patron, combined with Ye Qin's slap, had made Tang Chong lose his eagerness for something fresh. His heart was now filled with viciousness. What he wanted to do was to tear the wings of this little bird he could not get so that it could no longer flutter. Tang Chong smiled hypocritically and said, "It's too much for me. He's been aiming very high right from the beginning, hasn't he? He doesn't care for those of us who come from poor and humble families. Am I right, President Cheng?"

The meaning of those words could be understood by those present with little pondering. This obscure actor clearly had quite an appetite. Right from the beginning, he aimed too high, seeking connections with the unsympathetic young master of the Yi family. Now that his unsavory intentions had been disclosed, and he had been humiliated in public, he was going to have a hard time.

Eyes flashed to the side of the private room. There seemed to be an invisible circle around the corner Cheng Feichi occupied. He stayed in his own space and only raised his head casually when his name was called.

He glanced at Liu Yangfan sitting amidst the crowd, stood up, and said expressionlessly, "Gentlemen, take time to enjoy yourselves. Please excuse me."

From head to toe, he looked incompatible with the crowd. Even as he was leaving, he refused to give anyone anything but a sullen look. He didn't even pause for a second when he passed Ye Qin by.

Tang Chong had set the trap, but it was for nothing. There was no explosion whatsoever. With his fun spoiled, he gritted his teeth in anger. Tang Chong returned to the table, picked up the glass of wine, and poured it into his throat in a single gulp.

He then sat down. Seeing Ye Qin still standing in the doorway, Tang Chong ordered maliciously, "Come here. What are you doing, standing there acting dumb?"

"Now, President Tang, you're making it difficult. President Liu has come a long way here. Shouldn't you put your guest first?" someone clearly enjoying themselves was trying to add a bit more spice to the scene.

Liu Yangfan had fallen silent with a guilty conscience from the very minute he had seen Cheng Feichi, afraid that he might bring up what had happened long ago. Only now did he finally feel like he regained some control. Hence, he waved Ye Qin over

as if saving him from the scene. "Come here," he said with a face filled with undisguised smugness.

Ye Qin felt that the scene was ridiculous. He was actually relieved that Cheng Feichi had already left. At least he no longer needed to hold himself back anymore and could spread his arms to do whatever he wanted.

First, he raised them high, and then, dropped them with force, slamming the two bottles of wine in his hands into the ground.

The tremendous shattering sound made several people in the private room leap to their feet. Tang Chong pointed a finger at him and said wide-eyed, "You...you...you've gone mad! What do you think you're doing?"

Ye Qin kicked the broken glass on the ground. The neck of a bottle, still corked, rolled to Tang Chong's feet. Its sharp fracture reflected the cold light, stinging his eyes.

Ye Qin's chest rose and fell as he took several large gasps of air. "I've always been mad. Don't you all know that?"

He'd been enduring this for a long time now, and he decided not to put up with it anymore. Suddenly, Ye Qin figured out that as long as he stayed in this line of business, this sort of thing would never cease. The worst thing that could happen was having to quit being an actor and be rejected by the circle.

That sounded terrible, but there was nothing more terrible than Cheng Feichi's contempt.

He could beg for forgiveness without any dignity in front of Cheng Feichi, but he could not accept a single word of slander, even if Cheng Feichi did not care.

The waiting staff outside came in at the sound of glass shattering. Tang Chong told them to hold Ye Qin down, saying that this man was crazy.

The waiter saw nothing but broken bottles and spilled wine on the floor, with no signs of armed struggle. As Ye Qin glared and gritted his teeth fiercely like he was about to kill someone, the waiter regarded this as a tricky situation. Just as he was about to go downstairs and contact management, he turned right into a tall man.

Cheng Feichi, who had returned to the room, gave the current situation a quick glance. He did not ask anything, but pulled Ye Qin into his arms by his shoulder and brought him away from the mess of shattered glass on the ground.

Ye Qin had not yet realized what was happening when he heard Cheng Feichi say, "Have you vented your anger already?"

His voice wasn't loud, but it was loud enough for the whole room to hear.

Before Ye Qin could think of an answer, his hand, still shivering, suddenly fell into a broad, warm palm.

Cheng Feichi took it and led him to the door while speaking to the waiter, "Those two bottles of wine were broken by accident. Please clean it up. If there's any other damage, put it on my account."

CHAPTER 20

AFTER they got on the ground floor, Ye Qin followed Cheng Feichi slavishly. Even when Cheng Feichi's car stopped at the gate, he didn't dare move until Cheng Feichi called him to get in. Then, Ye Qin closed the door behind him gingerly, looking very much different from his fierce self earlier in that private room.

"Where are you going?" Cheng Feichi asked, starting the car.

Night had fallen, and it was still raining outside. When he had arrived in the afternoon, Ye Qin hadn't expected to return to the shooting location that day. His plan had been to get an hourly room in the city to spend the night and go back tomorrow morning when the sky cleared.

Ye Qin held his hands together as if trying to preserve the temperature that did not belong to him. Yet he was also afraid that Cheng Feichi would grow impatient and said after short contemplation, "Just drop me off at a hotel. Any hotel will do."

So Cheng Feichi took him to the Garden Hotel not far from the club.

With the car parked in an exclusive lot reserved for Cheng Feichi's use, Ye Qin thanked him, summoned his courage, and got out of the car. While walking towards the elevator, he wondered if he had enough money on hand to stay for one night, since buying those two bottles of wine had cost him all his money left on WeChat, and the money he had on Alipay had just been withdrawn to pay off the family debt.

"Ye Qin."

Ye Qin was still doing calculations in his head when his name was called. In a daze, he let out an "ah," and turned his head, meeting Cheng Feichi's eyes, which looked straight into his own.

Again, it was Cheng Feichi who averted his eyes first. He tilted his chin slightly to indicate the direction he was going. "This way," he said, sounding as detached as his expression.

In the end, the thin reasoning was no match for the yearning in Ye Qin's subconscious. By the time he came back to his senses, he had already arrived at the door of Cheng Feichi's suite on the top floor.

The set of toiletries Ye Qin had used last time was still there. Cheng Feichi fetched them from the bathroom and put them in the cabinet in the foyer. Ye Qin squatted down to change into a pair of slippers before going in. He felt ill at ease standing in the center of the suite.

Cheng Feichi took off his jacket as if no one was there. He rolled up his sleeves and quickly washed his face in the bathroom. Then, he opened the refrigerator in the kitchen and took out something to drink. All the while, Ye Qin stood aside and watched.

When a bottle of soda was handed to him, Ye Qin withdrew his eyes and did not dare to continue staring. He was about to take the bottle when Cheng Feichi suddenly withdrew his hand to unscrew the cap before handing the bottle to him again.

Ye Qin was stunned. He lowered his eyes subconsciously, eyelashes twitching a few times following the movement of his eyelids. When Ye Qin opened his mouth, he felt a lump in his throat and almost couldn't cough out a simple "thank you."

Back in the kitchen, Cheng Feichi took out two tomatoes and a few eggs from the fridge. He stir-fried them in a pan for a few seconds. It wasn't until after putting them on a plate that he realized that there was no carb to accompany the dish and that the only remaining noodles had already been eaten.

After washing his face with cold water from the kitchen tap, Ye Qin's scattered thoughts finally returned to their own places, no longer intruding and hindering his normal thinking.

When Cheng Feichi had finished the day's work, he saw seven or eight phone calls and text messages from Cheng Xin on his cell and thus, immediately pressed the off button. He didn't go to the Yi family residence or Cheng Xin's place. Nor did he return to the Garden Hotel suite. He randomly found a club nearby, wishing to spend some time alone.

While walking through the main doors, he bumped into Tang Chong and Liu Yangfan. Mingling with them had not been his original intention, but when Tang Chong made eyes at him inviting him to "a good show," Cheng Feichi suddenly felt apprehension. And so he agreed to join them.

What happened later was the sort of thing he expected: unforgiving verbal taunts, harmless mockery, things almost anyone would experience in this Darwinian society. He didn't take part in it, nor did he want to intervene. He had been about to leave when Ye Qin had entered the door.

Cheng Feichi had made his position clear when he had given Ye Qin his card number that he didn't want unnecessary dealings with Ye Qin. It wasn't necessary for this relationship to continue to exist, nor should he maintain it. They should not have anything to do with each other, not before, not now.

However, the sound of glass bottles shattering stopped his feet in their tracks, and the scene inside the private room involuntarily popped into his mind. Before his brain could make a choice, his body had gone ahead and made its way back.

Just like now, when he was about to give Ye Qin a drink, he would subconsciously unscrew it for him first before handing it over.

According to behavioral psychology, a new habit is formed after repeating the same action for more than twenty-one days. This is especially true in regards to major changes in one's life. But they had been separated for five years; a countless number of twenty-one days. Even a habit carved into bone with a knife should have been worn away with no trace by now.

Cheng Feichi wiped water across his face with a hand. The next time he opened his eyes, his eyes, which had always looked cool and emotionless, had more than a wisp of chaotic confusion.

The food they had rung for arrived quickly. It was lightly seasoned seafood congee with a few side dishes.

Cheng Feichi recalled that Ye Qin liked seafood, but did not eat congee much. His chopsticks, however, frequently went to the plate of scrambled eggs with tomatoes.

In the end, the whole dish almost all went into his stomach. After he finished eating, Ye Qin stood up and volunteered to clean up the table. Cheng Feichi stopped him, and he stood at the kitchen door, wanting to enter but not daring. "I know how to wash the dishes. I'm quite good at it," he whispered.

Cheng Feichi of course knew that he was capable of doing the dishes. Last time, he not only cleaned the dishes but also finished all the chores that could be done in the house short of going into the bedroom to fold his blankets.

This Ye Qin was new. He had become very different from before, which was something that Cheng Feichi had noticed during their first meeting after these years. Since their reunion, everything Ye Qin did had given him a hazy sense of surrealism.

Only the Ye Qin in that club just now looked like the Ye Qin he once knew: grumpy, headstrong with a quick temper, unable to endure a little bit of aggression.

What kind of things he'd went through to change so much, Cheng Feichi knew better than anyone.

After cleaning up the kitchen, Cheng Feichi returned to the living room and saw that Ye Qin had found an unobtrusive corner to sit in alone. He held a disposable paper cup in his hand and sipped it. There were no big movements. He almost exuded no trace of his existence. As soon as he heard Cheng Feichi's footsteps, he immediately got to his feet. His dark eyes quickly glued to him nervously and expectantly, like those of a small animal waiting to be chased away.

Cheng Feichi did not stop on his way but walked straight to the room next to the master bedroom. Ye Qin followed him to the door and was now looking at him bashfully over the dust cover. "You sleep here tonight," Cheng Feichi said.

Before going to bed, Ye Qin went to the kitchen to pour himself a glass of water. When he passed by the master bedroom, he stared at the closed door for a long time, wishing he could grow a pair of eyes that could see through the door so that he knew what the person inside was doing.

Light spilled out from underneath, so Cheng Feichi was still awake, probably leaning on the bed reading a book, just like before.

When they had lived together in Jiayuan Compound, there had also been rainy, sultry nights like this one. Ye Qin did not like rainy days. The sound of the rain hitting the windows made him restless, and when he felt restless, he didn't want to do anything except pester Cheng Feichi.

Cheng Feichi was different from him. He was the kind of person who could concentrate on a single thing even in chaos. The more Ye Qin had watched his profile—his lips pursed, absorbed in the book he had been reading—the harder it was to restrain himself. He could not help but poke Cheng Feichi's waist with his fingers or rub his calves. He just would not let him quietly read a book.

Then? Cheng Feichi would put down the book, press down on his shoulders, give him a swift kiss, and ask if he was making trouble again with a feigned stern face. Ye Qin would remain stubborn, and Cheng Feichi would give him another kiss, so on and so forth. The next kiss always lasted longer than the previous one, until Ye Qin was dizzy and short of breath. He would use what little strength he had left to kick Cheng Feichi's book onto the floor and hook his limp arms around Cheng Feichi's neck, refusing to let go. He would play those little tricks until Cheng Feichi agreed to sleep beside him.

Without the host's permission, Ye Qin had never entered the master bedroom. He guessed that the head of the bed inside was pressed to the east wall.

When he returned to his room, he tiptoed to the connecting wall, leaned over, and pressed one cheek against it. He closed his eyes and flattened his body there for a while as if he could be closer to Cheng Feichi like this and feel the reassuring warmth of his body.

The next morning, Cheng Feichi's biological clock woke him up at precisely six o'clock.

After doing his morning routine and returning to the living room, he realized after the fact that the guest who'd stayed overnight was gone.

The bedroom next door was ajar, the blankets were neatly folded on the bed, and the disposable toiletries were folded and placed in the corner of the sink, just like last time. They looked as if they had not been used last night.

Cheng Feichi took a look at his phone. No messages. Thinking that Ye Qin had probably left already, he put on the kettle, turned on the stove, and got an egg from the refrigerator.

When breakfast was ready, he suddenly got a phone call from the hotel security team.

"President Cheng, we found a suspicious person in front of your reserved elevator in the underground parking lot. He said he's your friend who went downstairs to buy breakfast and that he's taking this elevator to go back."

Without a thought, he knew who it was. Cheng Feichi gave the security team permission to send Ye Qin up.

Five minutes later, he heard someone knock. Cheng Feichi opened the door to find Ye Qin standing in the doorway carrying two paper bags, his head drooping. Apparently, he had been too despondent to lift his head. Cheng Feichi could only see the blushing tips of two red ears.

After following Cheng Feichi inside, Ye Qin saw the fried egg and sliced bread on the table and cast his bashfulness to the wind. He immediately unpacked the breakfast he had bought, put the items on the table, and aligned all the dishes. "Have these. I took a public bike to buy them. It's still hot."

Cheng Feichi looked up and saw Ye Qin's expectant expression as if he were presenting treasure. He couldn't say no.

The soymilk was steaming hot, and the deep-fried dough sticks were golden and shiny. This was Cheng Feichi's first hometown breakfast since coming back to the country. After the meal, his stomach felt warm and comfortable. He put down his chopsticks and thanked Ye Qin in earnest.

Ye Qin almost leapt from his seat. "No, no, no. There is no need for you to thank me. I should thank you for taking me in for the night..."

He was behaving like a good boy, but in contrast, his gaze held unconcealed eagerness. Ye Qin eyed the fried egg next to the breakfast he had bought intensely, and his longing was overwhelming.

Cheng Feichi was used to arriving at his office early to sort out the day's work, and when the two of them took the elevator down together, it was not yet seven. The fried egg had only just gone down Ye Qin's belly.

He asked Ye Qin where he was going and offered to book him a taxi, but Ye Qin shook his hands hurriedly and said, "You just go work. I'll call a taxi myself."

Cheng Feichi paused before getting into the car. With one hand holding the car door, he turned to Ye Qin and said, "The pin is 0215."

Ye Qin stood there dazed for a moment before realizing that he was talking about the pin to the reserved elevator. No verification was needed to take that elevator downstairs, but a pin or fingerprint scan was needed to go up.

Twice, he had come here with Cheng Feichi. Not once did he pay attention to the fact that Cheng Feichi had used his fingerprint to move the elevator. Ye Qin was very ashamed recalling how he had been caught by the security team. He nodded his head furiously, not daring to look at Cheng Feichi.

Turning with the steering wheel in his hand, Cheng Feichi saw Ye Qin in the rearview mirror. He stood in place, staring after him.

This time he held his head high. He wore a loose, almost dangling T-shirt on his lean body. His pant legs were rolled up casually, one side long and one side short, each revealing a fraction of his thin, bony ankles.

Cheng Feichi's eyes swept down to the pair of white shoes Ye Qin wore, now a weird color from the wine stain that splashed on them yesterday. The shoelaces on his left shoe were undone, like he was waiting for someone to help him tie them.

Originally planned for fifty days, the shooting period was now down to its last twenty. Having gained an acute feeling of urgency, Ye Qin made a call to Zhou Feng during his mid-day break from shooting.

"Gah! You stayed overnight at his place, you know the pin to his home, and you're still coming to me to ask what to do?" Zhou Feng, who had made considerably less progress than him, was blinded by envy and yelled on the other end. "Just march to his door! Show up next to him and make a statement. Make your presence known!"

"No, if I do that without a good reason, he'll get annoyed at me." Ye Qin made a face.

Zhou Feng was exasperated by Ye Qin's resistance to making an effort. "A-Qin, you weren't like this before. When we went to school together, what did you not do in pursuit of our straight-A guy? You bought that ring, didn't you? Just give it to him. What are you waiting for? New Year's, so you can give it to him as a present?"

Ye Qin lay down on the deck chair the crew had just sent to him. "I can't. You don't understand," he sighed.

The day he returned to Cangquan Mountain from the Garden Hotel, Ye Qin sensed that the whole crew had changed their attitude toward him. They became more polite and respectful than ever. When the assistant told him that a place in the lounge had been vacated for him to take a nap there after lunch, not only had he been amazed at how quickly these people had gotten the news, he'd also realized how powerful the Yi family was.

No wonder Cheng Feichi only needed a single sentence to rescue him completely from that precarious situation that day in the club.

He hadn't told Zhou Feng about this. After all, Liu Yangfan had been a friend to them both, so whatever Ye Qin said would be suspected of sowing discord. Now, thinking back, Ye Qin couldn't help but blush. "You don't understand..." he whispered again with a peek at the skin on his hand.

"Okay, okay, I don't understand," Zhou Feng simply sounded speechless. "Then couldn't you take advantage of this and get involved in his life? Just to repay the favor? Repay a spring for a little drop of water in need. Can't you play the mythical Lady Snail and make him meals and do housework for him while he's gone?"

Even though years had passed, Zhou Feng never managed to quit his habit of talking nonsense. Though Ye Qin was speechless, he continued to think about what Zhou Feng said after hanging up. After several failed attempts to dismiss the thoughts from his head, he really began to consider the feasibility of this method.

Their history aside, since their reunion, Cheng Feichi had twice offered his home as a sanctuary. He had also saved him several times, and now Ye Qin wanted to return the favor. That was solid reasoning, was it not?

To help untangle him from the mess and keep him safe, Cheng Feichi had gone out of his way to pretend to be his patron. Now it was Ye Qin's turn to do something for him.

He had simply been a taker in the past. He hadn't known what giving and devotion meant. Now he would not make the same mistake again. To express his love with real action was the need of the hour.

The first thing to do now was to bypass the many heavy ears and eyes and infiltrate Cheng Feichi's home.

This task, which he rated as "difficulty: high," was in reality accomplished with casual effort. The code that opened the door was the same one that started the elevator: 0215—February 15, the first day of the last semester of high school, the day when

Cheng Feichi had left the country to go abroad.

These four numbers were exceedingly heavy to Ye Qin, like stones tightly pressing down on his chest. Each press reminded him of a road he had once taken that year. People coming and going at the airport, whistling planes taking off, the application form for C University, and the bitter tears that slipped into his mouth.

Fortunately, those were all in the past now. Ye Qin took a deep breath and forced himself to face the present. All would be well if Cheng Feichi did not find out. As long as they didn't stand face to face, as long as Ye Qin didn't stare into that pair of cold, frosty eyes, he could summon infinite courage from thin air.

Maybe he was really careful, or maybe Cheng Feichi was too busy to pay any attention, but the first few times that he tried, he actually made it.

He had been there to clean up, boil water, and do the laundry. Once, he'd filled the fridge with a lot of produce, and Cheng Feichi hadn't found out. Or maybe he had, but he hadn't said anything.

All the better if that turned out to be the case.

Feeling encouraged, Ye Qin became bolder. On a morning when no shoot had been scheduled, he came down early and bought a bunch of flowers from nearby while doing groceries. With bags of all sizes in his hands, Ye Qin went upstairs. He found a vase in the suite and put the flowers inside. Now, this cold and empty place finally felt a bit like home.

After Cheng Feichi went back home last night, the refrigerator was missing two eggs and the water jug was only half full. Ye Qin carefully restocked the fridge with produce. He folded the jacket that had been thrown on the sofa before putting it aside, rearranged the toothbrush and towels in the bathroom. He wiped down the floor, wiped down the range hood, wiped down the bookcase. He thoroughly wiped down every piece of furniture that could be wiped.

Ye Qin was not up for the more technical tasks, but he was okay with those that required physical strength and patience. When they were living together, Cheng Feichi had taken over all these chores. However, after Ye Qin had been on his own in recent years, he gained some general knowledge of housekeeping. While wiping down the furniture, he thought that he might be able to leave a fried egg for Cheng Feichi.

By the time he came back, Ye Qin would already be gone. Without facing him personally, Cheng Feichi would be left with no choice but to finish the egg. Surely he couldn't bear to see food wasted.

Ye Qin let himself indulge in wishful thinking. When he finished with that, he walked around the suite and decided that there was nothing left to be done. Thus, he washed his hands and prepared to leave.

Right at this moment, the door beeped and someone opened it and entered the suite.

Ye Qin thought Cheng Feichi was back. A chill crept onto his back, yet he could not help but look at the door. When he met eyes with the girl who came home, whom he had met twice, they were both stunned.

Yan Hong had not expected to run into Ye Qin here.

She had called Cheng Feichi in advance to tell him that she had something for him. Since Cheng Feichi was still busy with work and unable to meet up with her conveniently, she volunteered to drop it off at the Yi residence. When Cheng Feichi said that he hadn't been living there as of late, Yan Hong immediately guessed that he was presently living at the penthouse suite in the Garden Hotel.

She had not told Cheng Feichi she was coming. She also

hadn't asked for anyone's permission to come upstairs. The hotel staff knew her and sent her up directly. The room's pin was a guess. She had peeked at Cheng Feichi's cellphone password when they had both been studying abroad, and they turned out to be the same.

The shock of running into Ye Qin almost made her lose composure, but she quickly adjusted herself and carried her things inside calmly, as if she hadn't seen Ye Qin at all. She put various bags down on the table. When she saw the bouquet that clearly hadn't been bought by Cheng Feichi, she half-snorted, half-laughed in disdain.

Ye Qin had dealt with Yan Hong once. He had taken her as a headstrong, straightforward heiress. She asserted domination with her provocative words, but it was nothing too much to bear, so he decided to pay her no heed. After washing his hands and taking off his apron, he walked to the foyer to change his shoes, ready to leave.

"What are you doing here?" Yan Hong took the initiative to ask.

Not knowing how to answer, Ye Qin thought about it for a moment. "Returning something."

Yan Hong took another glance at the flowers on the table as if trying to gauge whether he was speaking the truth. "Don't come here again," she then commanded.

Ye Qin straightened up and met her eyes. "If he doesn't want me to come here, then I won't come anymore," he said.

"He" referred to Cheng Feichi, the owner of the house. Ye Qin tried his best to speak with assurance as if justice was on his side.

Before, he had thought Yan Hong was who she had claimed to be—Cheng Feichi's fiancée. He hadn't been without hesitation. Sure, they had once been a match made in heaven, but that was all in the past. If Cheng Feichi truly had someone now and was living a happy life, Ye Qin could convince himself to let go.

Based on his understanding of Cheng Feichi and various signs that he had picked up on, this girl wasn't even his girlfriend. And so there was nothing to worry about. He still had the right to fight for himself.

After all, Cheng Feichi himself hadn't asked him to stop.

After hearing Ye Qin's unhurried reply, Yan Hong's face turned gloomy for a moment. Then, as if recalling something, she lifted the corner of her mouth and held her chin high. "You two are high school classmates, right? As far as I know, he transferred to High School No. 6 in Beijing in his second year, so did you even know each other for more than two years?"

Confused, Ye Qin stared at her blankly. For a moment, he wasn't sure if he understood the significance of her question.

"He was in America for five years, and I was by his side for four." Yan Hong paused and withdrew her smile for a somewhat serious expression. "Do you know how he spent these five years?"

Ye Qin's eyes blanked again.

Those five years were a blind spot for him and Cheng Feichi, like a river broken down the middle with a tall wall. Water at this end did not flow through to the other. After the reunion, neither of them told the other anything that had happened in the past five years. They could only use speculation to paint a vague picture.

Back when his mother Luo Qiuling was still alive, she also wanted to send him abroad while she still could. Ye Qin had thought that since the Yi family had both money and power, Cheng Feichi's life studying overseas had probably not been too hard, at least not as hard as his life at home.

"He was very smart and good at studying. When all the boys born with a silver spoon were out clubbing, gambling, drinking, he was the only one who took his studies seriously. He

was the only one of us who completed both his bachelor's and master's in five years with no gap in between." Yan Hong could not help using a prouder tone when she spoke of what Ye Qin didn't know. "Every time he got praise from the professor, every time he won a scholarship, I was sitting offstage, watching. Everyone clapped for him."

For a moment, Ye Qin blinked as if he was also seeing Cheng Feichi, free from shackles and bursting with spirit.

Years ago, even he had believed that Cheng Feichi shouldn't stay in a mediocre school like High School No. 6. He shouldn't have rotated between endless part-time jobs or gone to an ordinary university like C University.

Even when Cheng Feichi dipped his hands in dirty water, Ye Qin found those hands out of place. He had not known it then. It took a long time for him to figure out that he had seen Cheng Feichi with different eyes right from the beginning. He'd thought that Cheng Feichi was special. Cheng Feichi had been different from anyone he had met before.

Cheng Feichi was born to sit on high places, not to be burdened by the mundane or bow from the weight that he never should have carried.

After hearing Yan Hong's words, Ye Qin felt slightly relieved. At least, in the end, Cheng Feichi had chosen his own future. He hadn't given up the more important things for Ye Qin.

"But he never even felt a little bit proud of all that he achieved," Yan Hong then said. "He wasn't happy at all."

Ye Qin's eyelids trembled, and he instantly tightened after relaxing just a little, especially upon her last two words.

"Do you know what other people called him behind his back? 'The bastard son' was among the better names. Just because he didn't want to change his surname and kept to himself. Just because he never mingled with the others, they all said that the Yi family bought him as a footman to help with household chores. His stepmother, the current lady of the Yi family, flew over repeatedly to spread rumors in the school under the excuse of visiting him. Even his advisor got wind of her slander. In his last term, his advisor even asked him, in front of everyone, if he wanted to solve his family issues before coming back to continue his studies.

"The most outrageous part was when his stepmother lied to him that his mother was critically ill. She froze his cards to stop him from buying a ticket to fly home. He asked the other international students to borrow some money, only for them to laugh and mock him to his face, asking if he was going to be the wooden horse for the real young master of the Yi family after graduation."

Hearing this, Ye Qin's mouth opened and closed reflexively. His hands at his sides were now clenched into fists, and his eyes were wide with panic and helplessness.

Seeing his reaction, Yan Hong suddenly laughed again. "You didn't expect that, did you? That someone like him can stand that kind of insult. He's clearly not someone who would bend over for money or power."

This time, the pause was longer than any previous ones.

Finally, Yan Hong breathed a sigh of relief and regained the expression of confidence in victory. "So you see, I'm the only one who can help him stand firm in the Yi family, while you——" Her gaze swept over the handful of sunflowers on the table before turning back to Ye Qin. There was pity in her condescending gaze. "You will only drag him back down into the mud and destroy everything he fought so hard for."

On that day, Cheng Feichi didn't work in his office, but took a car to a neighboring city to inspect another hotel chain owned by the Yi family. He stayed there to host a business meet-

ing, and when he got off work, the sun had already set. The sky was pitch dark when he came back to S-City.

After responding to several emails in the office building next to the Garden Hotel, Cheng Feichi picked up his car from the parking lot. He leaned back in the driver's seat and closed his eyes for a few minutes to rest. When he reopened his eyes, they were still full of fatigue.

Recently, Yi Zheng passed him a significant portion of the family business. This, added to his other responsibilities and business's expansion to the capital—which he had been doing behind Yi Zheng's back—made his days quite busy. Now, he seldom finished work before 10 p.m.

He managed to squeeze in a few free minutes to go over, filter, and reorganize the smaller issues that he couldn't make time for in the day. Aside from Cheng Xin's routine call and extortion, Cheng Feichi recalled that Yan Hong had also called this morning saying that she had something for him.

And Ye Qin. Cheng Feichi wondered if he had come today.

The first time Ye Qin had entered his place, Cheng Feichi had noticed it. He had not asked Ye Qin why he was doing this, partly because he was too busy to be distracted from his work and partly because he didn't feel it necessary to make everything super clear.

Cheng Feichi more or less understood what Ye Qin was thinking. He was doing all of this because he felt that he had owed Cheng Feichi a favor and wanted to make up for it in his own way. He used to be like this too. If Cheng Feichi got his clothes wet picking him up, Ye Qin would buy him a new set the next day. If he lost his temper for no good reason, he would let go of his dignity, hook his arms around Cheng Feichi's neck, and shower him with kisses to get Cheng Feichi's forgiveness.

He would wait until Ye Qin felt that he had repaid enough.

There was no need for him anymore to come forward and speak out, to prevent Ye Qin from doing this. On the other hand, Cheng Feichi thought that getting in touch with Ye Qin just for this seemed like deliberately giving him leeway.

If he really had to do something about this, the only correct thing would be to immediately change the PIN and take the SIM card out of the mobile phone. That way, there would be no future trouble.

As he took the elevator upstairs, Cheng Feichi fiddled with the PIN buttons. When the electronic voice prompted him to reset the pin, he couldn't think of any other combination. His birthday was too easy to guess, but apart from that, the only combination he now used regularly was 0215. In the few seconds he was hesitating, the system had jumped back to standby mode. Then the elevator made a *ding* sound as it reached the top floor.

It wouldn't be too late to change it tomorrow. Cheng Feichi was extremely tired now. He entered the room without taking off his shoes. His sense of smell, however, was stronger than the other senses, and he unexpectedly caught a wisp of fresh floral fragrance.

Then he heard a sequence of strange movements.

Cheng Feichi switched the light on. With a *tick*, the room filled with brightness.

The person who had been trying to hide under the table had been in a hurry. His head hit the corner of the table and a gasp of pain inadvertently escaped him. He had just covered his head and straightened up when his red eyes met Cheng Feichi's.

Several times Ye Qin had come and gone in a rush, but he didn't today. Even though he knew that he would be caught on the spot, he stayed until now.

Cheng Feichi stood in place for several seconds, as if he

could think of nothing to say. He cast his eyes down at the things on the table.

Before he could open his mouth, he heard Ye Qin say, "Yan... Miss Yan brought you that." Then he pointed at the sunflowers nearby. "I brought you this."

Cheng Feichi did not say a word. He went to the bathroom to wash his face and refresh himself. Ye Qin followed and stood beside him, handing him a towel. While wiping his face, Cheng Feichi looked at the ground and saw Ye Qin still wearing disposable slippers. The thin cloth that covered his feet was so worn out that Cheng Feichi was afraid that his toes were going to make holes in it.

Then, Ye Qin had transformed thoroughly into a shadow following Cheng Feichi everywhere. When Cheng Feichi raised his hand, Ye Qin brought him a cup of water. When Cheng Feichi took off his jacket, he helped hang it up. When Cheng Feichi walked to the foyer, he fetched slippers for him. Whatever Cheng Feichi did, Ye Qin was always one step ahead of him as if he could read his mind.

Ye Qin followed him to the bathroom, but this time he was blocked by the sliding door. Pouting, he simply leaned against the wall and waited.

In less than half a minute, the door was opened again. Cheng Feichi, shirt still entirely unbuttoned, held the door frame with one hand and asked expressionlessly, "What on earth are you trying to do?"

Nevertheless, the cold words lit a light in Ye Qin's eyes as if he'd been long waiting just for this moment.

The soft light from the bathroom shone directly on Ye Qin's face, and his dried tears couldn't be concealed whatsoever. His eyelashes were clumped together like little bushes, and his eyes were swollen. It was hard to tell how long he had been crying.

Despite looking miserable, he gave Cheng Feichi a grin.

"Don't you know?" Ye Qin raised the pitch of his voice slightly, rolling his eyes. "I want to pursue you."

The calm lake in Cheng Feichi's eyes surged violently.

Throughout the years, he never took time to think about the past. Now, he had already chosen his path, he had no intentions of looking back. Memories would only add to his troubles.

After returning, none of the people he met or things he experienced managed to summon those dusty thoughts, including Ye Qin. After they met again, Ye Qin was always apprehensive and cautious, overcautious even. He was completely different from before, like he had flattened all the sharp spikes that he had once put out.

Cheng Feichi had actually felt relieved to see him in such a state. But when Ye Qin had said that he was going to pursue him, the sense of security, paper-thin, suddenly shattered. A raging tide rolled over all the past events Cheng Feichi deliberately buried and spread them out in front of his eyes.

There was a bleak autumn evening, an empty classroom, the fragrance of food drifting in the air, the boy with a bright smile saying he wanted to pursue him. At the time, Ye Qin had been fearless. His eyes had been full of light so dazzling that Cheng Feichi couldn't tell whether it was reflections of the lights overhead or shot out directly from his pupils.

It was this light that had beckoned him closer step by step, made him sink bit by bit, and finally smashed all illusions like a hammer. When he had woken up from that, he had been so overwhelmed by pain and grief that he had wanted to die.

After so many years, he felt a similar tingling in his heart again. It didn't matter whether it had appeared because what he was seeing now reminded him of the past, or because of old pain

revisiting his heart. Cheng Feichi averted his gaze to a random, empty spot and got a grip.

"You should go," he said.

For a moment, Ye Qin's smile froze on his face. He knew this was the same as rejection, yet he didn't seem to have taken a blow. Instead, he raised the corner of his mouth again and kept smiling. "It's so late now. Can't I spend the night here?"

Cheng Feichi didn't answer. He applied so much force on the balls of his fingers on the door frame that they turned white.

Seeing his chance, Ye Qin redoubled his efforts. "I can do housework now. I can sweep the floor and wash your clothes. I can also fry eggs for you. I can learn to cook whatever you want, and I promise not to cause you any trouble."

"There's no need. I don't need anyone to take care of me here."

"Are you afraid of being found out by other people? Don't worry, I'll keep my mouth shut the moment I step outside. I'll take extra care when I come. I won't..."

"I don't care what other people say," Cheng Feichi interrupted him. "Go back to where you should be, and don't come again."

With that, he went back to the bathroom and closed the door, locking Ye Qin out.

Ye Qin didn't have time to say what was on his lips. His face almost slammed into the door.

Cheng Feichi probably needs time to digest the message, he thought. Resisting the urge to break in, he went back to the dining room and sprayed some water on the flowers. "I'm leaving," he said in the direction of the bathroom. He finally left, but not without looking back three times every step.

That night, the stars he made were a bit shriveled, as if aggrieved, but the handwriting inside was neat, normal, and full of life. It read: *Will you please let me be your boyfriend?*

The sun scorched in the sweltering summer. Since Ye Qin made a trip to the Garden Hotel from time to time, his life was actually quite busy. The scene he needed to shoot was coming to an end. Zheng Yueyue took him to two other shoots for the local magazines. He still had friends here.

Liao Yifang had made an appointment with him in advance, but Song Xu didn't call him until his plane had landed in S-City. Liao Yifang and Song Xu happened to be on the same flight, seated next to each other. They struck up a conversation because they were holding the same book. When the flight landed, they found out that they were traveling to the same place, so again they chatted all the way.

When they both arrived at Cangquan Mountain, they found that they were looking for the same person. Marveling at the coincidence, the two of them talked freely for the whole afternoon. Ye Qin felt completely ignored, like a wisp of transparent, odorless air.

Anyhow, the arrangement suited him. He was glad to take a break from his busy schedule. With his cellphone on hand, he kept sending Cheng Feichi bad puns.

Ye Qin had only said that he wanted to pursue him. Sincerity, especially at this early stage, was especially important. However, he still had several such tricks which he himself had used once. If they worked once, they would probably still work now.

Cheng Feichi banned him from his door, but he could send text messages, right?

"One day, Nüwa was laughing while shaping the clay figures that would transform into human beings. Pangu asked her what she was laughing at. Nüwa said, 'Happiness is what it takes to make one human.'"

Ye Qin read those words aloud while typing and got the attention of the two people discussing academic problems. They

found yet another common thing: it was super easy to make both of them laugh.

When the two again shook with laughter at hearing "Xiao-Ming and Xiao-Hong rushed to meet each other out back, and then they both got concussions," Ye Qin still didn't receive a reply from Cheng Feichi. He didn't dare send him too many for fear of distracting Cheng Feichi from work. Thus, each one had been carefully selected. He could tell from Liao Yifang and Song Xu's reactions that these jokes were in fact quite good.

So the lack of a response was particularly disappointing. Just as he'd said, Cheng Feichi was going to keep him at bay. Even if Ye Qin wanted to clear up everything that had happened in the past and express his attitude, he couldn't find an appropriate opportunity.

Moreover, even if he had the opportunity to say it, Cheng Feichi still might not believe him. Cheng Feichi had seen these things with his own eyes and heard them with his own ears. They had grown in his heart like a forest and become so intertwined that a mere few words were not enough to let him make peace with them.

Ye Qin couldn't say that his path of pursuit had been smooth, but this time he was definitely on hard mode. It was a console game, and Cheng Feichi was as harsh and impartial as a computerized opponent. Ye Qin, who never had a silver tongue, felt even more at a loss.

Amidst Liao Yifang and Song Xu's laughter, he took a deep sigh.

Ye Qin settled his two friends who had come from afar in a B&B not far from the set. Liao Yifang asked in amazement why the place was so deserted. "Shouldn't there be fans chasing after you stars?"

Ye Qin told him that the crew had kept the filming location a secret. Furthermore, this mountain was a scenic spot, and the crew reserved most of the place for their use. The fan clubs and "frontlines" were also playing by the rules and not revealing the idols' whereabouts casually. Otherwise, such a big place couldn't even hold a large crowd of fans.

Liao Yifang nodded with understanding. "I know a friend on Weibo who's your fan. He named himself 'Soft Brother Is Not Iron Sister.' Do you know him?"

Only after Liao Yifang had reminded him did Ye Qin remember that his fans had the title "Soft Sisters." In fact, this Weibo username, silly in the extreme, already revealed the identity of its user. Ye Qin was amazed at Liao Yifang's very friendly attitude towards that so-called "Soft Sister," and he couldn't help but applaud Zhou Feng's cunning methods.

Liao Yifang came to S-City for an academic seminar, so he was only dropping in at Cangquan Mountain. Ye Qin accepted the huge gift package of snacks he and Song Xu brought. As he turned the corner of the corridor in the B&B, he ran into someone who shouldn't be there.

"Shh!" Zhou Feng pulled him to the corner. His eyes were fixated behind Ye Qin, clearly in the direction of Liao Yifang's room. "Did that kid come from thin air? Could you send him away? I'm sure he has his eyes set on my Yuanyuan. Fuck!"

By "that kid," he was referring to Song Xu.

Ye Qin took a moment to digest the fact that the person in front of him was indeed Zhou Feng. "What are you doing here? Don't you have work?"

"I asked for leave. When I go back, there'll be two weeks of night shifts waiting," Zhou Feng said anxiously. "Thank god that I came along. Otherwise, I wouldn't even know someone's about to lure my love away!"

Ye Qin was speechless. "Song Xu is straight."

Zhou Feng stared at him, eyes about to pop out, and pointed at his own nose. "Didn't I used to be straight? Weren't you once straight? Aren't we both gay now, thorough and thorough?"

When he put it like that, that did indeed seem to make some sense.

At Zhou Feng's insistence, Ye Qin went back and knocked on Liao Yifang's door. Using "there's something your big brother wants to tell you" as an excuse, he called Song Xu out. He was, in fact, hanging out with Liao Yifang. Determined to be a loyal wingman to Zhou Feng, he dragged Song Xu along with the excuse, "Since you've recently put on some weight, Yueyue-jie asked me to take you out for exercise." They then ran ten laps around the B&B.

Afterwards, Song Xu practically lost his desire to live. He returned to his own room to take a shower before going to bed. Ye Qin took a brief rest before he was about to go back himself, but barely took two steps before seeing two people in the empty courtyard.

Liao Yifang walked hurriedly in front with luggage in his hands. Zhou Feng, tall and long-legged, caught up with him in a few steps. As soon as he grabbed Liao Yifang, he pulled the latter into his arms, and the luggage fell to the ground with a *thump*.

At first, Liao Yifang struggled hard. Then, because of whatever Zhou Feng said in his ears, he gradually stopped beating his hand down on Zhou Feng's back. There were muffled sobs and whispers, and then the two figures in the shadow of the trees blended into each together as if they were one.

From Ye Qin's vantage point, he could see Liao Yifang grabbing onto Zhou Feng's arm and Zhou Feng's head slightly bowed over.

They were kissing.

Ye Qin held his breath and did not let it out until he walked to the other side of the B&B's fence. He gazed at the full moon above. There was a sense of accomplishment that made his heart swell. He wanted to ignite firecrackers for the two of them and set up several dozen tables for their wedding guests...if he had the money.

Ye Qin hadn't had such a relaxed and happy moment for a long time. On his way back to the crew, his steps were light and brisk, as if he had seen a little bit of hope for himself through this. There was hope for him to have his gege back in his own arms.

The next day, Ye Qin had planned to see them off at the airport. But just when he had gotten out of bed, he got a phone call from Liao Yifang saying that he had to leave early to deal with an emergency. He promised to catch up again when Ye Qin got back to Beijing.

After a while, he got another call from Zhou Feng, who was in hot pursuit. Only then did Ye Qin realize that the two of them hadn't really come to an agreement yesterday and the kiss had been a forced one. No one knew how much Liao Yifang had actually been moved. Still, Zhou Feng thought that there had been revolutionary progress. While relaying to Ye Qin what had happened, his face was animated with joy, and the frustration at his erstwhile unsatisfactory progress was gone.

Zhou Feng was in a hurry to go after Liao Yifang, so Ye Qin didn't say much, not wanting to hinder him. When Ye Qin went back to filming, he was so absorbed in his work that he actually forgot to ask about it. When he finally picked up the phone that evening, Zhou Feng already knew what he wanted to ask.

"Actually, I didn't do anything grand or special," he offered. "Remember how he wants a stable life? I gave him the bank card where I receive my salary, my car keys, real estate deeds, and all

other valuables I had on me."

Ye Qin was speechless with astonishment. "And the class monitor accepted?"

"Not at all. He wouldn't take it. He asked me to give them to someone else and to go as far away as possible. I said, 'But where can I go when you're here?' He got up, packed, and ran outside, so I just chased after him and said 'I love you.'"

Having heard this, Ye Qin became sure that this was not a method he could borrow. If he said those things to Cheng Feichi, he would not be welcomed by a kiss, but by a cold door.

"The class monitor is still so soft-hearted," Ye Qin sighed.

"Whoever said he wasn't?" Zhou Feng was still immersed in joy. "All thanks to my shamelessness. Not everyone can stand sleeping at the foot of his beloved's house. Last time, when I was injured during an assignment, I stayed downstairs with a plaster cast. He could see me the moment he got up and opened the window. How could he not feel sorry for me?"

Well, Cheng Feichi wouldn't. Had that happened to him, he would send the person straight to the hospital with a blank face, turn around, and leave right away.

Thinking of this, Ye Qin didn't know whether he should feel a sense of loss for Cheng Feichi's impartiality to everyone or be grateful for opportunities to spend time with him just because he always appeared in front of him in a state of embarrassment.

On the other end of the phone, Zhou Feng continued to sum up his experience, "Anyway, you only need to keep eight words in mind: do whatever he wants, say whatever you want. Just do what you want in your heart. One sincere heart can definitely be exchanged for another." After a pause, he continued in puzzlement, "Hey, isn't that something you told me before?"

With only three days left in the shoot, Ye Qin, who had

enough theoretical knowledge to write a book on pursuit, managed to find time to visit the Garden Hotel again.

The PIN for the reserved elevator hadn't been changed, but the PIN for the door had.

That was to be expected. Cheng Feichi had indeed told him the elevator PIN, but the one to his room was a pure guess, and without the owner's consent at that. If not for Ye Qin inviting himself in so many times and practically making it his home, Cheng Feichi probably wouldn't have taken the trouble to reset it.

Back in high school, Cheng Feichi's first smartphone didn't have a password. Ye Qin had repeatedly reminded him that it was unsafe and urged him to use one, but Cheng Feichi hadn't heeded his advice.

Later, when Cheng Feichi was reading a book, Ye Qin played a trick and secretly set his real birthday as the password for Cheng Feichi's cellphone. He told himself that if Cheng Feichi could manage to unlock it, he would tell him that the birthday he had revealed earlier was a small lie; just a harmless lie to get his attention.

It turned out that Cheng Feichi had no idea. He tried and tried but couldn't get it right. He tried 12 22 countless times, since he thought that was Ye Qin's birthday. In the end, after trying too many times, the phone locked itself.

Ye Qin had laughed at his "silliness" and hadn't taken this weighty trust to heart. Now he wanted it desperately, but couldn't have it. He knew that he had to regain that trust first. Only then would Cheng Feichi believe his words. Despite this, he had no clue where or how to find it.

Cheng Feichi had always been open-hearted and upright. There was nothing for him to hide. He was fundamentally different from Ye Qin, who lied continuously and tried to hide whichever way he could.

That thought forced Ye Qin to face the gap between him and Cheng Feichi. They were not a match made in heaven. They had never been, and they still weren't. No one who saw them together would think of them as a suitable pair.

Today, Cheng Feichi returned home very late again. Two steps out of the elevator, he ran into Ye Qin squatting in front of the door.

Although he didn't show too much surprise on his face, Ye Qin could see from his half-second pause that he was not exactly unaffected.

Ye Qin dared to follow him inside. Unable to find a pair of disposable slippers, he stepped on the floor with bare feet. Although he walked quietly without making any obtrusive sounds, his mouth didn't remain idle for a moment.

"Have you had dinner?

"Would you like some tea?

"Which book are you looking for? Let me get it for you.

"Did you get my messages?"

Ye Qin continued to pursue him, chatting randomly about anything and everything. Cheng Feichi continued to stay silent in lieu of rejection.

After hearing the last question, Cheng Feichi, at last, gave a small response. As he set the cup down on the table, his eyes fell on the book. "That number is no longer in use."

Ye Qin was slow to reply, and it was a long time before he finally said, "Oh...Oh."

After tea, Cheng Feichi took a shower. The tranquility in the room continued for about half an hour, and the final evacuation order was issued though the closed door.

Ye Qin looked at the closed door and summoned his courage. "Then...can you tell me the number you're using now?" he asked.

The person inside didn't respond, and instead, turned off the light, taking away the last bit of light spilling out from the crack beneath the door.

Ye Qin stood there for a while before squatting down against the door.

He felt like he was being shameless, acting on the ground that Cheng Feichi would not forcefully drive him away. Well, he was shameless, and so he decided to stay there.

He hadn't had his say yet. He couldn't leave now.

"I know you're still mad at me," Ye Qin said and pondered for a moment. "What happened in the past...I wasn't thinking clearly back then. I acted like an asshole. It was all my fault. You can beat me or yell at me, whatever you want. If you're still unhappy, then you could return the favor. You're welcome to mock me and laugh in my face, but please, never...be so nice to me again."

That last sentence was said with difficulty. No one knew how afraid he was when faced with Cheng Feichi's indifference. It was precisely because he was too afraid that the darkness that had once terrified him became easier to endure. In a reckless way, it could even be transformed into courage.

"I'm quite sincere. I don't want anything else, really. I don't want anything..." He gradually lowered his voice but forced himself to cheer up again. "I-I like you."

That last try was stammered, and Ye Qin repeated seriously, "I like you very much, not because you're beautiful, not because you're rich, but because you're Cheng Feichi. I like you only because you are Cheng Feichi.

"I was so bad and stupid. I thought...I thought you would always stay by my side, that you would never leave. I was so bad. I wanted to tie you to me. I was really so bad..." The words he had organized in his mind were now an entire mess. Ye Qin thought he might as well speak his mind freely. Maybe this was

the only chance he had. He lifted his head and tried his best to make his voice clear, "Not anymore. I'll treat you well and make you happy every day, just like before. No, even happier than that. I'll work hard. I won't bring you any trouble. You longer need to think everything through for me. I've grown up, really... I've grown up a lot."

That day, after seeing Yan Hong off, Ye Qin had sat alone in this empty suite from morning until evening. He sat on the cold floor with no lights on, just as he was doing now.

In darkness and silence, he forced himself to think through whether to leave or to stay. If he left, then he would never come back. If he stayed, he would never let go.

The choice between continuing and giving up had always been very difficult. What Yan Hong had said indeed had a big impact on him, and she succeeded in making him think of letting go.

In others' eyes, Cheng Feichi lived a good life now. He had a car and a house. Both of his parents were alive. Not only was he living in luxury, but he also had everything that came with it; the places he visited, the people he socialized with. Perhaps, just like what Yan Hong had said, Ye Qin's appearance might well drag him back down.

But no one asked Cheng Feichi if this was what he wanted. No one asked what he considered the swamp.

The Cheng Feichi that Ye Qin knew was not afraid of being left alone, nor was he afraid of a life of drifting. He was only afraid of being used, deceived, and forced to do things that he didn't want to do with various lofty-sounding reasons as excuses.

Back then, Cheng Feichi would rather be with him, even if he had to give up his future. He never had a second's hesitation because it was his own choice. Despite the bumpy road with many obstacles ahead, he remained full of confidence. Despite leading such a hard and busy life, he smiled with a joy that exuded from his heart.

Yan Hong thought that his unhappiness was because of his complicated family and uncertain future. Only Ye Qin knew why he had that indifferent face and eyebrows that wouldn't smooth out even in his sleep. It was because he had chosen a seemingly smooth but completely unfamiliar path. Others only saw how fast he walked and how high he flew. No one asked him if he was tired and wanted to take a break.

And the initiator who had forced him to make that choice was Ye Qin himself. Because of his naivety and ignorance, their bright and lively hopes had turned into boundless despair, and the young and unsophisticated love Cheng Feichi had tried his best to defend was also buried. By Ye Qin, with his own hands.

When he thought of this, Ye Qin bit his lip and buried his face in his knees. His eyes felt sore, and he wanted to cry again.

That day, he sat here alone and cried his eyes out. As he let the tears fall freely, he gritted his teeth and told himself that this was the last time. He would never let himself cry again. He hoped that every Ye Qin Cheng Feichi saw from then on would be as enthusiastic and fearless as the teenage Ye Qin.

The only difference was that this time, the enthusiasm was as pure and clear as the morning sun, without any impurity. He wanted to go back to being Cheng Feichi's little sun, the little sun that belonged to him alone.

Ye Qin swallowed hard and tried to hold back the tears gathering in his eyes. He tried to multiply the tiny bit of courage in his heart in hopes that it could leave no room for the shyness and lack of self-confidence looming inside. He prepared to advance.

Facing the closed door, he clenched his fingers around the ring at his chest and said the words he'd been holding back for a long time. "I'll never trick you again...gege."

He believed he could make Cheng Feichi happy.

This was an indestructible certainty, no matter how many long years and how many storms were to come.

CHAPTER 21

THREE days later, Ye Qin temporarily bid the crew good-bye and boarded the plane back to the capital.

Zheng Yueyue had bought the ticket for him. Ye Qin originally wanted to take the high-speed train, but she said that this wasn't the time to be thrifty. After broadcasting for a week, the variety show Ye Qin had filmed earlier received good reviews. Maybe there would be fans to see him off and pick him up at the airport.

Before leaving, Ye Qin hurriedly finished his last magazine photoshoot. With barely any time to spare, he grabbed a taxi and raced to the airport where he actually ran into several fans who had come to see him off, snapping a flurry of pictures with cameras pointed at him. They followed him to the security checkpoint, and, waving their hands, urged him to look after his personal belongings.

Heaven knows the last person Ye Qin had seen who could be called a fan was that peasant, Zhou Feng; he couldn't get used to this sense of fanfare. He sat on the airplane for a while before remembering that shortly after making his debut, he had once lost a wallet at a signing event.

Unafraid of embarrassment at the time, he tossed his pen

aside and got up, looking for it everywhere. His fans, thinking him innocent and cute, nicknamed him "Little Ditz." No one knew that those several hundred RMB were his living expenses and losing them meant he would have to live on air for the next month.

The reason he was going back this time was to take part in the fifth anniversary of their group's debut. Despite the group only existing in name, they still had to keep up with appearances so that those arrogant boy groups currently basking in success knew of their pioneering predecessors. Also, it was a good opportunity to sell some of the albums, photos, and such collecting dust in storage.

When he turned his phone back on after getting off the plane, the first thing Ye Qin did was send a text message.

Regardless of whether Cheng Feichi's old number was still in use, Ye Qin couldn't stop sending him a daily greeting until he got his new number.

He used the time on the shuttle from the airport to scroll through his Super Topic on Weibo. The photos taken at S-City airport had already been posted. Given such a short period of time, they obviously hadn't been touched up. Zooming in on one photo, Ye Qin was shocked by dark circles that could well belong to a panda!

A hundred percent, that was on the eyeliner the make-up artist used for the magazine photoshoot. Ye Qin wiped his eyes with a damp paper towel using his phone as a mirror and thought, *Not much of a chance to get famous again. Yueyue will probably be disappointed.*

...No, wait. He was never famous to begin with. How could he get famous again?

After a bit of despair, he comforted himself, *Thank goodness Cheng Feichi didn't open the door that day, and have to see this hideous face.*

Ye Qin switched to public transit downtown, planning to visit Chengdong Prison first before the anniversary event in the afternoon.

He had applied for visitation recently and just so happened to be granted permission for today. In a hurry, Ye Qin went completely empty-handed.

Ye Jinxiang was still the same, putting on a big smile as soon as he saw him. He asked Ye Qin across iron bars if he had eaten and what was going on in his life now.

In recent years, Ye Qin visited twice per year on average and offered no more than ten sentences each time, nine of which were responses to Ye Jinxiang's questions. He also never stayed longer than five minutes, like he was just completing an assigned task.

Ye Jinxiang wasn't mad at him, either. He spoke with Ye Qin patiently and told Ye Qin not to work himself too hard, to wait for him to pay their debt after he'd served his time, as there were still a couple of old friends he could try his luck with, and so on.

In the past, Ye Qin let his words go in one ear and out the other, as if he hadn't heard anything at all. Today, though, he re-acted differently. "Do you have an old friend called Mr. Yi from S-City?"

"Yes, we were university classmates," Ye Jinxiang said cheerily after a moment's pause. "Did you run into him? You give him dad's name, and he'll definitely help..."

"Give your name to him or his mistress?" Ye Qin cut him off ruthlessly. "You think I don't know what you were up to back then?"

Ye Jinxiang smiled in deprecation. "It's all in the past. I'm a different man now. When they reduce my sentence in a few years and I get discharged, I'll make it up to you. Don't get hung up on this now, or you'll be the one to suffer... Why don't you give me his number, and I'll ask him for a favor..."

"A favor for what? I'm doing great," Ye Qin snapped.

After having his family destroyed and spending over five years in prison, any superiority Ye Jinxiang once had had been completely weathered away. Seeing his son struggling in life, Ye Jinxiang only felt guilt. "I made some money in here doing work," he said, pondering for a bit and humbling himself. "Take it. Ask C University to take you back and continue your studies. Singing and dancing isn't a long-term solution. Your mom wouldn't want to see you live like this from heaven."

In the end, Ye Qin didn't tell Ye Jinxiang about him and Cheng Feichi.

The old man still didn't know that Ye Qin not only hated him for indirectly killing his mother, but also for having messy relationships with women which had caused him to misjudge Cheng Feichi. That then ultimately progressed into the irreparable relationship they had now.

Despite the lasting antagonism aimed at his father, Ye Qin also knew very well that Ye Jinxiang wasn't fully to blame.

If Ye Qin had called Luo Qiuling before going out that morning, reminding her to drive safely and come home early, she might not have driven tired and ended up in an accident. In his short relationship with Cheng Feichi as well, if he had been honest with himself earlier instead of stubbornly remaining in denial for the sake of a false bravado, he wouldn't be in this situation.

If none of this happened, they would probably be like any other couple: going to school, eating in the cafeteria, holding hands in the empty lecture hall, praying to Buddha in the library right before final exams, walking back in the trees' shadows after the library closed, sharing a kiss on the shady, deserted boulevard.

They would also fight. After every falling out, Ye Qin would always be the first to cave in. He'd find Cheng Feichi and make amends. Cheng Feichi would also slowly open up and fix his "bad habit" of expressing more through actions than words.

After graduation, they would rent a small apartment not far from either of their workplaces. In the morning, they would compete for the chance to cook breakfast. At night, they would squish into the tiny shower. Each would flail in excitement when the other got a promotion and use it as an excuse to buy all sorts of meats and seafood for a giant feast. After eating, they would lie together on the bed with rounded bellies and joke about the other being a hungry ghost reincarnated. In the end, the person who got to the dishwasher first would be hugged from behind by the other, heated breath tickling his neck. Halfway through washing, he would forget the stuff he was holding, turn around, and initiate a loving, lingering kiss.

Even if imagination was the cheapest, freest thing in the world, Ye Qin still took care to restrain himself from thinking of those expired memories and impossible what-ifs.

But that afternoon, as he looked at the gigantic "5" flower arrangement on stage at the memorial event, his thoughts inadvertently drifted back to the same day five years ago, when he had signed his name at the bottom of the contract. Later that night, he had moved into the dilapidated dormitory and stowed his offer letter from C University in the dirty cabinet. As he lay on the bed, staring at the rusty iron handle of the drawer, he had let himself freely imagine a future with someone who was now far, far away.

Fortunately, the auditorium today was packed with fans, and there wasn't much time for his imagination to run wild.

After a few songs, a cake with a candle shaped as the number 5 was rolled on stage. Ye Qin took the knife and sliced it, secretly taking a large piece. While other group members vied for the microphone, he hid in the corner and had his fill. Even dinner was taken care of. As soon as the event ended, he'd buy a

high-speed rail ticket and get back to S-City pronto.

During the signing session, a fan asked about his eyes earlier that morning.

"I was just tired from staying up all night," he laughed.

The fangirl didn't believe him. "Did you get that from filming? 'Avancez!' really is going too far. They wouldn't even stop after you fell."

She was referring to their skating in the most recent episode.

"Did that make the final cut?" Ye Qin passed the signed photo right to Song Xu and raised his head. "I haven't seen it yet. Do I look good in that episode?"

She nodded frantically. "Yes, yes, you look really good! The on-screen comments are all asking who the tumbled beauty is. They wanted to do you right there in that position."

This startled Song Xu, and he looked over with wide eyes.

Ye Qin slapped on the table with feigned savagery, but then his shoulders loosened. "You little girls..." he sighed helplessly.

When the group had first made its debut, Ye Qin had assumed the persona of the proud and arrogant young master. After, he somehow turned into the cute boy next door.

His facial features, softer than they were harsh, didn't give him any sense of aloofness. After shedding all the unparalleled arrogance he once had, he became overwhelmingly approachable, especially when he laughed. He treated what precious few fans he had as if they were friends. It was clear that he was one of those people who were naturally easy to get along with.

When Ye Qin found Liao Yifang off-stage, he asked him why he hadn't come up to get an autograph; Ye Qin could even give him an extra copy to set on fire for fun. Liao Yifang waved the neon sign printed with "Ruan" in his hands.

"A friend mailed this and asked me to keep up appearances for you, just on his behalf."

This must be that friend, "Soft Brother, not Iron Sister," who refused to reveal their real name. Same-city express mail service truly wasn't easy.

Ye Qin had originally planned to go chat with Liao Yifang at a nearby café, but Zheng Yueyue suddenly called and asked where he was. She told him to meet up with the others at the back door for the celebration party the company had thrown them.

"Go ahead," Liao Yifang told him, very accommodating. "I have to mail off this neon sign and deliver the photo album you gave me. Otherwise, the little girl will be impatient."

"Little girl?"

"Yeah. She can't come because of school." Liao Yifang pulled up the address on his cellphone. "I'm sending it to the Chengdong Police Station where her father works."

Ye Qin's lips twitched. Was Zhou Feng not afraid of developing split personalities from role-playing all day?

Worried about what his terrible friend had told him, Ye Qin used every excuse in the book to stop Liao Yifang from meeting Song Xu and only made for the back door after sending him off in a taxi.

On the way, he called Zhou Feng and asked when he was planning to reveal his true identity. Zhou Feng said that there was no need to rush, since he had already invaded Liao Yifang's life in every imaginable way. When the right time came, Liao Yifang wouldn't be able to escape even if he fled to the ends of the earth.

"What about you?" Zhou Feng asked after his fellow man in misfortune afterwards. "Are you going back to S-City?"

"Yeah. He's there, so of course I'm going back."

"I have two pieces of news for you," Zhou Feng said after a moment's hesitation. "I don't know how real they are. Do you want to hear them?"

By the sound of that voice, this was related to Cheng Feichi.

Of course Ye Qin wanted to hear.

"There's good news and bad news. Which one do you want to hear first?"

Ye Qin couldn't stand Zhou Feng's dawdling. "The good news," he said casually.

"So I heard that Straight-A Cheng is looking for an office building in downtown Beijing. Seems like he wants to expand his business here."

Hearing this, Ye Qin's heart almost leaped into his throat. No wonder Cheng Feichi had been staying out all night recently. Even the food in the refrigerator would often go untouched for days. It turned out he was coming to the capital.

Naturally, Ye Qin wanted to stay in the capital. This was his hometown. It was Cheng Feichi's as well. It was the place where they'd met and fallen in love. Everywhere here, there were roads they had walked together and traces of them being together.

"What about the bad news?" Ye Qin didn't forget to ask despite all his excitement.

Zhou Feng stammered on the other end, peppering in a bunch of cautious words like "gossip...not very reliable...it's probably fake..." After a fair amount of stalling, he finally said, "Straight-A Cheng is getting engaged to an heiress from a very prestigious family in S-City. Word has it that her last name is Yan."

The so-called celebration dinner party was actually just a formality. After eating, drinking, and posting on Weibo, everyone separated into their own small cliques.

Ye Qin had already filled up on cake that afternoon on stage. He also wasn't in the mood to eat. After Zheng Yueyue led him in a circle to toast the company's executives, he downed drink after drink as if the glass was glued to his hand.

Somewhat worried, Song Xu asked if something had made him unhappy.

"With such a powerful financial backer holding him up, what can he possibly be unhappy about?" He Hansong sneered close by. "He probably wakes up from his dreams laughing."

Ye Qin grinned, pressing the half-empty wine glass against his face. "Yeah, I'm so happy. So happy that I just want to drink more, unlike you, who have to be on your best behavior even as you wait to attend someone else."

Ye Qin used to ignore He Hansong's provocations as much as possible, unwilling to get into a dispute. It was very rare for him to match He Hansong tooth for tooth. He Hansong had just touched up his makeup in the car before coming. Despite glaring at Ye Qin so hard his eyes went round, given the present company, he simply hmphed and walked off in huff.

After dinner, Ye Qin was booking a high-speed rail ticket on his phone outside the hotel when Zheng Yueyue stepped into his way. "Is there another shoot scheduled for tomorrow?"

"Mm, yeah. The crew might still need to take a few more shots."

"In such a hurry? Can't you wait 'til tomorrow morning?"

Ye Qin shook his head like a rattle drum. "No, no. I need to go… I have some business there."

With no other option, Zheng Yueyue took out her own cellphone and booked him a flight. "Regardless of popularity, you're still a celebrity. I can't believe you're thinking of taking the high-speed rail while this drunk. The sun's going to come up by the time you reach S-City."

Zheng Yueyue shoved a tipsy Ye Qin into a taxi headed to the airport. When he got the boarding pass, he realized she had booked him a business seat. Endlessly grateful for her huge splurge, he took out his cellphone and sent her *xoxos*.

Ye Qin boarded and found his seat by the window. Settling in, he pulled down the fold-away table and propped up the tablet he'd snatched from Song Xu, using hotspot to continue loading

a video. He wanted to see how stupid he looked on that show, that even fans who had long forgotten him were digging him out from the dusty corners of their minds.

When the video finished buffering, he plugged in headphones and began to watch.

Seats in business class were comfortable and could even recline. Before he saw himself appear on the show, Ye Qin was hit by delayed drowsiness from the alcohol, head falling askew. He only lifted an eyelid every now and then to take a peek when he heard laughter in his earbuds.

As he was too sleepy to even keep up with the show, Ye Qin naturally didn't notice who came to the seat next to his.

Cheng Feichi had seen him as soon as he'd stepped into the cabin.

Normally, on shorter flights, he opted for economy. He could just take a short nap before landing, so it didn't really matter where he sat. This time, there were only business class seats left on this particular flight, so took out his laptop, planning to work through some files on the plane.

Although these seats were more spacious than economy, they still weren't entirely secluded. As he browsed the web, he could constantly see the person beside him out of the corners of his eyes.

Ye Qin was fast asleep and completely slumping in his seat. His toes were pointing outwards, his head almost tapped on the window, and his hands were in his pockets. Even when the flight attendant passed by with a cart, offering beverages, he didn't wake up.

The video continued playing on the tablet on the foldaway table. Cheng Feichi inadvertently glanced at the screen showing someone pushing Ye Qin down on the ice. Despite wearing a thick coat, his legs shook. Even without a close-up, Cheng Feichi's eyes were sharp enough to see that Ye Qin's hands were red with cold as he grabbed the handrails for balance.

Ye Qin barely regained his balance before falling again. The video was edited to hide the culprit, only showing him sprawled on the ground. When the camera zoomed in on Ye Qin, he immediately curved his eyes into a smile and waved his trembling hands, saying that it was okay. However, his pale face and the beads of sweat rolling down his forehead completely exposed all the pain he tried his hardest to hide.

So this was how he injured his tailbone.

Cheng Feichi couldn't help but remember how Ye Qin had once been afraid of pain and prone to crying. He had put on a fierce face as he drove Cheng Feichi out of the house. Then, after thinking things through and deciding to fetch him, Ye Qin's tears had fallen freely as he held him in a tight grip. Crying, Ye Qin had forbidden him to leave, so upset that it had been as if *he* was the one being bullied.

Cheng Feichi looked away from the screen to the person.

It was the same, restrictive posture. Ye Qin's neck was so shrunken into his collar that his chin could no longer be seen. His legs, thrown about just a moment ago, were now crossed, and a pair of exposed ankles rubbed together instinctively as if trying to generate warmth from the friction.

When Ye Qin woke up from his nightmare, the flight attendant was asking the passengers to lift up their window shades.

He wiped cold sweat off his forehead and stroked his heart, which was beating wildly from fear. When he straightened his tense body, the blanket over it slid to the floor. He picked it up and examined it, puzzled as to where it had come from. Then, he folded it a few times and set it aside.

Owing to the alcohol and subsequent dream, Ye Qin still felt a bit muddled. He took off his headphones and slowly put away the tablet on the foldaway table. Just as he turned his head,

he caught sight of the passenger putting his own laptop away beside him. In an instant, the lingering panic hit his chest like a heavy hammer, shaking him profoundly together with the familiar profile before his eyes.

After shock came a shattering sense of loss, as if his soul had fled his body. This scene was like a mirage; only his face was clear. For a moment, Ye Qin thought that he was still inside a dream.

In the past five years, he had had countless dreams about Cheng Feichi. No matter whether they began in black and white or color, took place in summer or winter, in the end, they were all untouchable and unattainable.

His heart began to beat violently in his chest, so much so that his eardrums began to pound in a similar rhythm.

Even if this was a dream, Ye Qin couldn't let go.

He grabbed Cheng Feichi's hand as the latter closed his laptop. When Cheng Feichi turned to look at him, Ye Qin hurriedly pulled the corner of his mouth into a smile. Just as how he'd practiced in front of the mirror repeatedly at home, Ye Qin moved his lips and offered some words in a hurry.

At the same moment, the plane's undercarriage touched the ground, and the roaring sound of friction washed out his faint voice.

After a brief bout of ringing in his ears, Ye Qin suddenly came back to his senses, looking around and remembering where he was.

He turned back to meet Cheng Feichi's profound stare. Ye Qin didn't dare interpret their meaning. In a panic, he lowered his head, just to see the hand that he was holding onto tightly.

Ye Qin's throat tightened. Still breathing erratically, he reluctantly loosened his own fingers.

Cheng Feichi was silent the whole time.

After getting off the plane, he walked in front of Ye Qin, who stared at his back almost greedily without caring for anything else. When they reached the exit, Ye Qin tripped over the steps but couldn't even be bothered to tie his loosened shoelaces, getting up and continuing to follow.

Around the corner, a group of girls held up cellphones and cameras. Ye Qin burned with anxiety at the road blockade. As he squeezed through the cracks, he also looked in the distance. "Excuse me. I'm just passing by. Your idol is behind me."

The girls all exchanged puzzled looks. "But we're waiting for you."

Ye Qin, who had not had the privilege of being picked up by fans for ages, was stunned. It was only a moment before he was completely encircled. The girls snapped pictures and asked him questions nonstop.

"Qin-Qin, are you here to film? What kind of drama is it? Are you in a relationship on screen?"

"Now that the group has no fixed schedule, are you going to make a solo album, Qin-Qin? I'll buy all the copies."

"Qin-Qin, have you seen He-He? Did he not come with you after the ceremony?"

"'Soft Girl' is so outdated. How about you give us a new nickname?"

"Here, take these: all your favorite snacks... They don't cost much, so just take them!"

After being passed between a bunch of people, Ye Qin was still unable to escape after receiving a pile of gifts and patiently answered every fan's questions. In a moment of desperation, he turned and pointed at the time on the flight information display. "Look at the time. Shouldn't you all be going home? It's quite dangerous for you girls to stay out so late."

"Not as dangerous as you staying out late," they all giggled.

"Your company is so caring that they won't even assign you a bodyguard and even let you drink. What if someone takes advantage of you?" one girl asked worriedly.

Ye Qin lifted his forearm and sniffed it. Sure enough, he could smell alcohol. He wondered if Cheng Feichi had smelled it sitting beside him just now.

"I have an assistant up ahead. I'm going to find her."

Finally finding an excuse to escape, Ye Qin cut through the path that the girls spontaneously parted for him. Even as he ran, he still took time to turn back, remind them to be careful going home, and warn them not to take any unlicensed taxis.

With untied shoelaces flinging about, Ye Qin dashed to the plaza outside the airport, looking all over, but how could there be any traces of Cheng Feichi left?

With the spirit of a defeated fighting cock, Ye Qin took a taxi to the city center where he paced in front of the Garden Hotel and sniffed at his clothes, catching the scent of alcohol that even he disdained. After glancing down at the time on his phone, he decided against going in, afraid of disturbing Cheng Feichi, and instead made do with a cheap hotel nearby for the night.

The next morning, he felt fully revitalized. On the way to set, he planned out a trip to the Garden Hotel later that day. His assistant, Xiao-Yun, called as soon as he arrived, asking if he was back yet and telling him that the director wanted him to come in today for a shoot.

After shooting, he left without delay. Xiao-Yun stayed behind with the cast and crew. When she saw him carrying a handful of bags of snacks up the mountain, she clapped in delight.

Lead actress and major foodie Liu Yuqing was overjoyed as well. "Is my didi blowing up? Does that mean I'll have to ride your popularity from now on?" she exclaimed upon hearing after hearing these were all gifts from his fans.

"Blowing up *again*," Xiao-Yun said, knowing on chicken feet. "Mr. Ruan was quite popular when he first debuted. He used to be the super popular member of the group."

"You must have debuted early, then."

Ye Qin unwrapped a lollipop, stuffed it in his mouth, and said with his mouth full after making a "ten" followed by a "seven" with his fingers, "—years old."

"But I heard from the director that you're twenty-four now?" Liu Yuqing asked doubtfully, doing the math.

"The age on his ID card is actually one year older," Xiao-Yun rushed to explain.

"Everyone is so eager to fake a younger age. Why are you doing the opposite?" Liu Yuqing laughed.

"It's fine as long as I have a baby-face," Ye Qin chuckled, moving the lollipop to his other cheek.

As the heroine's 18-year-old brother, Ye Qin really did look baby-faced. He had casually messy short hair and wore a loose short T-shirt paired with school pants and sneakers. Standing there with the uniform shirt tossed over one shoulder, he looked every inch the Boy Next Door.

They were shooting the scene of him coming back from the county seat and finding out his sister was leaving for the city. As the staff adjusted the camera, Liu Yuqing, leaned into his ear and made eyes at him. "Did your schoolmates ever say that you look very nice in a school uniform?"

Normally, Ye Qin would happily play off this kind of comment and brag about himself. But this time, he had a thought that made his eyes briefly zone out. "In that case, jiejie, you've probably never seen the best-looking guy in my school," he said, quirking his mouth.

"Is he very handsome?" Liu Yuqing raised her eyebrows.

The director yelled at everyone to start the countdown through loudspeaker, and Ye Qin kept his voice quiet beneath his hand. "The handsomest in the world," he said, barely concealing his pride.

They called it a shoot, but they were really only there to cater to the stars. Most of the time, Ye Qin stood aside as a prop in the background, either reacting to the star actors' dialogue or merely giving a cameo of his back.

When they heard Ye Qin had been doing an event in Beijing just yesterday and that he had come back to S-City just for these few scenes, several staff members urged the director to hold a dinner for him. "Don't make the kid travel back and forth in vain," they said.

Ye Qin declined their kind offer and told them he didn't come back for the shooting. It just happened to pop up. But the director, feeling obligated after all their heckling, immediately called a restaurant and booked tables, telling him to accept this as a reward for completing his scenes.

Now that he could no longer find an excuse, Ye Qin had to pretend to be overjoyed despite feeling bitter inside. In the car ride to the restaurant, as he chatted with everyone else, he was also sending bad jokes on his cellphone. The road downhill was full of sharp twists and bumpy turns, making him want to vomit even before eating.

There was almost no time for anyone to sit down at this kind of banquet. As a no-name newbie, Ye Qin could only make himself look meek and small.

Although a few people there knew he had some sort of connection with the young master of the Yi family, he still had to toast them out of unspoken showbiz etiquette. After being taken care of by the crew for so many days, he would look insincere if he didn't drink a few glasses. Otherwise, who would think of him when a suitable role turned up in the future?

After drinking for two nights in a row, Ye Qin began to feel uncomfortable midway through. His stomach churning in pain, he excused himself to the washroom and hid there for a while.

Before coming back out, he rinsed his face and shook his head, still very dizzy.

He walked weakly to the end of the hallway, only discovering that he had gone the wrong way when he saw the exit sign. Turning around, he suddenly bumped into a human wall.

The wall moved. Still dizzy, Ye Qin was shoved forcefully into a corner with his back against the door. His chin was wrenched up, and an arm looped around his waist. Before he could clearly register the person in front of him, he heard a greasy, male voice. "You're even more beautiful when you're drunk."

Ye Qin's tolerance for alcohol wasn't poor, but he really did drink too much this time. The alcohol also had a strong and delayed effect, making him muddled and unable to focus his eyes.

Frowning, he raised his hand and gave the man a push. Not only did the man refuse to move, but he even giggled. "What is it? Are you saving yourself for your protector? The elder son of the Yi family? I can't believe you'd dare to brag about this bullshit."

Ye Qin blinked his eyes hard, finally seeing the person pressing against his body. "Director? Wh-what are you doing?"

The middle-aged, mustached director not only did not panic, but even wanted to negotiate, gradually tightening his grip on Ye Qin's chin. "What a pity that someone with such a striking face is still struggling amidst the no-names. In my opinion, you don't need to flaunt your connection with the young master of the Yi family as leverage. I still haven't cast a supporting male actor for the series I'll be filming next month..."

Ye Qin's brain was sluggish, and it took him a while to understand what the director meant.

Not knowing whether to laugh or to cry, he asked himself what kind of luck he was having this year with all these wannabe financial backers. As soon as he scared one away, another emerged. It was unfortunate that he didn't have a liquor bottle

in his hands this time, or he would have instantly scared this fat slob into fainting.

Zheng Yueyue had called him every now and then to warn him to be careful around this Director Li, and yet he hadn't believed her. A while ago, there were rumors amongst the staff of the director rushing to the supporting actress's room as soon as they finished shooting and telling anyone he ran into they were "discussing the script." Truthfully, everyone knew as clear as day. They just turned a blind eye, is all.

Who would have thought that he played on both teams?

In light of their cooperation in the past, Ye Qin planned to reason with him at first. There was no good in offending this man, after all. But unexpectedly, Director Li had gone crazy after a few drinks, pulling his chin up for a kiss as his other hand audaciously moved towards Ye Qin's butt.

Ye Qin barely had any meat on his body. There was no hope that he could match the strength of this middle-aged man weighing more than 200 pounds. He couldn't break free even with all his strength. He had just closed his eyes and made up his mind to burn this bridge and use the old trick in the book of weaponizing his forehead when a woman suddenly cried out next to him.

"Ah! Sorry, I didn't think there was anyone here."

The director blanked out and Ye Qin stomped on him hard, making him topple over. Ye Qin then scrambled on all fours to the elevator, only relaxing his tense nerves and letting loose inside.

The woman who had spoken was Liu Yuqing. She got in the same elevator as him and clapped her chest in panic. "My god, you scared me to death... Didn't you go to the bathroom? How'd you end up in that isolated corner?"

Ye Qin knew she had deliberately spoken up to save him. Squatting in the elevator, he took a few deep breaths and thanked her over and over, lacking the strength to explain anything else.

Liu Yuqing helped him to the resting area in the restaurant lobby. Even with people constantly walking by, she couldn't let down her guard. She asked him where his assistant was. Too dizzy to respond, Ye Qin left her no choice but to get his cellphone from his pocket, grab his hand to unlock it, and scroll through his address book.

"I can't believe you're so careless," she harped on. "Were you blind to the look I gave you at the table earlier hinting at you to drink less? Director Li is a famous pervert. He's been interested in you for a while now. He's always ogling you while we shoot. I even invited you to the rest lounge that day because I was afraid that he would catch you alone, but you gave him an opportunity anyway, you silly boy. If I hadn't had the heart to follow you, you'd be crying your eyes out tomorrow morning..."

Overwhelmed by the heaviness of his head and eyes, Ye Qin could hear what she was saying but couldn't open his mouth to respond.

"Which one is Xiao-Yun here?" Liu Yuqing jabbered on. "Do you young ones not use names anymore when you save other people's numbers? If you're not going to answer, I'll just call someone random. How about this 'gege'? Is this your real brother? Is he in S-City? Hey! Hey! Don't fall asleep now!"

With his last thread of consciousness, Ye Qin caught the word "gege." The taste of sweetness passed through his lips, and he couldn't help moving them into a faint smile as he fell asleep on the table.

When he woke up, it was still dark outside.

For a brief moment, Ye Qin stared at the gently swaying car roof. Moving his stiff neck and lifting his head up, he heard a familiar voice. "Are you awake?"

By now, most of his drunkenness had subsided, and his head no longer hurt. After double-checking for half a minute

that he was lying fully intact in the back seat of Cheng Feichi's car, Ye Qin helplessly closed his eyes and sighed inwardly. He lifted off the blanket on his body and shifted himself upright using the back of the seat.

"Sorry to have troubled you," he whispered.

Cheng Feichi glanced at him in the rearview mirror and said nothing.

"Is someone bothering you again?" he asked, back facing Ye Qin while the red light counted down at the intersection.

The word "again" made Ye Qin feel ashamed. Despite constantly thinking about staging opportunities to run into Cheng Feichi more often, he didn't want it to happen through getting into a predicament. This kind of clinginess and refusal to let go was no different from deliberately setting up an accident.

"No, no one's bothering me. I just...drank too much."

Ye Qin racked his brains for an explanation of how the phone call to pick up a drunk made its way to Cheng Feichi. The more he thought about it, the more he felt that any explanation would be superfluous. He wouldn't even believe it himself.

While Ye Qin was annoyed at himself, Cheng Feichi parked his car on the side of the road. "I need to buy something."

"Oh," Ye Qin said absentmindedly, watching him get out of the car. He pressed against the window and stared at Cheng Feichi's back as the latter went into the convenience store.

Cheng Feichi wasn't wearing a suit today. His casual clothes accentuated his narrow waist and long legs as he moved like the wind. Ye Qin was reminded of the sneak photo someone had once posted on the high school forum calling Cheng Feichi High School No. 6's mobile scenery.

Back then, Ye Qin had hypocritically ridiculed them for being nymphos, yet he himself had saved the photo afterward and admired it in his bed at night. He had even logged into the forum and reported the post as spam, requesting to delete it. *This is my boyfriend,* he had thought pettily, *don't even think of it.*

Upon returning, Cheng Feichi first opened the back door of the car first and handed him a plastic bag with two bottles of water.

Ye Qin reeked of alcohol. Afraid the scent would suffocate Cheng Feichi, he shrank back. But Cheng Feichi suddenly crouched over and poked his head in, looking into his eyes. "Who did it?"

"Huh?"

For a while, Ye Qin didn't realize what he meant. It was the pain he felt on his butt that reminded him of Director Li's forcefulness back at the restaurant. He'd already felt pain when Director Li had squeezed his waist, so his chin, having been pinched with a strength hard enough to break bones, naturally hadn't been spared.

Ye Qin had fair skin. It was easy to leave marks, especially after such rough handling. It had only been slightly red at the time, but after a while, terrifying blue marks emerged as if he had been beaten.

"It's nothing. Really. I accidentally hit—" Ye Qin quickly covered his chin, hiding it from Cheng Feichi.

An outstretched hand interrupted him as he was speaking.

Cheng Feichi peeled away Ye Qin's hand on his mouth. The warm fingertips of his middle and index fingers pressed together touched the soft flesh between Ye Qin's jaw and Adam's apple. Cheng Feichi gently lifted Ye Qin's chin, moving his whole face into the glow of the street lights outside.

Having spent a while in the dimness of the car, Ye Qin was a bit unused to light directly shining at him. With his head raised, he blinked several times, still barely able to make out the shape of the person in front of him.

Cheng Feichi stood against the light, making it difficult

to see his expression, and yet Ye Qin could sense the air around him gradually become more sunken.

"Who did it?" Cheng Feichi asked again in a low voice.

"N-no one did it. I hit it." Ye Qin insisted, not wanting to cause him any more trouble.

"How did you hit it?" Cheng Feichi pursued. His hand stayed fixed on Ye Qin's chin.

Ye Qin felt slightly uncomfortable with his head tilted up, and his eyes drifted in every direction. "Just, you know. I hit it on the table. I drank a bit too much and was careless..."

Examining marks that were obviously fingerprints, Cheng Feichi pursed his lips in a small frown before letting go and moving out of the car. He slid the back door shut and returned to the driver's seat.

As he drove on, the atmosphere in the car became more and more depressing.

Cheng Feichi was angry.

Ye Qin didn't dare think too much into the reason behind his anger, but he couldn't help it.

As his thoughts lingered, he couldn't help but feel a little sad. He lowered his head, burying his chin into his chest. Suddenly, he thought of when he had told Cheng Feichi that he would no longer lie to him. Not knowing if this counted as a lie, he felt even sadder.

After arriving at the Garden Hotel, Ye Qin followed Cheng Feichi upstairs.

His steps were still somewhat weak after getting drunk, and he staggered sideways on a straight path, nearly bumping into Cheng Feichi as he went through the door. When Cheng Feichi glanced back at him, Ye Qin immediately grabbed the door frame and stared back. He forcefully cleared his mind, pretending to be sober.

It wasn't until he saw himself in the bathroom mirror that Ye Qin realized how serious the bruises on his chin were—a mix of blue, red, and purple. It was obvious at a glance that this wasn't something that could be caused by hitting a table.

Feeling extremely upset, Ye Qin braved himself before going out. "May I use some ice cubes?" he asked Cheng Feichi, who was sitting on the sofa with a laptop, after pulling his collar up over his chin to conceal the incriminating evidence.

Cheng Feichi told him yes. Ye Qin took three ice cubes from the refrigerator and pressed them to his chin. When his left hand got too cold to bear, he switched to his right. The ice dripped as it melted. Afraid of dirtying the floor, he went to the sink instead to apply it.

The ice hadn't melted much by the time Cheng Feichi made his way over. He silently grabbed a towel, wrapped it around a couple of new ice cubes, and handed it to Ye Qin. "Use this."

Ye Qin put his ice cubes down and dried his wet hands on his T-shirt before taking Cheng Feichi's ice pack, stammering thanks.

It was really cold. The bruises didn't fade much, but the skin around them turned red. Unable to see his own face, Ye Qin was unaware of this as he continued to press the pack on his face and endured its iciness. For a while, Cheng Feichi stood and watched. Then, he took the ice pack back from Ye Qin's hands, turned around, got an egg from the fridge, and offered that instead.

Ye Qin's head hadn't fully cleared yet, and his brain wasn't at its usual capacity. Without knowing why Cheng Feichi swapped out ice for an egg, he took the egg and continued rolling it on his skin. Cheng Feichi had already left but came back after only a few steps. He took the egg from Ye Qin's hand, cracked it open on the chopping board, and peeled it.

Ye Qin was still in a daze when his chin was lifted again. Across from him, Cheng Feichi warmed the hardboiled egg in

his hands before pressing to Ye Qin's skin and rolling it.

Ye Qin held his breath on reflex. He kind of wanted to close his eyes but couldn't bring himself to.

From this angle, he could see Cheng Feichi's entire face: his high nose bridge; his thin, tightly pursed lips; his sharp jawline; and his eyelids that hung heavily over his eyes. But even so, Ye Qin could still catch his focused gaze through his thick eyelashes.

Cheng Feichi's hands were gentle. Though his face contained no expression, Ye Qin could feel great patience and tenderness.

Ye Qin couldn't get by just gritting his teeth, so he switched to biting his lip.

"Does it hurt?" Chen Feichi asked when he noticed his reaction, lifting his eyelids.

Ye Qin shook his head a few times and opened his eyes wide at the ceiling. "No, not at all."

Despite saying that, the corners of his eyes turned red.

Cheng Feichi looked at him for a moment and parted his lips slightly as if wanting to say something. In the end, he didn't, averting his eyes as he continued to roll the egg.

It was past nine when they had returned, and they both went to bed alone after taking a shower.

The next day, Ye Qin was roused by the ringing of his cellphone. As soon the call connected, Liu Yuqing got straight to the point. "Are you all right after last night? How are you feeling?"

Rubbing his temples, Ye Qin shook his head. "I'm fine... Thank you. I'll treat you to a meal when I get back to Beijing."

"That's good. No need to treat me," Liu Yuqing said courteously. "Do you still have any scenes left to shoot? Stay away from set for now. Director Li isn't a generous person. Wait for him to calm down a bit before coming back. He wouldn't dare do anything to you."

This made Ye Qin's head hurt even more. "I still have a few

more scenes. They can probably be shot in half a day. Is Director Li ...very angry?"

"Not really. When I returned to the table yesterday, he was slumped over pretending to be drunk. They had to carry him back to set. He didn't say a thing to me this morning, like he forgot about everything... He often plays stupid as a coverup, but I'd still recommend taking a few days to come back."

Ye Qin agreed and expressed his sincere thanks once again.

With the formal business over with, Liu Yuqing immediately jumped to another, completely unrelated topic. "Was that really your brother yesterday? He doesn't look like you at all."

"Huh? Oh, he's not my...actual brother."

"Your cousin then? Mom's side or dad's? Your family has really good genes. When he stood in front of me yesterday, I thought he was that latest actor. I was even wondering if I could find an opportunity to film with him."

Speaking of acting, Ye Qin remembered that he used to worry Cheng Feichi was so good-looking that a scout would one day whisk him away to do showbiz. He'd even firmly instructed Cheng Feichi not to go with a sense of justice with the excuse that his face was too serious and stern and would scare everyone away.

Now, hearing this kind of praise from a fellow actress, the inexplicable jealousy faded from his heart, leaving only admiration and pride. "Really? I told you he was the handsomest man in the world."

"Not just handsome, but so full of boyfriend energy. If you didn't put him down as 'gege' in your contacts, I would have thought that he was your partner."

Ye Qin's heart raced for a moment. "Ah? You're so funny," he joked, too embarrassed to ask her where Cheng Feichi's *boyfriend energy* came from. "Aren't you scared my brother-in-law will get jealous?"

"Speaking of the devil, your brother-in-law just called to check in on me," said Liu Yiqing chipperly, as she was already in an established relationship. "Let's talk next time."

After hanging up, Ye Qin got out of bed.

In August, S-City was only slightly cooler early in the morning. The air conditioner in the apartment was set to dehumidification mode, so it didn't feel hot even though the temperature wasn't low.

Ye Qin made breakfast, fried egg sandwiches with lettuce. He even sliced two pieces of tomato to put inside, cut them diagonally, and placed them on a plate. The reds, whites, greens, and yellows made for a very nice aesthetic.

Cheng Feichi brushed his teeth, washed his face, and entered the kitchen where Ye Qin fed leftover tomato slices into his mouth. When he turned his head and saw Cheng Feichi, he was like a little kid caught with his hand in the cookie jar. Without even chewing, he swallowed the tomato and said with round, stuffed cheeks, "Morning..."

Cheng Feichi looked at a drop of clear red juice dripping down the corner of his mouth. Ye Qin quickly licked it away with a bright, red tongue. For a moment, Cheng Feichi forgot what he was going to say and nodded in response.

Neither of them spoke during breakfast. Occasionally, dishes clinked on the table.

Ye Qin was afraid that Cheng Feichi would drive him away. "How was the sandwich?" he made small talk after dinner, standing up and clearing the table. "This is my first time making it. I make fried eggs a lot. My roommates all say they're good. This pan...is really good, non-stick too, easy to wash. It'd be nice if we had soymilk. But would it be weird to pair sandwiches with soymilk?"

Cheng Feichi helped him tidy up, occasionally humming to

indicate he was listening.

Every time he made noise, Ye Qin visibly got more excited. He gradually rambled on from what he ate every day to the difference in climate between Beijing and S-City to when domestic plane tickets would lower in price. It was as if the timid, cowering Ye Qin from last night was fake and this incessant chatterbox reminiscent of the old days was his real self.

Ye Qin was so caught up in chatting that he neglected the time. When they left the kitchen, the shorthand on the mounted clock already pointed eight. Ye Qin remembered that last time Cheng Feichi left, it hadn't even been seven.

"Sorry," he said, walking him to the door to see him off. "Once I started talking, I ended up going on and on..."

About to change shoes in the foyer, Cheng Feichi paused as if suddenly recalling something. Ye Qin held in his breath, fearful he was about to be evicted. Only, Cheng Feichi just went back to the kitchen, got a boiled egg, and put it on the table.

"Roll it on your chin," he instructed before leaving.

He neither drove Ye Qin away nor told him the apartment password.

This meant that Ye Qin could stay there for a little longer. But once he left, forget about coming back in.

Ye Qin's heart was filled with mixed feelings, and he didn't know whether to be happy or disappointed. He walked to the table and slowly peeled off the eggshell, then went to the bathroom and rolled it on his chin in front of the mirror.

On him, scars and bruises were easily formed but never easy to fade. After a whole night, his chin was still purple. He pulled open the waistband of his pants and twisted his head to look back. There were more visible fingerprints in the area between his waist and butt.

Thank goodness Cheng Feichi hadn't seen.

The person in the mirror thought of something, and a blush slowly spread on his cheeks. He rubbed the egg on his chin for a while longer, suddenly feeling that there was no need to get rid of this bruise too quickly. For a brief moment, he held up the tender, white egg in front of his eyes, examining it. Then, he shoved it into his mouth.

Cheng Feichi didn't come back at noon, so Ye Qin made some noodles to tide himself over. After that, he rolled up his sleeves and continued tidying.

From the state of the room, he could tell that Cheng Feichi had been very busy recently. The most he could manage was to do the dishes. Not only were there books scattered everywhere and the furniture dusty, but there were also several dress shirts left in the bathroom waiting to be washed.

Ye Qin looked up and carefully read up on how to clean dress shirts. Some articles said to apply toothpaste to the collars and cuffs while others said to sprinkle some salt, invoking his fear of making decisions. Thankfully, Cheng Feichi's clothes weren't very dirty. In the end, he chose the gentlest method, to soak the shirts for a few minutes and scrub them softly with his hands. After that, he spread them out and hung them up.

As he wiped down the bookshelf, Ye Qin accidentally knocked off the rightmost book on the shelf level with his eyes. An open envelope fell out with it.

He picked up the envelope from the floor. Out of curiosity, he examined it a bit more closely. It was evidently sent abroad, as the addresses of both the sender and recipient were written in English, and the letter was stamped with the mark of a certain university.

Ye Qin took out his cellphone and copied the school's name into the search engine. He browsed through the school's introduction and photos of campus life. As he zoomed and looked closely at the neat, spacious library and huge sports turf, his eyes curved into a smile.

This type of school was what Cheng Feichi deserved, not the no-name C University.

From the moment they met, he felt an indescribable admiration for Cheng Feichi. Ye Qin thought that he knew everything and could accomplish anything easy as pie. Cheng Feichi didn't need anyone to worry about him.

But before, Ye Qin was too caught up in saving face and refused to accept this. Now, he finally knew why he felt a sense of security whenever he was with Cheng Feichi.

After a busy day, he fetched the clothes from the drying table at sunset. He smoothed them out carefully on the sofa and folded them one by one.

When he thought of how Cheng Feichi had to wear these clothes to work, Ye Qin felt that the smell of detergent was too cheap, not worthy of his current status. Looking around, he found an unopened bottle of cologne in a cabinet in the foyer. He was going to spray it on the clothes, but when he looked at the packaging, he found that this was one of the things gifted by Yan Hong.

Thinking of the rumors he had heard from Zhou Feng, Ye Qin felt terribly suffocated. And since he didn't know what would give him the right to ask Cheng Feichi about this, he brooded even more.

In the end, he didn't spray any, just kept the original scent of detergent and sunshine.

Since he hadn't received permission, Ye Qin followed the rules and stayed out of Cheng Feichi's room. He temporarily stacked the folded clothes on the sofa. With the water already boiled, there was nothing else to do. But he didn't want to leave either, so he sat and read the book that Cheng Feichi had been

reading last night.

The book on economics contained too many specialized words. It was dry and dull. Before long, Ye Qin felt tired. He put it aside and lay down on the sofa cushion. As he massaged his waist, he accidentally touched the bruises, scrunching his eyebrows and gasping in agony.

It only got more comfortable when he flipped over and massaged the other side. Slowly, he closed his eyes and let his head drop. Smelling the faint fragrance of freshly washed clothes, Ye Qin fell into a deep sleep to the ticking of the mounted clock.

When Cheng Feichi returned home, it was already dark outside. He thought that he would turn on the lights to an empty living room as usual. Unexpectedly, the first thing he saw was Ye Qin curled up around a stack of clothes, fast asleep on the sofa.

Ye Qin used to love sleeping. He slept in class, after class, and continued to sleep when he got home. Even while doing homework, his head could drop to the table in a blackout. Cheng Feichi had heard that actors were very busy while filming and often couldn't get enough sleep. No wonder Ye Qin had been looking a little haggard recently and was missing flesh on his once plump cheeks.

Cheng Feichi couldn't help but lighten his steps. Upon entering the kitchen, he saw a disposable cup set aside, still half-full. He could still feel a bit of warmth as he touched it. Half a pack of dried noodles was missing from the refrigerator, as well as another egg. Clearly, Ye Qin had taken care of his lunch here and hadn't left all day.

It was very late. If he started cooking now, who knew how long it would take before he could eat. After going into his bedroom to change clothes, Cheng Feichi made a call to the hotel kitchen behind closed doors, requesting two dinners.

After hanging up and leaving his room, he had a thought,

came back, and fetched a blanket. He walked back to the sofa and tried to wrestle his shirts from Ye Qin's hand several times to no avail. With a light sigh, he gave up, unfolded the blanket, and put it over Ye Qin's body.

Ye Qin was a deep sleeper, the kind that couldn't be woken up by thunder or lightning. Yesterday, he had been the same. Cheng Feichi had carried him all the way from the hotel lobby to the back seat of the car. Afterwards, when he had covered him with a blanket, Ye Qin had even tugged it and muttered a thank you but still hadn't woken.

Thus, he didn't hesitate to pull the blanket up to Ye Qin's chin, glancing at the still obvious bruises as he did.

Even though Ye Qin didn't want to explain, Cheng Feichi could more or less guess how they came to be. He had only been back in the country for three months, and already he'd seen his fair share of filthy chaos amongst the rich and famous. He could infer through these past years of experience what would happen to a person without a strong backing or connections.

He just didn't think that, despite admitting his relationship with Ye Qin in front of so many people back at the club, there still existed those who harbored ill intentions.

Cheng Feichi's eyes darkened as his thoughts drifted. He didn't even notice Ye Qin opening his eyes.

It may have been because they kept running into each other recently that Ye Qin frequently dreamed these days. Even during a short nap, he would dream of Cheng Feichi standing under the ginkgo tree in front of the back door of their high school, though he could neither see him clearly nor touch him. Every time he woke up, he would space out for a long time, too immersed in the turmoil of the dream to extricate himself.

This time was no exception. When their eyes met and Ye Qin saw Cheng Feichi right in front of him, he subconsciously

grabbed Cheng Feichi's hand and forced an unnatural smile.

"Gege...gege, you're back," he said hurriedly.

His voice was hoarse and shaky, with traces of tiredness from just having woken up. It was not clear and pleasant like usual, yet it pulled Cheng Feichi's consciousness back to the present. The lingering voice turned into silk threads wrapping tightly around his heart so that he could only stand stiffly in place, devoid of the strength to pull his hand away.

He remembered this sentence.

This was what Ye Qin had said that day when the plane had landed.

Right now, he looked very happy but also somewhat nervous. The hand he used to grab onto Cheng Feichi's was shaking hard. This time, Ye Qin didn't contain himself too much. His eyes teared up and wavered in sync with his rapid breaths. He was obviously terrified but still forced the corners of his mouth up in a stiff smile.

This was like finally getting an anticipated reunion after years of longing. No matter what, he must not spoil the mood of this moment.

Cheng Feichi looked at him intently. Those threads wove into a net around his heart, plucking hard as they tightened.

That day, on the other side of the door, had Ye Qin curled up like this, barely withholding tears, waiting for him to open the door?

CHAPTER 22

YE Qin was still hiding in the bathroom when dinner was delivered. After a few more minutes, he came out. His eyes were no longer red, and a few strands of wet hair stuck to his forehead as if he had just washed his face.

When Cheng Feichi handed him chopsticks, he whispered "thank you" in a voice that remained a little hoarse. Ye Qin still didn't have the guts to lift his head, wanting to disappear into a hole in the ground. Cheng Feichi felt at a loss as to what to do or say to melt the frozen air.

Ye Qin had been the one to let go first. Like a rabbit startling out of a nightmare, he jumped and fled to the bathroom, closing the door behind him. Cheng Feichi had been left to stand there alone in the living room, looking down at the hand Ye Qin had been holding. He hadn't moved for a long time.

Now things were back to normal, yet they could still clearly feel the difference. Even though they had only been separated by a door, it hadn't been the same as laying things out in the open. Now, a large hole was smashed into the door between them. They could cover it with paper, wooden boards, or with their own bodies, but that jagged hole would still exist, forcing them to look each other in the eye.

The person on the left harbored the tiniest bit of self-confidence. His actions were still governed by fear, and he kept reminding himself to be rational, but between heaven and earth, he had nowhere else to go. Only through this door was he able to find a safe home.

The person on the right seemed completely put together, but the truth was that he had already lost his ground. Every movement, every word from the other spoke to emotions that had remained stagnant for many years. His dull heartbeats started thumping once again.

At this moment, the wind scattered away the fog between the two to its thinnest form. They only had to take a few steps forward to see each other clearly.

"You…"

"You…"

They spoke at almost the same time. Ye Qin cleared his throat, trying to make his hoarse voice return to normal. "Y-you go first."

Cheng Feichi didn't refuse, but he mulled over it for a moment. Just as he was about to speak, there was a knock on the door.

He was the one to get it. He returned with a new pair of slippers in his hand, walked around the table to Ye Qin, and placed them at his feet. "Put these on."

Dinner and everyday supplies were sent up by the kitchen and room service, respectively, in full compliance with the hotel's standard operating procedures. However, there was no set standard to follow for how to pick up a topic again after being interrupted.

Ye Qin tucked his feet into the linen slippers. This pair was not disposable and much more comfortable. And yet, wearing these, he didn't feel as free and comfortable as stepping barefoot on the floor.

They ate across from each other silently as if finding a buffer zone in this way.

"Did you catch a cold?" Cheng Feichi spoke again when the meal came to an end.

"Huh?" Ye Qin sniffed, still spacing out. "I don't think...so."

Then, he sneezed loudly.

When it rained, it poured. On top of being injured, he'd caught a cold. Ye Qin couldn't be more unfortunate.

After eating, he took medicine and pondered whether that was the only thing Cheng Feichi had wanted to say. For a moment, he thought yes, but then he felt like there must have been something else. With nothing to base this on, Ye Qin scooped up water with a teaspoon—one sip yes, another sip no, over and over again.

He used the new cup just sent up via room service.

After doing this gleefully several times, he finally dispersed his dejection and even tasted a hint of sweetness in the warm water that he usually disliked. Even though this cup was different from Cheng Feichi's, at least it was ceramic, not paper. It was as if his status had been elevated from a guest to a friend who visited frequently. He could walk about the place with his chest puffed.

But before he could finish, Cheng Feichi took away the cup. "The water's cold now. I'll pour you a new cup."

With his secret divination interrupted, Ye Qin was too embarrassed to explain. His hesitance made Cheng Feichi think that he wanted a cold drink. Taking full preventative measures, Cheng Feichi stacked all the soda bottles in the fridge on top of the kitchen cabinet. A little less than five foot nine, Ye Qin couldn't reach them even if he stretched his hand up.

After taking a refilled cup of warm water from Cheng Feichi, Ye Qin dragged his feet. Finally, he sat beside Cheng Feichi who was reading on the sofa. Only when Cheng Feichi didn't

show any objection did he relax, inconspicuously leaning against him. He put in earbuds and played the episode that he hadn't finished on the plane. Sneezing, Ye Qin belatedly remembered that he had a cold and moved towards the opposite side, afraid of giving it to Cheng Feichi.

Little did he know that next to him, Cheng Feichi was aware of all these little movements.

From the corner of his eyes, Cheng Feichi saw Ye Qin move like a bee before him and inch tiny steps towards the sofa. Then, when he sat down, he seemed to measure the distance, precisely controlling himself to sit in the closest place he was allowed to by social standards. When he played the video, he even stole a glance at Cheng Feichi, afraid the latter would peek at him. Afterwards, he sneezed into his hand and moved away a few inches reluctantly, thinking that this tiny bit of space could prevent a cold from spreading.

Since the cold medicine had a sedative effect, Ye Qin began to doze off after a while, his head swaying from one side to the other. However, this time, Ye Qin managed to hold out until he appeared and even laughed at the sight of himself on the ice, legs shaking as he grabbed onto the handles tightly. In the end, he couldn't hold back his heavy eyelids from sinking. Dropping his cellphone in his lap, he fell asleep sideways against the back of the sofa.

Cheng Feichi "profited" again by reexperiencing the whole episode.

There were the subtitles at the bottom. After Ye Qin fell, someone else used the excuse of talking about the group to mention Ye Qin's education. They spoke with an undertone of ridicule. Ye Qin's response was much more unexciting. He said to the camera very candidly that he hadn't gone to university, so please don't laugh at him for not knowing how to skate.

His lips curved up, but there was no smile in his eyes.

Seeing him, Cheng Feichi held his breath. His amber eyes gradually darkened, like he was contemplating something.

The next morning, the one in the guest bedroom woke up first, as usual.

Cheng Feichi pushed open the semi-closed bathroom door to see Ye Qin telling himself good morning in the mirror. When Ye Qin turned and saw him, he hiccupped in alarm and swallowed half the foam in his mouth.

By the time they ate breakfast, Ye Qin was still a little embarrassed. He didn't dare raise his voice, instead muttering like a mosquito, when he asked if he had fallen asleep on the sofa last night. Cheng Feichi nodded and said yes, making him so embarrassed he couldn't even raise his head.

"Next time...if there is a next time, I promise it won't happen again," Ye Qin promised with a raised hand.

When they had been living together in the Jiayuan Compound six years ago, this kind of thing had happened more than once.

Cheng Feichi attended class in the day. After returning in the evening, he had to do homework, review, and still find time to write lesson plans. Often, he was too busy to pay attention to Ye Qin. Too restless to stay in his room, Ye Qin often went to the living room to play Legos or video games, falling asleep halfway. When he opened his eyes the next day, he would always be tucked in bed.

"You sleepwalked into bed," Cheng Feichi told him, smiling, when Ye Qin asked him what had happened.

Ye Qin was not stupid enough to believe him, but Cheng Feichi refused to reveal anything no matter how he asked. This thing took root in Ye Qin's heart, and he told himself that he couldn't sleep too deeply from now on; he had to wake up when Cheng Feichi got close to him and see whether Cheng Feichi

helped him up or dragged him.

Fate had other plans, though. To this day, Ye Qin had yet to master the art of choosing when to wake up. Now, he had a new, more pressing concern, which was not bringing Cheng Feichi any more trouble.

"Don't worry about it," Cheng Feichi said across the table, putting down his chopsticks.

Ye Qin wasn't sure if he also remembered something. He hoped Cheng Feichi still remembered. At the same time, he hoped Cheng Feichi would quickly forget and only remember the less hateful side of him.

Ever since their reunion, it was like two little human figures with opposite opinions moved into his heart, constantly fighting. They wore him out even before he came to a decision. All the fear he had or would ever feel throughout his lifetime was probably condensed here, he thought.

Another whole day of staying in.

As he had been too diligent yesterday, Ye Qin found himself with finite things to do. After cleaning, he picked up and read the sticky note Cheng Feichi had left on the table. In the end, though, he still didn't call the kitchen. Instead, he filled his stomach with a bowl of noodles.

The freshly washed shirts had been crumpled in his arms yesterday when he slept. Thinking of smoothing them out, he found a hanging iron in the storage room, filled it with water according to instructions he found online, and turned it on.

Steam came out of the nozzle. Ye Qin wasn't sure if this much was effective, so he stupidly put his hand there to test it and got burned so badly that he almost screamed. Even after running it under cold water for a while, he still couldn't get rid of the burning sensation.

By the time Cheng Feichi came back, those shirts were once again smooth and hung up on a drying rack, fluttering in the wind.

It had rained in the afternoon, and the temperature dropped slightly. The air conditioner was turned off in the apartment, and the windows on the upper level were open wide. The evening wind took away any stuffiness, leaving behind cool and humid air.

"I'll be leaving tomorrow." Ye Qin stated at dinner. "I'm going back on set to shoot some scenes."

Hearing this, Cheng Feichi looked up at him and hummed.

After waiting for so long, he still didn't even get a door code. Dejected, Ye Qin couldn't help but wonder what he had done wrong. The burn on his palm was still easy to spot, so he deliberately hid it while they were eating. Cheng Feichi wouldn't have seen it.

So just what did he do wrong? Or was Cheng Feichi just impossible to sway no matter what he did?

As he pondered, Cheng Feichi's cellphone rang on the table. He was taking a shower in the bathroom, unable to hear anything outside. Ye Qin didn't plan to answer at first, but it wouldn't stop ringing as someone called over and over again with great patience.

On the fifth call, Ye Qin finally had enough. He picked up the phone and went to knock on the bathroom door, but when the burn on his palm touched a hard object, his hand jolted and accidentally tapped the answer button.

"Gege! Gege, are you coming home to have dinner with Huihui today?" someone yelled from the other end before he could react.

Having heard the knock on the door, Cheng Feichi came out without drying his hair. He wore a loose bathrobe only held together with a tied sash. With one hand, he took the phone. With the other, he grabbed a towel and dried his hair while

speaking to the person on the other side.

"Yes... Not today, just eat by yourself... No, I don't hate you... When school starts next month, I'll drive you... Okay, bye."

Ye Qin pretended to fold clothes, but his eyes kept glancing over at Cheng Feichi in his disheveled robe. His ears were perked as well, and he caught every word.

That was a boy's voice on the phone, calling Cheng Feichi "gege" so sweetly, telling him to "come home for din-din." Ye Qin couldn't help but let his mind wander.

Before even finding out who that boy was, he already got jealous in spite of himself. At some point in time, he started seeing "gege" as his exclusive address for Cheng Feichi. Despite this being a common thing to call someone, he still felt unhappy hearing someone else call Cheng Feichi that.

After drying his hair, Cheng Feichi came out to see him sitting silently, yet to touch the cold medicine on the table. He walked over. "My younger brother," he said, picking up folded clothes.

Ye Qin was caught unaware by these words that seemed to have come out of the blue. His eyes widened a bit, and he looked up at Cheng Feichi.

"My younger half-brother from my father's side," Cheng Feichi explained again seriously.

Despite Cheng Feichi tiding over things with a few words, Ye Qin had seen and heard many secrets of the rich and powerful since childhood. He could infer the situation with the Yi family from how Cheng Feichi acted.

Moreover, the story had already been spread everywhere: Cheng Feichi had only been brought back to inherit the Yi family business because his father's wife gave birth to a disabled son. Only, Ye Qin hadn't realized that Cheng Feichi was actually on good terms with this "brother" and was even closer to him than to his biological parents.

"He often called me when I was abroad. He's an interesting kid."

Ye Qin felt depressed hearing this. Why should the grudges of the last generation be passed down to this one?

But thinking back, wasn't that exactly what he had done? Blamed Ye Jinxiang's sins on Cheng Feichi, which then led to a series of misfortunes and even changed the lives of two people.

As he felt a sense of regret and loss, Ye Qin suddenly recalled yesterday's scene where he'd grabbed Cheng Feichi's hand and called him "gege." That was so embarrassing that he wanted to find somewhere to hide away again.

Grabbing a change of clothes, Ye Qin ran into the bathroom. With his back to the door, he lifted his shirt to look at the injury on his waist.

This was his only chance in the past two nights to see how much the bruises had faded. The ones on his face clearly faded faster. They should be unnoticeable after applying makeup tomorrow. He didn't know how much longer it would take for the ones on his body. Fortunately, he had no naked scenes. At most, he'd still be in a vest and underwear.

He was too focused on looking to notice footsteps approaching from outside.

"Your hand..."

The voice sounded at the same time as the door, and both came to an abrupt stop.

Cheng Feichi held a jar of ointment. His eyes fell directly on Ye Qin's waist where there was a motley of bruises even more striking against fair skin. Deep and long, the winding bruises disappeared into his waistband. There were probably more still covered by his clothes.

Ye Qin's heart pounded as he turned, hurriedly pulling his shirt back down.

"Did you see the injury on my hand?" he played dumb, lifting it. "I accidentally burned myself with the clothes iron. Ha ha ha... Ow, it kinda hurts."

This diversion was much too clumsy.

Cheng Feichi looked at his face. Though his expression remained unchanged, his eyes turned very cold.

He set down the ointment near the sink and turned to leave, only to be stopped by Ye Qin's cry.

"It's not..." Ye Qin couldn't even pretend to smile. He took two steps forward and forced himself to take a big step back. "It's not what you think. I didn't...with anyone..."

He mumbled incoherently; head jumbled into a giant mess. Countless thoughts flashed through it, but there wasn't a single one he could grab onto to prove his innocence.

Last time, when Ye Qin had taken out makeup from his pocket as Cheng Feichi drove him from the club to Cangquan Mountain, Cheng Feichi must have already thought it then— that Ye Qin's private life was complicated, that he didn't keep himself clean.

Indeed, how many people could remain pure and principled in such a messy circle? Cheng Feichi had both been poor and a member of the rich and powerful. How could he not be aware of these dirty secrets?

Ye Qin was so anxious he was close to tears, and the more anxious he felt, the more he panicked. But besides "it's not" and "I didn't," he couldn't make a stronger argument.

Even if he told Cheng Feichi, would Cheng Feichi believe him? In his eyes, wasn't Ye Qin just a liar who played with other people's feelings?

The words he used in his own defense slowly died down. Ye Qin couldn't continue. He hung his head in defeat and covered his eyes with one hand. Maybe if he didn't see Cheng Feichi, he would pretend nothing ever happened, and Cheng Feichi also wouldn't see him in a helpless, embarrassing state.

One second, two seconds, three seconds...

With his eyes closed, Ye Qin silently counted to ten in his head. Instead of hearing fading footsteps as he'd expected, he heard a deep voice that immediately gave him shivers.

"I know," Cheng Feichi turned around and said over his head.

The next morning, Ye Qin was not the first to get up. When he opened the bedroom door, Cheng Feichi was already drinking coffee at the table.

Ye Qin brushed his teeth and rinsed his face. Rubbing his eyes, he looked intently in the mirror.

Though he had gotten used to living an ordinary life, some parts of his body still wanted to be pampered, like his stomach, skin, and eyes. So long as he cried the night before, he would wake up with bloodshot eyes the next morning, and eyedrops offered very little help.

Brushing his bangs out of his eyes, Ye Qin went out bashfully and sat down. It looked like breakfast had been sent up from the kitchen. There were two cream custard buns carefully arranged on the plate, and the sandwiches were cut neatly and beautifully. A single bite filled his mouth with the light, fresh taste of the ingredients coupled with the strong taste of dressing. The bread was toasted crispy on the outside and soft on the inside. It had an amazing texture, many times better than what he could make.

No wonder Cheng Feichi would rather have room service than what he made. Ye Qin couldn't help but feel down. Despite taking great care to learn how to cook over all these years, he still couldn't really master this craft. Even if he followed the recipe down to a T, he would still end up with a pot of burnt food. He

was only somewhat good at frying eggs.

"Finished?" Cheng Feichi asked, seeing him put down the cup and wipe his hands.

Ye Qin nodded. Cheng Feichi stood up and walked to the foyer to fetch a small box. He opened it while walking and picked up the ointment Ye Qin had used last night from the coffee table on the way.

Ye Qin focused as Cheng Feichi stopped in front of him. Upon finding that the new bottle contained safflower oil, he jumped and snatched both bottles, gunning for the bathroom without looking back. "Thank you. I-I'll apply this by myself."

Inside, Ye Qin let out a long breath with his back against the door.

Yesterday, it was here where Cheng Feichi had guided his hand while applying ointment to his burn. Cheng Feichi had even asked if the bruises on his waist still hurt and said that he would take him to see a doctor.

How had he responded? Ye Qin braced himself and went over everything that happened in detail. At the time, he had been caught in the aftershock of Cheng Feichi's "I know." Though he had wanted to look up to see what kind of expression was on Cheng Feichi's face, he feared it would be one of disdain or ridicule like Ye Qin himself used to do.

Despite knowing well that Cheng Feichi wasn't that kind of person, Ye Qin had still been terribly afraid, burying his head deeper and curling into a ball in an attempt to stall and evade the blatant truth.

Then, Cheng Feichi had grabbed the hand hanging at his side. Next had come the stinging smell of safflower oil. Cheng Feichi had asked questions while applying. However, seeing Ye Qin only nodding and shaking his head, reluctant to remove away the other hand covering his eyes, he hadn't pursued. He'd only said, "Don't stay up too late," and left.

Ye Qin hated himself for being a useless coward, especially in front of Cheng Feichi. He always start to crying uncontrollably.

That was not clearly how he usually behaved. He had suffered through things a hundred, a thousand times worse. The number of times he had been pushed around could not be counted on both hands. He'd already grown accustomed to it and had also received many words of comfort from others. However, none of them could make him feel more heartbroken than that one phrase from Cheng Feichi or make him want nothing else but to throw himself into Cheng Feichi's arms and cry his heart out.

To him, Cheng Feichi was that special. He could make Ye Qin fight with everything he had, and he could also break down Ye Qin's last line of defense.

Ye Qin didn't care whether others liked or hated him. All he cared about was how Cheng Feichi thought of him, whether Cheng Feichi believed him, whether he was willing to give him another chance.

But fantasies were just that. Ye Qin still didn't have the guts to throw himself into Cheng Feichi's arms.

As Ye Qin applied ointment on himself, he also adjusted his mood. By the time he came out, Cheng Feichi was fastening his cuff links in the foyer with his shoes at his feet.

"Would it be too late to go back on set now?" he asked, turning when he heard a door opening.

After going downstairs and seeing a multi-purpose vehicle parked at the hotel entrance, Ye Qin belatedly realized that Cheng Feichi was going to drive him back. "I can just take a taxi by myself," he said hurriedly. "It'll take a long time to go there and back. You should take care of your..."

His voice gradually died down to near silence as a chauffeur opened the back door for him. Cheng Feichi sat on the other

side of the back seat, waiting for him to get in. The situation was getting a bit difficult.

Wanting to staying by Cheng Feichi's side a bit longer, Ye Qin compromised and got into the car.

On the circular highway surrounding the city, with the Cangquan Mountains rolling in the distance, Ye Qin gradually noticed something unusual. Normally, Cheng Feichi drove by himself. He wouldn't drive this kind of business car, either. Today, however, not only did he change cars and have a chauffeur, but he also brought along a sharp-looking assistant dressed in a suit and skirt.

Presently, he was working through files on his laptop in the back seat while the assistant gave directions in front. It clearly seemed like they were on the way to work instead of dropping someone off.

The more Ye Qin thought about it, the more he felt something off. Unable to sit still, he craned his neck and looked around. "Please drop me off here. It's just up ahead," he said as soon as they got off the highway.

The assistant turned to Cheng Feichi, awaiting his order.

Cheng Feichi was so buried in his work that he didn't even lift his head. "Keep going until the original destination," he said calmly.

As soon as they arrived, Ye Qin leaped out of the car like his butt was on fire and rushed inside before the door even closed. "Thank you! Thank you, I'm going now. Please take care on the way..."

"Wait for me."

With just three words, Cheng Feichi made Ye Qin freeze in place.

Ye Qin helplessly watched everyone in the car get out. Cheng Feichi walked up to him and straightened out his pleated collar. "Let's go."

A notice had gone out yesterday saying that today's shoot would take place indoors. The crew had started early. By now, the cameras and props were all ready. All staff was present, some of them chatting as they took bites out of steamed buns.

"Didi, you here already? Have you had breakfast yet?" they greeted as soon as they saw Ye Qin.

Cheng Feichi let Ye Qin walk in front. Ye Qin said hello to a few people he knew well, but didn't have the guts to cross the threshold and go inside.

He didn't want to cause a disturbance, but every single crew member had sharp eyes, especially the personal assistant, who looked at Ye Qin, then the person standing behind him, then slipped away to fetch more people. Soon, all the important staff members assembled in this small courtyard.

Including the insanely lustful Director Li.

He probably didn't expect to run into these troops. "This is?" He smiled broadly, casting a glance at Cheng Feichi's attire and the car parked outside.

Cheng Feichi stood still, his unsmiling appearance and heavy aura rendering the surrounding crowd silent.

When the head of the crowd, Director Li, didn't get a response, he laughed dryly for a bit and looked at Ye Qin awkwardly. "Xiao-Ye, why haven't you introduced us yet?"

At this time, the assistant beside Cheng Feichi stepped forward and handed over a business card. "Mr. Ye is a friend of President Cheng." She then made polite conversation in a very level voice. "Please take good care of him."

Though her words were dressed up as a request, they actually had the obvious meaning of a threat.

Director Li took the business card. After seeing the name and company job printed on it, he didn't even have the guts to

put on airs anymore. Faced with the assistant's superficial smile, all he could do was nod and respond, "Okay, sure, yes, no problem." In less than three minutes, he broke into cold sweat despite the it being the blazing midsummer.

The people around them had never seen an actor's financial backer coming directly on set to speak for him, but they could all probably guess why. Everyone had seen what happened at the so-called celebration party, how Director Li had hurriedly followed Ye Qin out and came back later leaning on someone. There was a lot of private discussion about it afterwards.

Having obtained their objective of forcing the director to restrain himself, Cheng Feichi and his assistant left early.

Director Li and his party walked them out cordially. At the doorway, they received a frosty glance from Cheng Feichi and didn't dare step further. "President Cheng, please take care on the way. We'll just see you off here..."

The well-trained assistant and chauffeur stood a distance away, leaving Cheng Feichi and Ye Qin as the only two people within twenty meters.

Momentarily stunned, Ye Qin hadn't spoken. Now that no one else was around, he finally changed his expression. "I... Y-you don't need to help me like this. What if you end up making trouble..."

Seeing the person in front of him look panic-stricken, Cheng Feichi suddenly thought back to six years ago.

On an early autumn night, on the sidewalk outside the school, Ye Qin had been the same as he was now. Frightened others would find out about their relationship, he wouldn't sit in Cheng Feichi's back seat or walk beside him. He'd been scared to death that someone would spread rumors and jeopardize Cheng Feichi's chances of higher education.

He still remembered Ye Qin scratching his hair and frowning.

"You finally got the award," he'd said angrily. "If anyone finds out now, everything will be ruined. No school will ever accept you."

The past overlapped with the present. These two things felt miraculously similar.

And the effects achieved were also the same, something stabbing into the soft flesh in his heart. Dumbfounded, Cheng Feichi came back to his senses and met Ye Qin's anxious, worried eyes.

"It's okay. I won't get into trouble because of this," he finally said.

Although Ye Qin still couldn't momentarily dispel all his concerns, he felt much reassured by Cheng Feichi's words.

As he watched Cheng Feichi get into the car, he crouched over and looked into the rear window with one way mirror film applied on it. Even with his nose almost stuck to the glass, Ye Qin still couldn't see anything. Just as he was about to back away, wilted, the window suddenly rolled down.

Inside, Cheng Feichi sat upright with a pen in his left hand. With his right, he passed a business card out the window. "Call me when necessary." After a short pause, he added, "Don't forget to apply ointment."

The scheduled half-day of shooting turned into two and a half days.

This time, it wasn't because the crew saw Ye Qin as a pushover and deliberately stalled to slight him. On the contrary, their attitude towards him changed drastically, afraid one moment he would be tired and hungry, afraid the next he'd get a sunburn. The shooting schedule kept getting revised, and things were pushed back again and again. As a result, apart from eating, sleeping, and filming, Ye Qin also sat there spaced out in the rest lounge for a good part of the day.

"You didn't even call me over to watch when your gege came to speak on your behalf? That's so ungenerous."

In the cool lounge, a bunch of fruit trays covered the table. Liu Yuqing tossed a few grapes into her mouth and accused Ye Qin of "inhumane behavior" as she munched.

"There was nothing to see," Ye Qin muttered, fiddling with the business card in his hand.

"I wanted to see Director Li humiliated. He used to say I couldn't properly portray an ordinary citizen fawning over others, told me to go out in the world to see and learn. Wasn't that such a great opportunity for me? He personally came on stage to demonstrate what 'fawning' really is."

Much amused by her remark, Ye Qin laughed, but she sighed ruefully instead, "What a pity such a handsome man isn't an actor."

"He has a job! He's very busy!" Ye Qin insisted, very defensive when it came to this topic.

It was Liu Yuqing's turn to laugh. "Ha ha ha, look at how nervous you are! If you're so possessive, you should quit acting in the future. It's exhausting and dangerous. Better to stay at home and watch over your gege. He's rich enough to easily support you anyways."

"Then...wouldn't he really become my sugar daddy?"

Ye Qin said "sugar daddy" extremely quietly, afraid of being overheard.

Liu Yuqing imitated his cautious demeanor, leaning over and blinking fast. "So you don't want him as a sugar daddy?"

Ye Qin instantly went red. "N-no."

For Ye Qin, the only temptation about the whole "sugar daddy" business was that he could see Cheng Feichi often.

He wanted them to get back together and date again like before, even though everyone in the circle knew Cheng Feichi was providing for him.

Cheng Feichi surely had no such intentions. He only offered Ye Qin all this help because they were once acquainted. If there were only ever two options, Ye Qin would rather be a normal friend for Cheng Feichi than a casual lover.

Ye Qin looked at Cheng Feichi's business card day and night. Initially, he wanted to text Cheng Feichi giving his proper thanks for accompanying him on set. However, he also didn't want to waste this opportunity.

After finishing all the scenes, Ye Qin took a taxi down the mountain and went to the Garden Hotel again, uninvited.

That night, Cheng Feichi came back very late as usual. Turning on the light, he tossed aside his coat at the foyer before loosening his tie as he walked inside. When he raised his head, he bumped into Ye Qin coming out from the guest bedroom. Both of them froze in place.

Ye Qin didn't think that Cheng Feichi would come back today. After all, this wasn't his only residence. Thus, when he'd heard the lock moving, he had jumped out of bed, almost tumbling to the ground.

He could also guess why Cheng Feichi was surprised. There were four numbers hand-written on the back of the business card Cheng Feichi had given him that day. Ye Qin had known immediately that it was the door code, but when Cheng Feichi had handed it over, he'd said to get in touch "when necessary." Clearly, he had been implicitly telling him not to go there randomly.

The password was for when he was in need, not for him to come and go freely as if this place was his home.

Sure enough, Cheng Feichi abandoned his tie. "What's the matter? Something happened?" his first reaction was to ask.

Ye Qin shook his head, heart filled with bitterness.

This was what he had been struggling with for the past few days. Cheng Feichi did things in a clear and orderly manner. He drew clear boundaries between close and distant relationships.

There was obvious meaning in giving Ye Qin his number and password—*I can help and protect you, but you mustn't go too far and hope that I would ever break my principles for you again.*

Ye Qin had come here this time to get to the heart of the matter. Even if asking for forgiveness was a protracted battle that couldn't be won overnight, he at least had the right to know whether he was working in the right direction.

Cheng Feichi had the habit of reading before bed every night, no matter how late it was.

After showering, when Cheng Feichi sat down with the book in his hands, Ye Qin seized the opportunity. "I want to ask you a question."

Cheng Feichi looked up at him. "Ask."

Ye Qin licked his lips nervously as he clenched and loosened his fist. "What's wrong with your hand?" he said after long deliberation.

Cheng Feichi subconsciously lowered his eyes to his right hand. With his palm facing down, his knuckles shifted a little. "It's nothing. Nothing to do with you," he finally said indifferently.

Ye Qin knew "nothing to do with you" meant that it was none of his business, but that wasn't the answer he wanted.

No matter how calm and steady and strong, how completely impenetrable Cheng Feichi appeared, he was a mortal human being. He was just used to hiding sadness in his heart and taking on all burdens in silence. He used to be like this, and he still did the same now.

If Cheng Feichi really was so invincible, he wouldn't have lost hope, wouldn't have given up everything and left just upon hearing those unbearable words.

If he wanted to make Cheng Feichi happy, Ye Qin had to find the crux of the problem. He could no longer just rely on Cheng Feichi and accept his kindness like he once did.

"That day, you heard everything I said outside the door, didn't you?" Since Cheng Feichi didn't want to answer this question, Ye Qin asked another.

For all he appeared with perfect assurance, Ye Qin actually had no confidence at all. His palms sweat profusely. In particular, the calm, composed demeanor Cheng Feichi maintained pushed back his psychological defenses more and more until they had nowhere left to go.

"I already answered a question." Cheng Feichi's eyes moved back to the book. He pressed his lips together and said no more.

The courage Ye Qin had gathered in his chest was once again broken by cold resistance. He slumped his shoulders and let out a sigh of relief. At the same time, a heavy wave of despair washed over him.

He seemed to have screwed up another great opportunity to open up their hearts.

He really shot himself in the foot.

Like a zombie, Ye Qin walked to the kitchen, poured a glass of water, drank it, tidied up the apartment, and hung up the coat in the foyer. Then, he saw that bottle of cologne.

Picking it up and looking at it, Ye Qin frowned and asked the bottle what he hadn't gotten a chance to ask Cheng Feichi, "Are you getting engaged then?"

As it was a private question to himself, Ye Qin could set free his sour grievances. His whisper come out in nasally tone.

But then there was a reply.

"Who said that?" Cheng Feichi asked, looking up at Ye Qin, even though he'd always been too absorbed to hear anything while reading.

The abrupt voice frightened Ye Qin so much that he almost smashed the perfume on the ground. Ye Qin put it back in its

original place and stood up straight. Running the back of his hand across his back, he pretended to be calm. "No one. No one said anything."

"Did you guess that yourself then?" Cheng Feichi stared at him. "No. No. I didn't..."

Mid-denial, Ye Qin suddenly realized that apart from hearing from others and guessing this himself, there was no third way for him to know. His denial was too false and completely full of holes. Thus, he lowered his head and simply kept his mouth shut. The more he spoke, the more mistakes he made. At least if he didn't talk at all, he could give a good impression of being calmer than before.

Before going to bed, Ye Qin knocked on the open door of the master bedroom. Twisting his neck to avoid looking inside, he passed a glass of warm milk in through the crack and bit his lip to stop himself from saying nonsense.

Cheng Feichi thanked him and took it. As Ye Qin retreated and almost closed the door, he randomly added, "No."

"Huh?" Ye Qin looked at him with one eye through the crack in the door with his mouth pursed and neck tilted.

Cheng Feichi looked away, avoiding eye contact. "I'm not getting engaged," he added after a few seconds.

Ye Qin didn't sleep for a whole night. Early next morning, as he was telling his panda-like self "good morning" in the mirror, his heart still soared with joy.

Since Cheng Feichi was willing to explain to him, that must mean Ye Qin still occupied a fraction of his heart. He didn't dare assume anything else, but at least Cheng Feichi wasn't against him showing up here. Things were finally starting to move in a good direction, and Ye Qin decided to make persistent efforts from now on. He would be more proactive and let Cheng Feichi feel his sincerity.

He had originally set aside two weeks for shooting, so for the next few days, Ye Qin didn't have work. In addition to getting up early to make breakfast, he also took over laundry and cleaning the apartment.

One time, when he got a call from Zhou Feng, Ye Qin said that he was scrubbing down the floor and asked him to call later.

"Are you really being Snail Lady?" Zhou Feng asked, making a big fuss. "Men don't like people they can get for nothing. Don't sell yourself too short."

"Then what about when he used to cook for me every day?" Ye Qin retorted, throwing the cleaning rag on the floor. "This is a way of showing your feelings. The hell do you know?"

"Okay, okay, I know nothing," Zhou Feng sighed. "You're right. Thinking back now, if Yuanyuan didn't agree to date me so easily, I wouldn't have dismissed him like an ass. I was so childish back then."

"You're no better now, still childish and an ass," Ye Qin snorted in rare agreement.

The two rambled on about nothing and everything for a while before returning to the everlasting topic.

"When are you coming back to the capital?" Zhou Feng asked. "I want to use you as an excuse to invite Yuanyuan to dinner, but I can't even reach you with you being in S-City all the time."

"Why don't you shut it." Ye Qin tucked his phone between his shoulder and ear as he continued laboring away at scrubbing the floor. "I haven't settled things with you yet for all your helpful advice!"

There was a pause, and then, "What did I do?"

"You said he's getting engaged. Where did you hear that?"

"At the party. You know, with those dudes."

"What dudes? Stop hanging out with them. They're so obsessed with the sound of their own voices, even though they

only know how to talk nonsense." Here, Ye Qin couldn't help but get a little smug and show off. "He told me himself that he's not getting engaged."

For a moment, Zhou Feng was stunned. "Impressive!" he exclaimed, slapping a table. "You even got Straight-A Cheng to explain this to you?"

"I asked, but I didn't expect him to give me an answer."

"He must have been afraid you'd misunderstand. Why bother to explain otherwise?" Zhou Feng stroked his chin in affirmation and clicked his tongue. "I feel good about this. Definitely good."

Ye Qin smiled ear-to-ear, eyes curving into a line. "Right? Right?! When we get back together, I'll bring him back to the capital, and we can have dinner together."

That being said, there was an unavoidable degree of embellishment. After all, Ye Qin's old fear of losing face in front of his friends was not entirely gone. In all honesty, he was not so blindly confident.

It wasn't that Cheng Feichi would reject all gestures of goodwill. For example, when Ye Qin couldn't find any clothes to wash in the past few days, he brazened asked Cheng Feichi about it, and Cheng Feichi said that they had naturally been sent to the hotel's laundry room. Before, the laundromat cleaners would always come up to collect dirty laundry.

So Ye Qin had actually been robbing someone else of work?

Ye Qin felt ashamed. He was an amateur at these sorts of things, and the professionals could do the job much better. Cheng Feichi probably didn't tell him straight out to save him from embarrassment. That was why he used these indirect measures to get him to stop.

But Ye Qin only felt down for a little while before quickly regaining his energy. Laundry was a no-go, but he could still do something else.

When they had lived together before, Ye Qin went grocery shopping every now and then when he felt like it. Now that he knew the password and could come and go freely, he went to get produce every day. After returning, he carefully examined recipes for lunch. He had even bought a beautiful bento box. Today, feeling like he made some passible dishes, he packed a portion to take to the office building nearby.

Though the two buildings seemed close, he actually had to walk through a long underground passage and two overpasses. A round trip took 40 minutes even if he walked fast. No wonder Cheng Feichi preferred to drive around when he went to work.

Without an ID card, Ye Qin couldn't enter the building, so he waited downstairs with the bento in his arms. It was impossible to run into Cheng Feichi, but he would sometimes catch his assistant. Ye Qin asked her to bring it upstairs but she said, very business-like, that this kind of thing didn't fall within her responsibilities and to contact President Cheng directly.

But it was precisely because he was too embarrassed to contact Cheng Feichi that he resorted to this instead. Desperate, Ye Qin had no choice but pull out the trump card, showering her with "jiejie"s. One day he praised her beautiful complexion, the next day how her lipstick shade really matched her clothes. Then, once she was put in a good mood, he quickly pleaded for help in his softest voice.

No longer able to hold her poker face, the assistant finally mentioned this to Cheng Feichi one day after a meeting.

Cheng Feichi stopped flipping through the documents and pondered for a moment. "Let him deliver. No need to stop him."

And so, the next day at noon, when Cheng Feichi returned to his office from the conference room, he saw a blue bento box on the table.

Opening the lid, he saw tomato-egg stir fry, sweet and sour prawns, and sauteed green beans on top, all easy, home-cooked dishes. The two meat, one vegetable pairing looked quite tasty.

The whole bottom layer was packed densely with white rice. It was even topped with a carrot sliced in the shape of a heart.

That night, when Cheng Feichi returned to the Garden Hotel suite, he found a white tablecloth placed over the dining table.

"I bought it while grocery shopping today," Ye Qin said proudly. "Doesn't this look much better? The color matches the decor too."

Instead of responding, Cheng Feichi walked into his bedroom and came out two minutes later, placing a card on the table.

"What's this for?" Ye Qin stared at it blankly.

Cheng Feichi lowered his eyes and undid his cufflinks. "Use this card when you shop in the future."

"This stuff isn't expensive at all," Ye Qin insisted hurriedly. "It's just some groceries, daily necessities, and the like..."

Cheng Feichi looked up at him. "I used them and ate them, so I should reimburse you appropriately."

Ye Qin's heart tanked again.

At night, as he watched videos, he sat more than a meter away from Cheng Feichi.

His heart was filled with pain. If they had to measure things with money, then when how long would it take him to "reimburse" the feelings he owed Cheng Feichi?

This must be Cheng Feichi's way of using goods and money to define their relationship and also warn him not to get any other thoughts.

Not that he had any other thoughts. Couldn't Ye Qin just want the best for him?

At a loss, he suddenly remembered Cheng Feichi had also insisted on paying rent when Ye Qin had invited him to stay together at the Jiayuan Compound. That was his nature, seemingly gentle but actually stubborn, unwilling to take advantage of or owe anything to anyone else.

Thinking of it this way, Ye Qin's bad mood vanished completely, and he felt much better. While Cheng Feichi concentrated on his book, Ye Qin employed an old trick and discreetly inched towards him.

After some effort, he finally got one foot closer. Ye Qin glanced at Cheng Feichi's expression out of the corner of his eyes. Seeing no change, he boldly shifted another a few inches closer. When he leaned over to get a glass of water, he shifted again until their shoulders nearly touched. They were so close that Ye Qin could hear Cheng Feichi's even breathing. He was so happy that not even seeing He Hansong's disgusting face in the video could spoil his good mood.

The next day was bright and beautiful. Ye Qin got a call from his manager, Zheng Yueyue, asking him why he hadn't returned to the capital yet.

He switched speaker mode and put his cellphone on the table while folding stars. "I just finished filming. Yueyue-jie, please be merciful and give me a month off?"

"A month?!" Zheng Yueyue roared. "Are you getting married or giving birth? How on earth do you have the nerve to ask for a month?"

"Just pretend I'm taking time off to get married or for both... I have something very important to do," Ye Qin said guiltily.

"Isn't making money the most important thing for you now? Or did President Cheng pay off all your debts?"

The "sugar daddy" news clearly rode the wind southward from S-City to the capital. "No, no, we don't have that kind of relationship," he quickly denied. "I'm still going to pay off the debt by myself."

"I don't care what kind of relationship you have. You can't just stop working. It's clearly written into the contract. See? The fifth line on the second page..."

"Then, Master, will you please find work for me in S-City?" Ye Qin interrupted with a pained expression, sensing that she was about to recite scripture again. "Let me rest for another week at least."

After fifteen minutes of negotiation, both parties finally step backed from firm ground and reached a verbal agreement of five days.

As soon as he hung up, Ye Qin let out a long sigh. *Only five days left...* he thought, counting every star he folded. *What can I do to move my gege?*

He hadn't carried the stars with him in a while, so today he caught up on missed homework.

After delivering lunch, Ye Qin stopped by the supermarket to buy dried chili peppers. He remembered Cheng Feichi had strong taste and liked spicy food. In the past, he always used to put a few dried chilis in his cooking. After finding out Ye Qin couldn't eat spicy, he had changed this habit.

Now that Ye Qin was cooking for him, he naturally had to cater to Cheng Feichi's taste. S-City food was traditionally on the sweeter side, so Cheng Feichi probably wasn't used to it.

The reserved elevator was located in the parking lot. Ye Qin thought it too flashy to enter the front door of the hotel, so he always took the back corridor used for delivering goods and went down to B1 to take the elevator. He rarely saw people on this route, and after learning the delivery schedule, he could even avoid running into a single person.

Today, the path was unobstructed as usual. Almost at the elevator, Ye Qin sped up his pace with the groceries in his hand. But then, unexpectedly, he bumped into two people around the corner.

Two middle-aged women, to be precise. The one standing at the back was a complete stranger, but the one sitting in the wheelchair looked familiar. She had a thin, sallow face and shoulder-length hair. Right now, she was looking at him with a pair of eyes that resembled Cheng Feichi's, except they were much gloomier.

B1 was dimly lit, so they moved to a secluded area behind the hotel to speak.

With the weather turning colder these past few days, Cheng Xin began getting headaches again and had to be wheeled when she went out. Not to mention that she couldn't even stand a breeze. Wrapped in a thick coat, she waited for the woman who looked to be her caretaker to place a blanket over her body. Coughing several times, even as she flicked her arm to dismiss irrelevant people from the scene, there was no strength in it.

Six years ago, Ye Qin had hated this woman because of a misunderstanding. Now, other reasons prevented him from facing her calmly. He couldn't help feeling a little timid, not knowing what to say.

"Are you Ye Jinxiang's son?" Cheng Xin spoke first in the end.

This opening remark was not within Ye Qin's expectations. "Yes, auntie," he said after a second of consideration. "My name is Ye..."

"I know your name," Cheng Xin suddenly interrupted even though she had just been speaking slowly enough to pause between each word. "What I want to know is, what are you doing here?"

Faced with harsh words from an elder, it was impossible for Ye Qin not to be afraid. He tried his best to steady his mind and spoke on the principle of not causing trouble to Cheng Feichi, "I'm staying here temporarily."

He hadn't expected Cheng Xin to laugh. She cast a glance at the tote in his hands with the supermarket's logo on it. "Temporarily? Would you need to make food or do laundry or run to the office building across the road every day if you were only staying temporarily?"

Obviously, she had come prepared, having looked into everything. There was no way he could hide this.

"I'm in love with him. I'm pursuing him," Ye Qin said, closing his eyes and taking a deep breath.

Cheng Xin's eyes shot open as if she had just heard a fantastical tale from 1001 Arabian Nights. "He'll be engaged soon," she said, looking up.

Hearing this, Ye Qin actually relaxed from his tenseness. Since Cheng Feichi himself had told him there was no such arrangement, rumors of this so-called engagement were likely being spread by his parents. As long as Cheng Feichi didn't admit to them, Ye Qin wouldn't believe them.

"I asked him, and he said he's not getting engaged."

Impatience appeared on Cheng Xin's face. "Sooner or later, he will be. If not this year, then next. Don't bother him anymore. You'll hurt him if you do."

For a moment, Ye Qin froze, unable connect the dots between "bother him" and "hurt him". His eyes went a little dazed.

Watching his expression, Cheng Xin lifted her lips into a smile. "Do you really not understand, or are you pretending to be dumb?" she drawled. "I know with my son's current position, it's hard for him not to attract uninvited attention, especially from people like you who want something from him. If I can tell with one glance, do you think that he can't?"

As Ye Qin stayed frozen, Cheng Xin tilted her chin up, acting like she had seen through everything. "I'm not being unsympathetic. Since I was once friends with your father, I can help pay off your family debt. Don't bother him anymore. He can't have his bright future ruined by these insignificant things."

Only after hearing such straightforward words did Ye Qin finally understand what she wanted. But he didn't even know what kind of answer he should give.

He just knew why Cheng Feichi had been unhappy, had rarely smiled during these years. Five years hadn't been enough for him to come to a closure. Instead, he became colder and more taciturn, completely sealing himself in as if using silence to fend off any disturbance and interference from the outside.

"Then why did you come find me instead of making him drive me away?" Ye Qin asked with trembling lips, swallowing dryly.

Cheng Xin looked up at him again, this time in disbelief. Before she could say anything, he pressed onwards, "You came to me because you can't make him do anything. He doesn't accept your plans, so you can only come find me on your own."

He hit the heart of the matter. Cheng Xin went pale, clasping her hands tightly underneath her blanket. "He is my son!" her voice finally contained outrage. "I gave birth to him. I raised him and educated him so well! How can he possibly not listen to me?!"

"Then you're welcome to talk to him. As long as he tells me to leave with his own mouth, I won't stay another minute."

Ye Qin held his head high, trying not to show any trace of cowardice on his face. In reality, he was shaking from head to toe, inside and out, all the way down to his fingertips.

It wasn't that he wanted to leave a bad impression on Cheng Feichi's mother. The situation forced it. If he chose to concede and back down now, he wouldn't do right by the tears he had shed or the resolution he had reached in the past five years.

More importantly, he wouldn't do right by the reckless persistence Cheng Feichi had shown back then.

Thinking of this, Ye Qin's throat choked up as if blocked by a

soaked ball of cotton. He finally knew now: back then, in order to be with him, Cheng Feichi had forsaken what many people could not have achieved in multiple lifetimes. He had carried several mountains of burdens. In comparison, the frustrations and hardships Ye Qin had endured were as light and small as a feather.

"You'll ruin him, you'll ruin him!" Cheng Xin attacked furiously, face twisting when she sensed that Ye Qin could not be persuaded. "Everything I do is for his own good. If you really love him, you wouldn't get in his way!"

As Ye Qin looked at the woman in hysterics, his heart became colder.

Although his mother died an unfortunate death, Luo Qiuling left him with an impression that was nothing but kind and gentle. She had always thought of him, not only in major life events like choosing schools but even little things like food and clothing. She would always ask for and respect his opinion.

Ye Qin wasn't qualified to judge whether Cheng Xin was right or wrong as a mother. He just felt sad for Cheng Feichi. His heart ached for him openly.

"Way? What way? The way you want him to go, or the way he wants to go?" Sorting out his thoughts, Ye Qin met Cheng Xin's eyes under heavy pressure and said word by word, "You are welcome to make him drive me away. No matter his decision, I will respect his choice."

Venting had sapped Cheng Xin of almost all her strength. She opened her mouth, but either couldn't find her voice anymore or was just too tired. Her eyes gradually lost focus, and she fell into a long silence.

With the tense confrontation finally coming to an end, Ye Qin breathed a long sigh of relief and loosened up. His eyes drifted into the distance. "He has no obligation to live for anyone. He should only live for himself."

It didn't seem like he was directing his words at Cheng Xin, but more like talking to himself.

As he stood beside Cheng Xin on the porch, Ye Qin used the cool breeze of late summer to calm his mood, which had gone up and down several times in just a few minutes.

When a freight truck arrived and workers began moving things in and out, Ye Qin exhaled one last heavy breath from his chest. "Auntie, I have to go now. Please excuse me."

He had just turned around and taken a few steps when he heard someone yell "be careful, out of the way" from behind. He glanced back, and that passing glance scared him out of his wits.

Two people in work clothes were lifting a one-meter square refrigerator, but because the path was so narrow, they could barely pass by Cheng Xin. One of them knocked into the left wheel of the wheelchair with his foot, making it slowly slide towards a flight of stairs in front. Sitting in the wheelchair, Cheng Xin was still in a daze, utterly unaware of the impending danger.

Ye Qin's mind blanked completely. He threw away everything in his hands, turned around, and leaped for the wheelchair's armrest.

At that moment, more than half of both front wheels hung over the top step. Logically, Ye Qin should still be able to pull Cheng Xin and the wheelchair back with a bit of strength. However, a third worker hauling boxes immediately followed the other two. The three boxes stacked in front of him blocked most of his sight, so he relied on old habits and his memory of the shape of the corridor to walk forward, stepping up every time the tip of his toe touched the edge of the stairs.

"Wait!"

By the time Ye Qin called out, it was already too late. The man with blocked vision didn't even know that Ye Qin was yelling at him. His foot landed on the wheelchair pedal. Upon

meeting an obstacle, he conditionally stepped back, dragging the wheelchair along with him.

Cheng Xin's body was about to fall forward right in front of Ye Qin. All he had the time to do was push the armrest to the side, lift his arm to protect her, and put his body in front as a shield. A second later, there was a loud crash as the wheelchair and two people fell down the stairs at the same time.

Ye Qin landed at the very bottom with his left calf twisted. It had slammed on the edge of a step. With all that weight pressing down from above, an extreme, piercing pain suddenly attacked him. His vision blacked out, and he struggled to take another breath.

An ambulance arrived promptly. As Ye Qin was loaded on a stretcher, Cheng Xin's eyes were still full of panic. She had probably spent too much time alone indoors. After running into a sudden accident like this, she couldn't pull herself away from the shock.

The doctor, hearing that she had also been involved in the accident, urged her to get into the ambulance so that she also get checked at the hospital. She shook her head and shrank back. Her middle-aged caretaker behind the wheelchair said that she had just been checked and wasn't injured. There was no need to go to the hospital. After a few more questions, the doctor left her alone.

Just as the ambulance doors were about to close, Ye Qin suddenly propped his upper body up from the stretcher. "Auntie, please do me a favor," he implored Cheng Xin, who was outside.

His legs had been hit so hard that his pants were half-soaked with blood. The two nurses cleaning his wounds discussed broken bones amongst themselves.

Ye Qin's face was pale. Every word he said seemed to sap him of strength. Even so, he tried his best to lift his body up and hold his head high as he spoke to Cheng Xin. "This accident, don't tell him about it. I don't want him to know." He took a few breaths, licked his chapped lips, and continued, "And you don't want him to know that you came to see me, do you? So please, don't...don't tell him."

That night, it drizzled in S-City. This kind of weather always made people want to go home early.

Halfway through the meeting, they took a break. Cheng Feichi stood in front of the window wall looking at flashing neon lights through the water droplets on the window and the fine threads of rain in the air.

The staff beside gathered in small groups, chatting about economy trends and the housing inflation and their children's education. He didn't know who brought it up first, but the topic shifted to everyday life. One person said that eating out often wasn't healthy. Another sighed that a Manchu-Han imperial feast paled in comparison to a home-made meal.

As Cheng Feichi listened, his eyes lost focus as if remembering something he shouldn't be thinking of at the moment, but he couldn't help it.

"Tell them the meeting is adjourned," he told to the assistant beside him, refocusing his gaze. "We'll resume at ten tomorrow morning."

When he returned to the penthouse suite at the Garden Hotel and turned on the light to see an empty, deserted room, he felt a discomfort he couldn't quite pinpoint.

As he set the empty lunch box down on the table, he saw a red box placed in the corner on top of a sticky note.

There were only two lines on it: *I'm going back to the Capital for work. Eat well and sleep well!*

It was signed Ye Ruan, followed by a chubby heart.

After showering, Cheng Feichi carefully examined the red square box on his bed. He didn't know how long Ye Qin had

been hiding it. The corners and edges were already frayed, probably because he carried it often with him.

As soon as Cheng Feichi saw the logo in the middle of the
box, he already guessed what was inside. No matter how much
he prepared himself, he still felt inexplicable nervousness as he
put his hand on it.

He opened the lid, and, as he expected, there was a ring.

But upon closer inspection, this wasn't the ring that he
remembered. This ring was wider and larger in size. It was also
inlaid with a diamond that sparkled with a slight change of angle.
Without warning, the closed gates in his mind were suddenly
smashed open under this dazzling light, and a torrent of memories
surged out.

Cheng Feichi thought he had almost forgotten everything,
especially the details that had once penetrated deeply into his
flesh and caused enduring wounds. Out of self-defense, he had
buried them all in the deepest parts of his heart, refusing to even
touch them, let alone remember.

But why did he still clearly remember the meaning he had
given this ring when he was young?

He put the ring back and closed the box, then put the box
back on the bedside table as if avoiding something. Inadvertently,
his eyes landed on the sticky note with writing on it. Under close,
direct light, he could make out the strokes that had escaped his
notice before.

Picking it up and turning it over, Cheng Feichi saw four
words written in neat and proper script on the back side: *With
all my heart.*

CHAPTER 23

FALL came a little earlier in Beijing than in S-City, and the same bout of rain fell in a monstrous torrent.

When Ye Qin's bullet train arrived at the station, Zhou Feng was already waiting for him at the exit. Zhou Feng scooped him out from the busy crowd, grumbling about how there were too many people at the station and how he'd been looking forever for him. Then, he saw the cane in Ye Qin's left hand and followed it down to his bandaged leg.

"Shit!" he cried, speedily ushering Ye Qin away from the crowd. "Didn't you say you 'just' twisted your leg? This looks a lot worse?"

Ye Qin tossed Zhou Feng his backpack and did his best to hop along. "I broke a bone. They put a steel plate in."

Zhou Feng paused. "Can you not say that as casually as if you're going out for dinner?"

Ye Qin curved his lips into a smile. Though it looked quite weak and dispirited on his wan face, he didn't seem to think so. "I'm still growing," he said casually. "The doctor told me it'll be good as new in no time."

They took the elevator up to the parking lot. Zhou Feng's

car was parked far off, so they had to walk a distance.

The more Zhou Feng dwelled on it, the more he felt that something wasn't quite right. He looked down at Ye Qin's leg, too swollen to even put on shoes. "Did the doctor really say that? You know they say fractures don't heal for 100 days. Why didn't you stay in S-City for a bit longer before coming back?"

"It's not like I can't use my medical insurance card here—ow!" Ye Qin accidentally banged his leg on the front seat as he was getting into the car. With great care, he used his arms to lift his injured leg inside. "I'm usually in great shape, so I've got no need for it, and now it's finally useful. I haven't paid all that insurance for nothing."

Now that Zhou Feng knew his situation, he couldn't help but feel for him. In all the years they'd known each other, Ye Qin's life could be considered carefree, if not extravagant. When had he ever needed to worry about something as minor as hospital fees?

As they drove away from the train station, Zhou Feng offhandedly asked if he wanted to check into the Army General Hospital for a few days. His dad was apparently well-connected there. Naturally, Ye Qin refused.

"You can recuperate anywhere. I just need to go to the hospital for a daily antipyretic IV injection. There's so many people there. It's so loud. If I can't sleep, it'll prevent my bones from healing."

Unable to persuade him, Zhou Feng gave in. "Call me anytime if anything comes up, then; twenty-four hours round the clock. Don't be courteous if you really think of me as a brother."

"Cool," Ye Qin joked, nodding. "As soon as it hits twelve, I'll call you up to bring me a late-night snack."

When they got back to a certain dorm in one of Chengbei's residential neighborhoods, Zhou Feng helped him inside and took a glance around. Seeing the Lego Technic placed inside a glass case on the top bunk, he suddenly thought of something.

"Hey, why didn't Straight-A Cheng come back with you if you're injured?"

Ye Qin, who had just bragged that he would bring Cheng Feichi to Beijing so that they could all go out for dinner, felt embarrassed at being exposed and made up an excuse. "Well, he's busy. The whole company is waiting on him to give orders. I can't keep him from working because of me."

"He's so busy that he didn't even have time to buy you plane tickets?" Zhou Feng questioned.

"I wanted to take the bullet train," Ye Qin babbled, having developed some acting skills after years of working as an actor. "What's so good about planes? The pressure's low at high altitudes. What if my new steel plate cracks from the vibrations?"

Zhou Feng scratched his head. He'd never broken a bone before, so he didn't know if it really was possible to fly with a steel plate in, but since Ye Qin said it wasn't, he tentatively believed him.

"But you didn't give him a call when you arrived?" he then reminded. "He must be worried over there..."

Ye Qin threw a pillow at him. "Okay, okay! What time is it now? Hurry up and go home."

After seeing Zhou Feng off, Ye Qin used the wall's support to get back to his room. He picked up his phone, tapped into the contact list, then to the texting interface, then back to the contact list. After a long struggle, his eyes finally settled on the time in the upper right corner.

2:30 a.m. He should sleep.

Since Cheng Feichi didn't contact him, it meant that he hadn't raised any suspicions. After lying down on the bed, Ye Qin took a deep breath and let himself relax.

Against the doctor's orders, he'd left the hospital right after surgery, but it hadn't been for nothing, since he'd been able to make a trip to the Garden Hotel. He'd tidied up all that needed to be tidied and left behind a note clearly detailing where he had gone. Unable to help himself, he even left behind something that shouldn't have been taken out yet.

Once the effects of anesthesia faded, his wound flooded with the pain of a thousand ant bites. Now that no one was around, Ye Qin could finally stop pretending he was alright. Gritting his teeth, he clutched his pillow and took deep breaths to ease the pain. The doctor prescribed painkillers for him back in S-City. He crawled out of bed and swallowed two. Only when the horizon started turning pale white did he fall into a dazed sleep.

The Cheng Feichi in his dreams was even colder than reality. When he opened that red box, he curled his lips into a sneer and held the ring at eye level in front of him. Then, he counted down from three and let go, letting it fall to the ground before spinning and rolling into some obscure corner.

Startled awake, a cold sweat covered Ye Qin from his chest to his back. The first thing he did was grab his phone. At the sight of an empty screen, he let out a breath of relief, closed his eyes, and lay back down for a while longer. He let his erratic heartbeat even out and then got out of bed and washed up for the day.

The rain had already stopped. Because he couldn't walk well and the ground was still ponded with water, Ye Qin made a rare splurge for a taxi to the hospital.

On the way, as he sent bad jokes to Cheng Feichi, he also took a call from Song Xu.

"Gege, gege, how's your leg? Is it okay?"

"It's fine. It'll recover in a few days."

"Did you go back to Beijing? I'll be going around to gigs with Yueyue-jie for a few days. Take my bed. It's wider."

"You don't have to tell me. I'm already sleeping in it," Ye Qin teased.

Seeing him in good condition, Song Xu relaxed. "That's good then. He Hansong's also out of town for a while, so he won't be back. The dorm's conveniently reserved for your recuperation."

That counted as good news. At least his mood wouldn't be killed by He Hansong's cold sneers and heated scorn. After hanging up, Ye Qin continued sending text messages, inexplicably feeling that the bad jokes he had chosen today were extra funny. He giggled like an idiot as he looked at the text message interface, forgetting the pain of his injury for the most part.

Cheng Feichi would laugh too, wouldn't he? If he could see.

Though he already got Cheng Feichi's new number, Ye Qin obstinately continued to send texts to his old one.

It wasn't entirely out of fear. Privately, he thought that this number had special meaning. It was evidence of all the little things he had with Cheng Feichi from when they met up to the present.

Unless someone else took this number, he would continue texting it forever.

Ye Qin sat in the IV room of the hospital, dripping antipyretic. Liao Yifang, having heard what happened to him, called to double-check his location and arrived in less than an hour.

Someone as conventional as the class monitor naturally wouldn't visit a patient empty-handed. He arrived carrying a couple of bags of fruit, milk, and walnut powder, just to see that Ye Qin was only getting an IV.

"How can you be an outpatient after breaking your bones?" he asked in shock. "What if they grow back crooked? What if your wound gets infected? What if you need to get up at night?"

Ye Qin was caught between crying and laughing at his same old worrying tendencies. "Class monitor, why are you the

same as the doctor just now? All that's missing is either one of you holding my hand down to sign a hospitalization form." He clapped his thigh. "Don't worry. I'm doing great. It's *my* leg. How can I not know?"

When he finished the IV drip, they went looking for a restaurant. They'd barely sat down before Liao Yifang started looking up information on broken bones. "In the early stages of a fracture, blood clots up and swelling occurs," he read worriedly. "In the early stages, the patient must not be fed greasy, hearty foods. He or she should have a light diet with items such as pork bone soup, chicken soup, stewed softshell turtle—goodness!" Here, he quickly got up and yelled into the kitchen of the restaurant. "Excuse me, boss. Did you already start cooking the fish we just ordered? No? Please cancel that dish then. Thank you!"

Unable to hold him back, Ye Qin could only let him call the shots.

As they waited for their food, he and Zhou Feng messaged back and forth on WeChat. Despite Zhou Feng's line of knife emojis, Ye Qin still didn't share his location and only revealed that they were eating somewhere close to the hospital.

[*The class monitor's my friend too. I can't be biased towards you and betray him. If you can find us then it's a sign that fate is on your side.*]

Zhou Feng sent a line of wilted flower emojis followed by, [*Pleaseee eat slowly. Give this humble man a bit of time!*]

As a result, Ye Qin underestimated him.

Zhou Feng found the restaurant only fifteen minutes later. A glance behind him revealed that he had brought a helper to look for them, their mutual friend Zhao Yue.

When Liao Yifang saw Zhou Feng, he wanted to leave. But now that there was another friend there, rushing out would look rude. Presuming that Zhou Feng wouldn't start spouting nonsense in front of so many people, he calmly sat in place and continued eating.

However, Zhou Feng surprisingly didn't follow common sense. "Yuanyuan, I'm making a promise to you in front of my two best bros," he began with a shocking sentence. "As long as you accept me, from now on, if you want me to go west, I'll never go east; if you want me to dive into the sea, I'll never jump into a ravine."

Thin-skinned as always, Liao Yifang reddened at once. "S-shut up."

"Okay, okay," Zhou Feng said quickly, "then tell me. Please tell me what you want. If you can stump me, I'll never bother you again."

As a witness, Ye Qin couldn't help but marvel at how well Zhou Feng excelled at "retreating to advance." The class monitor was kind and soft-hearted. He wouldn't be able to come up with anything outrageous.

"Your family won't accept me," Liao Yifang said after a brief moment of thought.

Zhou Feng tugged down his shirt collar to show him a long scar on his shoulder. "I already got beaten. It's taken care of."

Liao Yifang quickly looked away, eyes wavering. "My parents won't accept you either."

"I'll come around and show my face every day. I'll play chess with your dad, and knit sweaters with your mom. I refuse to believe that I can't move your kind and charitable parents," Zhou Feng laughed.

Rascal! Ye Qin scolded him inwardly.

Across from him, Liao Yifang set down his chopsticks and sighed. "You're not incapable of dating girls. I'm not either. Since neither of us is the other's one and only, why must you persist and make our families sad?"

A whole meal was rendered tasteless. When Liao Yifang

left, Zhou Feng gave chase, leaving behind Ye Qin and Zhao Yue to exchange stares. Only, these two friends who hadn't seen each other for many years had nothing to say at this moment.

Ye Qin asked the waiter for a new set of tableware and nudged it in front of Zhao Yue. "You haven't had lunch yet, have you? Eat up, or it'll go to waste."

Zhao Yue picked up pair of chopsticks and put a mushroom into his bowl. "Ah-Qin," he said after a moment of thought, "I'm sorry for what happened before."

This was the very thing Ye Qin was most afraid to hear. It made their family's bankruptcy sound like it had come from someone else's sabotage. "Don't worry about it. Everything's in the past," he quickly made his stance clear. "Thank goodness you lent me money back then. I'm doing well now, other than recently breaking a leg. I just look a bit unlucky."

But Zhao Yue clearly still dwelled on it. "I heard what happened with Liu Yangfan," he said, eating the mushroom. "He's just got too much time to fool around. Don't stoop down to his level. Let's all remain friends in the future, okay?"

Ye Qin didn't know who told him or what he heard, and he didn't want to dig. He already heard from Zhou Feng that Zhao Yue changed after taking over his family's company. He became much steadier, more reliable. That was why Ye Qin didn't say no when Zhou Feng suggested for them to have a get-together. Even if he believed he no longer had any way of fitting in with them, couldn't get used to the vague pity they had in their eyes whenever they looked at him.

"Of course," Ye Qin said with a smile.

"Are you still on good terms with Straight-A Cheng?" Zhao Yue asked, not quite reassured yet. "I heard Zhou Feng say you're about to get back together?"

"Not yet... Not quite yet," Ye Qin said awkwardly.

Zhao Yue nodded. "Back then, I could see that you really loved him and he really loved you. He didn't date in the five years that he was in America."

The news of Cheng Feichi made Ye Qin's ears perk up. "You saw him in America?"

"Only once. I saw him at a university Lego creation contest. Our diploma mill can't compare to his university. We wouldn't have had a chance to meet under normal circumstances. I only heard rumors from fellow international students."

"Lego?"

"Yes, didn't he tell you? It was about three years ago," Zhao Yue recalled. "I think he came with their school club. But what's strange is that their team clearly had a very good machine blueprint that he was mostly responsible for making, but they didn't end up using it. His excuse was that he had already made a similar one for someone else before, so it belonged to that person alone. He didn't have the right to take it back by himself."

When Ye Qin got back, he stood in front of his bed and looked up at the broken Lego Technic inside the glass case. For the first time in days, he got the urge to call Cheng Feichi.

Did you really not miss me these past five years? He wanted to ask. *You still think about me, right? Why else would you still be so good to me?*

Several times, he swiped from his contact list to his text messages and back. Before he could even think of what to say, his cellphone suddenly vibrated, and a new notification appeared on the screen.

Cheng Feichi had sent a message from his new phone. *[You left something behind.]*

Ye Qin's heart sped up and his calm, steady steps suddenly lost rhythm. Thinking that Cheng Feichi was talking about the ring, he stalled for ages after typing out a text before finally sum-

moning his courage to send it.

[What?]

Evidently not as torn up as him, Cheng Feichi responded very quickly, *[Your cellphone charger.]*

Seeing these four words, Ye Qin let out a heavy sigh of relief. Then he felt a bit disappointed. Had Cheng Feichi not seen what he'd put on the corner of the dining table, or had he seen it and was just pretending he hadn't?

Ye Qin wanted to know Cheng Feichi's reaction and at the same time, was afraid of knowing. He typed and deleted, typed and deleted. Thinking that this was better said face to face, he ultimately chickened out and chose to continue playing dumb.

Cheng Feichi had just hung up his call with Yi Zheng when he got Ye Qin's reply.

When he'd first come back to China, Yi Zheng had only called him for work. Recently, perhaps due to Cheng Xin's influence, he started to veer towards meddling in Cheng Feichi's private life. The conversation would barely start before Yi Zheng told him to go home and have dinner, and the topic of adding him to the family register was revisited again and again. Neither did he forget to urge Cheng Feichi to take Yan Hong out for afternoon tea. Yi Zheng was dying to schedule all 24 hours of his day.

Unfortunately, it was no use. Cheng Feichi wasn't a helpless chick hiding underneath his parents' wings. The reason he agreed to come back in the first place was to grow independently. Otherwise, he wouldn't be balancing managing the Yi company while expanding his business to Beijing.

In all honesty, the Yi estate wasn't something he wanted to take over. Neither did he believe that it was his right. Since he didn't covet it, no one could use it as leverage and truly control him.

He tapped open Ye Qin's message, overflowing with four

lines of text. *[Sorry! I left in a rush and forgot it! I'll get it when I'm finished working here! But I won't have any free time for half a month... Please hold on to it for me!]*

Cheng Feichi knitted his brows, feeling off. This long message clearly seemed like he was hiding something.

He'd had the same feeling the day he came back to an overly tidy apartment. If Ye Qin had been in such a rush, where would he have gotten the time to put everything back in its place first? And the fridge still had half a chunk of pork belly and a few chicken wings. The wings had been marinating, clearly intended for dinner.

When he got back to the Garden Hotel suite, Cheng Feichi saw that red box. He walked over, picked it up, and stared at it for a while. Before he had a chance to open it, there was a knock on the door.

It turned out to be Yan Hong, who told him she had gotten together with some friends nearby and didn't want to go back because it was too late. Planning to spend a night at the Garden Hotel, she dropped by to see him.

Cheng Feichi thought it was too late to let a woman in, so he grabbed his coat from the foyer and put it on, intending to escort her downstairs and help reserve a room.

But Yan Hong stalled, refusing to move. "So did that guest leave?" she asked, stretching her neck to peer inside.

Though it was phrased as a question, she actually appeared quite confident. She looked happy, as if she'd already known that Ye Qin wouldn't be here.

"How'd you know he was a guest?" Cheng Feichi asked after a moment of thought.

On the third day of dripping antipyretic IVs, the swelling on Ye Qin's calf finally eased somewhat. His knee had been so swollen that he could neither fully straighten nor bend his leg.

Now, he could touch the ground with the sole of his foot with minimal pain.

The doctor said he had never seen a patient like him, who ran around and troubled himself with transferring hospitals right after breaking his bone. He wrote a note for Ye Qin to get X-rayed to see if his bones had grown out of place.

Ye Qin hopped downstairs with the support of the wall. Thankfully, a kind nurse came to help partway and helped him to the Radiology Department. When he took off his mask to thank her, she almost recognized him.

"Are you what's-his-name from AOW?" she asked excitedly, pointing at him.

Ye Qin hurriedly waved his hands. "No, no. If I was that popular, this street would be in chaos from end to end."

He didn't expect that to be a prophecy.

When he finished X-raying and took the images back to the doctor, Ye Qin shot down Zhou Feng's suggestion to skip work and go see him. He continued hopping down the stairs on a cane. He hated crutches for being ugly and heavy. The day before yesterday, he'd tossed them aside in his dorm.

Diagonally across the street from the hospital was a middle school. Ye Qin never took much notice of it passing by before. Now that he'd broken his leg and couldn't walk fast, he had time to look around. He found that the school had very similar gates as High School No. 6, and the uniforms were also alike.

It was right at the end of the school day. Small groups of students filed out of the doors, among them boys riding bicycles. Though none of them were as handsome as Cheng Feichi, Ye Qin still couldn't help thinking back to those days when he sat on the back seat of Cheng Feichi's bike.

Thinking back some more, he found it funny. He should have been solely focused on revenge, yet at some point, he had quietly begun to indulge. If the heavens could give him another chance, he promised to hold on tightly to Cheng Feichi's waist and never hide his thoughts, never say those insincere words again. He promised to only tell himself how much he loved Cheng Feichi.

By the time he moved to the bus station, Ye Qin's heart was pounding from the sudden flood of memories. He had also forgotten to wear his mask and was recognized by a schoolgirl waiting for the bus beside him.

"Qin-Qin. You're Qin-Qin, aren't you?" The schoolgirl, a hot-blooded fan, didn't even wait for Ye Qin to confirm before yelling on the spot, "Everyone look! It's Qin-Qin in the flesh!"

They were surrounded by students waiting for the bus, who appeared to have all watched the hottest new variety show. Hearing the familiar name, they all crowded around him.

Ye Qin was just one person, and his voice couldn't overpower a crowd of chattering people. Even if he refused to confirm his identity, it was no use. Even aunties and uncles came up to him asking, "Who is this?" And so, more and more people gathered, wrapping around him and jamming the station so that not a single drop of water could flow through.

Thankfully, one of the teachers who had just gotten off work couldn't stand the scene and stepped in to maintain order. He steered the students to disperse and let the disabled person go through. After missing one bus, Ye Qin finally got on the next one ten minutes later.

There were two schoolgirls on the same bus as him, but they weren't as extreme as the one who had just been yelling. They sat behind him and blushed as they asked him what happened to his leg. Did he fall dancing?

Ye Qin knew he didn't have many real fans. If they were, they would have known by now that everyone in the group had

gone their own ways long ago.

"I hurt myself singing," he blatantly lied. "I got too excited, and my blood flowed down. My veins couldn't hold it in, so they burst open and broke my leg."

Perhaps it was because he had been quite serious on the variety show, but the two schoolgirls didn't get that he was joking.

"You have to be careful singing in the future then, Qin-Qin!" they exclaimed, eyes wide, hands covering their mouths.

After getting off the bus, Ye Qin walked cheerfully, feeling more and more like he had a natural talent for telling jokes. Next time why not tell Cheng Feichi some jokes he'd already thought up, he thought. That way, it'd seem more sincere. He might even get lucky and get a laugh out of him.

Humming the group's debut song, Ye Qin walked towards the compound. From afar, he saw someone standing in front of the building, but didn't pay them much mind. With the cane in one hand, he took out his cellphone in the other and typed his joke into a memo for later use.

After hopping for a bit, Ye Qin took a thirty-second rest. He was almost at the entrance of the building. When he looked up from his cellphone, he came face to face abruptly with the person coming his way and thought he must have started to hallucinate from overexertion.

As those strong hands helped him into the elevator, Ye Qin's soul was still floating in limbo, unable to get a grasp of the reality that Cheng Feichi was right beside him.

Why was he in Beijing?

Oh, right. Zhou Feng said he was expanding his business here.

But why was he *here*?

Did Cheng Feichi run into him while visiting friends and relatives? But that was too much of a coincidence. The capital was packed with people. What was the possibility of them being in the same complex, in front of the same building at the same time?

He'd have to ask Liao Yifang to help him calculate later.

It just so happened to be the evening rush, with the elevator stopping every two floors. With people continuously coming in and out, the small elevator was packed to the brim.

Cheng Feichi maintained a circle of open space with his arms, tucking Ye Qin safely into the corner. But right now, Ye Qin had no time to be moved. His brain was filled with thoughts of escape and how to avoid talking to Cheng Feichi so he wouldn't give anything away.

The elevator stopped on the 23rd floor. As a housekeeper next to the door moved and opened up a path, Ye Qin extracted his elbow and slid out of the elevator.

Then, he reached inside his pocket for a key. The corridor was small and narrow, and he only had to hop a few steps to the dorm room. Ye Qin stuck the key in the keyhole, opened the door, and hopped inside with a hand on the doorframe. "Sorry," he rushed out before even fully turning back. "The place is a mess today, so I won't invite you in to sit, but you're also busy so you probably don't have time to idle here anyway."

He spoke very fast, panic written all over his face. Anyone else may not be able to tell, but Cheng Feichi could see this as clear as day.

"I'm not busy," he said, standing in the doorway. "I came to see you."

Still in a state where he couldn't quite see or hear with full clarity, Ye Qin turned around, about to close the door. "Let's meet another day then..."

He couldn't. Something was in the way.

Cheng Feichi's hand pushed against the door. Even as Ye Qin looked at him with panic verging on the point of tears, he didn't relent.

They stood in a deadlock for a few seconds. In the end, Ye Qin was the first to let go. All these years, the door in his heart had always remained open for Cheng Feichi, no matter if Cheng Feichi wanted to come in or not. All he could ever do was wait. He never had any strength to close that door, to begin with.

He shouldn't be afraid. Five years was enough time for him to be prepared.

But he still hung his head, awaiting Cheng Feichi's sentence like a criminal waiting for trial. He cut his entire being—his entire heart—open and put it under the sun. He waited for either Cheng Feichi's light glance or heavy stomp of rejection, a turn and flick of the sleeves.

Yet the anticipated interrogation never came, and the ring that he'd only dared to leave when no one was home wasn't thrown on the ground.

"Didn't you say—"

Cheng Feichi paused after merely three words. He pursed his lips like it was hard to speak about this, like he was mulling over it.

Ye Qin had never seen Cheng Feichi struggle like this. The Cheng Feichi in his eyes did everything in an orderly manner and never muddled about. Even their break-up five years ago had been quick and clear-cut, and Cheng Feichi never looked back afterward.

But now it was different. Besides the usual indifference and self-control, Ye Qin could see something else in his eyes. It was an emotion that he had seen once before, long ago. Most of the time, it was fading. Now it appeared to emerge.

The night was descending now, and it was dark in the corridor. Every second, the setting sun took back some of the light splayed on the floor.

So it wasn't long—just two breaths, in fact—before Cheng Feichi parted his lips again.

As he looked at Ye Qin in the light of the sunset coming through the doorway, his voice was calm and clear, "Didn't you say you would never lie to me again?"

Ye Qin still felt stuck in some world all by himself. At the same time, he felt like he had already been stripped out of it, suspended in mid-air and dizzy from being flung too far. He couldn't touch the ground, couldn't see the road ahead, didn't know which direction he should go.

He felt like this until the sound of boiling water whistled in his ears. Then he leaped to his feet, back ramrod straight like he'd suddenly been yanked back to reality with all five senses back online. Right before he registered the pain of his injured leg, a hand pressed him back down by the shoulder.

"I'll go. You sit here."

The sound of footsteps gradually faded away. There was a gurgle of hot water being poured into a cup. The sound of footsteps gradually approached. While all this was happening, Ye Qin regained all his senses, fidgeting even more like an easily startled bird. When he leaned over to touch the cup, the hot water scalded his fingertips.

Cheng Feichi went around the table and sat down on the other side. "The water's still very hot," he reminded. "Wait a bit to drink."

Ye Qin took his hand back, rubbing his fingers on his shirt. The more he rubbed, the more it stung. Song Xu and He Hansong weren't there, so he was the default host of this dorm, but for some reason, he felt more awkward and helpless than the guest who was coming for the first time.

It all went back to those words he'd heard in the doorway.

He looked up inconspicuously to the man sitting on the curved edge of the sofa. That man's gaze was fixed on his leg.

Ye Qin knew he couldn't hide anymore, but deep down, he

still held onto a bit of hope that Cheng Feichi wouldn't ask despite already knowing the cause.

Unfortunately, things didn't go according to his wishes.

"What happened to your leg?" Cheng Feichi asked very evenly.

"I fell when I was sing—no, when I was dancing," Ye Qin replied, not daring to beat around the bush too long, intending to offer anything as an excuse except the actual truth.

That was close. He scared himself into shuddering. But seeing as Cheng Feichi was questioning him, he probably didn't know yet. Cheng Xin must have made sure of that. She was the last person who wanted Cheng Feichi to know about this incident.

This isn't lying, Ye Qin assured himself. *This is not lying.*

Cheng Feichi didn't speak or nod. He just cast a glance at the master bedroom, where the light came from. "Do you still have work?"

"H-huh? Yes, I have work. I was just at work. I also still have a live broadcast in a bit." Afraid that Cheng Feichi wouldn't understand what a live broadcast was and even more afraid that he would misunderstand, Ye Qin continued to explain, "That is, I'll be video chatting with fans, the innocent kind."

Then, he thought he was too extra. At first, this had been no big deal, but now his strange description made it sound fishy.

"Okay," Cheng Feichi said without raising suspicion. "Just take care of your stuff."

What was there for Ye Qin to take care of? When Zheng Yueyue had heard that he'd broken his leg, she'd yelled at him, all the while adding another fifteen days of vacation to his original five. He had nothing to do from now until the last week of September.

After giving the excuse, however, Ye Qin had no choice but to find work. He resigned himself to hop back to his room, shutting the door as part of the act. "Then I'll just...take care of my stuff. Feel free to do whatever."

The live broadcast was neither long nor short, lasting about an hour. Ye Qin spent most of this time in a daze.

It wasn't hard to guess how Cheng Feichi found his dorm. Even back in high school, he himself had been able to use shady methods to find Cheng Feichi's address and household information, so how hard was it for someone of Cheng Feichi's current status to find where a nobody like him lived?

But why had he come here?

Right. Hadn't he said, outside the door, that he had come to find Ye Qin? What for? When they'd been talking just now, he hadn't said anything?

Ye Qin felt somewhat restless in his seat. When the hour had passed, he turned off the music on speaker. With a single slipper on, he used the move to the door with the support of the wall and opened it.

Cheng Feichi had already left. He'd put the two glasses on the table back in the kitchen. The room appeared tidy, like no one had been there.

Ye Qin poured himself a glass of now lukewarm water and took a few slow gulps. Suddenly hearing knocks on the door, he hopped over and peered through the peephole. Cheng Feichi was back.

When the door opened for him, Cheng Feichi cast a glance at the bedroom. "Is the live broadcast done?"

"Yup...it's done," Ye Qin answered, without a trace of confidence and feeling guilty.

Cheng Feichi asked no further questions. He angled himself to enter and then went into the kitchen with several full bags.

Seeing him take out the groceries and arrange them item by item on the kitchen counter, Ye Qin couldn't just stand there. He followed Cheng Feichi into the rather narrow kitchen and leaned on the fridge for support. "I can just have takeout for dinner. No

need to trouble you…"

"This is also for me," Cheng Feichi said as his hands continued to move.

Ye Qin was helped into a seat in the living room. Five minutes passed before he realized the logic was all mixed up. This was his place. How could he let Cheng Feichi make dinner?

He hurriedly hopped back to Cheng Feichi cutting vegetables with his sleeves rolled up. Cheng Feichi's skillful motions momentarily brought him back to those days when they had lived together.

Whenever it had been time for dinner prep, Ye Qin tiptoed behind Cheng Feichi and hugged him, catching him off guard. Or so he'd thought. He would tickle him and ask him what delicious dish he was making, and Cheng Feichi would tip his head back. "Go hang outside a bit longer," he'd say with a smile. "It'll be ready soon."

Now, Ye Qin no longer dared to hug him, but Cheng Feichi still tipped his head back like before and offered similar words, "Wait a bit longer. It'll be ready soon."

They ate two lightly seasoned stir-fried dishes and a chicken soup. Overall, the meal was considered bland, well-suited for an injured person.

It was only Ye Qin who cooked in the dorms occasionally, so the kitchen lacked a full set of wares. The chicken soup had been cooked in a wok and brought to the table glistening yellow in a wide-lipped bowl. It looked really mouthwatering.

Cheng Feichi skimmed off the oil with a ladle and scooped out a bowl for Ye Qin. He then skillfully picked up a chicken drumstick with his chopsticks and dropped it inside. As the steam of the soup rose into Ye Qin's nostrils, his nose suddenly felt stuffy. Tears almost slipped out of his eye sockets and fell into the bowl.

Dinner was oddly peaceful. Neither of them spoke.

Ye Qin didn't dare speak, lest he raise Cheng Feichi's suspicions. Staying silent was the most dependable way to approach things.

They cleaned up the kitchen wordlessly. Cheng Feichi washed his hands, rolled down his sleeves, and prepared to leave. Ye Qin shifted a few steps towards the doorway after him and then asked, "A-are you leaving now?"

Cheng Feichi hummed yes.

"Wait a sec," Ye Qin said before hopping back into his room. He opened his wardrobe and fetched a jacket that he had just bought last year and didn't have the heart to wear often. He took it outside and gave it to Cheng Feichi. "It's chilly in the capital. Stay warm." After a pause, he added, "It might be a bit small for you, but you can still drape it to block out the wind."

Whether it was because S-City was too hot or because he had been in a rush, Cheng Feichi had come in just a shirt. He hadn't worn a jacket. He looked at the grey windbreaker with hooded eyes, hesitating for a moment. "Thank you," he said in the end, taking it.

Ye Qin answered Zheng Yueyue's call the next morning.

"I told you, keep a low profile while you're injured. Keep out of the public as much as possible. Why can't you just stay put?"

She'd found out about yesterday's incident where he'd been walled in by the crowd at the terminal.

Because he couldn't move his legs, Ye Qin's stayed in one position the whole night. His back ached and his neck was stiff. "I did keep a very low profile," He replied weakly, raising the phone in an awkward posture. "I just went to the hospital to get an IV. Who knew those students had such sharp eyes?"

Zheng Yueyue lectured him in the same way that Tang Sazang cast a gold hoop around the Monkey King. She repeated

the same few words over and over: "In the end, you're still a celebrity. That variety show gained you a lot of fans. Stop thinking of yourself as some average guy on the street."

Then, she reminded him to be mindful and not say anything that would give rise to speculation, especially since the idol drama was still airing. If he made unscrupulous paparazzi go wild with conjectures and pissed off the crew, then he'd be in big trouble. He couldn't do that, even if he had an impressive patron.

After hanging up, Ye Qin made a Weibo post using a document that Zheng Yueyue sent him. In short, he explained how his leg injury came from accidentally falling after leaving the set. They shouldn't worry about him. He would officially meet them all once he recovered.

After posting, he spent eight minutes sitting up before lifting his injured leg off the bed onto the floor. Taking a break to catch his breath, Ye Qin looked at his cellphone and startled at the thousands of unread messages that had come in in just a few short minutes.

Swiping back to his profile, he found that he had somehow gained two million fans. No wonder he'd been recognized by those students yesterday.

Completely fitting the current standards of "cute," Ye Qin propped up his tablet on an upside-down rice strainer and played the most recent episode of the variety show that he hadn't finished. As he watched, he ladled a bowl of leftover chicken soup from yesterday, added a scoop of rice, and put it in the microwave.

At that moment, there was a knock on the door.

He assumed it was the downstairs landlord with another important notice. They lived here for two years now, and the landlord knocked on their door once per week on average. Apart from urging them to pay rent, he bothered them about all sorts of strange trifles. When he and He Hansong argued once, their landlord heard He Hansong kick the door and came upstairs huffily. He inspected their apartment for ages and rolled his eyes at them, walking away only after seeing that nothing had been damaged.

Ye Qin braced himself before opening the door, thinking that the landlord was probably here because he's been hopping too loudly recently. He even thought of what to say. But when he opened the door, he froze.

It was Cheng Feichi, not the landlord, who came.

They sat across the narrow, foldable dining table, each with his own bowl of chicken soup and rice.

Cheng Feichi picked up a few custard buns he'd brought with chopsticks, put them on a plate, and slid it in front of Ye Qin. Ye Qin picked one up and nibbled on it. The sweet, thick, golden custard filling mixed with the savoriness of the chicken soup, and yet it didn't taste bad.

When they finished eating, neither of them moved. They silently watched the program to the end.

On the tablet, the female anchor was very considerate of Ye Qin, always prompting him to make a comment. At the end of the program, after reading out an advertisement for a skincare product, she asked Ye Qin what he ate to grow such delicate features. Ye Qin very intentionally replied that he didn't look like this before debuting; it was all thanks to skincare products from the aforementioned brand that made his skin taut and supple and gave him more confidence in public.

Every program had to say this kind of thing to curry favor with their sponsors. Ye Qin didn't think much of it in the first place. But now that Cheng Feichi was watching, he was embarrassed beyond belief. He reached out and slapped the tablet face down on the table, looking up just to see Cheng Feichi staring back at him.

Five years ago, in their honeymoon phase, the two of them

had traced each other's faces countless times. Ye Qin envied Cheng Feichi's deep, defined contours. After school, pressed up against the wall in the silent, empty hallway, he would always caress Cheng Feichi's face in darkness after a prolonged kiss.

"I like this mouth. Your nose is pretty. Your eyelashes are very long," he said as he did, until Cheng Feichi couldn't help but tug up the corners of his mouth.

Cheng Feichi leaned down and gave him a few pecks on the lips, leaned into his burning ears, and told him, "You're prettier."

So Cheng Feichi was the most qualified person to speak on how he'd changed after his debut, both in terms of appearance and character.

The distress of being seen through became more and more intense.

Averting his eyes, Ye Qin leaped up to put away the tableware, and yet across from him, Cheng Feichi stopped him by the wrist. "Let me."

When they finished tidying up the kitchen, it was already 8 p.m. Ye Qin was in the middle of worrying about how to co-exist with Cheng Feichi in the same room when Cheng Feichi announced he was leaving.

He opened the long, rectangular box he'd brought with him and took out a silver, carbon fiber crutch. Before handing it to Ye Qin, he first tried to bend it at different angles with both hands to test its sturdiness. "Use this. You can adjust the length and also attach a footpad to the bottom."

Ye Qin took it, aware that this crutch was the farthest thing from an old man's walking stick that you could find on the market. He felt warm inside and a little embarrassed to take the gift at the same time. "I only need to use this for a few days. Isn't it too wasteful?"

"I just bought it," Cheng Feichi said offhandedly as he drifted to the door, picking his jacket off the sofa away with him.

Ye Qin didn't want him to stay too long but also couldn't bear for him to leave. In the end, though, his internal struggle was dominated by the fear of being discovered.

The temperature rose quite a few degrees today, and there was no breeze despite the open windows.

As he saw Cheng Feichi to the door, Ye Qin wanted to tell him to return his windbreaker, so he wouldn't have to come back another time. Hand on the doorknob, Cheng Feichi turned around and beat him to it. "I'm going to S-City. I'll come back tomorrow."

The flight from Beijing to S-City landed peacefully a little before noon.

Right after exiting the terminal, Cheng Feichi ducked into a business van that had been waiting for him for several hours already. He took the tablet that his assistant handed him, opened it, and worked through files.

He'd left in a hurry yesterday, leaving behind a pile of documents to go through. He hadn't brought his laptop along or a change of clothes. This trip was not only for all the things he'd left behind, but also to make a work schedule for the following week. Everything was already planned out: files, he could get through email; meetings, he could attend remotely on video call. Leaving for a few days would not cause any disruption.

It was already 4:30 p.m. by the time he finished holding meetings. Cheng Feichi didn't have lunch and didn't have time to worry about lunch. He drove to the Garden Hotel and went into the suite. As he opened the wardrobe to pack his clothes, the doorbell rang.

After arriving at an empty office, Cheng Xin rushed straight over and was wheeled inside by her caretaker. One look at the suitcases open and spread out on the floor, and she asked

with wide eyes, "Where are you going?"

Cheng Feichi casually folded the clothes he had tossed on the sofa and piled them up in the suitcase. "Beijing."

"Are you going to find..." Halfway through the sentence, Cheng Xin deliberately trailed off and changed the topic. "Are you going on a business trip?"

"In passing," Cheng Feichi said. "A friend of mine is injured. I'm going to take care of him."

Cheng Xin's face turned austere. "What friend?"

Cheng Feichi's hand paused and he finally looked at Cheng Xin. "You know," he stated calmly, meeting her eyes.

Cheng Xin panicked. She hadn't mentioned a single word of that incident to anyone. Even when Yan Hong asked, she only told her *that* person had already left. How could Cheng Feichi possibly know?

"Did he tell you?" Eyes aflame, Cheng Xin slapped her hand down on the wheelchair armrest. "He said to my face he wouldn't tell you, only to reach out in secret behind my back. I knew he's a nuisance."

Wheeling forward, she grabbed Cheng Feichi's arm. "Don't go to Beijing. Don't go looking for him. Trust your mom, just this once. Just one more time. He's only after your money. He wants to break our mother-son relationship. He doesn't have good intentions!"

A simple sentence was broken into bits and pieces. Cheng Xin choked on the breath she took at the end, clutching her chest and coughing incessantly.

Cheng Feichi set down his clothes to help, giving her light pats on the back. He waited for her to stop coughing and then said, "I'll decide what kind of intentions he has. No need for you to worry."

This was the same as saying he didn't trust her. Alarmed

and furious, Cheng Xin had a slight premonition that she could no longer control him. Recalling that Cheng Feichi responded better to persuasion rather than force, she clutched his hand desperately, tearing up.

"Xiao-Chi, Xiao-Chi, we're *so* close to success. We've almost pushed that woman and her son out, and then you'll be the only young master of the Yi Family. We've already come so far. You can't give it all up for someone like that... Mom is begging you. Mom is begging you, okay?"

When he finished listening to this tearful spiel, Cheng Feichi pulled his arm out of her hands and went back to packing his clothes.

He already repeated everything he could say many times. He had also conceded many times and even walked down a path that he didn't like. Now, he no longer wanted to foot the bill for his mother's endless list of selfish desires. Let her make threats and promises. Let her use persuasion or force. He would only follow his own heart and do what he thought was right.

Seeing Cheng Feichi unmoved, Cheng Xin, overcome with fear and panic, switched to a nasty face. "If you dare take one step out of this suite today," she snapped, "if you dare go looking for him, I will never forgive him!"

If she had said these words when Cheng Feichi was a teenager, before he spread his wings, they might have had the intended effect of intimidation. But he was now twenty-five. All the while Cheng Xin had obsessively pushed him to grow up and take revenge on her behalf, she also allowed him time to develop his own strength and grow into a man who could take charge. Now, even if he left the Yi family, Cheng Feichi still wouldn't be afraid of any threats that his mother made.

He leisurely finished packing his suitcase, closed it, and stood it up. After walking to the door, he stopped and took a

deep breath with his back to Cheng Xin.

"Mom, forgive yourself."

Night had just fallen by the time he got back to the capital. When he turned on his phone, he got a new email from his assistant. After a quick skim over the contents, Cheng Feichi more or less understood what had happened in front of the back doors of the hotel that day. Before reaching out, he had done a bit of guesswork based on the clues he had picked up. Now he finally saw the whole picture.

At first, he merely thought it was strange that Ye Qin suddenly left. Then, Yan Hong's behavior when she came knocking on his door made him more suspicious. Even if Yan Hong didn't snitch on Cheng Xin under his interrogation, he only had to use the slightest bit of brainwork to rule out all but a few possibilities. Just by the process of elimination, he could get a general idea.

Not to mention he could also get the security footage in the elevator.

Yesterday he had gotten the tape of the day Ye Qin left. Fast-forwarding through it, Cheng Feichi saw him skip down the stairs at noon holding up the bento box with both hands. Before it got dark, he returned on crutches and had trouble walking. Something must have happened in between, and definitely not something as simple as what Ye Qin had told him.

Just now, he'd casually probed Cheng Xin and confirmed that she had indeed been involved. On his way to the airport, Cheng Feichi told his assistant to go to the hotel lobby on his behalf and ask if anything unusual happened that day.

It was much easier to investigate with an objective. The manager in the lobby left a trail to the back kitchen, then the food transportation department. A few porters Cheng Xin had bribed initially refused to say anything, but when Cheng Feichi's assistant used her identity as leverage and laid the pros and cons out for them, they all became alarmed, no longer daring to lie. Each scrambled to tell the whole story about what had happened that day.

Exiting out of his email, Cheng Feichi closed his eyes and pinched the space between his eyebrows, bone tired from having taken two flights in a day.

Everything was as he had predicted, except for Ye Qin's secrecy.

What made him feel the most helpless was that he could guess why Ye Qin did everything he could to hide this from him.

Since he finished sorting out his affairs ahead of time, Cheng Feichi stowed his suitcases in a hotel in Beijing and went straight to Ye Qin's dorm.

Ye Qin opened the door, still wound up.

"Didn't you say you'd come back tomorrow?" he asked quietly, trailing behind Cheng Feichi with new crutches for support.

Cheng Feichi's silence made him aware of his own slip of the tongue. "I was just asking... I didn't mean to make it sound like I'm not welcoming you."

And then he made a beeline to the kitchen to pour water.

Cheng Feichi didn't take it, but Ye Qin still put a glass of hot water on the table to cool.

Ye Qin sat on pins and needles, unaware of what he said or did wrong. He was all too familiar with Cheng Feichi's angry expression. Before, he could lean over and give him a kiss to dissolve the anger. Now, he had no way of dealing with it and could only sit there and worry helplessly.

Soon, the hot water cooled down completely. Ye Qin got up and went to the kitchen to pour a new cup. Cheng Feichi stood at the same time, but he went towards the master bedroom in the shared dorm.

Ye Qin panicked at once, putting down the glass and turning around to follow him. "D-don't go in there."

The living room was small but filled with a lot of things.

His crutch caught on the edge of the table and slid out of his fingers, clattering to the floor. Completely zoned in on stopping Cheng Feichi, Ye Qin stepped on the crutch that had fallen with his still-weak leg and lurched, tipping right over.

Thankfully, Cheng Feichi turned on quick reflex and hooked an arm around his body, stopping him from falling flat. Unfortunately, they happened to fall in a corner of the living room that had stacks of wooden boxes. Ye Qin accidentally knocked his injured leg on a hard edge and grunted, face draining of color.

Cheng Feichi helped him sit on the sofa. Though Ye Qin insisted that everything was alright, that it didn't hurt, after two minutes, bright red blood began seeping through his white gauze.

"Come, we're going to the hospital."

Cheng Feichi's face turned even paler as he helped him up. Seeing Ye Qin's lips tremble and his face drenched in a cold sweat from the pain, Cheng Feichi lowered him back down onto the sofa. Then, he turned over, got down, and turned his head back. "Get on."

"Don't worry about it," Ye Qin continued to push back. "It's been stitched up for a few days already. We can just undo the bandages and disinfect..."

"Get on!" Cheng Feichi demanded forcefully, not letting him finish.

This was the first time Ye Qin had seen Cheng Feichi so aggressive, eyes brimming with oppressive anger. His voice, always steady and unwavering, raised several notes.

Clenching his teeth, Ye Qin tried to get on his feet by leveraging the sofa armrest. His arms and legs were sapped of strength, possibly due to how wound up he was. Several times he almost succeeded only to fall back at the last moment.

He took several deep breaths and closed his eyes weakly.

The last thing he wanted was for Cheng Feichi to see him

in this useless state, to gain sympathy under these circumstances. But from when they had first reunited up to the present, all of his wretched, miserable states had been witnessed firsthand by Cheng Feichi. Having fallen so low, he couldn't even offer the words, "I can't. I can't stand up."

He didn't want Cheng Feichi to pity him. He wanted to be a strong, independent man who stood beside him.

With this conviction, Ye Qin relaxed his strung-up body and took control of his involuntary shivers. He suppressed the panic and cowardice he felt towards the unknown and summoned all his strength to take a deep breath.

As he rose, his body suddenly became light. At some point, Cheng Feichi had turned around. He slid one hand under Ye Qin's arm and the other under his knee, lifting him in a bridal carry.

In the rental car on the way to the hospital, they sat shoulder to shoulder in the back seat. Cheng Feichi placed his hand on the knee of Ye Qin's injured leg. Every two minutes, he asked how he was feeling and if he still hurt.

Actually, Ye Qin hurt a lot. Afraid Cheng Feichi would be worried and afraid that he wouldn't be able to hide it at the same time, Ye Qin compromised and said he only hurt a little.

They registered for treatment at the nearest hospital. The doctor removed the gauze to examine the injury and then disinfected it with alcohol. He informed them it had reopened but he was unsure if the bone was affected, so he instructed them to get an X-ray.

As they waited for the images, Cheng Feichi set Ye Qin on a chair in the hallway and sat beside him. Worried that Ye Qin would aggravate his injury if he put his leg on the floor, he made Ye Qin lean on him and dangle the left half of his body in the air to avoid putting force on it.

In this position, Ye Qin almost sat entirely in Cheng Fei-

chi's lap. It had been so long since he was this close. His heart skipped several beats, and his breaths hitched, jagged.

There were still advantages, however. In this position, Ye Qin couldn't see Cheng Feichi's face and didn't have to meet his eyes. The fear that had gripped him a moment ago slowly dissipated into thin air.

It might be purely in his mind, but Ye Qin didn't feel much pain anymore as he pressed his cheek against Cheng Feichi's arm. "Are...are you still mad?" he probed in a small voice.

About half a minute later, by the time Ye Qin was sure Cheng Feichi wouldn't entertain him with a response, a bony hand grabbed his own in front of him. Warm, dry fingertips rolled on the back of his hand, pressing down gently before letting up. Then, five fingers tightened, wrapping Ye Qin's smaller hand into Cheng Feichi's palm.

This hand was as soft and cold as it had once been. "I'm not mad," Cheng Feichi said, looking down at the scallion-white fingertips out of his hold.

Feeling heat flow from his hand throughout his body, Ye Qin licked his lips and plucked up courage. "Then give me a smile, okay?"

This time he didn't have to wait long. "Okay," Cheng Feichi said in a timbre.

His voice passed overhead again. Ye Qin couldn't see his expression, didn't know whether he was smiling or not, but he could hear Cheng Feichi's vigorous heartbeat.

Just like six years ago, in the dark, narrow car repair shop. The boy who held his hand and pressed paper stars into his palm also had the same heartbeat. Little by little, step by step, that boy calmly entered his world.

And then became it.

CHAPTER 24

THANKFULLY, the results of the examination showed that the bone was fine. Suddenly feeling confident, Ye Qin straightened up. "I knew there was nothing wrong. My bones are sturdy, I tell you."

Cheng Feichi didn't express his opinion, but the doctor who heard grunted. Jotting down notes on a clipboard, he reminded, "As sturdy as a steel plate. Or you'd run out of legs to break."

Now that he was relaxed, Ye Qin dozed off askew on the back seat of the taxi ride home and even had a dream in the fifteen short minutes. For once, the Cheng Feichi in his dreams was so close that he could reach out and touch him. He had a small smile on his lips, a curve of the most familiar warmth.

After waking up to Cheng Feichi's tranquil face, even though the idyllic dream wasn't shattered per se, Ye Qin still felt the dim loss of being yanked back to reality. It appeared Cheng Feichi only agreed to his requests in the hospital because he looked pitiful. Ye Qin was exploiting his injury. That didn't count.

Even so, he still heartened up, visibly becoming livelier—or rather, hyper. He hopped all two hundred meters from the gates of the compound to the apartment building, climbed the stairs without Cheng Feichi's help, and continued hopping into the elevator.

An elderly couple on the same ride up watched with apprehension and asked Cheng Feichi, "Young man, why don't you offer your didi a hand? It's too dangerous."

Cheng Feichi responded in kind and reached out to offer support.

Ye Qin panicked upon hearing the word "didi." Being supported actually gave him less stable footing than hopping on his own. As soon as he entered the room, he shook Cheng Feichi off and laughed, "Sorry to trouble you."

They had no blood ties. Their features were not resemblant in the least, and their personalities were also poles apart. So why was it, then, that people always thought they were brothers? Before, this could have been justified by their close relationship. Now, it was puzzling that they still thought that.

Cheng Feichi couldn't possibly not bear a grudge for what had happened, so even though Ye Qin called him "gege" now and then, he only did so while Cheng Feichi wasn't present.

He didn't want to cower like this. He wanted to be brazen and passionate. But he worried that acting without proper thought would make Cheng Feichi mad at him, just like he had been before they went to the hospital.

Ye Qin had just boiled water when Cheng Feichi announced that he was going out.

Aware Cheng Feichi was going to make a grocery run, Ye Qin grabbed his crutch. "I'm coming with you."

By now, it was pitch black outside. Cheng Feichi made him stay in on the grounds that it was unsafe to walk at night, and the door shut in front of him.

A second later, Ye Qin leaped up and hopped into the bedroom, gathered all the stars on the table there, and put them in the jar. He put the glass jar on the top bunk and covered it along with the Lego.

After looking at the lump from three angles and making sure there was no way to make out what was underneath, Ye Qin dusted his hands in accomplishment.

He refused to exploit his misfortune to win sympathy points, so Cheng Feichi couldn't see these things for the time being. He wanted to win him over with his own abilities like he had once before.

...Even though those small scuffles hadn't taken any real skill.

First things first, Ye Qin couldn't let Cheng Feichi break his back for him.

He laced up an apron and took out leftover produce from the refrigerator, rinsing and chopping up enough to make a vegetable stew. The wok had just been oiled and the vegetables were about to go in when a knock came at the door.

Ye Qin opened it without any preamble, thinking that Cheng Feichi had returned. Who knew it was actually his landlord from downstairs.

Every time this mean, middle-aged man came knocking on Ye Qin's door, he glared and fumed through his mustache as if he had anger that he could never get to the end of. "No wonder I've been hearing *thump-thump-thump* nonstop for these past couple of days," he blurted once he saw Ye Qin's broken leg. "It's been you knocking around with your crutches the whole time."

"I've never used my crutches in the apartment. I only use them when I go out."

The landlord rolled his eyes. "Then it's the sound of you hopping about that I've been hearing non-stop day and night and even in my dreams. The noise is giving me high blood pressure."

Ye Qin had carefully followed the doctor's orders during his recovery period. Most of the time, he either sat or lay down. His steps on WeRun didn't even add up to fifty per day. He had

no clue how the landlord could hear noise loud enough to carry over to his dreams.

But in the end, Ye Qin was still renting the man's apartment, so he reined in his temper, didn't argue, and conceded, "I'll take my time from now on and try my best to be quiet."

The landlord hmphed and went into a tirade about how group renting was illegal and he only let them live together out of the kindness of his heart; if they were caught, he would be fined; he was really risking a lot; and so on and so forth. Finally, he summed it all up in one sentence, "I'm raising the rent next month."

Originally, the company paid rent for this dorm. After everyone started pursuing their solo careers, two people moved out and the rest seldom lived there. And so the three of them sat down to reallocate the rent.

Originally this wasn't a problem. They would have had to pay rent for school dorms even if they went to school let alone now that they were part of the working force. But this landlord thought that they were young and easy to dupe. He had already raised rent twice this year and now again with this kind of pompous excuse. The only reason for this was that he could tell they had grown used to living there and didn't want to find a new place. As a result, he couldn't help but push them around.

Unable to hold back, Ye Qin turned, pointing to the wooden boxes stacked against the wall in the living room. "You're always saying that it's illegal, you're taking a huge risk, but maybe you should take back all these things you piled up in our apartment first before raising the rent?"

"What are you saying?" the landlord demanded. "Can't I store things in my own apartment?"

"But your apartment is rented to us, so we have the right of use. You putting your stuff here takes away from our living space. We signed the contract based on net area, so we have to subtract your pile to get the real usable area, which, hmm...would be at least three to four hundred square meters. Added up over the number of years we've been renting, it's not a small amount. *You* should actually be paying *us*."

The landlord listened dazedly and took ages to finally react. "You're talking twisted logic! I've put a bit of stuff here, so what?! Just be more careful! I have family heirlooms in those wooden boxes! If you break them, you have to pay!"

"Ah, now you've gotten to the point," Ye Qin said immediately. "Right now, it's not me who broke your things; it's your things which were blocking the corridor that made me injure my leg." Here, he pointed to it. "They almost caused a second injury. I just came back from the hospital, so my medical records are hot and fresh. You wanna take a look?"

With his own logic turned against him, the landlord glared in rage. "You have the nerve to blackmail me, you crook?!"

Ye Qin had been waiting for him to say this. He pulled up the rental contract on his phone and read, "The landlord shall ensure that the structure, equipment, and installation of the apartment follows construction, fire, security, health, and other safety requirements and must not pose a risk to personal safety... So you see, you have not only posed a risk to my personal safety, but you are actually responsible for an injury. You want to pay my medical bills?"

The landlord was originally in the wrong, and on top of that, he couldn't win an argument against Ye Qin. Red-faced with anger, he shot out, "You're a cheapskate who deserves to never make it big," before storming off in a huff.

In light of his overwhelming victory, Ye Qin thought that he hadn't lived all these years in poverty in vain. A penny saved was a penny more towards paying off this debt and escaping from a miserable plight. Essential costs must be spent, but he

could not let an opportunity to save slip through.

Nodding his head in satisfaction, Ye Qin was about to close the door when he suddenly saw Cheng Feichi emerge from the hallway to the elevator, looking like he had borne witness to the battle for quite a while now.

Cheng Feichi more or less began to eavesdrop when Ye Qin told his landlord to clear his stuff from the apartment.

Just the landlord's unscrupulous, scathing tone told him his demand for raising rent was groundless. At first, Cheng Feichi wanted to go over and help, but unexpectedly, Ye Qin not only didn't take it but also scared the man off with a sharp tongue. He could picture Ye Qin with his head tilted back in utter fearlessness just hearing that familiar voice.

As if the haughty kitten had come back.

Sadly, it had only been a few minutes. After going into the dorm, that kitten went back to being well-behaved, trailing behind him without a single sound. He carried plates and bowls and helped out in the kitchen. He even asked how long the scallions should be cut, dotting his i's and crossing his t's more than writing an exam.

Cheng Feichi remembered now that the kitten who had brandished his fangs at every small thing had his claws and teeth pulled out long ago. Only when he was backed into a corner would his fur explode in defiance. Normally, he wouldn't dare go about doing as he pleased, wouldn't reveal his nature that easily.

Especially in front of him.

As they ate, Yi Hui called asking if he was coming home for dinner for the Mid-Autumn Festival.

When Cheng Feichi said that there was still a month and then some, Yi Hui said petulantly, "Then let's make a promise first. Huihui wants to eat a huuuuge mooncake with his gege."

Because Yi Hui was similar to him in age, he was even closer to Cheng Feichi than his own mother, who accompanied him from dawn to dusk. Like all innocent kids would, Yi Hui wanted to share everything fun and delicious with Cheng Feichi.

In the end, Cheng Feichi didn't have the heart to say no. After putting down his cellphone, he looked at Ye Qin, spaced out and chewing on his chopsticks across the table. Suddenly, he remembered that Ye Qin's mother was already gone.

He also remembered that Ye Qin really loved and cherished his family a long time ago, else he wouldn't have mistaken him as his half-brother and done all those stupid things.

After dinner, the two curled up on the sofa, each minding his own business just like at the Garden Hotel suite.

Cheng Feichi brought his laptop and had just begun typing when he heard a male voice from a phone speaker. "Shit, shit, shit, I've been exposed! I'm done for! A-Qin, save me! What should I do?!"

Ye Qin blocked the mic in a drastic response, gripped with panic. "I-I'll go talk in the room," he announced.

Cheng Feichi hauled him back down by the wrist right as he stood up. "Just talk here. You won't disturb me."

And so Ye Qin put in earbuds and brought the mic up to his lips to whisper, "What are you yelling for?! Keep yelling and I'll block you!"

Cheng Feichi could tell that the voice had been Zhou Feng's, but now he could no longer hear anything. Ye Qin angled away from him and spoke in a very quiet whisper that he could only make out a few words of if he concentrated.

"Didn't I tell you not to dig your own grave? 'Completely invade his life,' like seriously! ...No. If I call the class monitor, he'll know my intentions for sure... Okay, fine. I'll try tomorrow... The same old. I don't think I made any progress, but today he hugged me... Not that kind of hug. My injury reopened so he

took me to the hospital… Shouldn't be very heavy. I weighed less than 110 pounds at last year's examination… Hey, say, I've been hopping on my right leg for so many days now. Am I going to gain muscle?"

Here, Ye Qin stealthily peeked back at Cheng Feichi and saw him focused on the screen. Knowing that anyone absorbed in work wouldn't hear anything outside of it, he relaxed, turned back, and continued, "So say if I moved the bandage, would I have one thick leg and one thin leg? …No, it's not idol baggage. How ugly would that look? It might even leave a scar… I'm scared he'll see…"

As he spoke, his voice became quieter and quieter until finally, Ye Qin slumped his shoulders and sighed. "Drop it," he murmured sullenly. "He saw me arguing with the landlord to-night. Tell me, should I keep playing dumb or tell him I'm not usually like this?"

This question tormented Ye Qin for an entire night.

Cheng Feichi left before 10 p.m., saying that he had booked a hotel in the area. Not bold enough to keep him for the night, Ye Qin quietly saw him off at the door.

"I'm going somewhere tomorrow, so I'll be here later," Cheng Feichi announced before leaving.

Still not quite understanding why Cheng Feichi letting him know of his whereabouts, Ye Qin went back into the room and let out a long, confused sigh.

The next morning, he called Liao Yifang as per Zhou Feng's instructions. Ye Qin had prepared a script beforehand, but Liao Yifang seized control of the conversation first. "Ye-tongxue, Did you already know that the 'girl' is him?"

Ye Qin rediscovered the terror of being dominated by the class monitor that he'd felt back in high school. "No," he said in his most sincere performance since his debut. "What girl? Is Zhou Feng womanizing again?"

"No. I'm talking about the girl that you told me was your fan," Liao Yifang sighed. "Never mind. I'm the idiot. I couldn't even see through such a stupid trick."

"No, no, no. It's because Zhou Feng's such a crafty guy," Ye Qin probed and upon discovering that he wasn't angry, asked, "How did you find out, class monitor?"

"He posted a picture of the school's entrance on Weibo. It had his location."

"Maybe that girl just happened to be passing by?"

"I was sitting in the reception office at the time. It was just him at the gates."

Ye Qin was speechless. This irredeemably stupid guy had been caught red-handed. "Crafty" was too much of a compliment for him.

But since he was there to speak on Zhou Feng's behalf, he had to put in some good words for him. "He just wants to get back with you so much that he'll try anything. He means well."

Liao Yifang went quiet for a while before humming in understanding.

Ye Qin still wanted to put in a few more good words for Zhou Feng, but Liao Yifang nimbly cut him off. "We're going to have a class reunion on the 15th of next month. Are you coming?"

Ye Qin knew about this. His QQ account was still in the class group chat, and he would always be tagged with everyone else around this time of year. Occasionally, he would browse a thread or lurk the chat, never daring to say anything.

After going through such a radical upturn in his family, not even going to university, Ye Qin knew clear as day how everyone saw him. He'd seen too many people who rejoiced in the misfortune of others and hit them when they were down. Even if all his

old classmates were kindhearted, he couldn't bear having them look at him differently.

Perhaps it was the pride left in his bones. He had never been able to fully adapt from the unrestrained generosity of granting favors with a wave of the hand to bowing his head and having others look after him.

"Nah," Ye Qin found an excuse. "My leg's still a bother. It's pretty hard to go out."

Liao Yifang, as sensitive as he was, naturally knew what Ye Qin worried about. "Everyone's worried about you. We'll just have dinner and chat for a bit. We also only met up once a year in the past, and it's always been very friendly. We won't make you feel embarrassed."

Ever since going into showbiz, Ye Qin hadn't kept in contact with his former friends. He only gradually started talking more with Zhou Feng after the latter got discharged from military service. There was no way he didn't miss any of them at all.

"Let me think on it for a few days, okay?" Ye Qin scratched his head and left his answer ambiguous.

Due to his leg injury, Ye Qin didn't shower for several days.

After hopping for a distance yesterday and sweating all over, Ye Qin could almost smell body odor. And so he decided to shower while Cheng Feichi was out.

He couldn't let his injury get wet, so he had to take ample precautionary measures. He wrapped a plastic bag on his leg and secured it in place with several rounds of duct tape. To ensure no water would get in, he aimed the sprinkler at the shower wall as much as he could and kept the shower door open, propping his leg up on a small stool outside.

But the execution was never as thorough as the plan. It was not smooth or easy as Ye Qin had imagined. The old showerhead sprayed water everywhere, splashing outside and making the tiles slippery. He couldn't keep his foot stable on the stool either. Several times, he almost slipped and only didn't because his arm had a solid grip.

Ye Qin, who had recently been using his arms to make up for his injured leg, thought that if he continued like this, his biceps would be the first to bulk up.

He still worried about the class reunion. *Should I go or not?* He asked himself, straining to scrub his back. If he did go, how should he present his career? Did he have to buy a set of new clothes? Fall fashion had just hit the market, and boy did it cost a pretty penny. Why hadn't Cheng Feichi returned his jacket yet?

His thoughts drifted in circles but always came back to Cheng Feichi. *Yesterday he said he would come by later,* Ye Qin thought worriedly. *Later as in when? Will he come for dinner? If he comes later, does that mean he'll leave later?*

These questions didn't bother him for too long. After finishing his shower, as he sat on the sofa undoing bandages on his leg, Cheng Feichi arrived.

Ye Qin opened the door eagerly and only then realized how weird he looked right now. Awkwardly, he shifted his leg, still wrapped in a plastic bag, out of sight behind him.

Cheng Feichi came in and cast a glance at him, silent.

Just as Ye Qin thought that he would go into the kitchen, as usual, he fetched a dry towel from the bathroom and covered Ye Qin's head without explanation. Behind him, Cheng Feichi began drying him off.

Ye Qin once enjoyed this kind of treatment, so it wasn't the first time ever. But for some reason, this time he stood frozen with his neck hanging and eyes cast down, like a young student waiting to be scolded by the teacher.

It was a conditioned reflex because, in the short time that they had lived together, Cheng Feichi would always check his

homework at this time.

He would lazily hold up a test booklet and Cheng Feichi would look it over while toweling his hair. "You used the wrong formula for the third question," he would say, his low voice sounding both clear and muffled through the towel covering Ye Qin's ears. "The topic isn't clear in the seventh question. Over on the other side, for English, look closely at the last sentence. There's a word spelled wrong. If you can't find it, then you'll have to copy it fifty times."

Back then, he always complained about Cheng Feichi's ruthless pushing. Thinking back now, those were the happiest days of his life, and he would be willing to write a hundred more test booklets.

They ate pork bone soup and sweet and sour eggplant for lunch along with the vegetable stew left over from yesterday.

There was a clay stewing pot in the kitchen. Ye Qin had gone out to buy it yesterday, but when Cheng Feichi asked, he said he found it in the cupboards and after a wash, saw that it was quite new. The landlord also let him use it.

He did so to prove that he normally had a good relationship with the landlord and to observe Cheng Feichi's response to yesterday's incident. Cheng Feichi just nodded his head in silence. He soaked the clay pot completely for a few minutes before using it to stew.

After lunch, Ye Qin hid in his room under the excuse of an afternoon nap.

Everything was going well. Cheng Feichi took care of him and didn't reject his advances. He also didn't react to his abnormal behavior and even held Ye Qin's hand. These were all good signs.

But he still felt uneasy, especially right after coming back to the present from a memory. He felt uneasy when he didn't get an answer and uneasy when he did. It was just as Zhou Feng had said, things were as bad as ever.

Ye Qin turned over in bed, dangling his injured leg off the edge.

What would happen after he recovered? Would Cheng Feichi leave? Go back to S-City and get married?

He thought of Cheng Xin's words: if not this year, then next year. Cheng Feichi would have to get married next year. Ye Qin had landed him once due to luck, but what did he have now? Enough stupidity to fall and break a leg just by walking?

Ye Qin had always been someone who craved assurance. The things he had done to hurt Cheng Feichi were a way of testing him. Even if they seemed petty and childish now, he had used Cheng Feichi's reactions then to ascertain his standing in Cheng Feichi's heart.

All that effort Ye Qin had spent to get Cheng Feichi to sleep with him was only for a sense of security. He had wanted to stay in his life, if only for a moment longer.

Now, it became his trademark. Everything he did to show and get proof of love broke his muscles and bones and tore his lungs and heart.

It had been five years, and he still hadn't been able to become as steady and collected as Cheng Feichi. The flame in his heart always burned. When Cheng Feichi ignored him, it dimmed a few measures, and when he got a response, it flared up again. But from the start, it had never gone out.

Ye Qin sat up and put both feet on the ground.

He couldn't keep hiding like this forever. This so-called "waiting for the right time" was nothing but an excuse to stall and let opportunities slip away.

He wanted to ask Cheng Feichi. If luck was on his side, he would receive a few drops of oil; if not, then a basin of water.

Since that flame would never go out, there was nothing to

be afraid of.

When Cheng Xin called again, Cheng Feichi was cutting up fruit in the kitchen.

He didn't plan to take the call, but after recalling what his grandmother had said to him that afternoon, he thought for a bit and answered in speaker mode with the phone set aside.

Cheng Xin changed strategies this time, playing the role of a caring mother worried about his life in the capital. She told him to put on more layers and drink more water. After sufficiently padding the conversation, she then indirectly probed his location.

"His place," Cheng Feichi said truthfully.

Cheng Xin audibly choked on the other end and sneered after a long pause. "He really is something, to charm you so much that you don't even want your own mother anymore."

Though he had known for a long time that Cheng Xin's obsession was deep-rooted to the point where she couldn't let go, Cheng Feichi still felt inescapably helpless as he stated the truth, "He saved you. Under such dangerous circumstances, he couldn't possibly have any ulterior motives."

"Did he tell you?" Cheng Xin zeroed in on the first sentence, leaping on it like someone had stepped on her foot. "I knew he would. That kind of person would do anything to get out of poverty. His broken leg is just a scheme to get your sympathy. Xiao-Chi, my good son, listen to your mom. Do not fall for it!"

Words reached the tip of Cheng Feichi's tongue before he swallowed them back. He knew that Cheng Xin had already gone mad, and would no longer listen to anyone. What his grandmother and grandfather couldn't do—breaking her out of her obsession—was even more impossible for him as a member of the younger generation. All he could do was fulfill his duty as her son and care for her until her final years.

After hanging up the utterly pointless call, Cheng Feichi

turned and caught a glimpse of Ye Qin's hastily fleeing back.

Cheng Feichi followed him to the bedroom door, pausing for a moment before pushing on the narrowly open door. Walking in, he set down a plate of fruits and picked up the crutch that had been knocked to the floor, leaning it against the wall.

Ye Qin was sitting completely silent on the bottom bunk. Cheng Feichi stood less than a meter from the bed, also not making a sound.

He remembered that Ye Qin used to love talking. When Ye Qin had been with him, his mouth had never paused for a single moment, as was seen from his WeChat call with Zhou Feng yesterday.

So how did he turn into this? Cheng Feichi vaguely knew why but didn't really want to get clarification. The Ye Qin he remembered shouldn't be like this.

Finally, it was Ye Qin who broke the silence. He was always the one to take initiative. Perhaps he knew of the somewhat forceful nature of the smile on his face, as he dropped the corners of his mouth. "You...know everything?"

Cheng Feichi nodded.

Ye Qin didn't feel as bad as he'd imagined, just a little hurt and a little relieved as if he'd just come out of a disaster. It was a bit like someone stabbed him meticulously with a needle for several days, all the false bravado inside deflating and spiraling to the ground.

At least he no longer had to be stretched taut like a tense bowstring, hiding a secret. He thought, *No wonder he came over to take care of me. No wonder he didn't bring up that ring. Staying here is an obligation for him, a duty, not an obstacle that couldn't be passed over or some kind of hidden motive.*

The two of them were different. While aging made Ye Qin weaker, it didn't wear down a single bit of Cheng Feichi's

extensive integrity.

"S-so you..." Ye Qin disliked awkward silence, but didn't know how to continue after those two words. He wanted to cover his hands over his eyes and also didn't want Cheng Feichi to see him in this broken state again. Pinching the edge of the bed until his fingers turned white, he said, "Auntie had a mishap that day. I just happened to be close by, so I..."

It was a typical accident, and at most he could be commended for having bravely done the right thing. As these things usually go, her family should have come in person, thanked him, and that would be that. He'd already gotten enough.

"You still have work, don't you? Just focus on your stuff. I'll be fine on my own. I'll be better in a few days. I can already walk really, really slowly."

These words came from his heart and also contradicted it. Ever since meeting Cheng Feichi again, Ye Qin often put himself between a rock and a hard place. But the ball was ultimately in Cheng Feichi's court, so even if he tormented himself over it, it was no use.

Knowing this, he was unexpectedly calm. It was Cheng Feichi, who while silent, wavered as ripples moved through the calm waters of his eyes.

"You think I pity you?" he asked slowly.

Ye Qin shuddered hard at the word "pity." His first instinct was to object, and he shook his head, but he said what he was actually thinking, "D-don't you?"

Suddenly, it was all clear.

They were both afraid.

Cheng Feichi was afraid to uncover the truth with his own hands once again. He was afraid that Ye Qin was serious this time, even more so that he was mistaken, and it had been yet another joke this whole time. If everything was fake, then even if he had put up brick walls, he couldn't bear having them smashed a second time.

That was why he waited passively. He had already gotten used to Ye Qin's initiative, both before and now. However, Ye Qin was no less scared than he was—scared of rejection, scared he behaved out of line, scared to the point of fleeing at the tiniest response. If he had any courage to spare, it would have already been depleted by this constant push and pull.

They both had changed, but it also seemed as if they both hadn't changed. Cheng Feichi still hoped to see that brave and passionate little sun. Ye Qin still wanted him to take a step closer. Just one step would be able to sustain his heat stores and let him keep emitting rays.

It wasn't just Cheng Feichi trapped in the same place. Now came the time to break away from habitual passiveness and give Ye Qin, as well as himself, an answer.

Cheng Feichi slowly let out a breath. He extended his right hand and laid out his palm to reveal that winding scar. "Do you pity me when you see this?"

Ye Qin was taken aback. Once, he had examined this scar closely while Cheng Feichi had been drunk. He'd also stolen a few glances here and there. Every time, he felt something tearing up his heart.

"No," he mumbled, shaking his head.

All he knew was how to feel pain for Cheng Feichi, like a sharp knife twisting the same wound into his heart. Despite it having healed over, every time he thought about it, it felt too painful for words. Cheng Feichi was the absolute singularity of his life. Whoever hurt Cheng Feichi also stabbed a knife into Ye Qin's heart, even if that person was Ye Qin himself.

Cheng Feichi's fingers curled into a fist that hid his wound, not letting Ye Qin look anymore and tear himself apart.

"Me too," he said. "I'm the same. I also don't pity you."

As his voice faded, Ye Qin abruptly reached over to catch the hand he had been about to take back.

When he caught it, he didn't know what to do. His hand was small, covering only half of Cheng Feichi's. Even so, he refused to let go.

His breaths came short and fast, as if he somewhat understood what Cheng Feichi had meant but not fully. For the moment, he could only grab onto Cheng Feichi first and make Cheng Feichi wait for him.

Ye Qin barely used any strength. Cheng Feichi only had to move his wrist a tad bit to break free. But he didn't. He stood silently and let Ye Qin hold his hand, soothing every restless worry with comforting warmth and a steady pulse.

After Ye Qin repeatedly verified, thoroughly digested the words, and let them seep into his brain, he let go of Cheng Feichi's hand and shrunk back. Before he could, Cheng Feichi caught his hand again.

He easily wrapped his hand around Ye Qin's entirely. "Is there anything else that I don't know?"

Ye Qin's heart pounded like a drum. He couldn't stand, couldn't sit. He bit his lip and shook his head. "No," he said stubbornly.

The corners of his eyes reddened as if he was being bullied.

Cheng Feichi wasn't in a hurry to know right now, so he just caressed the back of Ye Qin's hand with his thumb and let go. "Then tell me in the future."

Ye Qin floated on cloud nine into the evening, now thinking he dreaming, now hearing a voice in his ear: *It's real. He forgives you.*

Even if his heart was shaken and his thoughts restless, he could still vaguely sense that the "future" Cheng Feichi mentioned had already begun.

Maybe even earlier, when Cheng Feichi showed up at his place, standing in the doorway, asking him why his words held no weight. Since then, their "future" had already been slowly opening its doors to him.

Even if Cheng Feichi didn't say it explicitly. Even if Ye Qin didn't think he'd done anything.

When Cheng Feichi was about to go for a grocery run before dark, Ye Qin grabbed his crutches, wanting to go with him. Seeing him in a tense and nervous state, Cheng Feichi didn't have the heart to tell him to stay and rest at home, and the two of them went out, one walking, one hopping.

There was a big supermarket chain nearby that they'd been buying pretty much everything from. Injured but determined, Ye Qin leaned on his crutch with one hand as he pushed the shopping cart with the other. After a while, he felt that this was too strenuous and put the crutches away, finding balance with one foot on the ground and two hands on the cart.

Cheng Feichi, seeing how he was more natural like this than leaning on his crutch, let him do as he pleased. He walked ahead and picked out produce, turning back once in a while to check that Ye Qin was keeping up, even though this was clearly unnecessary.

Ye Qin's eyes were glued to him, unwilling to drift off even a little. He followed him closely with every step, afraid that Cheng Feichi would run away in the blink of an eye.

Cheng Feichi kept a very slow pace which let Ye Qin keep up with him and gave him ample time to examine the produce he put in his cart at the same time. He even had time to chuck in a few things he wanted to get for himself.

Like a new mug, and size 45 male slippers.

Ye Qin was much worldlier than before, comparing prices even for a pack of toothpicks. However, this kind of careful

budgeting was a habit instilled into him by the circumstances of life, not one he had naturally been born with. Neither had there been anyone to teach him, so he actually only expressed it somewhat superficially.

For instance, when Cheng Feichi picked up a carton of eggs worth 29RMB and put it in the shopping cart, Ye Qin picked it up. He found that the eggs on the shelf beside it were 3RMB cheaper and took it upon himself to swap the produce.

Falling back into his role as a tutor, Cheng Feichi held both cartons in his hands and had Ye Qin count the number of eggs in each one.

Biting his finger, Ye Qin counted a few times and found that though the second carton was a very large square shape, it actually held five fewer eggs than the first.

"Y-you get the groceries," he immediately stuttered in defeat. "I'll just push the cart."

In the end, though, Cheng Feichi chose the carton Ye Qin picked out and put the other one back. "The number of eggs isn't the only thing to consider," he explained to Ye Qin's puzzled expression. "The ones you chose are bigger."

Despite Cheng Feichi softening the blow, Ye Qin became even more embarrassed and so humiliated that his ears turned red.

It was the busiest time for the supermarket. Even with a dozen cashiers, the lines still backed up all the way to the shelves. Worried Ye Qin would get tired standing for so long, Cheng Feichi told him to sit and wait in the exit area.

But how could Ye Qin sit still at all? The line only moved forward half a meter before he went back to tell Cheng Feichi that there was something he forgot to get and to wait for him here.

Cheng Feichi couldn't leave with a fully loaded shopping cart. Watching Ye Qin's hopping back vanish into the crowd, he couldn't help but worry.

He had just left the line and was about to stow the shopping cart in a corner and follow him when he heard someone yell, "Mr. Cheng!"

Cheng Feichi looked to the voice. A man wearing a khaki jacket sauntered over, staring at him. "Teacher, it really is you!" he cried happily after confirming.

The man was Wei Jiaqi, a student Cheng Feichi once privately tutored.

As it had been a long time since anyone had called him "teacher," Cheng Feichi spaced out for a moment. Then, he smiled. "Wei-tongxue, long time no see."

After exchanging greetings, they chit-chatted for a bit. He found out that Wei Jiaqi now attended a famous school in the capital. Cheng Feichi was happy that he got to reap the benefits of many hard years of studying.

Wei Jiaqi also recalled what had happened before and felt guilty for his mother always having made things difficult for Cheng Feichi. After exchanging numbers, he promised to visit him one day. He thanked Cheng Feichi for teaching him good study habits and told him he was one of the main reasons he could get into his dream school.

Chen Feichi told Wei Jiaqi not to view him in such a great light, that he had just been doing it to get paid.

"What kind of tutor 'just doing it to get paid' would extend every lesson and even give out lectures at lunchtime?"

When running into someone, it was unavoidable for some vivid memories to be evoked. As they reminisced about how occupying a table in the cafeteria for lessons had made the cleaning lady roll her eyes at them countless times, they both laughed.

When the conversation came to a lull, Wei Jiaqi sighed, "Originally, I used you as my goal. I wanted to get into your university and be your junior. I never expected you to go abroad."

At the time, everyone assumed Cheng Feichi would go to university in China, so going abroad without notice had indeed been quite unexpected. There was a sense of melancholy when Wei Jiaqi brought it up.

But Cheng Feichi grabbed onto the key point. "How did you know I went abroad?"

He remembered he left in such a rush that he had to get someone else to change his school registration. Even the class monitor didn't know where he had gone. Wei Jiaqi had gone to another high school, so how would he know?

"He told me, the student named Ye from High School No. 6," Wei Jiaqi said. "He came to find me and asked if I was in contact with you."

Cheng Feichi asked him when this had happened, and Wei Jiaqi thought for a moment. "Two or three years after the beginning of my freshman year, so he should have been...a senior? He came to my classroom, told me you went abroad, and asked me if I had any way of reaching you. I only had your China number, which was already out of commission. He left me his number and told me to call him immediately if I got any news of you."

Here, Wei Jiaqi fished out his cellphone and scrolled to Ye Qin's number. "See? This one. I kept it even after changing phones. Every now and then, he'll send me a text and ask if I heard from you. He's going to be so happy to get my call—or maybe you can call him, Mr. Cheng? Give him a surprise?"

On the way back from the supermarket, Ye Qin, insisting on dividing the groceries, carried the plastic bag with the vegetables. Stuck to the surface of the bag was the pack of dry red chili peppers he'd raced against the clock and charged back into the supermarket to get.

They made two sweet dishes and two spicy dishes for dinner.

Ye Qin picked up a few pieces of hot pepper with his chopsticks and swallowed them without so much as changing his expression. Only then did Cheng Feichi believe that he wasn't just bragging about his spice tolerance.

He did change his expression after dinner, however, when they were eating fruit, because Cheng Feichi told him he was going back to S-City tomorrow.

"Tomorrow is September 1st. I promised Yi Hui I'd drop him off at school."

"Okay, go," Ye Qin said, feeling extremely twisted and uneasy inside. But unlike before, he felt a much deeper reluctance to part with Cheng Feichi, even a bit of indefinable fear and panic.

When he woke up the next morning, Ye Qin stared at the ceiling for several long minutes until the cellphone by his pillow vibrated. Then, he pulled his drifting senses back to reality.

It was a text from Cheng Feichi.

[I've boarded.]

These two simple words somehow grounded him again. Ye Qin closed his eyes and took several deep breaths. He got out of bed, did his morning routine, and ate breakfast. As he was drying clothes on the balcony, he got another text from Cheng Feichi.

[I've arrived.]

Ye Qin didn't quite understand why he was sending these texts. Clutching his phone, he texted back, *[You've arrived at his school?]*

Two minutes later, Cheng Feichi replied, *[Yes. They're raising the flag.]*

The school was already very far away, but Ye Qin lifted his head to the sky and imagined the scene. As the chilly autumn wind scattered the clouds and a few gentle rays of sunlight fell on him, Ye Qin's thoughts drifted farther and farther.

It was like he had entered an alternate universe. In this

universe, he and Cheng Feichi got into the same university. In the welcome ceremony, they stood in a corner of the back row that no one paid attention to, holding hands. They leaned in and whispered things in each other's ears like, "The professor speaking looks a lot like the director of High School No. 6," and, "Let's eat breakfast in the cafeteria after," and, "You look so good today."

If he could, he would still choose to go back to the time before all this happened.

Cheng Feichi left for two days and had just come back when a phone call summoned him to host a meeting in the new office.

If they didn't stay in touch through text, Ye Qin would have thought that he was still inside another imaginary daydream.

He found things to do for most of his day: watching movies, reading scripts, walking back and forth with the support of the wall to rehabilitate his leg. But in the moments in between, he still couldn't grasp any real sense of Cheng Feichi accepting him.

Perhaps it was because it all happened too suddenly.

All reconciliations need time. They had separated for so long. In those five years, Cheng Feichi must have met many extraordinary people. Everyone said that horses never ate old grass; those with ambition never looked back. This mouthful of old grass could choke anyone. He needed time to digest.

Moreover, acceptance did not equate to forgiveness.

Even though Ye Qin had been steadily drip-exposing his guilt and regret to Cheng Feichi, the two of them had yet to sit down for a frank and open discussion about what had happened.

That was a quiet river flowing between them that could never be drained dry. He could only wait for it to evaporate slowly over time and leave behind a gully that could not be leveled.

Later on, Ye Qin decided to go to the class reunion. The day before, he made a hasty last-minute effort, overturning closets in search of an outfit.

After recovering for several days, Ye Qin could now limp with the aid of his left foot. The doctor told him to walk more in his free time to deter muscle atrophy and rest if he felt tired so as not to overexert himself.

Last night, Cheng Feichi came over and examined his leg. After brushing the injury with his hand, he limited Ye Qin to walk for at most twenty minutes per day. Cheng Feichi stayed for a bit after dinner and then left. Ye Qin wanted to tell him to stay longer but the words didn't even have enough time to fester before they were due to leave his mouth.

And he couldn't really say them out loud. His place was so small that he didn't even have a large enough bed. Where would Cheng Feichi even sleep? A 1.2-meter-wide lower bunk?

After packing clothes for tomorrow, Ye Qin got ready to take a shower. Cheng Feichi would come back at night, so if he could use half an hour for a shower now, he'd be able to stay and chat with him a little longer.

Halfway through, the showerhead stopped spraying water. Wrapped in a towel, Ye Qin left the bathroom to investigate. The kitchen taps were still running, so it wasn't a piping problem.

He threw on a random outfit and went downstairs to look for the landlord. His landlord had been acting weird ever since their last argument took a turn for the ugly. He found all kinds of excuses to push back. The showerhead was blocked because they were sloppy and lacked diligence when it came to cleaning it, he said, so he had to figure out how to fix it himself.

Thinking of how Cheng Feichi would arrive soon, Ye Qin threw in the towel. He found a wrench and decided to do it himself, twisting the showerhead a few times. It briefly put out two spurts of water before drying out again. Water splashed all over him, soaking the long sleeve T-shirt he'd just changed into.

Anything that could go wrong, would go wrong. Ye Qin

had been too fixated on the showerhead to notice his cellphone, He only just saw the text that Cheng Feichi had sent half an hour ago saying that he would be there immediately. Setting his phone aside, Ye Qin had just wiped his face when a knock came on the door.

Even after changing into a clean outfit, he couldn't hide his raggedness. Cheng Feichi had waited at the door for quite some time.

"What happened?" he asked immediately when he saw Ye Qin's drenched hair.

"A little situation." Ye Qin pointed to the washroom. "The shower won't work."

Cheng Feichi went in. After fiddling with the lever and confirming that it really wasn't working, he rolled up his sleeves to try to fix it.

He was ten centimeters taller than Ye Qin, so he barely had to reach to get to the pipe connected to the showerhead. Ye Qin looked at him, head raised in focus, jaw clenched, Adam's apple bulging in his neck. Only now did his heart, suspended for so long in Cheng Feichi's absence, find a solid spot to land and floated back into place.

As he lost himself in watching, he overlooked a certain thing.

When the thought suddenly came back to him, it was already too late to warn Cheng Feichi. Ye Qin only had time for a rushed, "Wait!" before the shower sputtered out water right at Cheng Feichi's chest, immediately drenching his upper body.

The two of them went back to the living room. Ye Qin handed him a dry towel, lifting his head right into Cheng Feichi's white, skin-tight shirt. With a jolt, he lowered his eyes.

A moment later, he couldn't help but steal a glance.

Cheng Feichi had a tall, slender figure, and the wet shirt was stuck so completely to his body that Ye Qin could see the muscles that stretched as he lifted his arms to wipe down his hair in detail. Skin, hidden behind just a translucent layer, made Ye Qin's mouth water. He turned, picked up a glass of water on the table, and drank it all.

While Ye Qin was occupied with the shame of his own perverseness, Cheng Feichi remained calm the whole time. He picked up his jacket and prepared to leave.

"I'm going back to the hotel. The leftovers in the fridge from yesterday should last you another meal. I have work tomorrow so I might come back late..."

Before he finished speaking, Ye Qin enveloped him from behind.

"D-don't leave today." He wrapped his arms tighter. Despite having just wiped his face, he nestled it deep into Cheng Feichi's wet shirt uncaringly. "Don't go. Stay here, okay?"

Cheng Feichi still had his jacket in his hand. He'd staggered a step forward when Ye Qin had crashed into him. Only when he got a hold of himself did he realize how fast Ye Qin had run. How could his leg take that kind of treatment?

Tossing his jacket onto a nearby cabinet, Cheng Feichi placed his hand on Ye Qin's arm. "Let go. Your leg..."

Ye Qin shook his head firmly and tightened his grip even more. "Don't go. Promise me you won't go first."

Cheng Feichi didn't know what had gotten into him. "Okay, I won't go," he said helplessly, afraid another mishap would cause permanent damage to Ye Qin's leg.

But after receiving confirmation, Ye Qin went back on his words and didn't let go. His breath fanned over wet cloth, creating a constant stream of vapor. Holding onto this steady body, Ye Qin finally saw clearly the reason he had been so on edge for the past couple of days and lit up with an abundance of confidence.

"I-I know you're good. You can be good to anyone," he

rushed out hoarsely, "but I still—still want to be with you. Since you're s-still willing to accept me, let's get back together. Or we can forget everything that happened and start over. You can choose, okay? I'll follow your decision."

Ye Qin spoke so fast that his brain blanked out momentarily after he finished. Suddenly remembering something he missed, he tightened his fingers. His breaths came out hot against Cheng Feichi's back. "I'm sorry, gege. I love you. I love you so much…"

This was a hard-earned chance, and he spilled his heart out. But because he couldn't see Cheng Feichi's expression, he didn't know of the tumultuous waves set off in Cheng Feichi's heart by his stumbling words.

It was like they dredged up something he had forgotten in the depths of his memories while pushing back the regret and dissatisfaction pervading his heart.

He had already accepted compromise the day that he rushed to the capital. Moreover, he'd gotten proof from various conversations that what happened back then was not entirely what he thought. But only now did he truly feel relieved.

He hadn't always looked so calm and open. He had been born into poverty. Growing up, dating outside of his class triggered his overly sensitive pride, causing him to hate that "deception" down to his very bones.

It also blinded him to the truth.

Cheng Feichi pulled off Ye Qin's hands and turned around to face him. When Ye Qin ducked, he pursued him. When Ye Qin lowered his head, he took his chin and made him look up.

Ye Qin's eyes were filled with tears. He panicked at being on the receiving end of Cheng Feichi's direct stare, but he had nowhere to hide. As he blinked, a teardrop spilled from the corner of his eye and trailed down his cheek to his chin. Dry hands wiped it off.

"Why are you crying?" Cheng Feichi asked.

Ye Qin shook his head. It was all he could do. He also didn't know why he was crying. It was probably because his feelings had been piling up from the moment Cheng Feichi began to accept him. Now, they were finally given an outlet.

Now, he had no more fears. Even if Cheng Feichi didn't like him back, he wasn't scared anymore. He said everything he could, everything he should have. The ball was in Cheng Feichi's court.

But his heart still trembled nonstop, and his tears dripped down, gradually wetting Cheng Feichi's palm.

"Don't cry."

Ye Qin nodded with all that he could. He sniffed and bit his lip, trying to hold back tears. He didn't know why Cheng Feichi was telling him not to cry, and he was also completely unaware of how pitiful he looked right now, how seductive.

By the time he realized the meaning of Cheng Feichi's eyes going dark, there was already a large shadow in front of him. In the same position that he tilted Ye Qin's head up by the chin, Cheng Feichi lowered his head and kissed him.

Whenever Ye Qin's brain was fuzzy or he'd gotten liquid courage, he thought about what his first kiss after getting back together with Cheng Feichi would be like. He was sure that he'd be the one shamelessly initiating. Even if Cheng Feichi kissed him back, it would be steady and restrained, like the slow movement of lips against each other from before, lengthy and warm.

Not like this. Their lips crashed in a kiss full of friction, and then Cheng Feichi's hot lips sucked on his tear-stained chin. There was a moment when he moved away, before quickly crushing his lips against Ye Qin's. His tongue pried open Ye Qin's teeth and reached in without resistance. Cheng Feichi was so eager it was like he wanted to take him apart and eat him. His breathing was loud and messy, and he was even forceful and rough.

It was like he had been holding this in for ages; more than Ye Qin could ever imagine.

Wet noises filled his ears. This kiss was completely dominated by Cheng Feichi. Ye Qin found it hard just to respond. It wasn't long until he stopped crying, only able to squeeze a few helpless noises from his throat. His head was all jumbled up too. Apart from knowing that he was kissing the man he'd just been calling gege nonstop, it was completely empty, too occupied for other thoughts.

When they broke apart, Ye Qin felt weak and boneless all over, like he'd almost died. Splayed out on Cheng Feichi's chest as the latter greedily sucked in air, Ye Qin searched for his senses drifting around them.

The saltiness of tears lingered in his mouth, mixed with the taste of Cheng Feichi. It made him reluctant to part. When Cheng Feichi's breaths evened, Ye Qin tilted his head in search of their origin.

He couldn't avert his eyes this time either, looking straight into Cheng Feichi's deep gaze.

For a moment, they both froze.

Finally, Cheng Feichi lifted his hand. The balls of his fingers brushed the fine droplets on Ye Qin's eyelashes. He recalled belatedly that he had been going to say something to soothe the heart of this boy who loved to cry. After holding it in for so long, the word broke from him, "No."

Ever since understanding Ye Qin's fear and unease, he tried to convey his feelings through all kinds of methods from texting him to showing up directly at his place. In any case, he couldn't keep living as he had been for the past five years, closed up. He couldn't leave Ye Qin's imagination running wild, making himself feel ill at ease.

Tickled by his touch, Ye Qin blinked. Before he could ask

for clarification, Cheng Feichi added solemnly, "I'm not good to anyone. Just you."

Ye Qin's breath hitched. He looked at Cheng Feichi with wide eyes lest he'd miss the tiniest change in his expression.

Cheng Feichi looked back at him.

He couldn't be sure how much he conveyed his meaning to Ye Qin. He only knew that Ye Qin's sincerity, laid bare in broad daylight, engulfed him whole.

For him, Ye Qin was both brave and a coward.

He should have shredded the lies lingering in his ears long ago, peeled away the illusion and layers of misunderstandings clouding his sight.

He should have seen the love in those eyes long ago.

CHAPTER 25

THEY didn't stay in the end. With the showerhead still broken, Cheng Feichi took Ye Qin to a hotel.

It was a normal business hotel on the main road nearby, a very average suite with a king-sized bed. Walking in, the whole room could be seen end to end.

It made Ye Qin think of six years ago, when he'd impulsively flown back from an island in the southern hemisphere to the capital with no money and checked into a little hotel suite with Cheng Feichi. He'd been shivering, so cold that he couldn't speak properly. Still, he'd disdained the hotel for being run down and the heating broken.

He even ended up borrowing money from Cheng Feichi to buy a small cake.

As he inserted the "18" candle, the 19-year-old Cheng Feichi didn't tell him it was wrong, eating spoonful after spoonful with Ye Qin. Cheng Feichi only looked cold and detached. In truth, he calmly accepted all of Ye Qin's unruliness and impudence.

There was the sound of flowing water as Cheng Feichi showered in the bathroom.

Partitions in business hotels were more decent than most,

and though this one was made of frosted glass, it concealed the form inside.

Still, Ye Qin felt restless. He circled around an area of 30 square meters, walking to the door, balling up the wet shirt Cheng Feichi had removed, and cradling it in his lap. Then, he circled again and put it back quietly, red-faced.

When Cheng Feichi came out, Ye Qin was on a call with Zhou Feng. Recently, this guy called him up at all hours of the day, crying and howling.

"What did you say? Our high school reunion's tomorrow?"

Ye Qin caught a glimpse of Cheng Feichi's loose bathrobe and quickly looked away. "Uh, yeah. You didn't know?"

Zhou Feng swore. "Yuanyuan didn't say anything to me. He probably doesn't want me there."

"If he really doesn't want you there, he would have told me not to tell you," Ye Qin comforted. "Besides, the group chat is public. Anyone can see."

"True." Zhou Feng's fighting spirit suddenly came alight. "Where is it? When? Send me the location so I can switch shifts."

"It's just going to be our classmates there," Ye Qin reminded him. "Don't bring a gang with you to crash the party."

Zhou Feng had not been making any progress in his courtship as of late and was not in the best mental state. Every minute he seemed to be on the edge of total collapse, so it wouldn't be surprising if he took things too far.

"What are you even saying? I've always been a proper, law-abiding civilian police officer. You think I can do something like that?! Don't worry, this time I have a trump card. As long as we meet, I can capture his heart!" Zhou Feng said with confidence.

Ye Qin sighed. Having heard these words too many times, he'd already developed immunity. He hung up, and before he

could think of what to say, Cheng Feichi spoke first, "You have a class school reunion tomorrow?"

Ye Qin looked over. "Huh? Oh, yeah. A high school reunion."

"At noon?"

"Yeah."

Cheng Feichi briefly checked his phone calendar. "I'll get someone to drive you there, and I'll pick you up in the afternoon if I can make it in time."

Ye Qin had good dreams that night, likely because he received words that were more comforting than a promise. Plus, he had seen a few images that made his imagination run wild. When he looked into the mirror the next morning, his cheeks were dusted light pink. It was only after splashing his face repeatedly with cold water that he put an end to those devious thoughts.

On the other hand, Cheng Feichi was calm and collected after sharing a bed with him for a whole night, pouring him water and passing him food at breakfast as if nothing had happened.

As if they'd never fought and ignored each other, never broken up, never left each other for five years; as if it'd just been time that passed too quickly, and they'd both grown up in one night, naturally developing into this.

At first, Ye Qin planned to address how he'd almost lost his composure yesterday. Seeing Cheng Feichi so peaceful, however, he swallowed back his words and appreciated this rare and wondrous morning with him instead.

Because he had been crying yesterday, Ye Qin's eyes were swollen red. Thinking of how it was rather important to keep up appearances with his former classmates, he sat after breakfast with his head tilted up and covered his eyes with a cold towel.

Despite seeming like he had closed his eyes and was in a state of zen, Ye Qin actually heard every movement in the room, including Cheng Feichi's footsteps.

Not long after, there was a rustle of cloth as Cheng Feichi put on his coat to leave.

Ye Qin was about to take off the towel and get up when Cheng Feichi walked over and gently pressed it back on his eyes.

"I'm leaving now," his voice drifted down into Ye Qin's ears. "The driver will be downstairs at 10 a.m. sharp. I texted you the license plate. Make sure you get in the right car."

It was like he was talking to a kid about to leave the house for the first time in his life. Ye Qin's face burned up, and he nodded with a grunt.

The hand on the towel lifted, and his footsteps faded away. Ye Qin almost got to his feet again, wanting to walk with Cheng Feichi to the doorway, see him off, and say things like "take care" and "work hard," but Cheng Feichi came back.

This time, it was to say goodbye. He tilted Ye Qin's chin up and pressed a light kiss on his lips. "Bye-bye. See you in the afternoon."

The class reunion took place in a Chinese restaurant close to High School No. 6. Their private room on the second floor had a suspended terrace, and they just happened to see the school courtyard through the lattice of the wooden window. Liao Yifang had chosen this place very thoughtfully.

His former classmates also put in effort. Out of a class of 52, 37 showed up. Those who didn't show included three ladies who were either pregnant or postpartum, and eleven others far off who couldn't make it in time. Only one person was unaccounted for, Zhou Feng.

Once seated, Ye Qin sent him another text. When he didn't get a response for ten minutes, he looked around.

"Qin-ge, why are you looking around everywhere?" a woman called from across the table just as he was about to excuse himself. "Are you scared your fans followed you here?"

"It's better to be careful," Sun Yiran replied, "Our Qin-ge's super popular now. I have a bundle of postcards all from distant relatives asking for an autograph. Especially my cousin. She told me a thousand times to make sure I get one with a personal message."

"Last time I watched a movie with my parents, I told them the guy on screen is my former classmate," another man joined the conversation. "They didn't believe me. I said, 'This guy used to copy my homework all the time,' and my mom said, 'He's so handsome, you should let him copy your homework.' My own mother!"

Two tables of people burst into laughter.

His classmates were as kind and friendly as they had always been. They didn't go too far with the jokes. Neither did they make Ye Qin feel uneasy at all, just that coming here, getting together with friends once in a while, was the right decision. It put him in a cheerful mood.

Ye Qin had already been feeling good before this. The two kisses from last night and this morning, as different as night and day, lingered in his memory. Just the thought of them made his face red and heart thump, and he drank glass after glass of water at the table without a single bathroom break. His classmates all thought that he was embarrassed and switched to another topic.

"Speaking of which," another man said, "is anyone here looking for someone? We've got hot singles running around at our company. Anyone wanna swap numbers and save your parents the trouble of sorting things out for you at the match-making corner of People's Park?"

As soon as he said this, several people voiced their grievances at how their elders were starting to press for marriage not even two years out of university. They were practically trying to kill these young professionals who had just gone into working society.

Sun Yiran, already engaged, held a contrasting opinion. "Marriage isn't necessarily the death of love. How nice is it for two people to be together and share both the happy and the sad?"

Ye Qin finally managed to finish the pile of food Liao Yifang handed him, listening to them chatter on. Almost everyone at the table was done, and half of them left early, saying they had things to do. The other half continued partying at a nearby karaoke bar as per the original plan.

Ye Qin hadn't planned on going, but Zhou Feng still hadn't arrived yet, and he was worried something had happened. On the way there, he texted Cheng Feichi his plans and told him to go back to the hotel after work since he didn't know how much longer he would be out. Immediately after that, he swiped to the dialing interface and called Zhou Feng.

Still no answer. Ye Qin had no choice but to copy the karaoke bar's address and send it in a message.

Just as he put his cellphone back in his pocket, Sun Yiran caught up to him and took hold of his arm. "You really are something, Qin-ge. You run faster on your broken leg than me with all four limbs intact."

"I'm still practicing walking on both legs," Ye Qin said. "I'm even faster on one."

Playing along, Sun Yiran pretended to be greatly shocked. Two people who hadn't seen each other in ages talked about nothing and everything until the topic veered to Ye Qin's current situation.

"Hey, are you back together with him?" Sun Yiran whispered, hush-hush, and nudged him with an elbow.

Of course Ye Qin knew who "him" was. He had a reflexive urge to shake his head and tell her no but suddenly thought of the two kisses.

"Yeah," he said, licking his lips.

Sun Yiran was even more pleased than he was. She told him that she was going to set aside gift money for his wedding as soon as she got home. "What about that guy and the class monitor? I saw that he didn't come today, and I didn't dare mention him in front of him."

Ye Qin looked ahead to Liao Yifang at the lead. Occasionally, he could see his smiling face as he chatted with their classmates.

Ye Qin took out his cellphone and checked it again. No new messages. He furrowed his eyebrows. "That guy probably got sidetracked with an urgent mission to catch some cat or dog."

Why else would he not attend such a rare occasion?

The guy whose name didn't even get a mention really did get sidetracked, and it wasn't a trivial task like his previous dispatches. This was a proper mission to protect the interests of the people: to catch a thief.

Two hours earlier, he took off his uniform and changed into the new clothes he'd bought just yesterday. Then, he combed a smooth slick-back in front of the mirror in the workroom. Just as he left the police station, car keys swinging, a man swiped past him, followed by the sharp cry of a woman, "My purse! My purse! Robbery!"

This would be okay in any other downtown center, but right in front of the police station? How could he let that happen? Zhou Feng immediately gave chase.

Who would have thought the thief had such good feet? He ran faster than a rabbit, and Zhou Feng had to chase him down several streets to catch him. Even then, the thief refused to give up without a fight. The two of them wrestled in the alleyway, but Zhou Feng was ex-military after all, so it was a walk in the park for him to subdue a civilian with no military training.

But that thief was very cunning. Knowing that he couldn't win with brute force, he snuck a switchblade out of his pocket during the fight and hid it in his palm. While pretending to be subdued, he suddenly swiped it at Zhou Feng, who was caught off guard. Zhou Feng had been distracted and in a hurry when he'd cuffed the thief, so the latter was able to slice a two-inch wound into his arm.

This wound was honorable, much more honorable than breaking his arm when he fell from the tree rescuing a cat for the old granny in the neighborhood. Still, his face darkened.

To him, the wound was a small thing. More importantly, he couldn't go out like this, with his clothes ruined.

He ran, huffing, back to change. By the time he saw Ye Qin's message and caught up with them at the karaoke bar, it was already well into the afternoon. The traffic never stopped in this area, and it was hard just to find a parking spot. Finally, he saw one, only for the Mercedes-Benz coming from the other side to squeeze in first.

"Fuck," Zhou Feng cursed, angry enough to vomit blood. If not for the fact that he was a member of law enforcement and couldn't knowingly break the law, he would have parked somewhere random, penalties be damned.

The Benz's driver saw him and paused after driving its front wheels in. Zhou Feng hastily pulled the handbrake into park, got out, ran over, and knocked on the window, planning to make him a deal to park in the open space out back instead. There were lots of parking spots there. Zhou Feng was in a hurry. He needed this spot.

The driver politely rolled down the windows to listen. Zhou Feng went on and on, waving his hands around. But the driver just listened. He didn't say anything. After a while, Zhou Feng realized that this driver really was just a driver, and the chief figure sat in the back seat.

"We'll let you have this spot, then," the chief figure in the

back seat said after listening to his entire spiel. "We'll go somewhere else."

This voice sounded familiar. Zhou Feng craned his neck, peering into the back of the car. His lips broke into a grin. "Hey, Straight-A Cheng!"

Cheng Feichi came to pick up Ye Qin.

He finished work earlier than anticipated today, so he got there early. No matter where he parked his car, there wouldn't be any delay. Thus, he let Zhou Feng have it and told his driver to go to the east side of the building where, sure enough, there was an empty lot.

Just as they parked, another knock came on the car window.

It was his window this time, but the same knocker.

Hunched over, Zhou Feng spoke across the window, "I've been thinking about it, and I have some things to say to you face-to-face." Cheng Feichi opened the car door for him, but he waved his hands. "I won't be sitting. I'm in a hurry so I'll make things short."

Though he said he was in a hurry and seemed to be truly burning with impatience, Zhou Feng didn't miss a single crucial word.

"First of all, I want to apologize on behalf of my two friends, Yang Fan and Zhao Yue." Standing outside of the car, he bowed deeply, hitting his head on the door and covering it with his hand. "Back then, we were immature," he continued, "and did some...stuff that would still be considered offensive now. Even if I didn't say or do those things personally, I did participate. I didn't stop them. Nasty, childish, low, you can call me whatever. I admit I was wrong. You don't have to accept, but I still have to make a serious apology after all these years. I'm sorry."

Inside the car, Cheng Feichi opened and closed his mouth, about to say something, but once Zhou Feng began speaking, he didn't plan to give anyone else a chance. "I don't necessarily want to ask for your forgiveness. I just hope that you can keep in mind that we were all young and stupid back then. Don't be angry at A-Qin."

At this, Cheng Feichi had a somewhat different reaction, lifting his eyelids.

"I'm not excusing him by saying we were young and stupid. I'm not preventing you from being angry at him either. He deserves it. It's just...just..." Zhou Feng couldn't find the right words. "It's just, some things aren't what you think. He actually started to like you really early on. None of the words he said then were truly from the heart. He's just that kind of person. Even if he suffers, he'll die to save face.

"The day you came to the club, he pretended to throw out your ring in front of us. Later, he took it with him when we weren't paying attention. Then, on the day you broke up with him, he bought you a cake and the same model ring. He asked me to get it for him but when I arrived, he was squatting at the door. No matter what I yelled, he wouldn't respond, just searched for your ring like a madman.

"After driving you away, he lived like a shell of his former self, and even then, he still insisted on going to university. Said he promised you to get into C University, and he did, but because of his family crisis, he couldn't go. I was already enrolled in the army by that time. I didn't know his life was so hard. You know, too, how pampered he'd been. His snacks had to be imported, bed had to be made of fragrant rosewood, even his duvets had to be made of real silk and filled with duck down... Anyway, I can't imagine how he got through those days.

"I heard that you didn't get revenge on him or even say bad things to his face. I admire your generosity from the bottom of my heart. I'm also happy for him. It means he fell in love with

the right person. It was worth it to wait all these years. I've been rambling on for so long, but my point is, if you also can't let go of him, give him another chance. Who hasn't made a mistake before? And I promise I'm not just saying this as his friend!"

Zhou Feng held up his left hand with a grave expression. Seeing Cheng Feichi's face looking just as solemn inside the car, Zhou Feng relaxed and put down his hands. Cheng Feichi didn't think this was a joke.

"That's all I wanted to say. Gotta go now. I'm in a rush. We'll talk more when there's time."

Then he turned and ran off for ten meters before coming back.

"Uh, I thought of something important," he said, scratching his head. "A-Qin is...quite different now. No one can keep their sanity after falling through the clouds into the mud. It's already impressive how he's been so strong. Even though I don't really know what you used to like about him, if—and I'm saying if— you don't like how annoying and meek and hesitant to move forward he is now, don't worry. The truth is he's never changed his nature. With your impact, you just need to give him a teensy bit of patience. Please don't be mad at him."

Here, Zhou Feng clapped his hands. "To give a really bad example, um, if you sprinkle a bit of water on him, he'll come back to life. He sees you as his world. If you ignore him, he'll still be able to live and breathe, but his whole world will have collapsed. It'll be the same as if he died."

Ye Qin came out of the second-floor karaoke bar when it was almost dark. At the doorway, he looked around for a moment and spotted the license plate Cheng Feichi had told him about. Then, he wobbled over with one crippled leg. Cheng Feichi came out of the car and caught him halfway, nearly carrying him into the car.

"Did you wait very long? I wanted to leave earlier, but Zhou

Feng's so sketchy I have to keep an eye on him," Ye Qin explained hurriedly once he sat down.

Cheng Feichi nodded his understanding and then asked, "What happened to him?"

It was rare for Cheng Feichi to show interest in his friends. "He's pursuing someone. Here I thought he'd come up with a killer plan, charging in with so much confidence, and then..."

"Then?"

Ye Qin suddenly realized he'd said too much. Afraid Cheng Feichi would be annoyed at having to listen after a full day of work, he stuck his tongue out and illustrated succinctly, "...And then he lifted his shirt. He had a tattoo on his chest. He carved the name of the guy he's chasing onto his body."

The thought of that fiendish scene in the karaoke bar alone gave Ye Qin second-hand embarrassment.

His idea was not bad, however. The reason the class monitor didn't trust him was because he had once liked girls. Zhou Feng had to make the class monitor realize he couldn't be without him. At first, tattooing his name on his body seemed absolutely stupid and a bit unorthodox, but it was actually the right decision. Besides, judging by Liao Yifang's reaction, it really did work wonders.

It was very peaceful in the car. When they passed by High School No. 6, Ye Qin caught a few glimpses of those familiar gates from the window side. His mood gradually became lively. One moment he looked down, scratching his knees; the next he reached back, scratching his nape; the next he lifted the hem of his shirt, poking at his belly.

Catching movement in his peripheral vision, Cheng Feichi moved his eyes over to Ye Qin lifting his left sleeve cuff, baring a fair forearm. His fingers made strokes of something on it.

After eating dinner at the dorm, each sat on the sofa reading his own book. When Cheng Feichi got up and fetched a

coat to wear, Ye Qin thought he was going to leave. He followed him, hanging his head, reluctant to see him go. And yet Cheng Feichi said, "Grab some clothes. It's inconvenient to come here all the time."

Going into the king suite again, Ye Qin was happy beyond words. Who'd have thought a broken showerhead could bring this kind of fortune? Thank goodness he hadn't fixed it.

While Cheng Feichi showered, Ye Qin ran a hand through his half-dry hair and sent Zhou Feng a reply. Zhou Feng said super excitedly that Liao Yifang welcomed him with open arms and then stopped replying. Likely he was showering Liao Yifang with attention or...being intimate.

A couple that had just gotten back together would blaze like a dry wood, unable to be extinguished by all the emperor's men. It was completely different from his own situation.

Ye Qin rubbed the bedsheets beneath him. Last night, he and Cheng Feichi just pulled up the duvet and slept. Their most intimate gesture was him shifting closer to Cheng Feichi once the latter had fallen into a deep sleep. The more he thought about it, the more he thought he felt uncertain.

After all these years, did he not...want it at all?

Despite getting a solid answer, Ye Qin still found ways to wind himself into a dead end.

He was an action-oriented man. He didn't like to leave a problem unaddressed, whittling at his nerves. The best way was to resolve it immediately. And so, when Cheng Feichi came out after showering, Ye Qin pulled him over to sit on the edge of the bed and then sat on his knees behind him, toweling his hair dry.

As he did, he leaned forward towards him.

Perhaps out of concern about hitting the injured man's leg, Cheng Feichi didn't push him away. It was only when he had been pushed halfway down and propped up by his hand from behind, that Cheng Feichi laughed. "What are you doing?"

Immediately, Ye Qin was dumbfounded. He couldn't remember how long it had been since he'd seen Cheng Feichi laugh. With one hand on Cheng Feichi's chest and the other cupping his face, he wanted to preserve this smile forever.

"Nothing," he replied, "Just looking at...how handsome my gege is."

When he no longer practiced his bad habit of speaking contrarily, Ye Qin was a straight-shooter who said the first thing that came to mind. He thought that he might look somewhat silly like this. He had no clue that his undisguised sincerity was what attracted Cheng Feichi above all. Being looked at by beautiful, bright, obsidian eyes, and being called "gege" with wholehearted dependence brought Cheng Feichi's quiet heart back to life and made it beat powerfully in his chest for the first time in ages.

Ye Qin's body was suddenly flipped over. Before he could even register what had happened, he was pressed underneath Cheng Feichi.

"Your leg isn't even better yet, and you're moving around like this?"

When he saw Cheng Feichi's dark eyes, Ye Qin knew it had worked. He raised his injured leg and wrapped it around Cheng Feichi's waist. "As long as...my gege's leg isn't broken."

He only felt embarrassed after saying it, hiding his eyes with the back of his hand. When nothing happened for a while, he parted his fingers to peek at the man above him, only to see a large shadow. Before he could close his lips, they were sealed.

This time, the kiss was very light and soft. Heated lips ran past the corners of his mouth down to his chin and neck. There, they quivered continuously at his throat before finally landing on his chest between his lapels. Again and again, they gently touched that delicious, sensitive area.

The warm breaths brushing on his chest made Ye Qin itch and his face burn terribly. Heat slowly started spanning through his whole body. "W-what are you doing?" he asked, moving his hands away from his eyes.

Cheng Feichi looked up at him with laughter yet to dissipate in his eyes. "Watering you."

At this, Ye Qin's whole body shook. He had clearly been the one seducing Cheng Feichi, yet he felt so embarrassed now he wanted to hide in a hole.

Biting on his lip so hard he almost drew blood, Ye Qin finally summoned the courage to grab Cheng Feichi's hand. He raised and folded his legs on both sides of Cheng Feichi's body. "I...already prepped myself while showering..."

Cheng Feichi paused and let Ye Qin tug his hand to his loose waistband. Then his lips curved up, coming to a sudden realization.

This little guy gave "showering" a seductive meaning in his head.

He extracted his hand and propped up his upper body. "Your leg hasn't fully healed yet. Just rest."

On a normal day, Ye Qin certainly would have listened to him, but now that they were in this situation, how could he not lose face if he chickened out? Going all in, he trailed his hand down to the already responsive bulge at Cheng Feichi's groin. He then withdrew his hand, somewhat embarrassed, but quickly put it back and gave it a firm squeeze. "You're...hard. Let me help you, okay?"

Then he peeled off Cheng Feichi's bathrobe and cupped his enthusiastic erection through the thin underwear.

Cheng Feichi's eyes instantly darkened. He wasn't a person of desire, physically or emotionally. There were very few things he'd wanted in the past few years, especially after going overseas.

He had become increasingly numb to his studies, work, and life, as if living in an ascetic state.

This wasn't bad, he had thought. Desire is a gateway to greed. Having nothing to yearn for meant that he wouldn't be hurt.

But ever since reuniting with Ye Qin, that state gradually shattered. This little guy always had a way of stirring up the desire hidden deep within his heart, just as he had six years ago.

If Cheng Feichi was a flammable object hidden in the dark, Ye Qin was a tiny spark that could set him alight.

What happened next came from unrestricted instinct. They tangled together, touching each other impatiently, removing each other's hindering clothes. Bending his torso, Ye Qin tilted his hips towards Cheng Feichi. He stroked Cheng Feichi's hefty erection clumsily and guided it to his lower parts.

"Gege...gege, come in, come in."

At first, Cheng Feichi wasn't in a rush, but his heart melted when Ye Qin called him gege over and over. He leaned down and sucked kisses on Ye Qin's neck before gently biting on his shoulder. He brushed the erect red nipples on Ye Qin's chest with his fingers and gasped in his ear, "What's the hurry?"

Already made weak by him, Ye Qin felt even more bashful hearing this. For a second, he didn't know whether to blame himself for lacking charm or feel angry at how composed Cheng Feichi was. Withdrawing his hand, Ye Qin turned to get out.

But Cheng Feichi caught his arm and put it on his own waist. "Where are you going?"

Cheng Feichi had a rather high body temperature, and the touch burned initially, but he felt so good. He had a thin layer of muscle on his torso that made him look lean and strong but not too over the top. His muscle contours undulated gently in tune with his breaths. His warmth transferred through the hand Ye Qin had on his body, spreading from Ye Qin's palm all over his

body and wrapping him in it. It didn't take long for Ye Qin to totally forget why he had been about to hide.

Cheng Feichi was scared to hurt him. Even if Ye Qin said he had prepared himself, he still reached down and stretched him patiently with his fingers.

Ye Qin couldn't see down there. Just the thought of Cheng Feichi's beautiful, slender hand moving in and out of him made his face blood red. Those buried fingers curved into another angle, nudging a sensitive spot somewhere inside. He arched back in a long moan and tightened the hand on Cheng Feichi's waist.

When Cheng Feichi actually entered him, Ye Qin felt the hard, thick erection split open his twitching little hole, stretching it wide and sliding in so smoothly. He only then started to respond, red lips trembling obscenely as he grabbed one of Cheng Feichi's arms that were propping him up.

"Does it hurt?" Cheng Feichi asked, warm and caring.

Biting his lips, Ye Qin shook his head vigorously. Cheng's Feichi's every motion was as gentle as could be. At most, he felt a bit full.

It was just, he was so happy. Joining together with his gege once more almost made him cry. He thought of that time five years ago. Neither of them had any skill. They relied on hot blood to fumble through the act. Back then, he didn't know how to be considerate and cried out for Cheng Feichi to stop at the tiniest bit of discomfort. Like an idiot, he didn't know why the man on top of him became more excited the more he cried, until his body was limp, and he could no longer protest.

This time, wanting Cheng Feichi to feel good, he didn't hold back his voice. When that member entered his body, pressing and rubbing against the sensitive flesh inside, Ye Qin openly moaned. He wrapped both arms tightly around Cheng Feichi's neck and coiled his legs around his waist, feet swaying in the air as Cheng

Feichi began to go faster.

At first, Cheng Feichi moved quite slowly. He held onto Ye Qin's injured leg with one hand, afraid that he would fall, and cradled his face with the other. Every few seconds, Cheng Feichi asked him if he felt okay. Finally, Ye Qin couldn't bear it anymore and told him to go faster, blushing. Only then did he let go, lift Ye Qin's waist and pound hard, pulling out and entering to the fullest with each thrust. The sound of slapping skin blurred together, spreading wantonly throughout the whole room.

Ye Qin felt his lower parts pounded to tenderness with a few thrusts. When that strong, thick erection ground past his entrance, squeezed open the folds deep within him, and rubbed against his sensitive spot, pleasure spread to the tips of his nerves like an electric current. His elbows pressed down on the bed sheets, his knees hooked around Cheng Feichi's waist, and his feet rocking to the motion all flushed crimson.

From his angle, Cheng Feichi could openly see the seductive look Ye Qin put on while aroused.

Ye Qin's skin was as fair as snow. Any touch could leave behind a trace of red. Right now, naked, his body was even warmer and smoother, as if Cheng Feichi could squeeze out water with a gentle press; particularly that round ass that looked like it was moving forward with every thrust. Lifting it with one big hand, he looked to see flesh rippling and the cleft fully red, like a peach in the summertime.

It was only a moment ago that Ye Qin had been loose and brazen, but now that Cheng Feichi did this, he cowered and stuttered, "D-don't look. G--gege, don't look."

It was embarrassing to have his lower body on display, after all. Ye Qin reached out to cover it, only for Cheng Feichi to stop him easily. The hand that Ye Qin could never appreciate enough gripped the erection on his abs. Cheng Feichi stroked him up and

down without stopping the thrusts into his lower body. Pleasure flooding in from both areas stripped Ye Qin of all thought and he was left to cry wantonly.

Since Ye Qin was skinny, Cheng Feichi particularly liked to search out the meatiest parts of his body. After thrusting quickly over a hundred times, he dragged up Ye Qin's two buttocks, kneading them round and flat, playing with them obscenely while smacking them back onto his own body. The position not only didn't place pressure on Ye Qin's injured leg, but also aroused him even more.

Cheng Feichi only had to lower his head a little to see himself moving in and out of Ye Qin's body. That red, swollen entrance gripped his shaft tightly. That soft flesh dragged as he pulled out and shrank obediently as he thrust back in. Squelches and slaps made it clear that they were doing the most intimate act in the world. This knowledge alone dilated Cheng Feichi's blood vessels and gave him spurts of unending strength.

Ye Qin came very quickly, hot liquid splashing on his own abs and Cheng Feichi's hands. After coming, his body was more sensitive, and his hole started twitching on its own. Dazed, he could only hear Cheng Feichi's rough pants above him. Eyes fuzzy and unable to see clearly, Ye Qin urgently reached out to touch him. Cheng Feichi read his thoughts with one glance and guided his hand to his face.

Ye Qin slowly slid his hand down Cheng Feichi's protruding browbone to the corner of his eye, his eyelashes, nose bridge, and slightly parted lips. The familiarity of these features blanketed him with comfort, and he laughed. "Gege, gege, you're back."

Then, he wanted to cry. Truly unable to hold back, his fingertips trembled, and tears flooded out.

Cheng Feichi's heart hurt like it had been stabbed. The last chunk of ice inside melted into the trickling waters of spring.

They'd spent so much more time apart than together. For more than a thousand nights, how did Ye Qin bear these memories? How did he force a smile in front of the mirror and urge himself to wait for Cheng Feichi's return?

Cheng Feichi leaned over and swept Ye Qin into his arms, still buried inside his lower body. Their skin pressed together, breaths intermingling, as inseparable as if they were one.

"Yes," Cheng Feichi whispered in his ear, "I'm back."

Afterwards, the tedious clean-up almost made Ye Qin flop down in the bathroom once and for all. With his eyes shut half passed out beside Cheng Feichi, he still stuck out his lips in a pout.

He had been the one pleading and crying for Cheng Feichi to come inside. Then, he had been the one pulling open the bathroom door with red eyes to say that he couldn't get it out. Now, after Cheng Feichi had cleaned him up, Ye Qin dragged his feet back to bed and took Cheng Feichi's arm hostage. It was as if his arrogant, unreasonable ways had returned.

I did not water him for nothing, Cheng Feichi thought.

The next morning, Cheng Feichi woke up from a tickle at the heart of his palm. When he opened his eyes, he saw Ye Qin's shaggy head pressed into his shoulder. He was lifting Cheng Feichi's palm, face down, and touching light kisses to that scar. Very patiently, he kissed from left to right and back along the same path. "No more pain, no more pain," Ye Qin whispered as he kissed, like chanting a spell.

Who did he learn that from?

When Ye Qin got out of bed and went into the bathroom for his morning routine, Cheng Feichi "woke up," opened the bathroom door, and "happened to catch" him putting a necklace on.

With nowhere to hide, Ye Qin closed his eyes and let him approach like he was peacefully welcoming death. Cheng Feichi slowly lifted the ring around his neck.

"Didn't you throw it away?"

Such an oppressing voice almost made Ye Qin cry from distress. *I can't believe you're questioning me when I don't even know where you threw the one I gave you,* he thought.

Whereas he said properly, "No, I never threw it away. I wear it every day, and I won't...ever throw it away."

Cheng Feichi had originally wanted to use this ring as a pretext to ask if Ye Qin was still hiding anything from him. However, after seeing Ye Qin scrunch his neck as if waiting to be punished for something he'd done wrong, he didn't have the heart. Detaching the ring from the thin string, he lifted Ye Qin's left hand and pushed it to the base of his ring finger.

Not too loose, not too tight. Perfect.

Ye Qin was still frozen. Cheng Feichi pulled Ye Qin's hand to his lips and kissed Ye Qin like he had kissed him. As Cheng Feichi lowered his head and touched his lips gently to the back of Ye Qin's left hand, he curved his lips and said, "It doesn't hurt anymore."

Ye Qin's eyes went red.

He knew, he knew it all.

He knew his old habits had returned—nothing was for certain without first giving something in return. What he did yesterday was no different than an offer of sacrifice. He still chose compromise and acceptance. He knew too that he hid a lot of petty thoughts he didn't dare show the world, but now Cheng Fe-ichi walked towards him. *Don't worry,* he said. *I'm willing to hear you say them slowly.*

In the past twenty years, even if Ye Qin had been silent about it, he also ran into hardships at times and suffered. In those times, he also thought he had a tough life. First, he hadn't been careful making friends. Then, he kept running into bad company. After going through so many lessons, not only did he stay an idiot, but also didn't improve his personality. The fall of their family mostly fell on Ye Jinxiang's shoulders, but as a member of the household, he hadn't been of any help and had even added oil to fire: he had a hand in his mother's death.

How could someone as bad as him deserve to meet someone as good as Cheng Feichi? Be loved by him? Protected by him? Ye Qin made such a big mistake, and Cheng Feichi still forgave him.

The world was so big. What was so good about someone so insignificant like Ye Qin?

When the person in front of Cheng Feichi threw himself at him, he was prepared. He caught Ye Qin and hooked Ye Qin's arms around his waist. "Your leg..." he reminded habitually.

Ye Qin didn't care about arms and legs and whatnot. Even if his life force was cut short, he would still throw himself at Cheng Feichi in a huge embrace.

"I'll...I'll—"

Despite being on the tip of his tongue the words still didn't come out.

A thousand words could not express his feelings and loyalty better than one solid action.

Ye Qin hugged Cheng Feichi tightly, burying his face in the crook of his neck. He inhaled Cheng Feichi's nice scent and closed his eyes. *I'll be good to you,* he said inwardly, *very, very good. I'll never make you suffer again.*

Whether it's the clear dew on flower petals or the gorgeous sunlight at dawn, you deserve all the good the world has to offer.

First of all, he had to give Cheng Feichi the best boyfriend in the world.

Okay, so that was impossible for now, but at least people should know what was good about him.

Barely a few days after the class reunion, Ye Qin busied himself going back to work. The two weeks of "Avancez!" attracted

quite a bit of praise. His natural, unembellished performance had surprisingly drawn a group of fans. The idol drama had also put out some stills, and Ye Qin in a school uniform managed to make it into a certain site's trending topic, "Top 10 Ten Actors with the Most Youthful Vibes."

Although his votes couldn't compare to popular young stars with their huge number of fans, many passersby noticed him because of his photo's excellent lighting. One of the posts in the trending topic said that seeing him made them think of green grass and blue skies.

On the last day of voting, Ye Qin had originally been ranked eleventh. But because the seventh actor had just been involved in a scandal and had his name taken off the list, he got ushered into the top ten by a stroke of dumb luck. Moreover, because of this, he got an invite to Star TV's Mid-Autumn Festival evening banquet to perform a song about youth with the other actors on the list.

Zheng Yueyue smiled so wide that her lips couldn't close. Two weeks ahead of time, she began to take care of Ye Qin's outfit for the banquet. She even told him to go try it on.

"Not bad. You didn't get fat. Looks like you took my words to heart." She looked even happier seeing him in person, clapping him on the back.

Ye Qin had a different focus. As he spread both arms out and turned around for her to assess the outfit, he craned his neck and asked, "Is there gonna be a reward for going to the banquet?"

Zheng Yueyue rolled her eyes. "Be glad you have a chance to go. He Hansong tried to worm his way in and still couldn't get an invite. Going to such a high-exposure banquet once is like plating yourself with a layer of gold. They didn't even ask you to pay promotional fees."

She thought it weird that Ye Qin had disappointment all over his face. "Once you get paid by the drama, won't your debts almost be settled? What, you got other problems?"

Ye Qin went through his accounts in his head. "No, no, but who doesn't want to earn a bit more? Right?"

Zheng Yueyue joked that he was money-obsessed and how, once he blew up, he'd have so much money he wouldn't know what to spend it on.

Ye Qin still felt vexed. He needed money so he could buy Cheng Feichi nice things!

He used to express his love through spending. If he couldn't even get what his partner wanted, then he wasn't qualified to be a boyfriend.

Though considering Cheng Feichi's current financial state, he probably didn't care about the things that Ye Qin wanted to give.

Ye Qin's first gig going back to work was a concert at a shopping center. Cheng Feichi had some rare downtime, so he drove him there personally.

"We've been here before... D'you still remember the mutton and bread stew in that restaurant? We ate barbeque here in second year..." Ye Qin chattered nonstop the whole time. Wherever they went, he had a story.

When they were almost at the shopping center, Ye Qin's eyes brightened at the overhead sign. "They just rebuilt Times Square two years ago. When you used to work here, you said you would take me upstairs to eat dessert without having to line up..."

Ye Qin self-consciously lowered his voice and pressed his lips shut.

For him, all these memories were beautiful and happy, but for Cheng Feichi, they might not be. Cheng Feichi's life had been hard in those times, especially with Ye Qin always tagging along and bringing him trouble. Even if they did have some beauty, it had probably faded away.

"Why'd you stop?" Cheng Feichi asked, turning left at the

intersection.

"I forgot what I was about to say," Ye Qin answered gloomily.

"I'll drop you off at the entrance," Cheng Feichi said, dropping the matter. "I won't be going in. I'll come pick you up after the event is over."

Though the event was scheduled to start at 2:30 p.m., it was actually pushed back forty minutes.

Because more fans had shown up than was expected, the shopping center urgently dispatched two security teams, refenced the area, and directed the fans to line up in an orderly manner.

Ye Qin didn't idle during this time either. With his left leg propped on a chair, he did some small physical therapy exercises as he chatted with Liao Yifang, who had come to watch him.

"What?" Ye Qin exclaimed with his leg bent halfway. "That was a temporary tattoo?"

Liao Yifang nodded. "Yes. Officers aren't allowed to have tattoos. I knew it was fake as soon as I saw it."

"Did he admit it?"

"It's not like he can deny it," Liao Yifang stated calmly. "It disappeared with one shower. When I opened the bathroom door, he was applying a new one on his chest."

Imagining that scene, Ye Qin couldn't help but look away and close his eyes. This was too embarrassing. He should just pretend not to know that guy from now on.

"So, do you still believe him?" Ye Qin probed.

At first, Liao Yifang's half-hooded eyes looked nowhere in particular. Then, he lifted his eyelids. "Yesterday, he didn't even go to the hospital after injuring himself, just to rush over to see me. His wound was still bleeding when I saw it. It dyed his clothes red."

This sympathy magnet of an injury came at just the right time, Ye Qin thought. On the surface, he appeared puzzled.

"Then, do you...forgive him, class monitor?"

Liao Yifang looked helpless. "Forgive? I couldn't resist him from the beginning. It's laughable how I act like the bygones are bygones and I have no grudges or complaints. The truth is I've never forgotten any of that, or him. The truth is I kept turning him down and treating him with indifference because I wanted to make things hard for him. Because I was unhappy and wanted him to taste what I suffered, and not necessarily because I truly can't accept his feelings."

Ye Qin seemed to understand his explanation and also seemed to not understand a single word. Only when he applied those thoughts to Cheng Feichi did he feel a little sympathy.

"But you're still kind, class monitor," he told him with a smile. "You obviously knew this would hurt him more than anything, but you still held back. You didn't sink to his level. I know that he also knows deep down. Maybe he even hopes for this situation to last longer so he can make up for what you once lost. But you cut it short out of kindness. You gave him what he wanted and with a lot less suffering. If you think about it that way, do you not blame yourself as much?"

Unexpectedly discovering a natural gift for comforting others, Ye Qin got on stage beaming. Then, he startled at the dense audience.

In the past, it would have already been impressive just to fill up the inner area lined off by the host at a concert in a shopping center. Now, he could see a sea of people from the stage. They were squeezed together even behind the railings of the second-floor balcony, holding signs that said "Ye Qin's Worldwide Fanclub." Someone had even printed out a still from the youthful idol drama and made it into a poster they were holding over their head.

Heaven knows how many years it had been since Ye Qin saw this level of support. For a moment, he felt nervous. He stuttered

through the hype-up segment, forgetting his words and missing jokes that the host sent his way. It wasn't until the fan interaction after that he relaxed a little.

A fangirl asked him how his leg injury was and told him to please, please not run around until it's healed. Ye Qin instantly demonstrated his high-low step. He told her that while his leg was broken, he was 170 cm on his injured leg and 180 cm on his good one. He switched seamlessly from 170 cm to 180 cm just like a seesaw.

The audience burst into laughter. "Qin-Qin, how are you 180 centimeters?" one fan gibed loudly.

"Shh," Ye Qin said with an air of mystique, putting his index finger to his lips. "All you insiders, please give me a bit of face. Baidu says I'm 180."

Even the Q&A that Ye Qin had been afraid of the most turned out joyous. Several new fans asked him what he planned to work on in the future. After that, a familiar old fan took the mic. They didn't ask anything but stayed silent and finally apologized, saying that in his hardest and most painful times, they had left him to be a fan of another idol. Now they came back and pretended to be one of the originals. They once promised to always follow him, but couldn't even do that.

Ye Qin squeezed the microphone, unsure of how to respond. He felt panicked and somewhat lost. He always thought that he didn't deserve their love. He only went into showbiz for money. When he ran into his fans, he normally tried to treat them as nicely as possible and satisfy their requests as best as he could. Suddenly hearing words of such devotion, *he* was the one feeling guiltiest.

Then, the mic somehow got passed to Liao Yifang amidst the group of fans. The surrounding fangirls all heckled this rare "fanboy" to say something.

Liao Yifang blushed and said evasively, "All hardships serve to strengthen our will. In other words, we go through hardships to become a better version of ourselves. It's not wrong to count our past mistakes, but more importantly, we should look forward... Go Ye Qin! Go everyone!"

That Liao-style optimism was the same as it had ever been, bringing great laughter to everyone.

On stage, Ye Qin laughed so hard he almost cried. Old fans and the class monitor's words touched a deep place in his heart that had never been reached before. Perhaps it was because of this that after six years in the industry, Ye Qin found meaning in his job for the first time.

He had gone into showbiz for the money as a completely clueless teenager, stumbling his way through until today. There had been times when he'd been tremendously popular with endless possibilities, and there had been times when he'd fallen into a deep hole and spiraled without moving forward. Fortunately, the people accompanied him step by step from ignorance to maturity, whether they helped him or stepped on him, whether they were still here or gone, all made a valuable and indispensable experience in his life.

"Happiness and hardship may come one after another but to me, you don't. Thank you. Thank you, everyone."

With that, he bowed deeply to the audience.

Since the event started late, it also finished much later than expected.

As it was too late to make dinner back at the hotel, Cheng Feichi and Ye Qin went out for hotpot.

They headed back on full bellies. Sitting in the front passenger seat, Ye Qin opened letters from his fans. Thinking that the car was too quiet, he read them aloud, lowering his voice and mumbling through the occasional embarrassing part.

He hadn't assumed Cheng Feichi would listen while focusing on driving, but Cheng Feichi suddenly asked at a red light, "What was that just now? I didn't quite hear."

Ye Qin jolted and reread, "Sometimes, I think you're like my didi, innocent and cute."

Long fingers tapped on the steering wheel. "Before that."

Ye Qin could never bring himself to lie to him. "Something I think you're like my boyfriend..." he forced himself to say, "... warm and considerate."

And then he shifted his eyes and stealthily examined Cheng Feichi's expression. The sight of him—silent, his lips pursed— sent bursts of panic through Ye Qin's heart.

"They don't come one after another?" Cheng Feichi asked steadily when the light turned green, and the car finally drove on.

Ye Qin had no idea how Cheng Feichi heard the words he'd said earlier in the shopping center. He felt too ashamed to hold his head up.

Back in the hotel, Cheng Feichi went about his own business in silence, eyes thoroughly glued to the laptop screen. Next to him, Ye Qin finally saw an opportunity when he got up to get a glass of water. Hugging Cheng Feichi's arm, he whispered, "Gege..."

"Hm?" Cheng Feichi looked over at him.

Ye Qin licked his lips and summoned courage. "They don't come one after another because you're always in my heart. You never, never left."

At that moment, his greatest fear was for Cheng Feichi to misunderstand him. All the words he had once been too embarrassed to say, he forced himself to say them now. But this was above his capabilities, harder than a direct confession. No words could capture a thousandth of what he wanted to express.

As expected, Cheng Feichi made a puzzled face. "Oh?"

Ye Qin felt that he couldn't wash himself clean of this

even if he jumped into the Yellow River. "I've said before that I won't lie to you anymore," he said, swinging Cheng Feichi's arm. "Whoever lies is a...is a dog."

That flag was raised easily and fell over faster than a passing typhoon.

The next day, before leaving, Cheng Feichi finally returned Ye Qin's jacket with a reminder to check the pockets to see if anything was missing.

Of course there wouldn't be. But finding a star scared the soul out of Ye Qin.

Cheng Feichi buttoned his cuff links leisurely as he put on his suit. "Where did the star come from?" he asked, casting a glance at Ye Qin's closed hand.

Ye Qin hadn't finished them yet. Based on his past progress of folding three a day, 520 stars would have taken close to half a year. Initially, he thought that he could almost get back with Cheng Feichi in that time. Who knew he would make such substantial progress? Ye Qin didn't want to finish folding them all in one day just for show, so he continued to do it according to his original plan.

Who would have thought he'd ruin the surprise from accidental negligence. Now wonder Cheng Feichi asked him if there" was anything else he should know."

With the way things were now, he had no choice but to play dumb. "What stars? I don't know about any stars," he said, putting his hands behind his back and looking up.

Cheng Feichi stared, but unexpectedly didn't expose him.

Two days later, Ye Qin finally couldn't hold back any longer and asked him about the ring.

"What ring?" Cheng Feichi answered with his exact words, blankly and innocently.

Ye Qin almost choked. *I'll have you wear that ring sooner or*

later, he later thought, touching the ring on his own finger.

He patted his anxious, racing heart. Thank goodness his gege was too handsome and kind to really make him learn how to bark.

This year, the Mid-Autumn Festival fell close to National Day, so the statutory holidays were combined.

But for those in showbiz like Ye Qin, holidays are never a regularity. He finished filming only two days before the banquet and had a magazine shoot on the morning of Mid-Autumn. Just as he had gotten off work, Cheng Feichi texted him that he had arrived at the airport.

Ye Qin quickly called him. "Is the plane delayed? Did you bring all of your stuff?" he asked. He kept stalling, clingy and unwilling to hang up.

He wanted to spend Mid-Autumn in S-City with Cheng Feichi, but he had work. Plus, Cheng Feichi didn't invite him, so he didn't have a proper reason for going.

Thinking of how he had to eat mooncake alone tonight, Ye Qin's mood plummeted. "Can I eat two pieces of chocolate tonight?" he negotiated with Cheng Feichi over the phone.

In the short time they were together, Cheng Feichi discovered that Ye Qin had gone back to his old habit of eating snacks for meals when work got busy. Thereafter, he limited how many snacks Ye Qin could have in a day.

"Yes," Cheng Feichi allowed, probably because Ye Qin sounded so sad over the phone.

"And another pack of gummies?"

"Yes."

"Can I stay up later then? I'm scheduled to go on late for the banquet tonight. I won't perform until after 11."

"Yes."

Having unlocked the achievement of receiving permission

three times in a row, Ye Qin's morale ran high. He used the momentum to ask the question he had been mulling over for several days already. "Then, what do you like most, the inner arm, inner thigh, or the side of my body?"

The sudden change in topic didn't manage to disrupt Cheng Feichi's thoughts. "No," he said without hesitation.

Ye Qin was silent.

Before hanging up, Cheng Feichi lowered his voice and reiterated with no room for argument, "No tattoos."

At night, Ye Qin lay on the bed listlessly. The lively, jubilant sounds from the TV couldn't cheer him up.

They stayed in the suite for so long that he felt increasingly in need of a place of his own. Even though Cheng Feichi was only living in the capital temporarily, Ye Qin wanted to give him a home here. He wanted Cheng Feichi to have a permanent place to go when his flight landed. A place with hot meals, fresh sheets, and Ye Qin always waiting.

Cheng Feichi didn't let him engrave his name on his body, fine. Could Ye Qin at least buy a house and trap him inside?

Ye Qin hugged his pillow and rolled on the bed at the thought. When he went back to browsing on his phone, his face was still red, the heat yet to subside.

But the cruelty of reality shattered his dreams. Housing prices in the capital remained sky-high. Ye Qin went from new home listings to second-hand housing sites, growing more and more despondent.

The prices were expensive enough to make his chocolate lose taste.

Frowning, he went for the next best thing and opened a rental website. It wasn't so bad to rent for the time being; better than burning money every day on this hotel room. He could take on a few more dramas and do a few more concerts. And

forget about buying anything within the ring roads; the air was fresher in the suburbs anyway. They didn't need a huge place for the two of them either. If he worked hard, he could still manage a down payment.

Even later, he got a call from Cheng Feichi.

"Did you get home?"

"Mmhm."

"Did you see Huihui?"

"Yes, he's eating mooncake."

Ye Qin heard Cheng Feichi's voice fade before another boy's voice came on the phone, "Hello, Ruan-gege, I'm Huihui!"

His loud, energetic voice made Ye Qin's eardrums throb. "Hello Huihui," he greeted, rubbing the base of his ear.

He and the kid debated the best filling for mooncake. As they were trying to choose between nuts and fruits or egg yolk, Cheng Feichi grabbed the phone back. "There's a key on the entryway cabinet."

Ye Qin got up from the bed and walked there to check. "Yes, there is. What about it?"

"I'll send you the address in a second. If you don't want to stay at the hotel, you can wait for me there."

There was a pause before Ye Qin reacted, "You bought a place?"

"Yes, an apartment. It's not very big. It'll make do for now."

Ye Qin didn't speak for quite a while.

"Ye Qin?" Cheng Feichi asked under the impression that he hadn't been listening.

That brought Ye Qin back to his senses. "Didn't you tell Huihui that my name is Ye Ruan? Now you're calling me Ye Qin?" he fussed, latching onto this while hyped up with excitement. He scratched his hair and made a sulky face. "If you hide anything from me again, I'll...I'll..."

He didn't finish because he couldn't.

He couldn't bear to threaten this darling gege, not even as a joke—this darling gege that he tried so hard to get, who already thought of and arranged everything before him.

Ye Qin was agitated by the current state of things. He didn't want to always be taken care of by Cheng Feichi. He also wanted to take care of him. He wanted Cheng Feichi to be able to work without worry and not have to rack his brains over these other trifles.

"Then you buy the apartment," he decided, "and I'll pay for renovations."

"Renovations?"

"Yeah. Think of it as dow—"

He promptly covered his mouth before blurring out the word, not even daring to breathe heavily. His eyes, exposed, were perfect spheres.

He almost said it. Thank goodness he pulled the brakes in time.

There was a temporary pause on the other side of the call. "As what?" Cheng Feichi urged.

Mouth covered, Ye Qin shook his head like a rattle drum. "Nothing. Nothing."

Quiet laughter came from the speakers, and Ye Qin's heart clenched. Before he could change the topic, Cheng Feichi asked, "Dowry?"

CHAPTER 26

THAT night, Ye Qin opened the door to his new apartment with a red face.

It was a very good place, a quiet high-rise in the middle of the city close to many subway lines. The dowry was forfeit, as the apartment was already elegantly designed and all the main furniture provided so that he could just pick up his bags and move in.

It might have been a coincidence, but the apartment layout was identical to the one they had been living together in in Jiayuan Compound. Ye Qin wandered back and forth between two rooms of the same size and finally chose the eastern one.

Back then, they also stayed in the east room. The feng shui was good there, auspicious.

The bedding and pillows were all new. Ye Qin spent a bit of time unpacking and laying them out. He jumped and rolled on the bed after, thinking that if the sun was nice tomorrow, he could air them out on the balcony. Then, Cheng Feichi would have warm, fluffy blankets when he came back.

Ye Qin only unpacked one blanket. After moving in chairs and a rug, he stuffed the other into the top shelf of the wardrobe. Done tidying, he lay down on the bed to measure it. It should be big enough for two people. If not, then...they could scooch closer together.

He rolled over a few more times and got up blissfully to have mooncake. It didn't feel too bad to spend Mid-Autumn alone anymore.

The mooncake with egg yolk filling was given to him by Zheng Yueyue. It looked and tasted okay. Initially, he planned on sending a picture to Cheng Feichi, but thinking of how Cheng Feichi had to spend the holiday with both his brother and his mother, Ye Qin thought he should be more considerate and not disturb him. Thus, he put his cellphone away.

After eating, he lay stomach down on the bed and went back to watching TV, focusing in anticipation of his sparkling entrance. Too bad he had gotten up early for work for several days already and was fighting drooping eyelids before it turned ten. Not even dialing up the volume helped. Halfway into the driest skit ever, Ye Qin's head lolled onto the pillow, and he fell asleep.

It was bright and sunny the next day. Dazed and feeling a heat source beside him, Ye Qin scooched over his limbs, hugging the ball of warmth. Smacking his lips, he slept for a few more minutes until he smelled a strong, chocolatey aroma and opened his eyes drowsily.

The first thing that entered his eyes was a half-open chocolate bar. Ye Qin instinctively opened his mouth, but the chocolate had legs and he didn't get a single bite. He tried again and again, and when he craned his neck forward, he was suddenly met by something warm and soft.

Lips.

Ye Qin hooked his arms around the neck of the man before him, deepening the kiss.

It was a while before they parted reluctantly. Ye Qin's eyes

were even mistier than when he first woke up. Looking straight at Cheng Feichi who looked back at him, he stuck out a bright red tongue and licked his lips.

"Good morning, gege," he gasped lightly.

As they ate breakfast at the dining table of the new apartment, Ye Qin suddenly came to a realization. "Did you already get back last night?"

"Yes." Cheng Feichi set down the glass in his hands.

Ye Qin's eyes grew wide. "Why didn't you wake me up?"

"You were sleeping so soundly. Why should I have woken you up?" Cheng Feichi laughed.

Never feeling more regret in his life, Ye Qin wished he had taken a few more cups of coffee and stayed up longer. Then he could have watched himself on TV with Cheng Feichi.

As if reading his thoughts, Cheng Feichi turned on the TV after breakfast, fast rewinding the program to the exact spot where Ye Qin came on.

Because he had performed in a group and had the lowest standing among the male artists, Ye Qin didn't get many angles. He did sing, however. Ye Qin's advantage of having been a singer for several years really showed under these circumstances. Everyone else's voices were wispy during the chorus even with post-production editing. It was obvious that he carried the group. No wonder some people joked that "so and so TV" probably invited Ye Qin because they were afraid that, otherwise, this trainwreck would cause controversy and be painful to watch.

Three short minutes passed by very quickly. Ye Qin's ears still burned after turning off the TV.

As they did the dishes in the kitchen, he peeked at Cheng Feichi's expression while jotting down what essential seasonings they needed to buy. Cheng Feichi naturally registered these burning hot looks. "I can only give sixty points this time," he said as he put back the kitchen utensils.

Barely a pass. Ye Qin felt shock and then dejection. "Why?" he asked with a bitter face, reverting back to when he had been a student always looking for Mr. Cheng's approval.

"Because you didn't dance," Cheng Feichi remarked, looking him over from head to toe.

As he had made his debut as a member of a boy group, Ye Qin knew a thing or two about dancing.

But how did Cheng Feichi know? Did he watch Ye Qin's previous videos? Reaching this conclusion, Ye Qin felt too ashamed to look at him, wanting to go hide in a hole.

Most people in showbiz had some dark history they didn't want to revisit. Ye Qin, who could admit that the first three years after his debut were black history in and of themselves, was no exception. Funky hairstyles, rainbow hair, the embarrassing arrogant young master persona—he once thought that when he got rich, he would pay someone to totally wipe this "criminal record."

Those images had already entered the public eye, however, and they were second to none at overstating flaws. Good looks would not necessarily capture their hearts, but one ugly appearance would be held onto 'til kingdom come.

There was a perfect example.

When Ye Qin went back to his dorm today after work to pack his things, the landlord downstairs heard the noise and came up once again. "Oh?" was his first reaction. "Did your career skyrocket after the Mid-Autumn Festival banquet? Do you no longer have to dye your hair blond and act out country romances?"

Ye Qin couldn't be bothered to clarify that he never played a role like that. He got straight to the point: "I'm not going to stop paying rent, and I'll drop by once in a while. Uncle, please don't bully the kid who still lives here. He's even younger than your son. Please, as an act of charity for your new grandson."

Before the landlord could snap, he got out a red packet from his pocket. "After living here for many years, I'm indebted to your care. A token of appreciation for your grandson."

Delighted by money, the landlord immediately swallowed back harsh words. He squeezed the thickness of the packet and coughed. "As long as you pay rent on time, it's not like I'll come just to look for trouble."

Once Ye Qin moved out, Song Xu would be the only permanent resident left in this dorm. Song Xu had always followed him, called him ge, and even done favors for him. Ye Qin was obligated to take good care of him.

After dispatching the troublesome landlord, Ye Qin continued packing, carefully taking down the Lego set in its glass case from the top bunk. He wrapped it securely in the bubble wrap he'd brought along. He also wrapped a ball around the jar of stars and put it into his backpack to carry with him.

Cheng Feichi messaged him in the afternoon, asking if he was done with work.

[Yup, I'm just about to go take a look at Appliance City.] Ye Qin lied, squished in a subway.

Right after he sent the message, there came a call. "Hello?" Ye Qin picked up nervously.

"Program...meeting..." Cheng Feichi said to his PA on the other end, and she addressed each of his sentences. Then, the sound of high heels faded, and Cheng Feichi's voice came back on the mic. "Whatever appliances are missing, I'll get someone to buy and ship over. Since you're off work, go back and stay there. Don't go running around."

"Don't worry, my leg's already healed. I'm just waiting for them to take off the steel plate next year. It's on the way from work. I'll just drop by. I might not even like anything. Besides, these stores always have someone to deliver. It's not like I'll have to carry anything myself."

Hearing a station announcement over the phone, Cheng Feichi thought for a moment. "Go home after you're finished, then. Take a taxi. You have my card on you, right? Do you still remember the pin?"

"Yeah, yeah."

Ye Qin greatly enjoyed Cheng Feichi taking care of him. He tugged up the straps of his backpack with a smile so big that his eyes narrowed into slits. *But I won't be needing your card today,* he thought secretly.

That night, Cheng Feichi saw a new fridge in the kitchen of his new apartment in the capital. A luxurious, grand, double door very in accordance with dowry quality.

The only thing was that it looked somewhat cramped in the corner of the kitchen.

When Cheng Feichi walked over and pulled on the handle, the refrigerator door knocked into the cooking counter.

Ye Qin ran over from fiddling with the soymilk machine in the dining room, took Cheng Feichi's hand, and examined it from various angles. "This refrigerator had a deal...a free soymilk machine with the purchase," he admonished himself. "I thought it was fine that it's a bit wider. Who knew it'd fit, but the door gets stuck on the wall." Seeing Cheng Feichi's hand unhurt, he let out a breath of relief before frowning. "Tomorrow, I'll go return it."

"It's fine. As long as it works," Cheng Feichi said and tested the other door with his other hand. It was able to open halfway, and he reached in to grab two eggs. "In the future, when we get a bigger house, this refrigerator will be just the right size."

Ye Qin had lived a life of luxury until seventeen, so he had often seen the excessive lavishness in the lives of the rich and wealthy. Yet he had no particular interest in a big house. Com-

pared to the Ye family's empty villa, he would much rather a small apartment like this, where he could always see his partner and catch his movements. This was warm and a comfort.

He liked the words "in the future" even more. As long as he could be together with Cheng Feichi, they could live anywhere.

Ye Qin was quite excited to use the soymilk machine for the first time. While fiddling with it, he pressed two batches; one with red and black beans, and one with soy and mung beans.

There were no sealable containers left in the kitchen, and the milk might go bad if he left it overnight, so he poured glass after glass for Cheng Feichi.

Cheng Feichi drank three glasses while reading. When he reached for his glass and found it filled again, he turned to the man beside him.

Ye Qin hurriedly pointed to his own glass as proof. "I'm drinking too."

Cheng Feichi put his glass back on the table and returned to reading.

After a while, Ye Qin leaned over with a rustle. "Cheers, gege," he said, lifting a glass.

Stomach full of bean juice, Cheng Feichi really couldn't drink any more, but neither could he bring himself to say no to Ye Qin's fluttering eyes and soft calls. "After I digest for a bit," he said reluctantly.

Ye Qin sprung up from the sofa. "I-I'll put on a show to cheer you on then."

Cheng Feichi closed his book and sat upright.

His posture, much too serious, caught all of Ye Qin's attention. Ye Qin swallowed, fiddling with his fingers and the hem of his shirt. Once he could no longer stall, he finally began.

He sang a children's song, the kind that came with its own dance.

He once used this to look cute shortly after his debut. It could be considered one of the dark moments in history that he couldn't escape from. But now it was just the right thing to charm his gege. Ye Qin used his hands to make bunny ears, twisted his butt to shake his tail, tilted his head while spinning in a circle, and made all kinds of childish moves. Then, he stood there with a pillow over his face, waiting for feedback.

He didn't get any. First, there was applause.

Face burning, Ye Qin reached over to stop Cheng Feichi from clapping only to be pulled down into his lap.

"That was good." There was a smile on Cheng Feichi's lips as he took Ye Qin's chin and turned Ye Qin to face him. "Very good."

Ye Qin didn't know whether Cheng Feichi was telling the truth, but seeing him smile gave him assurance. He also became bolder and took advantage of their closeness to pull open his lapels for Cheng Feichi to look. "Then what if I get a tattoo on my collarbone? Gege, don't you want to...mark my body?"

Eyes on Ye Qin's smooth, fine collarbones, Cheng Feichi's expression shifted ever so slightly as if he was moved.

No man could resist such an advance, especially from the one he loved.

Just as Ye Qin got his hopes up, Cheng Feichi lowered his head and planted a gentle kiss on his collarbone. Then, he took Ye Qin into his arms, leaning against his shoulder.

"We don't need that," he said. "Everything is perfect as it is."

According to Chinese tradition, one must invite guests over when moving into a new home.

There was no need to hold a huge banquet, but they could find an excuse to invite a few friends for a gathering. And so, one fall afternoon, Liao Yifang and Zhou Feng visited with gifts.

"You're starting already? No rush. Let's boil some water first."

Liao Yifang couldn't sit still after arriving, fussing on behalf of the young people nowadays who hadn't an inkling of tradition. He filled a basin with water and added salt before splashing it all over the apartment. Then, he walked to the door and threw down two coins. They clinked crisply just as the water started bubbling in the kitchen. Liao Yifang arched his eyes in a smile and announced that this was to, "Bring profits in the door and ride the economic bubble."

Ye Qin looked on, stunned. "Bringing in profit is good. That's good. Quick, class monitor, help me see where else we can do this ceremony and bring in more money."

Like this, lunch became afternoon tea. As they made small talk at the table, it already got close to sunset.

Mostly it was Ye Qin and Liao Yifang chit-chatting, from moving ceremonies to feng shui to everyday household tasks like how to wipe down the fume exhaust and how to get rid of smells in the refrigerator. Every now and then, Ye Qin took out his cellphone to note things down, just like a good student eager for knowledge.

Zhou Feng took a sip of wine, unable to take this any longer. "A-Qin, stop pretending. How many days can you be diligent with your lazy bones?"

Ye Qin shot him a fierce glare. "I'm not like you, who only knows fancy tricks and can't do anything useful."

"I can do some useful things, like handing over my pay slips and stuff." Zhou Feng scratched his head and asked Liao Yifang for confirmation, "Right, baby?"

"Congratulations to the two of you on your new home," Liao Yifang changed the subject, raising his glass. "I wish you sweet and happy days." He was never able to get used to Zhou Feng being intimate with him in public.

Having low alcohol tolerance, Liao Yifang's face was flushed after a few rounds of drinks. He laughed aloud as Ye Qin filled the silence with bad jokes. "I still remember...one Ye-tongxue told me before that was super, super funny," he cut in.

"What?" Zhou Feng asked, peeling shrimp for him.

Liao Yifang first slapped the table and laughed for three minutes straight before steadying his breath. "One day," he said, "goddess Nuwa laughed as she made people out of clay. Pangu asked her what she was laughing at, and Nuwa said...guess what she said."

Clueless, Zhou Feng looked to Ye Qin for help. Ye Qin mocked him for being an idiot and refused to say anything to build anticipation. It was Cheng Feichi who spoke up from silently pouring more drinks for everyone, "Happiness is what it takes to make one human."

"Cheng Feichi, you also know this joke?" Liao Yifang asked in surprise. Then he understood. "Ye Qin must have told you. Hahaha, it's hilarious."

Ye Qin propped his chin on his hands and swung his head from side to side listening to them laugh. Half a minute later, he suddenly straightened his neck.

He remembered! He once sent this joke to Cheng Feichi, but it was to his old number. Didn't Cheng Feichi say he no longer used it?

At around eight, after sending off their two drunk guests in a taxi, Ye Qin leaned his head on Cheng Feichi's shoulder and let Cheng Feichi lead him down a winding cobbled path inside the compound.

There was a wide arterial outside, so this small path through the greenery was rarely taken. But Ye Qin really liked it. Even while wobbling drunk, he could still remember which way to go at the crossing. "Liar...you're evil..." he mumbled out the side of his mouth as he walked. "You swindled me..."

"How did I swindle you?" Cheng Feichi asked when he never

got the rest.

Alcohol had a delayed effect on Ye Qin, and it was only now that he was somewhat drunk.

Burping, he jabbed Cheng Feichi's left chest with his finger. "You swindled me...swindled me into thinking you were no longer...using your number." After jabbing him several times, he realized it was the wrong place and stabbed his own chest instead. "D-don't swindle me. I remember...remember all of it."

Cheng Feichi hooked up his lips. "How else did I swindle you?"

Light steps came to a halt. "You swindled my heart." Ye Qin slapped his chest, frowning. "My heart. And then once you got it you ignored me. Bastard."

He let go of Cheng Feichi and went to hug a nearby tree, both feet in the mud, refusing to move.

Cheng Feichi didn't know whether to laugh or to cry at his faked accusations and silly, shameless fit. "C'mon," he said, walking over and tugging his hand. "Let's go back. It's cold outside."

Ye Qin shook his head hard and then yawned. Red cheeks pressed against the bark, he closed his eyes and pretended like he was going to sleep right then and here.

This was Cheng Feichi's first time seeing him drunk. Remembering how the last time Ye Qin drank, he slept like a piglet for two hours in the back seat of the car, Cheng Feichi thought it'd probably be okay once he got Ye Qin back to bed. "C'mon," he said, squatting for Ye Qin to ride piggyback.

Even with his senses drifting and his vision blurred, Ye Qin couldn't refuse this temptation. There were a few seconds of hesitation and he slowly crawled up Cheng Feichi's back through muscle memory.

Cheng Feichi's warm, wide back was much easier to sleep

on than the cold tree trunk. Not to mention his steps were even and steady. Ye Qin closed his eyes, listening to the sound of wind and steady heartbeats, and his mind flowed through fragments of memories like a small river.

"Do you still remember...the balloon cat?"

The sound came muffled from behind him, and Cheng Feichi turned his head. "I do. What about it?"

With his head propped on Cheng Feichi's shoulder, Ye Qin only shook it slightly. "Nothing." After a pause, he continued, "Then, do you still remember you were gonna take me to a tropical island after university entrance exams?"

For a moment, Cheng Feichi froze, recalling the promise he had been unable to fulfill. "Yes."

"The sweets on Times Square second floor?"

"Yes."

"The milk-flavored lollipops?"

"Yes."

"The popcorn in the cinema?"

"Yes."

Every response was an affirmation of Ye Qin's precious memories. He thought he was dreaming and smiled ear to ear as he tightened his arms around Cheng Feichi's neck.

When the warm breath on his neck became slow and steady, Cheng Feichi thought he had fallen asleep. Worried that the chilliness of late autumn would make him sick, he jostled Ye Qin by his thighs. "Ye Qin?"

Ye Qin really did fall asleep, mumbling when he heard his name. His legs swung along to Cheng Feichi's footsteps.

Cheng Feichi thought for a moment and said instead, "Ye Xiaoruan?"

"Yes!"

The man on his back replied immediately, a conditioned

reflex to a voice rooted in his heart.

Then, he leaned back, cheeks rubbing against Cheng Feichi's shoulder. "You also said...we would get married," he whispered. "You...you can't swindle me again...gege."

Drinking only felt good temporarily. The moment Ye Qin woke up, he learned what being hungover felt like.

His head felt like it was going to explode. He dragged his eyes open and struggled to get out of bed. Water sloshed in his head, pieces of memory bumping around everywhere.

Turning and seeing no one there, Ye Qin's breath hitched. Immediately, he regained control of every joint in his body and jumped out of bed, not even putting on his slippers first before running out.

When he opened the bedroom door, he smashed into someone else coming in. Like a drowning man to a floating log, Ye Qin hugged Cheng Feichi and refused to let go. It was only when Cheng Feichi asked calmly, "Why aren't you wearing slippers?" that he sulkily got off, turned around with sagging shoulders, and weakly walked back into the room.

Seeing him sit back on the bed cross-legged, looking in every direction, Cheng Feichi walked over, picked up the slippers he had kicked to the foot of the bed, and put them back beside it. Ye Qin didn't even get a chance to put his feet on the floor when Cheng Feichi took one of his ankles.

"Did you think I left?" he asked with hooded eyes.

Not daring to say yes, Ye Qin copied Cheng Feichi and tried to use silence to tide over this brief episode.

Cheng Feichi never pried. When Ye Qin didn't speak, he didn't ask further. Quietly, he put Ye Qin's slippers on for him and lifted him up by the arm.

Now that the sleepiness was gone, Ye Qin had a keen sense

of touch. He felt a metal object in Cheng Feichi's hand.

He had already felt it when Cheng Feichi took his ankle.

Looking over, Ye Qin saw something shiny on Cheng Feichi's left hand.

Cheng Feichi followed his line of sight down. He took Ye Qin's hand and raised both of them, mirroring his puzzled expression. "Didn't you put this ring on me?"

Ye Qin's heart ran wild. Had he not only said stupid things while drunk yesterday but also done stupid things?

This terrifying thought vanished in an instant when he saw the smile on Cheng Feichi's lips and knew that he had been pranked. Annoyed and embarrassed, he was about to slip away when Cheng Feichi hauled him back.

As Cheng Feichi held him in one arm, he laced four fingers in his left hand through the hand he was holding, palm to the back of Ye Qin's hand. Two rings of the same model glinted against each other on their ring fingers in the morning light.

"Why are you running?" Cheng Feichi leaned forward slightly; chest glued to Ye Qin's trembling back. "Don't you know to take responsibility for what you've done, Ye Xiaoruan?" he asked, pressing his lips to Ye Qin's slowly burning earlobes.

It was in late autumn that they finished all the beans Ye Qin had bought from the supermarket next to the appliance store.

Every time he pressed soymilk, he just needed a small glass. However, he had bought the beans by the half kilo and even though he substituted soymilk for tea, the pile of beans did not seem to diminish. Left with no other option, he had to find another way to use them—in congee.

At first, it was a novelty. The beans were soaked through the night and when he woke up the next morning, he tossed them in the pressure cooker together with rice. By the time he and

Cheng Feichi were done with their morning routine, the congee was almost ready.

Recently, Ye Qin had been on a health program and had been heavily brainwashed by the guest nutritionist to believe that fruits and vegetables were very important to maintaining a healthy physique. Adding spinach, greens, and carrots to the congee made it look colorful and delicious, but because there was no sugar and salt, the taste was exceedingly natural.

In other words, it was bland. Even Cheng Feichi, who didn't particularly care much about food, was at the end of his wits after eating this for a month, let alone picky Ye Qin. If it weren't for Ye Qin washing and soaking the beans first thing after coming back from work, waking up early in the mornings to prepare vegetables and make congee, and researching and changing up different nutritious pairings, Cheng Feichi would rather make do with two buns on the street.

One morning at the end of November, Ye Qin reluctantly crawled out of his warm blanket, draped on some clothes, and went into the kitchen. Yawning, he fetched the vegetables he had bought yesterday to wash. Before his hand even touched running water, Cheng Feichi, who had gotten up after him, hugged him from behind. "Don't make congee today. Let's eat out."

Thinking that Cheng Feichi had grown sick of his congee, Ye Qin wilted the whole trip. He was still looking up recipes on his phone after they got there and Cheng Feichi led him into the restaurant by the hand. He found one for a red bean walnut pie that looked pretty good. Walnuts were good for the brain, perfect for Cheng Feichi who sat in front of his laptop looking at documents every day. But looking through the ingredients, he thought that there was too much sugar—it wasn't healthy—and scrunched up his eyebrows again.

Cheng Feichi had taken him to a normal dessert shop. When

a chocolate cake came to the table, Ye Qin suddenly remembered that today was his birthday.

They had birthday memories carved into their bones, half amazing, half painful. Remembering he had lied to Cheng Feichi about his fake birthday twice made Ye Qin panicky. Even his favorite chocolate cake lost its taste, and after two bites, Ye Qin sat spaced out with the spoon dangling in his hands.

"Does it not taste good?" Cheng Feichi asked, seeing him zoned out. "I noticed you have a light taste recently, so I put less sugar."

Ye Qin grasped the main point. "You made this cake?"

"Mmhm." Cheng Feichi nodded. "Yesterday when I finished work and came here, I only had time to make it like this. I let it sit in the fridge for a night, so the taste isn't as good."

Ye Qin quickly scooped a giant spoonful of cake and stuffed it in his mouth. "Delicious. Super delicious," he said with cake still in his mouth.

Cheng Feichi smiled. "Don't force yourself. If you can't finish, just leave it here and the waiters will take it. I'll take you to buy a new one tonight."

"No, no, I want this one." Ye Qin circled his arms around the cake like a food-hoarding cat. "This is my birthday gift. No one else can touch it."

With the added layer of love, this cake became exceptionally precious to Ye Qin. He savored every bite before swallowing and licked any icing that he accidentally got on his lips. Not even the crumbs on the table could escape him.

In the end, he only finished half. The other half he told the waiter to pack as takeout.

They both had work today. Cheng Feichi dropped Ye Qin off on set. Ye Qin looked back repeatedly after getting out of the car, bidding him goodbye five, six times. Then, thinking of how

they would see each other in a few hours, he pleaded for time to move faster and faster so that he could go home and spend his birthday with his gege.

As he sat in front of the mirror in the break room doing his makeup, his phone rang in his pocket. Ye Qin took it out and looked. Cheng Feichi sent him a text from his old number: *[Put your hand in your other pocket.]*

The sight of the "gege" that hadn't appeared after "Sent" for so long made Ye Qin choke with emotion. Tilting his head to the sky, he had to take a few deep breaths to blink back the tears welling in his eyes.

He put down his cellphone and put his hand in the other pocket of the jacket. At first, he felt smooth plastic, and then the hard, round object underneath. When he took it out, Ye Qin froze again.

The stylist doing his hair behind him saw the object in his hands and laughed. "A lollipop? You're so skinny, I thought you don't eat snacks."

Ye Qin stared at six identical milk-flavored lollipops, also smiling. "It's a birthday present. One for each year."

By the time Ye Qin finally finished the last lollipop, winter had already quietly arrived in the capital.

Every industry was busy at the end of the year. Zhou Feng weaved through the streets catching thieves, Liao Yifang woke up early and burned midnight oil to prepare extra lessons for his students, and Cheng Feichi was so busy his feet hardly stayed in one spot. He traveled back and forth between the capital and S-City. Any free time he had while traveling was used for reading year-end reports sent in by every department.

Compared to them, Ye Qin was actually the idlest. He finished filming a low-cost art film and took on two variety shows for local channels, all of which he was only the guest star for one segment. Afterwards, he did a few concerts and after that, had no more work until after New Year.

When he got free time, he wanted to do something.

Like go back to school and get a degree.

Backstage after a concert, Ye Qin pulled aside Song Xu, the guy with the most knowledge of university entrance exams, and asked him if he had any advice.

"I just studied and did problems and then passed a bunch of exams," Song Xu said, blinking and bewildered. "Ge, how many years has it been since you graduated high school? Is there still any chance to take university entrance exams?"

Overhearing their conversation as he passed by, He Hansong taunted Ye Qin for daydreaming. He was already in his mid-twenties. How could he possibly still want to go to university? He wouldn't even be able to pass the self-examination for adults.

Ye Qin didn't lower himself to his level. Later, he called Liu Yuqing to ask for advice. He also asked her out for dinner as a token of appreciation for taking care of him back then.

Liu Yuqing came from a family of actors. Her steady boyfriend was also in showbiz and had graduated from a class in the acting department. Upon hearing Ye Qin's request, she prudently called up her family and summarized their opinions to Ye Qin. She told him that if he wanted to stay in showbiz, he might as well try to get into an arts academy. The entry barrier was relatively low. Plus, it would be a great help for his career.

That night, Ye Qin read every single thing in the enrollment pamphlet for the capital's film academy. With the thought that he would try, he sent Cheng Feichi a picture for him to take a look at.

Less than three minutes later, Cheng Feichi sent a video request from S-City. When Ye Qin answered, he got straight to the point, "You want to go to university?"

Ye Qin nodded a little sheepishly. "Um, yeah. I've wanted to for a long time, but I got some free time recently? So I did a bit of research, and I think I'm quite suited for performing arts, so...I should learn how to act. I can't always play myself as the lead actress's younger brother, can I?

At one time, his head had been full of C University. He didn't even consider the major, didn't know what he wanted or liked. Now he followed his heart and found his goal. All that was missing was his gege's approval and support.

Cheng Feichi had a bit of hesitation. Just as Ye Qin thought that he was under the impression that Ye Qin was setting his goals too low and not progressing, he said, "Balancing work and study will be very tough."

Ye Qin let out a breath of relief. "What's tough about it?" he laughed. "Didn't you also work while you were going to school? If you can do it, why can't I?"

Touched by his rare show of confidence, Cheng Feichi nodded his approval and even told him he would look at admission pamphlets for some similar institutions for him. It was best for Ye Qin, as a person who wanted to go back to school many years after graduating, to look at more schools and prepare for different possibilities.

It was already 8 p.m., and Cheng Feichi was still in the office. After informing him, Ye Qin considerately let him return to work.

"Have you thought of what you would do if you blow up in the future?" Cheng Feichi suddenly asked before hanging up.

Although Cheng Feichi didn't know much about showbiz, he knew from rumors alone that celebrities whose names everyone knew, whether real actors with ability or idols dependent on fans, were all glamorous on the surface yet miserable inside. All year round, they spent time away from home filming in different places. Everything in their lives was aired out for the public to see. Even a love life that any normal person would enjoy could become an obstacle hindering their career.

But Ye Qin had a one-track mind and didn't understand what Cheng Feichi was trying to say. "When I blow up, you won't need to work so hard," he voiced his thoughts valiantly, patting his chest. "You can stay at home. I'll take care of you."

For a moment, Cheng Feichi froze. Then, it suddenly became clear, and he laughed. "Okay."

Ye Qin very quickly chose his path with his friends' assistance and began urgently preparing for interviews with several universities in February of the following year.

At the same time, Cheng Feichi returned his flight ticket to the capital due to Cheng Xin's sickness and temporarily stayed in S-City hospital to take care of her.

Cheng Xin's health was always the weakest in winter, and this year especially so. Right after hospitalization, she went into a coma for three days and lost considerable weight. Even while sleeping, she furrowed her eyebrows in pain as if she was suffering a disaster.

In her second week of hospitalization, she finally managed to sit leaning against a pillow. Her hands still shook so terribly that she couldn't hold any utensils. Cheng Feichi sat beside her and fed her one spoonful at a time.

Sometimes, when she was in a clear state of mind, she spoke to him. Mostly she was the only one who talked, telling him that he should work hard and show his face to the Yi family more often. Then, she went on to mention how Yan Hong was such a nice lady; how could he not like her? Then, she told him she was tired, and after taking a few sips of water, stared at the sunlight outside of the window. When she looked away, she was mostly muddle-headed, unable to tell between past and present.

"Work hard for Mom," she repeated, clutching his hand.

"Go abroad. Please, Mom is begging you."

Knowing that she was weak and not in the right state of mind, Cheng Feichi replied with silence.

Occasionally, she would also get sensitive for no reason at all, like today. As Cheng Feichi got off the phone with Ye Qin and walked into the sick room from the hallway, Cheng Xin perked up. She stared at him, eyes bulging, and asked him what he had just been doing.

"Making a phone call," Cheng Feichi responded truthfully.

"To who?"

Cheng Feichi poured a cup of water and handed it to her. "Don't you already know?"

Cheng Xin immediately sat up, staring into Cheng Feichi's unperturbed face. She racked her brains but couldn't find anything to threaten him with. In her panicked state, she caught a glimpse of the ring on Cheng Feichi's hand around the cup, and her heart shot into her throat. "You...what kind of ring is that?"

Seeing she had no intention of drinking, Cheng Feichi set the cup down on the table beside the hospital bed and answered, "A wedding ring."

"To who? Who?!" Cheng Xin's voice shook, her twisted expression looking exceeding sinister on her ashen face. "That Ye kid? I won't accept it. Mom won't accept it. You can't be together with him!"

Cheng Feichi didn't speak. Rather, he picked up a cover and placed it on the cup to keep the water warm. Looking down, he then tucked in the duvet that had been pulled off by Cheng Xin's flailing. Even when he was grabbed by Cheng Xin, he didn't make a sound, just let her grip him with all her strength until his flesh made noise.

When Cheng Xin went into a fit, she became blind to the

severity of her actions. She accidentally touched his scar; the scar which had not faded to this day, an insurmountable mountain between mother and son. The moment she did, her face went even more ashen, and she let go in a panic.

Cheng Feichi withdrew his hand, turned, and walked to the door. "I'm leaving now," he said, putting on his coat. "The doctor told you to rest." He paused for a few seconds. "When you're in a stable condition, I'll bring him here for you to see."

Only then did Cheng Xin react from where she was sitting listlessly. "What's there to see?" she sneered with a curled lip. "Don't think he can get me to like him just because he broke a leg for me. I'll acknowledge him when I'm dead."

Cheng Feichi pursed his lips. He once heard those words before. This time, though, they seemed to have no effect on him.

In truth, Cheng Xin knew better than anyone that saying "I won't allow it" was useless. After years and years of threatening him with her life, she and her son had long become estranged. Like a kite with a broken string, he would no longer be controlled by her.

Her little son who had called her "Mom," trusted her, and relied on her with all his heart, would never come back.

Cheng Xin suddenly felt tired. She lay down her exhausted body, loosened her keyed-up nerves, and let her aching chest expand in a deep breath.

Eyes half closed, she took a quick glimpse back at her life, which seemed so thrilling when in fact it couldn't be described as anything but dark and ugly.

The images in her eyes slowed down and finally stopped one summer twenty years ago. At the time, she was holding her graduation certificate and endless aspirations for the future. Back then, she still believed in the saying that love would find a way. As long as she worked hard, she could have who and what she

wanted firmly in her grasp.

In her trance, Cheng Xin's consciousness floated out of her body, drifting slowly in mid-air. It split into two completely different people. Two sets of eyes looked at each other. One was bright and spirited, the other weathered and dying.

The once-radiant Cheng Xin looked down at the exhausted Cheng Xin lying on the hospital bed. Her eyes were filled with pity and disdain, as if saying, *If it were me, I would never end up like you.*

Right as Cheng Feichi was about to leave, he vaguely heard Cheng Xin's weak and decrepit voice behind him. "If he could have been like you back then...why aren't you like him?"

Cheng Feichi stopped his footsteps and pondered deeply. "Everyone has the right to choose," he said, turning around, "as well as the duty to take responsibility for their choices. I am not him, and I can't be like him."

Cheng Feichi rushed back from S-City to the capital overnight and got to taste Ye Qin's newest discovery on New Year's Day—pan-seared green chili peppers.

"How is it? How is it?" Ye Qin peeked at him taking a bite with a face of anticipation. "I hand-minced the shrimp. I had to do it for twenty minutes for it to toughen up. Does it taste very springy?"

Cheng Feichi chewed for a bit, and two wrinkles scrunched up in between his eyebrows.

Ye Qin's heart dropped. "What is it? Does it not taste good?"

Cheng Feichi finished one and picked up another. "The shrimp's texture is very good—" He turned the chili over. "—but you used the wrong chili. This is Er Jing Tiao."

Ye Qin never heard of this name before. He took out his phone and searched it on Baidu, looking from the image to what was on the plate. "No wonder they were so skinny," he said dejectedly. "I could barely stuff any shrimp inside... The shop owner even lied to me and said this kind of chili is best for making pan-seared green chili peppers."

As he was speaking, Cheng Feichi had another. "It's perfect to me," he assessed, "but too spicy for you, not suitable to have often."

Ye Qin's mood lifted. "No worries, as long as you like it. I'll just pick out the shrimp meat."

They each ate a whole bowl of rice with just this one dish, and Ye Qin's bowl was filled with the shrimp meat Cheng Feichi picked out countless times.

After the meal, Ye Qin rubbed his belly and rued that he had made nutritional meal plans for a month for nothing. It was all undone by one meal.

"Eating unhealthily once in a while can stimulate the body and increase metabolism," Cheng Feichi comforted.

"Really?"

"Yes."

Ye Qin, who always believed Cheng Feichi's words without question, left giddily to make soymilk at once.

When he came back, he loitered around the sofa. When Cheng Feichi's eyes drifted up from the laptop screen, Ye Qin immediately expressed his inner doubt, "Where did you hear about Er Jing Tiao? I saw on Baidu that it's a necessity for Sichuan cuisine."

"When I was overseas, there was a Sichuan native in my class who would bring back a bundle of chilies every year. He once told me these long, thin chilies are called Er Jing Tiao."

"Oh..." Ye Qin nodded. "Did you have a lot of Chinese people in your class? What did you usually eat? Study? Do?"

Cheng Feichi answered his questions one by one. "Are you interested in my school?" he asked at the end.

Ye Qin lowered his head and fiddled with a cushion. "Well, yeah. I mean, I'm about to go to university too, so I'm a bit curious."

That was an excuse. He was actually interested in all the places his gege had been and all the things he'd done.

But Cheng Feichi believed him. Going through next year's work plans quickly in his head, he told him, "Next summer I'll take you there, and we can also go to that tropical island."

Ye Qin screeched, flinging the cushion and leaping off the sofa. Then, realizing his reaction was too extreme, he slowly sat down and adopted an air of "I'll go along with anything you plan."

When Cheng Feichi closed his laptop, Ye Qin shook his arm and bugged like a mosquito, "Summer's still so far away... Before that, can you first come with me to High School No. 6?"

They made plans for February 14th, the day after Cheng Feichi's 26th birthday.

The moment they got off the plane, Ye Qin made a beeline for High School No. 6.

He waited under the ginkgo tree beside the road, not even smiling when he saw Cheng Feichi approach. Ye Qin turned his head and walked in front, pouting, his loose shoelaces swinging very distractingly. Even when Cheng Feichi went up to take his bag, he shook his head and refused. He only came around when Cheng Feichi gave him a rose from his pocket.

Ye Qin wasn't angry. He just thought that the timing was damn unlucky. They hadn't been able to spend Chinese New Year together, fine, but yesterday he had work in the capital and something had to come up for Cheng Feichi in S-City. Cheng Feichi went back, and they weren't able to spend his birthday together. The plans he had made far in advance all went to waste.

Birthday, birthday, it was the day on which you were born.

What meaning was there in the day after?

As the two of them walked shoulder to shoulder on the path toward the back gates of High School No. 6, Ye Qin looked at the rose in his hands and blushed. "Forget it. This time we didn't make plans beforehand, but your next birthday, and the one after, and all the ones after you have to spend with me."

"Okay," Cheng Feichi agreed and added, "If I don't spend them with you, then I'm a dog."

It was still winter vacation, so the parking area behind High School No. 6 was completely empty. Ye Qin hadn't been back for a long time. He grabbed the fence railing and peered in. Unable to go inside, he grumbled that if they'd installed the fence back then, there wouldn't have been so many cars stolen.

"If there was a fence back then, my tire also wouldn't have been slashed by a certain someone," Cheng Feichi expressed his agreement.

Even while knowing that he was teasing, Ye Qin still flushed red. "Th-th-that wasn't done by me," he argued futilely. "It was Zhou Feng and the others... I was only on the lookout... Besides, didn't I make it up to you by polishing your bike?"

Even though he only did so reluctantly, under threat, and felt so mistreated he almost cried.

Despite students being on holiday, there was still a guard at the main gate. Now that conditions improved at High School No. 6, the back gates became electric powered, and a security booth had been built beside it. Inside, the security guard sat dozing with the heating turned on. Suddenly woken up by knocks on the window, he grumpily opened a sliver. "The school is a restricted area. No idlers."

It was only when Cheng Feichi and Ye Qin greeted "hello sir" together that he opened his eyes and looked closely at them.

"It's you two!" he exclaimed.

The security guard was still the same man. Back when they'd been dating, they loved to sneak out the back gates after everyone else in the school had left. Several times they bumped into him. Sometimes the gates had already been closed, and they had to rely on Ye Qin's begging and chasing to get him to open them reluctantly.

"You little rascals—ahem. I can't call you little rascals anymore. You two alumni always brought me trouble when you were in school. Every day you stayed until the last minute and fed me some excuse like 'taking extra lessons,'" the security guard mocked as he operated the electric gate. "You think I'm blind? The school building was pitch black. There were no lights on in any classroom. Were you 'taking extra lessons' inside toilet cubicles?"

"We were taking extra lessons! We were really focused," Ye Qin laughed merrily, left leg stretched out for Cheng Feichi to do up his shoelaces.

The guard chuckled, the ends of his mustache fluttering. "Are you two brothers?" he asked after staring for a moment. "I think so. I see you coming in and out together so often that you practically share one pair of pants."

This time, Ye Qin didn't object so much to that label. As Cheng Feichi got up from tying his shoelaces, they exchanged a smile.

They both understood from a look why everyone thought they were like brothers: because as long as they were together, they only had the other in their eyes.

When it was almost dark, they said goodbye to the security guard who had opened the gates for them and walked on that familiar path.

Ye Qin had been chatting away for the good half of the afternoon, but now he suddenly fell silent. At the corner with the main road, Cheng Feichi saw him squeeze the backpack straps in his hands and guessed what he was going to do.

Sure enough, when they got on the sidewalk, Ye Qin unzipped his backpack and reached in, searching. After a while, he took out a square box.

"Valentine's Day gift." Ye Qin craned his neck awkwardly to avoid Cheng Feichi's expression. "Nothing expensive. You can wear it whenever."

Cheng Feichi took the box and opened it. Inside was a men's watch. He immediately took it out, swapped out the one he was wearing, and held up his hand, looking at it from every angle. "A flower for a watch," he said, smiling. "Worth it."

Ye Qin knew he didn't need this watch, but he really couldn't think of what else to give, so he chose an appropriate item worn close to the body and spent the first bit of money he'd saved after paying off his debt.

Now, seeing Cheng Feichi genuinely pleased, he could finally put down the stone suspended above his chest. He still upheld appearances, however. "It's just a typical gift. When I blow up, I'll be able to buy you a watch for every day of the month."

At Ye Qin's eagerness to keep him at home and take care of him, Cheng Feichi simply laughed. This was more like the little sunshine he knew, always dreaming big.

They strolled past a red light onto the road closest to where Ye Qin's home once was. Cheng Feichi acutely sensed that Ye Qin had gone silent again.

He likely still had something to take out.

Even though Ye Qin had moved out years ago, every time he came here, he both reminisced about the past and found courage that he couldn't summon out of thin air anywhere else.

Under the fuzzy yellow streetlights, one of them stopped and the other followed suit. The only sound left came from cars pressing down on the streets as they passed by.

Turning to face Cheng Feichi, Ye Qin finally took out the glass jar he had been hiding all this time.

"H-happy birthday, gege. Happy birthday." So keyed up that his voice shook, Ye Qin cleared his throat and added with fake levity, "It's just a normal gift. You can play with it whenever."

Cheng Feichi really did open the lid, take out a star, and play with it in his hands.

"Can't you...act a little surprised?" Ye Qin scrunched up his face, unsatisfied with such an unremarkable reaction.

Cheng Feichi thought for a moment and slowly made his eyes grow big. "Wow!" he said halfway through.

He was more governed by logic than emotion. Very rarely did his mood fluctuate. Even while pretending to be surprised, his face couldn't appear more wooden and fake, and Ye Qin couldn't bring himself to look straight at it. He lowered his head somewhat dejectedly and cheered himself on, "Wow... Amazing."

His voice was dispirited, and he hated himself inside for being careless. If he hadn't left a star in the pocket of his jacket, Cheng Feichi might really have had a big surprise.

How could Cheng Feichi not know what he was thinking?

For the sake of Ye Qin's face, there were many things that he turned a blind eye to and pretended not to know. For instance, he found the Lego Technic in the glass covers under the bed long ago, as well as the neat stack of test booklets underneath.

Once, he heard noise coming from the adjacent room and followed the sound to an old phone in a bookshelf drawer. When he turned it on and slid away the notification making the sound, he then saw an unmoving version of himself on the phone interface.

With all his wishes fulfilled, Ye Qin held up his script after dinner and began acting the role of the good student, peacefully preparing for the preliminary exam in the capital's film school.

One of the tasks was to produce a short skit. Ye Qin wasn't very strong in dialogue and found it hard to concentrate switching back and forth between two roles. Once he saw Cheng Feichi reading leisurely next to him, work having died down temporarily, Ye Qin dragged him over to read the other lines so he could find some emotion.

It was an emotional scene filled with tension. As soon as Cheng Feichi read the first two lines of the script, he furrowed his eyebrows. "I flew over the garden wall on the light wings of love..." he said stiffly after hesitating for half a minute.

"No, no," Ye Qin interrupted and pointed at the name on the script. "You read Juliet's part."

Cheng Feichi pressed his lips together and adjusted himself. "Tell me how you came here and why?" he said like reading from a textbook. "If they find you, they will kill you."

"I flew over the garden wall on the light wings of love, for walls of stone cannot keep love out." Ye Qin lifted his head and winked playfully at him. "Your eyes are more dangerous than twenty of their swords. So long as you look at me lovingly, they cannot injure my body...much less my heart."

Ye Qin slept late that night, a rare thing.

Cheng Feichi took the script off his face and carried him to bed. Seeing the glass jar beside the headboard, he picked it up and examined it carefully beside the bed.

This man sleeping soundly in bed was very smart. He knew what Cheng Feichi cared about the most, wanted the most, and gave him all of them in his own way. Although he was only sometimes smart and an idiot more often than not, he could stab at the softness in the deepest parts of Cheng Feichi's heart every time, the parts he allowed anyone to see.

This man didn't know that this jar of stars meant much more to him than something as simple as a birthday present.

Back then, he carried this jar of stars lifelessly down the pitch-black path. For a long time, he couldn't see anything in his surroundings, just his hand that was illuminated by this cluster so bright he couldn't look away.

There was a clock tower close to High School No. 6 that rang on the hour. It had been the day after his birthday. The last minute of Valentine's Day had passed, and the melodious bell sounds rang in his ear twelve times. Looking at the stars in his hands, he took one step after another.

Soon, he forgot where he had been going, who he was, what necessary burdens he had to shoulder. He abandoned all thoughts that disturbed his mind. Whether there were steep cliffs or ocean trenches ahead, he only had one thought—to fall in.

No one would ever know that six years earlier, on the midnight of February 15th, Cheng Feichi broke free of the layers and layers of shackles chaining him in place for the first time. He threw away the constraints trapping him like a prison, pushed open an unknown door, and walked into a new life.

It was a risk as much as a rebirth.

Behind the door was a glimpse of light amidst his lackluster life. He desperately wanted to give it and wanted even more to possess it.

If it was necessary to give an appropriate description, he had done things by the book for 99% of his life. Ye Qin was that 1% of unruly rebellion, a seemingly unremarkable 1% that constituted all of his heartbeats and passion in his cold, tedious life.

Cheng Feichi untwisted the lid, put a single star on his palm, and closed a fist around it.

The light flashing in his eyes gradually settled. As the second hand on the clock struck twelve, he leaned down and landed a soft, precious kiss on Ye Qin's forehead.

Five days later, as Ye Qin came out of his interview in the morning, some fans jumped out of the crowd gathered at the door, continuously taking pictures, asking him how he did and if he was certain he got into the second stage.

"Everyone inside is a 17- or 18-year-old beauty," Ye Qin said, scratching his head. "I might as well be their uncle at my age. Out with the old and in with the new, as the proverb goes. Why don't we leave confidence and certainty to them?"

A girl immediately told him not to underestimate himself. "So what if you're in your twenties? Qin-Qin, you have such rich experiences in life and on stage that you stand a head taller than them. Besides, it's never too late to learn something new."

Greatly embarrassed, Ye Qin waved his hands. "No, no, not rich at all. You're the impressive ones, to be able to close your eyes and blindly give praise to someone like me. You should all be instructors. You might even be able to save our wayward youth with your encouragement."

Laughing, the girls guided him to a taxi and waved, reminding him to remember to watch tonight's premiere.

He took out his cellphone. After watching the latest trailer, he skimmed through the comments below. The most popular ones were discussions and promotions for the leading actor and actress. Further down, he saw some that mentioned other supporting roles.

"Is this young man in uniform the same as the one who came in tenth in that youthful vibes poll last year?" one of them said. Below it were a dozen replies that seemed to regurgitate Ye Qin's entire Baidu page in bits and pieces. Someone even supplemented with a still that had been put through eight hundred filters.

No exaggeration. Whether he zoomed in or out, he could not find a single pore. Ye Qin shuddered just looking at it. His fans were too powerful; the filter in their eyes was probably eight

hundred times thicker than this.

Cheng Feichi was inspecting the hotel in S-City when he got Ye Qin's call.

Once Chinese New Year passed, the hotel industry could finally take a small breather after a busy holiday season. Everyone took a break and prepared to regroup for the next traffic peak.

Two receptionists got off shift, chatting about the drama airing tonight as they walked to the employee break room. Running into Cheng Feichi, they immediately suppressed their smiles and straightened, nodding their heads at him respectfully following the standard greeting procedure. Cheng Feichi nodded back and solemnly walked through the path they made for him.

As soon as he was no longer near, they relaxed and continued whispering in each other's ear, abandoning their former topic.

"Our President Cheng is truly handsome, but he always looks so severe. Isn't he afraid he'll scare off his girlfriend?"

"How do you know he has a girlfriend? For some reason, I always feel like President Cheng isn't like this to his lover in private," the other receptionist pondered. "I once heard that he can cook. He even personally oversaw changes to the kitchen last month."

"Ah, I really envy whoever gets to become his other half."

Meanwhile, the envied other half sneezed into the phone and pinched his nose. "You can't come back to the capital today either?"

The word "either" was enough to express his displeasure. As if he had clairvoyance, Cheng Feichi told Ye Qin to zip up his jacket. "I'll be free after this," he then said. "I can spend the next month in the capital."

Perhaps because he had just come out of a performance that he put his whole heart into, Ye Qin felt light all over, the ethereal kind of light. After spacing out for a brief moment, banal thoughts raced through his head unrestrained. Wrapping his jacket around him, Ye Qin tilted his head back on the car seat and stared blankly at the grey car roof. "If—and I mean if—I didn't run into you, would you have come looking for me?"

He was talking about when Cheng Feichi had just returned from abroad.

Maybe it was because these days were extremely happy, so happy that it seemed a bit like an illusion, Ye Qin would always think back to the first time they reunited. Sometimes he'd feel as troubled and ashamed as if he were actually there, and sometimes he'd feel that he had been lucky. As complicated as showbiz was, there had been such a small probability of meeting in that kind of place.

In this sense, the heavens had not been cruel to him.

However, he was still afraid of hearing no, so before Cheng Feichi could speak, he hurriedly took back his words, "I was just asking. It doesn't make a difference who goes looking for who."

And so, Cheng Feichi didn't answer. "How was your interview?" he changed the topic instead, sensing Ye Qin's depressed mood.

"Oh, you know." Thinking of how he was due to spend another night alone, Ye Qin couldn't summon any enthusiasm. "It was full of young boys and girls as delicate as pond cattails. Meanwhile, I look like the dry daylily in the kitchen left over from yesterday."

"Don't talk about yourself like that. If you don't make it this time, there's always next time. The most important thing is the experience."

Ye Qin raised an eyebrow. "Don't you bosses only care about the results and not the journey?"

He made Cheng Feichi laugh. "Says who?"

"Says the script." Ye Qin looked back at his phone screen.

He turned on speaker mode and read some of the lead actor's lines in the trailer.

As he listened, Cheng Feichi suddenly thought of something. "Is your drama premiering today?"

"Yeah. How did you know?" Ye Qin asked, a bit surprised.

Cheng Feichi didn't answer. "Tell me your opinion on it," he said, walking out of the hotel.

Ye Qin read a few comments on the trailer aloud in the same manner as delivering a work report. Mostly, these were promotions from various fans. When he finally found one that appeared to give counsel, it said the young man didn't look like a rural kid at all; he had the air of a privileged young master about him and looked a bit out of place.

Strictly speaking, looks and costumes were not in Ye Qin's control, but he thought that an actor had to feel like their role, and so he became dejected.

But Cheng Feichi offered a differing opinion. "A person's aura is more remarkable and distinctive than their appearance and figure. There's no need to change it for anyone or anything." He paused for a few seconds and continued, "You can forever be a pampered young master as long as you're with me."

As usual, his words were somewhat restrained, characteristic of his increasingly deep-rooted reservedness and composure.

And yet Ye Qin understood everything. Some feelings had to be declared loudly through dialogue, but a different person had a different stage. There would always be many things that couldn't be captured by words, that had to be attentively perceived by the audience.

What Cheng Feichi never declared but rather told through his actions was: *As long as I have it, as long as you want it, I'll give you everything.*

Two hours later, Ye Qin took Zheng Yueyue's call in the

waiting area of the airport.

"Time off? More time off? My good ancestor, do you know what's happening out there? Everyone is posting pictures of this year's new students at the film school, you included. You're telling me that you, at this time, are not staying home like a good kid, posting selfies and getting your face out there, but running around outside? Waiting for the headline that not only are you having an affair with the Yi family heir, but sending yourself thousands of kilometers straight to him immediately after your interview to hit the front page of tomorrow's news?

Bombarded with a string of words, Ye Qin's ears throbbed. "I don't have that kind of relationship with him," he lowered his voice, putting on headphones. "He's not having an affair with me. We're dating properly."

"Is there a difference? Everyone else will see it as an affair and can only see it as an affair. Don't you know this better than me?"

Head hung, Ye Qin spaced out. "But I miss him...I want to see him," he mumbled.

Somehow, those magical words made Yueyue-jie calm down.

Ever since going into showbiz, Ye Qin seemed to put on a smiling mask. Very rarely did he show his real thoughts in front of anyone, especially right after his debut when he had been smeared. All the sharp parts of his body had been sanded smooth overnight, and he had seemed more sensible for a young boy of his age.

Zheng Yueyue finally let out a sigh. "Go then if you want. Cover yourself up. Don't let anyone get any pictures."

Ye Qin's eyes curved into two crescent moons over his mask. "Okay. Thank you, Yueyue-jie."

The airplane took off on time.

As the wheels left the runway, and its wings soared into the clouds, Ye Qin took a deep breath and felt himself leave the

ground along with it.

The feeling of weightlessness caused him to relax and was particularly suited for pondering. It might have been why he suddenly realized that the question he had asked Cheng Feichi over the phone two hours earlier was quite funny.

Looking back in this state of mind, those messy worries that had taken hold of his heart, particularly the anxieties surrounding a misunderstanding that could never be erased, all became insignificant.

Ye Qin recalled that when he packed his mother's things, he found a sentence written in pen on the cover of the book she often read: *If you love somebody, even breathing gives you courage.*

Besides, he was never an indecisive person.

Since theirs was a reunion, they must bear scars. Since there always had to be someone to take that first step, one of them had to compromise. Whether he or Cheng Feichi, what difference did it make who did it first?

The past can be remembered but never sought. Every day they spent their lives together was one less, so they had to grab on tightly to every second of every minute.

As the airplane steadily ascended, Ye Qin closed his eyes, touched his ring finger with his right hand, and slowly let out the breath in his chest.

He had flown many times, gone to many different places. The more he saw the world and all its vastness, the more he realized how insignificant he was.

A tiny being like him would drift off at a hint of a breeze. Yet at this moment, for the first time, he found confidence in the direction he was headed.

The place you're at is the place I'll go.

Where you're at is where I'll fall.

Glossary

- *A-, Xiao-*: friendly prefixes attached to a person's name to show closeness.
- *-tongxue*: "classmate", added as a suffix to a school peer's name.
- *Ge, gege*: literally "older brother", but also used between people as a friendly nickname, or occasionally flirtatiously between romantic partners.
- *Di, didi*: literally "younger brother", but also used between people as a friendly nickname, or occasionally flirtatiously between romantic partners.
- *Jie, jiejie*: literally "older sister", but also used between people as a friendly nickname, or occasionally flirtatiously between romantic partners.
- *Mei, meimei*: literally "younger sister", but also used between people as a friendly nickname, or occasionally flirtatiously between romantic partners.
- *Da-ge, lao-ge*: literally "eldest brother" and "older brother, but also used as a friendly nickname between peers.
- *Laogong*: a term used to refer to one's husband.

Cheng Feichi x Ye Qin

Falling

Volume 03

An imprint of Via Lactea Ltd.

Copyright © Yu Cheng

ISBN 9781774085226